Penn's Woods Passages

The Tenant

PENN'S WOODS PASSAGES

BOB SOPCHICK

Outdoor Essays and Stories
Art by the Author

HARRISBURG, PA

COPYRIGHT © 2020 PENNSYLVANIA GAME COMMISSION

All rights reserved. No part of this publication may be produced or transmitted in any form or by any means, electronic or mechanical, including photocopy, recording or any information storage or retrieval system, without permission in writing from the publisher. For information, contact the Pennsylvania Game Commission's Bureau of Information and Education, 2001 Elmerton Ave., Harrisburg, PA 17110-9797.

First Edition, October 2020

Edited by Joe Kosack
Designed, written and illustrated by Bob Sopchick
Layout by Joe Kosack and Bob D'Angelo
Printed in the USA

For Terry,
Gardener to Rabbits,
Sister to the Mantis,
Friend of the Bat,
Watcher of Eagles,
Mother to the Moth,
Keeper of this Heart

INTRODUCTION

*"Come forth into the light of things,
let nature be your teacher."*
William Wordsworth

THROUGH MY LIFELONG RELATIONSHIP with the natural world, I have sought to understand it in as many ways as possible, and that has entailed immersing myself in it professionally, as well as personally. It has been a joyous, consuming pursuit.

I first saw nature through the lens of a scientific illustrator, a book illustrator, and as a fine artist. This culminated in trying to express nature not only accurately, but with a personal vision and style.

As a naturalist and nature writer, I came to know the birds and trees, the flowers and animals, the reasons for nature's onward march. The learning curve arcs high and far. I found, though, it was vital to not only write with authority about what I saw, but also how I felt about it, and how the natural world spoke to me.

I also have looked at and translated nature in the role of a museum exhibit designer, where the goals are to educate, inform, inspire and entertain. Museum exhibits require a combination of several disciplines on an enormous scale, using words and mural art, 3-D elements, engineered lighting and sound, architectural design and special effects. The museum designer literally envelopes the viewer, recreating slices of the natural world indoors.

But my greatest insights into nature have been through the eyes, actions and heart of the hunter. The essays and stories in this book are expressions of discovery and visions that came to me while hunting the woods and hills of Penn's Woods for more than 50 years. First traveled with gun or bow in hand, I was compelled to continue those hunts later with pen and brush.

Penn's Woods Passages is mostly a compendium of articles selected from four different columns that appeared over 15 years in *Pennsylvania Game News*. Some are new, but all have been reworked in one way or the other, and are accompanied by illustrations and paintings.

It is my hope that *Penn's Woods Passages* will help you look beyond the obvious, and help you see that art is inextricably bound to nature in an enduring partnership in which the whole always is greater than the sum of its parts.

Bob Sopchick
York, Pa.
2020

CONTENTS

WHITETAIL COUNTRY
Curtain Call 1
Home from the Hill 6
Openers 11
The Butcher's Deer 15
The Reenactor 19
The High Blue Lonesome 24
Better Late 28

NORTHWOODS PASSAGES
Now I Know the Hunter 34
Ursa Minor, Shades of Black 39
Ursa Major, Allegheny Elegy 43
The Bog Man 48
A Bugle from Afar 53
Rosetta Stone 59
Oh, Canada 62

THE TIDES OF AUTUMN
In a Dark Woods 68
The Tides of Autumn 72
October Solitaire 75
The Light of Older Days 78
Far-Off Fields 83
Nexus 88
A Reluctant Passage 92

CONTENTS

THE SULTAN OF SPRING
Aubade 98
The Bones of Spring 102
The Callmaker 106
A Hallmark Season 111
Spring Anthem 117
A Little Help 120

RURAL ROUTE
Poke Salad Days 126
Tram Road 130
Rural Route 134
The Qualified Buyer 138
Anonymous 145
The Potato Fires 150
Fresh Tracks 155
Pathfinder 160
The Compass Rose 165

CROSSINGS
Swan Song 172
Plain Brown Wrapper 174
Transgression 176
The Clearing 178
Flow 180
Upland Aesthetic 182
Spark 184
Banquet 186
Scrimshaw 188

CONTENTS

ON NATURE
    Forever from Here 192

    Meadow Magic 196

    Woodlander 199

    The Nature of Things 203

    Mountain Time 209

    A Day So Rare 212

THE EDGES OF HEAVEN
    The Witness Tree 218

    Along the River 223

    The Edges of Heaven 229

    A Blade So Bright 235

    In the Gloaming 240

    The Cross Fox 245

    A Stitch in Time 250

    Brass Mountain 255

GREAT GUNS
    The Golden Pear 264

    The Tiger and the Dove 269

    The Good Shot 274

    Quicksilver 279

    Big Medicine 282

ACROSS THE BIG FIELD
    Across the Big Field 289

FOREWORD

THERE ARE MYRIAD TRAILS in Penn's Woods that will take you deep into wild and isolated places. They accommodate adventure, harbor nature's essence and provide surroundings that almost immediately settle your soul. They're out of step with time, lack conveniences and harbor life-taking threats. But they are the places where Bob Sopchick has spent so much of his life watching wildlife and studying its behavior, hunting for everything from squirrels to elusive black bears, absorbing whatever nature presented, from its outermost extremities to its mystical core.

Bob's inspiration also comes from other places, other times and, of course, people. He finds great comfort studying a campfire's flames and in helping others; artistically reconstructing with pen and brush the secret lives of Penn's Woods' denizens; even searching for portals to the past in the ruins of abandoned homesteads or in gun shops and flea markets.

It is through Bob's wanderings and experiences, his associations and friendships, and his penchant to write on both sides of the aisle separating fiction from non-fiction that the stories contained in this book rose to prominence within the pages of *Pennsylvania Game News* over that last 30 or so years. He truly is one of the magazine's most significant contributors. Now his stories and supporting art, as well as some of his finest *Game News* covers and Working Together for Wildlife paintings and other fine art have been assembled into this fine book, *Penn's Woods Passages*.

Journalistically, Bob's writings flourish in self-proclaimed eclecticism. He freely admits his thirst to create sends him in many directions, from boyhood adventures and memorable hunts to fiction often centering on mysteries and the trying conditions our grandfathers and forefathers endured back in their day.

What immediately stands out in Bob's prose is his attention to detail, particularly with his historical fiction. His research often is so exhaustive that you'd swear he came from the era. The same holds true when Bob writes about game and other wildlife. You know he's been there; the level of detail leaves no doubt. Descriptive precision is his signature, in both writing and art.

Another element that Bob injects into his work is feeling. Know that you will not read this book without getting emotional. Bob's writing is that powerful. When you forget you're reading a chapter in this book, and simply are following the plot – and you won't until you finish the story – you'll reflect on Bob's gift. That it happens again and again throughout this book, will guarantee this book's place in your library.

Bob is a masterful storyteller and his fictional accounts, which will probably be the biggest surprise to new readers of his work, instill deeper understanding of what once was in Pennsylvania's past, including essays from the Commonwealth's colonial days, the Great Depression and World War II's aftermath. The stories, often set in yesteryear countrysides, have engaging characters and thought-provoking storylines. Some are mysteries, others pack a surprising punch of suspense, even humor. After you read your first couple, you'll be looking for more.

The true measure of any writer's or artist's work is its ability to weather time and I believe the contents of this book have what that takes. They capture for eternity what so many of us experience in Penn's Woods: the essence of the hunt, the sanctity of nature, the vitality of sharing the outdoors with family and friends, the legacy and history nature endows. Bob achieves this with his patented down-home delivery and engaging narratives, and reinforces it with his incredible capacity to understand and his gift to recreate what he sees. After your first pass through these pages, you will know what I mean.

If the outdoors wasn't so massive, it would be easier for everyone to understand it. But it's not. Most who finally get it, do so by assembling it piece by piece. But it takes a lifetime of involvement. Bob has made that commitment and it reverberates through this collection. The depth of his knowledge of things wild, from insects and wildflowers to game animals and songbirds is overwhelming. There is no doubt this man's life has been spent in the heart of the forest, atop lonely mountains, roaming feral fields; they're from where Bob summons his craft and builds on his insatiable need to be one with the land.

Bob writes like no artist has a right. To be so competent, so commanding in one medium categorically takes a lifetime. But Bob's eternal quest to understand, which has sent him down more rabbit holes in his life than the lives of a dozen others, has assembled a comprehension of biodiversity, human behavior and emotion, geology, paleontology, history and art – to name a few, that few, if any, who walk this Earth will duplicate.

Bob uses words just like a painter, adding strength where needed, but remaining true to his vision. It's an extension of his vocabular command, the essence of his artistic dexterity. He writes like he paints, building scenes with brushstrokes of words that strengthen his essay's architecture.

But let's not forget he's a tremendous artist, too. His brushwork and illustrations rival other influential Pennsylvania native artists, such as Earl Poole and Ned Smith, both of whom no doubt influenced Bob to become the artist he is. Bob's artwork drips with reality, capturing the moment and showcasing his subject with the clarity and sparkle that define its character and importance, its place in Penn's Woods. Add to that his years at the easel, his decades afield, his perpetual ambition to further understand the dynamic forces that made our mountains and rivers and assembled our wildlife communities, and it's easy to see from where his inspiration comes.

Not one to be pigeonholed, Bob, in one of his essays, notes his preference to be known as a *woodlander*, a distinction he borrowed from the name of a Spanish shotgun he once purchased. He tells us woodlanders come from all manner of outdoors pursuits: naturalists, birdwatchers, hunters, trappers, anglers, hikers, campers. But they share common traits: they are committed to the ecology of Penn's Woods and seem to always be in touch with nature, wherever they are. They are caring, sharing people, who always look for new ways to explore the outdoors and append their nature knowledgebase.

Following this woodlander theme, it's relatively easy to see who Bob is and what he cares most about – that is, after his wife Terry. His nature is compassionate, but complex; his drive, often punishing. And both figure strongly in his work. He never strives for less than excellence.

Penn's Woods Passages reflects Bob's beliefs in forces of nature, the fundamental necessity of all organisms that embody our outdoors and the value of family, friendship and, of course, a good dog. His patience as an observer and willingness to be afield in all kinds of weather have earned him backstage passes to some of nature's grandest shows. If you're ready to join him, read on!

Joe Kosack, Editor
Pine Grove, Pa.
2020

Run Silent, Run Deep

Whitetail Country

BIG, MATURE BUCKS, like the one in the painting on the opposite page, don't reach such size on luck alone. Their keen senses, and perhaps an undefinable sixth sense, alert them to intrusions and imminent danger, causing them to quickly seek the safety of thick, remote cover, to run silent, run deep.

Some deer sneak along cautiously, silent and difficult to detect as they slip through the woods. But when caution fails, and they must run, it is nothing less than pure poetry; an amazing combination of leaps, bounds, and flat-out running, even when flying down a steep hillside littered with logs and rocks.

This magnificent buck was painted based upon a 12-pointer I missed during a past bow season. It was leading a line of five other bucks chasing a doe, and was the largest buck at which I ever shot.

Heavy-beamed, with long tines and a wide spread, the buck was truly outstanding, but its painted image is more enduring than any wall mount, and being able to share it with scores of readers who dream of deer like this, far more satisfying.

Most of us appreciate the beauty and grace of deer, but when you're a hunter, you learn to see beyond that enduring presence, gaining insight into the characteristics that define the very essence of whitetails and the country they roam.

Curtain Call

THE MARQUEE SHOW among the many productions playing on autumn's grand stage is the annual white-tailed deer rut, and it is always nothing less than great theater.

Hunting the rut is the bowhunter's opportunity to become part of an ancient saga, involving the alchemy of boiling blood, endurance, violence, and necessity staged against a shifting autumnal backdrop. It is a timeless tale of relentless pursuit cued by light and fueled by hormones, when incensed travelers follow olfactory highways across autumn's burnished landscapes.

The story of the rut is classically familiar, a script scribed in time immemorial upon the hills and hollows, but with a different interpretation and presentation every year. The hunter in this drama plays the role of primary predator present at the cusp of life, who upon taking a deer becomes as integral to that rite as the progenitors themselves.

The visual markers of rubs, scrapes and trails are like showbills plastered throughout the uplands, advertising the play and its cast. Bowhunters, in their supporting roles, must know their lines and cues.

It is November, and there is a tension in the air. The hunts of October seem little more now than dress rehearsals. The actors take their places on the stage. The houselights dim and the footlights come up. The curtain begins to open.

FOR ME, THE RUT begins seismically, a vibration that hums beneath my boots urging me to seek, to move, to hunt. I do not hunt from a tree stand. After painting two miles of murals 50-feet up on a swaying scissor lift during one stretch of my career, I vowed never again to spend another day upon any type of elevated platform. I consider my style of bowhunting as roving. I roam as a buck might roam, seek as he would seek.

On a drizzly, in-season Sunday scouting trip, I spot two bucks walking along the edge of a clearing deep in the game lands. At first, I think they are livestock, such is their size. One is a 10-point, the other an 8. They are picking up acorns and occasionally shake the rain from their broad backs in prismatic sprays. I would expect them to not be tolerant of one another. They are, but that can change quickly.

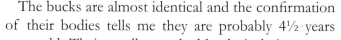

The bucks are almost identical and the confirmation of their bodies tells me they are probably 4½ years old. Their swollen necks blend nicely into muscular shoulders, with legs proportioned well to their stout bodies, having lost the lankiness of younger deer. Their silver-gray faces capture the soft light in the clearing and I notice they are slightly paunchy, yet still retain a relatively straight back, unlike 5½-year-olds; their backs sag a bit and legs appear short.

No ordinary deer, these brutes are exactly what I'm searching for. Although their antlers are respectable, I am equally impressed with body mass and age. These are mature public-land deer that know the ropes. Survivors extraordinaire.

After the bucks amble on, I slip away, moving down near the creek to a broad oak flat, where I discover a large, active scrape. A broken and twisted licking branch of a beech sapling dangles above the scrape. The exposed black earth is furrowed with deep grooves and in the middle is the signature imprint of a very large hoof, like the mark of a signet ring impressed in wax. This earthy missive is signed and sealed by its maker. I could smell deer, a blending of scents from several glands, further identifying its author. I am confident this is the work of one of the big bucks. Or both.

Nearby, I size up the toppled leafy crown of an oak hinged against its trunk that will break up my outline nicely. I'll start here tomorrow.

IT'S A LONG WAY back in. The night sky is a crystalline glass ceiling and I walk beneath the light of a river of stars. My boots crushing frosty grass makes a raspy sound and I'm careful not to skid on sheets of acorns. When I reach the toppled oak, I cocoon myself within and wait for first light. The deep bass notes of a great horned owl match the thud of my heart as the first blush of pink light spreads in the east.

Shafts of sunlight slant across the oak flat between my stand and the hemlock-shrouded creek, and, as if on cue, the barrel-chested 8-point steps into a single spotlight and stands, unmoving.

Enter the star, stage left.

The oily sheen of his winter coat and white antlers capture and turn the yellow light; he fairly glows, then steps forward into shadow.

The buck is 65 yards away and puts on a display of caution unlike any animal I have ever seen. He takes a few steps then stops to listen – radar-dish ears swiveling in concert, then moving independently, tilting this way and that. He walks noiselessly, then stalls, nostrils wide, licking his nose, inhaling an epicure of delicate tendrils of scent. He turns his head slowly and deliberately, looking toward the creek, then scanning the flat, then behind him. It takes him 15 minutes to cover 75 yards.

I wonder if his tentative, halting actions are due to his fear of running into his counterpart. As tense as he is, I am afraid to move. When he reaches a copse of young beeches, he works an overhead branch for several minutes. He ignores my grunt calls and vanishes with the ground fog. I remain alert, though, because he may be circling around downwind. But he doesn't show again.

THE NEXT DAY is cold and dark, with sleet and light drizzle. I cruise along the creek, still-hunt the edges of a thicket and, at mid-afternoon, filter up into a small hollow bisected by a narrow run. Ragged mists float through the dank hollow like fugitive spirits escaped from Halloween. I decide to stay here until quitting time.

No sooner do I hang my pack on a stub and start to nock an arrow when the 8-point trots across. He is not the study in caution as he was the previous day and appears to be on a mission. I grunt at him several times to stop him for a shot, but he suddenly torpedoes forward, neck outstretched and is gone. By day's end two small bucks have passed on the same trail. They are half the size of the big 8.

I TAKE A DIFFERENT route in the morning, high above the creek. Thin fog hugs the ridgeline and I drift along, through acres of ancient grapevines. This is one of my favorite haunts.

Far below, I catch movement. It's the 10-point and I watch him through binoculars as he moves through the grapevine tangles the way a person moves through the alternating cattle chutes of a ticketing queue line. If he continues up the slope, I will be most happy to punch his ticket. The buck stops at every hummock; sniffing, analyzing, drinking scent. This is a bedding ground and he is checking every nook and cranny.

At one point he stops, ears laid back and circles in place once like a dog then tucks his chin back and closes his eyes. He appears to have fallen asleep while standing. This moment is sublime. The huge buck is the paragon of the power and vitality of his kind, a living expression of the beauty and mystery of the woods itself and I savor this portrait framed within the gothic rigging of tattered grapevines.

Suddenly he snaps out of his trance and trots deep into the thicket out of sight behind some boulders, exploding back into view in pursuit of two does. The chase is on!

And now, it snows.

THE MORNING IS COLD, with a lacework of hoarfrost decorating the goldenrod and less than a half-inch of sparkling snow from the day before. I'm back at the oak flat and set up just below the lip of a 10-foot deep ravine cut by a tributary to the creek. From this lower eye level, I can see beneath low-hanging limbs far across the flat. I've killed several bucks with this setup.

A group of five does works across, feeding nonchalantly, when the big 8-point comes hustling down along the ravine, scattering them. Three does fly past only yards away and two others veer right as I reach full draw. At 8 yards, the buck stops hard, turns broadside along a log then surges ever so slightly just as I shoot. I can see the fletching of my bloodied arrow sticking out of the snow.

My shot went through the liver and had to catch part of the left lung, I reason. Usually, a liver-shot buck will lay down within a couple hundred yards and it is recommended that the hunter not push the buck for four hours. There is decent blood here with easy tracking on fresh snow, and I've got all day. I eat a ham sandwich, a raisin cookie and have some coffee, deciding to wait a couple hours before taking up his trail.

After an hour-and-a-half passes, I sense that something is out of sorts.

It is warming up fast. Not just a few degrees, but markedly, and the wind is steady and strong, like the hot breath of a hound.

I had experienced something similar in Calgary, Alberta – what they called a Chinook wind that can raise temperatures as much as 30 degrees in a few hours. Native Americans called the wind a "snow-eater," capable of melting all the ground snow in one day.

Although not a true Chinook, the effect is the same as the snow becomes a thin translucent veil, then gauze-like, then melts entirely. I follow the barely visible blood trail for 50 yards. Then there is nothing. Nothing; not even the slightest puddle of diluted pink held in a cupped leaf.

I searched for his big hoof prints in ever-widening circles and found them in several places across the big oak flat, but his tracks blend into others. It grows ever-warmer and I grow frustrated. All I have to work with is the suggestion of his general direction, and depending on where the liver was hit, there could be little blood anyway.

It was time to stop, to dismiss negative scenarios. I had to get positive logic on my side by defining the situation in clear, simplistic terms.

This is a large, muscular animal in a high state of excitement. He will run far. He will die today and may already be dead. The buck will seek safety in deep cover. The direction of his flight follows the creek.

Follow a deer trail along the creek.

I search fastidiously. Three hours later and 300 yards from where I arrowed him, I inch along a ribbon of a deer trail through a patch of weeds. An oak leaf impaled knee-high on a stick has a rusty freckle on its pale underside which smears slightly when I touch it.

Blood.

I felt at that moment the way the Apollo astronauts felt when they landed on the moon and planted the flag. Looking back at the Earth, they realize the magnitude of their journey. Looking in the other direction at the daunting enormity of infinite space, they face another reality: One small step.

I keep moving, heeding my own directives. Two more hours pass without a trace. I follow a deer trail on a tram road thick with rusty and bent ferns to where a huge black cherry tree had fallen across. The tree would turn him if he came this way, and another single drop of blood to the right on a punky chip of wood confirms that. I doubted he would loop around the windfall then back onto the tram. In his final hours he would head for sanctuary.

I decide then to let instinct take over. I must assume his role, to become the dying deer. I pick up a trail that crosses the creek into a dense bottomland.

I penetrate far into the thicket, almost 700 yards now from my morning stand. The afternoon shadows deepen. I sit on a fallen tree, my back resting against the tall arc of the root mass clotted with dirt and stones. I am exhausted, deflated, and drink the last of my water. I close my eyes, deciding to come back with help tomorrow.

After gathering my gear, I round the root mass and almost trip over the great buck, all 235 pounds of him, laying in the depression left by the tree when it uprooted.

I struggle to pull him out into the light. I look at him a long while. The bull neck; the blunt, coaster-sized hoofs; the broken tine and marks of battle on his face and white antlers; the green firefly luminescence of his eyes now in death.

He is the shining star of this woodland drama, who as sovereign of the hollow and monarch of the oak flats, knew well all the roles of his days and had this day given the stellar performance of his life.

THE HOUSE LIGHTS come up. There is no audience, no ovation for deer or hunter. No curtain call. The old story has moved ahead incrementally, one more scene added to that timeless script.

The grand stage of autumn awaits other acts, other players. Take your place.

The curtain opens.

Home from the Hill

THE LID on the kettle clanged like an alarm, waking Addy from her drowsy vigil by the window. She rose from her rocker then lowered the flame and stirred the hearty beef stew, or "farm-in-a-pot," as her husband Tom fondly called it. The comforting aroma of stew and freshly baked bread filled the farm kitchen. She placed her palms on the cooling loaves and knew she had slept about an hour, and glancing over at the clock saw she was correct.

Honestly, she thought, being able to gauge the passage of time by the warmth of a loaf. But after 40 years in the same kitchen and scores of loaves, she had proven the need of a clock was often secondary.

Addy wiped a fogged window pane with a potholder and slowly scanned the snow-covered cornfields all the way to the edge of the pine woods and beyond, to the high arc of the wooded hill that looked down on the farm. No sign of him yet. This was the first day of buck season, and some years he stayed out till quitting time. She had heard a distant shot earlier, and expected to see him dragging his buck in before lunch as he usually did. Maybe he missed, she thought, but that was not likely. Not Tom. Or, maybe the buck took off down the other side of the hill. This set her to worrying, and she returned to her seat and rocked to images of her stubborn, old farmer husband wrestling a buck up the steep, brushy hillside. She wished their son Jack was out there hunting with him, and at the thought of him she blinked hard, then took to worrying about him, too.

A fine, grainy snow hissed against the windows

and gathered on the sills. It was bitter cold and windy, and the creaking house complained in the same way it no doubt had complained to other generations of Stoughs for the past 150 winters. She tried to read, but lacked concentration. Instead, she studied her pale hands outstretched on the open book, and in them she read the story of her days.

She daydreamed of churning butter the old-fashioned way with her grandmother, and afterward, holding her red hands in the rush of clear water as her little sister worked the pump handle, recalling again the feeling of the cold stream numbing her very first blisters. Then came fleeting images of the busy hands of a young farm wife, nimble and calloused, picking snap beans, pulling weeds, peeling apples, plucking pheasants, and milking: 360 squirts to fill a pail. And now, the hands of a mature woman, knowing hands that seemingly worked without thought, kneading and rolling out dough, knitting colorful afghans, and always holding the ever-present broom, constantly sweeping away dirt – and along with it, anything that troubled her.

A breech in the clouds created a square of sunlight on the plank floor, and for a long while she watched its progress as it crept up a wall. Another shot, closer this time, echoed over the fields. Addy swept snow from the back-porch steps, and could tell by the shadow on the barn from the towering twin pines in the yard that it was a little after 2 at their Twin Pines Farm.

TO ADDY, THE FARM was a shifting, complex, multi-layered operation that required constant nurturing, but for Tom Stough, farming was as pure and simple as the black silhouettes of the twin pines against stark winter fields. He had a fascination and respect for all things that sprung from the soil, both domestic and wild, and from the very first time that he sat on a tractor and plowed a furrow, he became the quintessential farmer. He met every challenge with an unyielding will and stone-faced determination, and the farm survived. If it was something beyond his control, like weather, Addy was there to worry about it. When it came to hunting, particularly deer hunting, Tom's typically stoic demeanor changed to an animated exuberance that was a joy to behold.

Deer season was a time for fun, and there was nothing he enjoyed more than sharing that time with his son Jack. They were often joined by a few neighbors and Charlie, a longtime friend from town. The season opener was a grand event that began weeks before with careful preparation. Guns had to be sighted-in, equipment checked and rechecked, stand sites carefully scouted, strategies debated.

Over the years, many traditions developed. The day began with Addy's renowned buck hunter's breakfast, and an equally sumptuous feast at dinner. While the others put on drives in the huge thicket on the farm's west end, Tom and Jack always hunted together the first morning on the north hill. Another tradition concerned bringing in the deer: Under no conditions would a deer be hauled in by truck or tractor. The tractor was for farming, not for hunting, and dragging in a deer was part of the hunt. The ring of a big antique bell in the yard could be heard from anywhere on the farm, and whenever a lucky hunter pulled his buck in, he had to toll the bell once for each antler point. This was all tempered with a delightful competitiveness, and much kidding and boasting.

One year, Charlie rang the bell eight times, even though his deer sported a half-rack on one side and a broken main beam on the other. He reasoned that his buck would have had eight points had the other side not been broken. Charlie was an accountant, and this made what followed worse as he took a tremendous ribbing for counting points that weren't there.

But those enthusiastic times had passed. Most of the neighbors had moved on, and Charlie's health was declining. Jack said he might be able to fly in for a day later on, but the opener was out. Tom told him not to apologize, that he understood. But then made up his mind he wouldn't hunt deer at all.

The day before the opener, Addy bolstered Tom's spirits, gave him the challenge he needed. She said there'd be a fresh snow for tracking tomorrow and that she expected to hear the bell ringing. She added she was looking forward to making some venison sausage. The light in his eyes returned, like sun burning through a fog. She also mentioned he ought to take the tractor out and park it up near the pines, but he declined, clinging to tradition, then cheerfully rechecked his gear that had been readied weeks before.

JACK REVIEWED HIS busy year-end schedule for the third time while the jet held in a pattern above Atlanta. He managed his thriving business with Tom's same pragmatism and Addy's attention to detail. There were a lot of loose ends to be tied up before Christmas. He would call the farm on Thanksgiving morning and cancel out of buck season. Thanksgiving would be at his in-laws. Most of the weekend would be spent preparing for a presentation on Wednesday. If things snowballed after that, he would miss the remainder of deer season, too, but would make it up to them once things settled down.

While talking with his father on Thanksgiving morning, Jack felt strangely detached, as if he were listening to a voice other than his own, and the hitch in his father's voice bothered him.

After the call, he stared out the window and thought of how everything in Pennsylvania was becoming charged with the excitement of deer season, for the single largest participatory event of the year. A flock of blackbirds sailed over a magnolia tree and onto the lawn, reminding him of the geese that would sail over the farm's north hill and glide down to the pond. He placed the outline of the proposal back in his briefcase and looked out the window again, hunting for another memory.

TOM LEANED into the wind, plodding up the drifting lane that divided the cornfield. It was a long hike, and by the time he reached the pine woods, the stormy sky had a faint silvery cast. The wind in the pines sounded like the whispers of old friends urging him on. He continued up through the pines and farther up to Jack's funnel stand on the crest of the hill, where the woods constricted and deer came through spooky and fast, heads low and tails clamped tight in typical farm deer fashion. He hunkered in and waited for full light.

Addy's breakfast kept him warm and alert through the frigid morning. A shot cracked on the other side of the hill and Tom was happy to hear it. Soon after, several deer came sneaking through, the last, a bruiser of a buck. Tom tried to find the buck in the peep sight, but the aperture cup was full of the sugary snow. By the time he cleared it, the buck was already into the pines.

Without Jack to help him put on a drive, he would chase the deer around in there all day by himself. But then a plan emerged: he would ghost through the pines hoping to nudge the deer ahead slightly, then drop out of the woods, loop around the far end and ease back in through a little gully and wait there.

While sneaking through, he heard another shot from the big thicket, pleased that the Boyds, who always hunted there, were getting some shooting. An hour later, Tom peeped up over the rim of the gully and the deer were filing by, just as he had anticipated. His .300 Savage roared and the buck bolted downhill and out into the cornfield, where he went down.

It was a huge 11-point, the biggest buck ever taken on the farm. Even field-dressed, the big buck was difficult to slide over the undulating rows of corn stubble, but he managed to get it over to the lane. The farmhouse looked like a tiny toy in the distance, and without help, he knew the deer was more than he could, or should, try to drag. He knelt beside the buck, exhausted more from the emotions that buffeted like snow through his head than the rigors of the morning. He'd rest first, then go for the tractor.

ADDY SAW the speck of orange far down the lane that, for a long while, didn't appear to be moving. With her bird-watching binoculars, she could barely make out the hunter through the falling snow, but could tell it was Tom. She bundled up and went out to sweep the steps again, then stopped. She stared out the lane again and decided to find out what was going on, disappearing into a squall that swept in, enveloping her as she walked.

Tom stood when Addy called his name.

"I hope you're not gonna try and sweep this lane so I can drag in this big guy," he replied.

Addy looked at the broom in her hands, laughing, then looked at the big buck.

"Oh my, he's a whopper!"

She swept the snow off the maize-colored antlers and its long body and Tom's pant legs and coat. "I'll help you pull him in."

"No, he's too big; we'll get the tractor. I bet he goes more than 200 pou…"

He was cut off by six clear rings of the farm bell. It was one of the Boyds, no doubt, stopping by as they always did at noon on the opener. They waited as he started down the lane.

When the hunter emerged from a wall of flakes he whistled at the size of Tom's buck and offered his help.

"Looks like you could use some help dragging that buck in, and seeing that I already got mine, I have the time. Besides, I'm cold and hungry."

At the sound of Jack's voice, Addy dropped her broom and buried her face in her hands, shoulders shrugging, and leaned against Tom. Tom put his arm around her – helpless, speechless, breathless.

Jack told how he wanted to surprise them by showing up for breakfast on opening morning, flying in very late after several weather delays, then driving in through the storm only to get his rental car stuck on the other side of the hill. He got dressed there and decided to hunt his way home through the thicket, where he killed a 6-point. The Boyds helped get his vehicle free and he brought his buck around.

"We can talk more when we get back inside," Addy said. "I have hot coffee, fresh bread, apple cobbler and stew."

"Farm-in-a-pot?" Jack replied. "All right! My favorite!"

Tom and Jack each grabbed an antler, Addy with Tom's rifle slung over a shoulder, broom in one hand, the other in the crook of Jack's arm. They headed home from the hill as one, each bound to the other, and through the deer, to the frozen and furrowed earth.

Openers

SOME DEER HUNTERS refer to it as "First Day," while others simply call it "The Opener," but either designation describes the most celebrated day of the hunting year, the kickoff of Pennsylvania's rifle season for deer.

For some, the opener is the only day they will hunt during the entire season, while for others it's the first day of an entire season in the deer woods. It's that day when the greatest number of deer hunters head for destinations far and wide, to hills and hollows, mountains and swamps, deep forests and farmland; a time to bond with family and friends and to renew one's personal contract with nature. The deer opener is, in effect, an unofficial holiday.

Having been fortunate to hunt more than 50 rifle openers, I've found the dynamics of some opening days to be more memorable than their outcome. Following are a few openers from my half-century of participation. Surely, we have shared some of those days together: the same sunrise, the same wild winds, the same deep snows. That might have been your gunshot I heard across the hollow.

Winds of Fortune

ON CERTAIN OPENERS, weather determines the course of the day, and I can recall several where dense fog, torrential rains, snowstorms, ice, sleet and frigid temperatures presented additional challenges. The fickle winds of fate sometimes determine if one hunter gets a deer and another doesn't, but the winds on this opener were unlike any I've ever experienced before or since.

We climbed the mountain in the dark, a steep, tortuous climb through dense laurel thickets, around huge boulders and over rock slides. Once on top, though, the terrain was gently rolling and comprised mostly of classic oak flats interspersed with thicker cover.

The weatherman had issued an alert for high winds as a big storm front was sweeping in from out of the northwest. The day started with swirling, buffeting winds, and the first groups of deer moving through were very skittish, as they are when squally winds lend motion to trees and shrubs. I felt a bit on edge myself; there was a palpable element in the air of something ominous approaching. Far out in the river valley, I could see a ceiling of dark clouds edging in.

The winds suddenly changed their playful demeanor, uniting as a serious, sustained directional wind. It also was getting colder. A sudden, far-off roaring, like a thing escaped and unleashed upon the land rampaged down the river valley. The woods itself seemed to brace. When that gale slammed into the face of the mountain, I knew then that this was no ordinary storm front, but something hinging on disaster. And it was.

Thick oak boughs, snapping like toothpicks, thudded to the forest floor. Trees, uprooting and toppling, crashed violently in the distance, then closer. Tram roads, knolls and hillsides, once hidden beneath a foot of leaves, were laid bare as the leaf litter was driven horizontally far through the woods. I quickly moved into a patch of whippy sweet birch saplings, and out of range of any "widow-makers."

I was unnerved, and kneeled down behind a log, trying to get my bearings. Deer were the farthest thing from my mind when a tree toppled just down the hillside. A few moments later, four deer bolted up onto the flat.

They appeared panicky and disoriented and stepped about close together, ears laid back, uncertain of what to do next. One of them was a buck, a big half-rack five-point, and at my shot he bucked and bolted for the thick stuff at the edge of the laurel.

I found him 100 yards away, shot dead-center through the heart. As I dressed him out, I kept one eye on the overhead branches as the wind continued to roar. Just then, Dad showed up. He had gone out onto a nearby powerline to be safe, then came down when he heard me shoot.

"Let's get out of here!" he shouted over the whipping wind. At his words, a great hissing rushed across the woods as curtains of sleet pounded the mountaintop and the temperature plummeted.

It was several minutes before 8 a.m. when we brought the deer into the butcher shop. It was the first hunter-killed buck brought in. The other hanging there was a roadkill from the day before. The butcher said it was going to be a windy and freezing day with lots of ice and snow.

"But you're all done," he said, followed by an approving smile.

Later, on the evening news, it was reported that wind gusts of up to 65 mph had been reported. Some hunters who had parked on woods roads were stranded, because so many trees had come down.

No one can know what fortunes the winds may bear. But on that morning, a fierce wind pushed the gift of a buck to me, driving the events of that opening day, like a leaf, deep into memory.

The Bermuda Triangle

THE SEARCH FOR the perfect First Day deer stand can be an arduous, sometimes decades-long pursuit. It takes fieldwork, map research, and when hunting public land, strategizing for hunter pressure. Back in the early 1980s, my father and I located two promising stands, only several hundred yards apart.

Mine was on the cusp of a steep, 1,500-foot ridge overlooking a river valley where two powerlines merged creating a flat, 75-yard equilateral triangle. The powerlines were overgrown with broom grass, blackberry patches, sumac, tall weeds and truck-size clots of greenbrier, all of it interwoven with deer trails. Every deer that ran along that ridgeline passed through that small wooded triangle. It came to be called "The Bermuda Triangle," because many deer that went in never came out.

In the mid-1980s, the deer population exploded, and the year I discovered the triangle stand also was a banner year for the acorn crop. I was looking forward to posting in the triangle, but the weather forecast for the opener was unusual: record-high temperatures in the 80s were predicted. I didn't know what to expect.

It was just getting light when I eased quietly into the triangle. I was not alone, though, as a flock of more than two dozen turkeys were roosted everywhere. So much for an unobtrusive entry. A couple birds took off, but I quickly found my seat on the log and sat still. The flock was still on roost at legal shooting light and then began to fly down. Some approached within several yards of me, alarming others. For a while, it was total chaos with birds running and rocketing out of my woods right at prime time.

All morning, deer after deer ran into the triangle, then paused before continuing across. I lost count. This gave me plenty of time to look for antlers, but all were does and fawns. When the traffic slowed, I looked down and spotted a deer skull protruding from the leaves.

I pulled it from the ground and saw that it had two long spikes. A withered spider and a crazed eyeball stared at me, but the eye was only the spiraled shell of a snail stuck in the orbit. I hung the skull on a snag and watched as more deer filed in, then out again. The skull hung there for years.

Suddenly, a line of five deer, all of them bucks, hobby-horsed across the powerline. I was about to be surrounded by deer and quickly decided to shoot the first buck in. A long-tined spike fell to the shot from my new .280 Remington. The last deer was an 8-pointer that stopped momentarily only yards away. It spun, then took off across the powerline heading toward Dad's stand. I heard him shoot, but when he didn't shout for me, I knew he had missed.

I field-dressed and tagged my buck and noticed that the reason its spikes looked so long were because its ears were lopped off halfway down, most likely the result of frostbite.

Later, near quitting time, I heard another shot from Dad's 7X57, and was overjoyed to find that he killed the same 8-pointer he had missed earlier. There was no mistaking that deer, as it was the smallest mature buck we had ever seen. It was a very pale gray and tipped the scales at just over 85 pounds, even though it was acorn-fat.

That opener was a day of many firsts: both of us hunted with rifles that were new to us for the first time; it also was the first time we ever hunted in December in shirtsleeves, and it also was our first time on stands that proved, over the years, to be productive beyond our wildest dreams. Most memorable of all, though, is that the little 8-pointer was Dad's first buck.

Escarpment

THE DAY BEGINS with an odd geometry of shooting stars; perfect straight lines, like tracer rounds fired on each side of the moon. Water gurgles far down in the hollow like voices in the shadows or a conversation in another room. In the dim light, the boulders are barely discernible, the hulking shapes like a tragic beaching of leviathans on some dusky shore.

I am nervous and excited. In this rocky rampart, I am perched like some medieval guardsman on night-watch high in a castle keep. A sound of delicate footsteps interrupts my thoughts. Who goes there, buck or doe? The silvery light of a false dawn creeps across the western sky, and soon after, the faintest blush of pink on the opposing ridge.

Just up the hollow, a red fox barks sharply, as it always does here at this hour; a declaration to loosen oneself from night's grip, to shed the remnants of a last dream. All at once, the day steps forth, the shapes of familiar trees are recognized, and I am on full alert.

This is where the deer are, and will come as they are moved by incoming hunters. It's a stand that other hunters deem too steep, too difficult to hunt. Located on a thick, rock-strewn hillside below an escarpment, it's an obstacle course that few, if any, would attempt in the dark. I once shot a deer here in the first legal minute, that first shot of the day that causes everyone within earshot to snap to full attention.

As always, I am awestruck by the configurations of the enormous, tumbled boulders. Fortress and minaret, a lost Mayan ruin, perhaps a statuary of leering gargoyles or mythical beasts, or maybe a monumental frieze of creatures vaguely equine or Jurassic. Wrinkled gray boulders in tandem, all similar in size, could be a small herd of elephants. The imagination soars.

A flash of orange, high up in the rocks, draws my attention. Another hunter, I think. And it is; a handsome red fox dashes noisily down into the thicket. Right after, a doe trots out of the laurel, then another deer; this one, a buck. It stands at the edge of a shooting lane and when my .45-70 roars, the buck crumples.

The year before, while I was still-hunting here, a fox that I startled spooked a couple of deer bedded just ahead of where I was sneaking, costing me a shot. I wonder if it is the same fox.

As I drag the buck over the rocks, I notice a geometric pattern on the surface of a rock. The pattern is a couple of feet long and very precise, like large reptilian scales. What a discovery! It's a trunk section of a scale tree – lepidodendron – from 300 million years ago. However, these were not scales; they were the pattern of individual leaf scars from when the tree was developing. Scale trees topped out at 100 feet with a canopy of long, needlelike leaves.

Suddenly, I am thrust into a steamy, carboniferous forest thick with giant ferns and horsetails. I look at the buck and then the forest, deep in the heart of autumn. It is all a part of a saga begun in primeval Pangea, perpetuated on this bright and shining day in Pennsylvania.

The Butcher's Deer

STANLEY STOOD on a stump to get a better view of his little beagle Ruby bringing round a cottontail. When the rabbit bounded up a slope, he shot and it cartwheeled over the crest. Stanley knelt, holding the rabbit for Ruby to sniff, praising her for her fine work.

While dressing the rabbit, Stanley heard the strident grunting of a buck. A doe trickled through the hollow, followed by a handsome 7-point, like Ruby on a rabbit. A butcher by trade, Stanley studied the buck as it went by, drawing an imaginary butchering diagram on its form.

"One-twenty-seven on the scale," he said to Ruby as he held her under one arm. The beagle squirmed, eager to start hunting again, showing no interest in the deer, knowing that scent as well as any.

A few minutes later, he heard another deer hustling along the same trail. This buck was a bruiser, a 10-point.

"One-fifty-three," he whispered, wondering if it was the same buck he had seen behind his shop several times during the summer.

His butcher shop was a few miles from town. He and his wife Anna owned 54 acres out back that wound through a brushy hollow, looped around a hilltop cemetery and ran back out to the highway. Stanley had been seeing lots of deer, but only a few friends pushed it out each year, writing it off as a good place to run a beagle, but little else. Besides deer, he had seen turkeys, and one morning, a bear that had pulled down his suet feeders from an apple tree.

Deer processing was a big part of his business, and Stanley hadn't hunted deer in more than 20 years, as deer season was his busiest time. He tried bowhunting, but with three growing kids and a surging business, he couldn't devote enough time for even that. He was satisfied, though, knowing that his work was a vital link between the hunt and the many meals his customers' families would enjoy throughout the year.

His father had opened the butcher shop 50 years ago, and Stanley began helping out when he was just a boy. The shop now was a family business that provided a living for Stanley and Anna, as well as their daughter Jessie and her husband Frank.

To Stanley, deer hunting was as much about people as it was about deer, and many of his customers were close friends. He enjoyed the diversity of hunting traditions in the community, and hearing their hunting stories.

There was Pastor Phil and Father Mike, who hunted together. They always had their deer processed together and divided it equally. Jack, his mailman, liked to get done early and usually got a deer on the first day of archery.

Probably the best of the hunters was his friend Kenny, a bowhunter who always connected on a nice buck during the rut. What made Kenny really happy, though, was bringing in an antlerless deer during the late season as a donation to Stanley's Feeding the Hungry program.

Stanley really knew deer. He had seen it all come through the shop, and had developed an uncanny ability to guess a deer's weight just by looking at it. He had seen bucks with every configuration of antlers imaginable and antlered does. Some bucks had short, bristly manes running in a line down their back. There were whitewash-splashed piebalds and albinos. He even had processed three-legged deer, a tailless deer, a one-eyed deer and a deer with no ears.

Some had recovered from unimaginable wounds, like being impaled by chrome door strips from cars that had sideswiped them. Others had severe punctures from frenzied fights and long-healed hunting wounds that should have been fatal.

Most of the bucks were younger deer, but in recent years, he had seen an increase in mature, larger-racked bucks.

Most of all, Stanley enjoyed talking with young hunters who took their first deer and were eager to tell their stories. This was an important part of the hunt, too, and Stanley always took the time to listen. After the season, he sent every youngster a personal note of congratulations, along with a brochure on how to field-dress and care for venison in the field. Some of them now brought their kids to the shop with deer in tow.

Stanley was a stickler for proper field care, and if a hunter didn't do a good job, Stanley let him know it. On occasion, he would show some hunters how to sharpen their knives.

ON THE EVE of the opener, Stanley made sure everything was ready. If the weather cooperated, hunters would start bringing in deer around 8 o'clock, and then business would be steady late into the evening. The weatherman called for a cold, partly cloudy morning with increasing clouds and flurries in the afternoon, and this suited Stanley. It was the hot, meat-spoiling temperatures that bothered him.

Opening day, Anna and he got up at 3:30 a.m. and drove down to

Deb's Diner for breakfast. Deb was filling coffee cups at the packed counter, and motioned for them to go to the back room. When they walked through the swinging doors, the large room was dark; then the lights flicked on revealing a room full of applauding hunters.

A banner above the buffet table read HAPPY 50TH ANNIVERSARY – STANLEY'S MEATS. Everyone was wearing a blaze orange sweatshirt and cap with the shop logo. Stanley stood there slack-jawed, Anna with her head on his shoulder. Everyone was there: their children, relatives, friends and many regular customers.

Pastor Phil read a moving breakfast prayer of thanks written by Father Mike, who immediately remarked that he could have read it in half the time, so they could eat and get out in the woods. Then Stanley's oldest son Tommy came to the front of the room with a hunting outfit on a hanger, followed by Frank who was holding a rifle.

"Dad, this is for you," said Tommy. "A new hunting outfit and your old .30-06, refinished, with a new scope and sling, tuned-up, sighted-in and ready to go. Today, you're going deer hunting. We want you to have a great day off, and wish you the best of luck. You're welcome to hunt wherever you'd like. It's up to you."

Stanley cleared his throat, wiped away a tear, and thanked the group profusely. He said that he would enjoy most hunting in back of his place. Just a nice leisurely day.

"Aw, he just wants to get up on the hill to make sure everything's moving along down at the shop," Jack quipped. "Don't let him take any binoculars!"

STANLEY TOOK THE road to a picnic pavilion back in the woods and reminisced about the wonderful family picnics, parties and reunions he attended there. He recalled turning lamb on a spit there when he was a boy, while old-timers played accordions and mandolins. He could see his own kids building dams in the summer creek, and could hear the clink of horseshoes down at the pits.

Gray light accrued behind the hill. A cold wind swept through the pavilion, gathering leaves into a spiral that nudged him from his reverie. He set out with the wind in his face with no plan in mind.

The winter woods had opened up and showed deer sign at every turn. He skirted a helix of trails and took a stand on the rise where he had killed the rabbit recently, hoping a buck would sneak through.

The world seemed far away, and his familiar woods somehow appeared different now that he was looking at them through the eyes of a deer hunter. Geese flew low over the trees, and squirrels and jays complained in his wake. He climbed the opposite side of the hollow and watched the sun rise behind a tattered curtain of dark clouds that ignited in its passage. Stanley relaxed, admiring the sunrise, feeling snug and warm in the new outfit.

He walked quietly along the stream until it turned to black mire, and there put up a woodcock that set down again a short distance away. Soon after, he kicked out two deer, but saw only tails. He grew excited about the possibility of getting a shot.

Stanley had never killed a deer. That was something he never told anyone. Nor did he dwell upon it, as deer were such an integral part of his life. The butcher felt a surge of vitality, a joyous rush of energy somewhere deep inside him. His pulse matched that of the woods, and his next step was not that of someone out for a stroll, but the careful, predatory tread of a deer hunter.

Stanley still-hunted and posted alternately all day. Late afternoon found him with his back

against one of the tall, sentinel oaks surrounding the perimeter of the cemetery. His parents were buried not far behind him, and he knew that today they would be proud.

In the next instant, a lone buck came around the steep sidehill, and at his shot, it slid down the slope and piled up against a log.

It was the 7-point he had seen several weeks before. Stanley admired the deer a long time. He ran his fingers along the beaded antler.

His deer.

Stanley tagged the buck and rolled it over to dress it out. But after patting down all of his pockets for his knife, he realized he had forgotten it and laughed out loud. Here he was, a butcher, a man who made his living with a knife, standing in the woods with his first deer and without so much as the old pocketknife he always carried.

He got back at dusk, collected a knife from the console in his truck, and in a few minutes had the buck dressed out. He dragged it around the building and up the delivery alley where several weary hunters were standing in line with their deer.

When he pulled his buck into the shop, Tommy yelled, "Hey everybody, look what this guy brought in."

Anna looked up from her clipboard as the crew came into the counter room.

"Let's get him up on the scale and see what he weighs," she said proudly.

"Around 136, I'd say," said Stanley. "But I could have sworn he was heavier halfway back the hollow, but that's another story."

The needle settled at 131.

"Well, eagle eye, you're about 4 or 5 pounds off, but that's close enough," Anna said.

Stanley pulled out a plastic bag with the heart and liver from the pouch in back of his coat and set it on the scale.

"Like I said, 136," said Stanley. "And there's an even bigger one running around back there."

"Maybe you'll get him next year, Pop," said Tommy.

"Maybe," said Stanley. "Now let me tell you about my buck…"

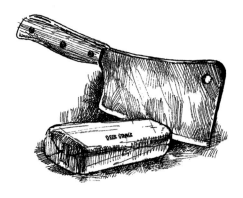

The Reenactor

JIM TACKED the shingle into place and slipped the hammer into a loop on his jeans. From his vantage point on the ladder, he looked around the yard, satisfied that everything was ready for winter: leaves raked, lawn fertilized, driveway sealed, deck stained.

Done and done – all of it.

Replacing this shingle was the last chore. He didn't want any tasks lingering into deer season. Beyond the neighborhood, the wintry hills beckoned, and now he could concentrate on getting ready for the opener.

He climbed down the ladder, and when he turned, a small elderly woman was standing there, smiling.

"I didn't want to startle you while you were up there. We've never met. I'm Jean Lubic. I live over on Pinewood. Do you have a minute?"

"Sure," said Jim.

"You might remember my late husband, Harry. He passed away earlier this fall. He was walking by when you were putting things out for the spring cleanup. You gave him some tires for his Jeep, even dropped them off at our home. He said that you were a hunter, and that he talked with you a long time."

"I remember him," said Jim. "I'm sorry to hear about your loss."

"Thank you," Jean replied. "The reason I stopped by is that I have his hunting things in the basement. Not much, just some clothes and such, and his gun. If you could come by and look these things over, you're welcome to them. No one in the family hunts, and I don't want to be bothered with trying to sell it. Harry took such good care of his things. He even was working on the gun when he passed

on; it's in pieces. It's an old gun, the only one he had, and I don't know anything about it."

"I just finished here, and can come over now, if that's okay."

Jim walked back with her, knowing full well that he wasn't interested in the old hunter's gear. If any of it was good shape, he would take it down to the sportsman's club.

She led him down to the basement.

"That wool hunting outfit hanging over there had just been cleaned," Jean said. "You're about Harry's size, and I'm sure it will fit you. Just take your time, I'll be in the kitchen."

A work light above the workbench cast a dense thicket of shadows from the double row of antlers on the wall. Most of the racks were above average, and one, a 10-point with lots of mass, was outstanding.

On the workbench was an old Remington Model 14, with a .35 Remington cartridge case headstamp on the left side of the receiver.

For a 70-year old gun, the pump was in fine shape. Harry had been taking it apart for only a thorough cleaning. A cleaning kit lay open on the bench, and a rod was still halfway down the barrel. Jim scrubbed out the bore, oiled the rifle sparingly, and reassembled it. The action was slick and sound, and he liked the immediate sight picture of the Lyman receiver sight.

Inside a cardboard box, among odds and ends, he found several boxes of ammo, a drag rope, an old thermos, a Marbles Ideal knife in a sheath, and a dog-eared topo map. The coat, a heavyweight red-and-black-plaid Filson Mackinaw Cruiser, was in excellent condition, as were the gray wool bibs. A red wool shirt, plaid vest and a pair of recently resoled L.L. Bean pac boots completed the outfit.

Jim went upstairs and sat at the kitchen table. Jean poured him some coffee.

"The gun's in fine shape," he said. "If you'd like, I could put an ad on the bulletin board at the sportsmen's club, I'm sure someone will be interested. It's probably worth $300 or more."

"Please, won't you keep it?" Jean insisted. "Harry liked to return favors; let's just call it a trade for the tires."

She poured more coffee and talked about her late husband.

"He loved his deer hunting. Eighty-three years old, and he was still looking forward to the upcoming season. He had slowed down a bit the last several years, but he always went out, no matter what the weather. We liked to try new venison recipes, and I'll miss that. Most of all, I'll miss his stories. He remembered every last detail, from first light to when he came home. That was his favorite thing – the telling."

IN STARK CONTRAST TO Harry's basement, Jim's resembled a sporting goods store. The room was subdivided into thirds with free-standing shelves; one area for shooting and reloading, another devoted to archery gear, and the third for clothes and boots. He owned a lot of the latest and greatest.

Jim spread Harry's topo map on the table and studied it carefully. It was of a mountain 9 miles north of town, a slice of public land Jim had hunted years ago. From what he could decipher, a hand-drawn red line was the route Harry took across the face of the mountain. It went back in almost a mile, terminating at a spot Harry had marked as "Shelf Rock." Various Xs marked along the route were most likely deer stands. The Xs closest to where he parked were probably more recent stands that he used as he aged, with the last one in only 200 yards. Jim could envision the old hunter carefully walking along the trail. If one could read between the elevation lines, here was the complete story of a deer hunter's days.

In the very bottom of the box, he found a black and white snapshot of a young Harry posing in his backyard with a big buck; stamped in the snow was "1955."

Jim sat for a while holding the old rifle, staring at the wool outfit hanging from a hook, now curious about Harry the deer hunter. He worked the lightning action and snapped the rifle to his shoulder and plastered the bead on an image of a running deer on a lampshade.

What sort of hunter were you, Harry Lubic? Did you see the woods the way I do?

THREE DAYS BEFORE DEER SEASON, Jim was about to take Harry's things down to the club, when he had a strange notion. A short time later, he was dressed in the hunting outfit.

It fit perfectly. He turned up the tall collar against an imaginary wind. Even the boots were comfortable with a double-layer of socks. He slung the rifle over his shoulder and looked at his vague reflection in the sliding glass door.

The old deer hunter himself.

He put the Marbles knife on his belt, cartridges in the loops and the drag rope in a pocket, then slid the thermos into the rear cargo pouch. All ready to go. It made him wonder why he lugged a heavy backpack full of state-of-the-art accessories.

Jim looked at the snapshot again. He had never taken a buck that big and it had been two years since his last deer, a bit of a dry spell that he intended to change. But his bad luck had continued through the recent archery season.

The next day, he was at the rifle range with a score of other procrastinators sighting in their guns. He had shot his synthetic-stock bolt-gun throughout the summer, and with carefully developed handloads, it was a real tack-driver. But now, here he was, waiting for a bench to open, anxious to sight-in Harry's little woods rifle.

Used to sub-minute-of-angle accuracy, he was less than excited with the 3-inch groups. Not too bad, he supposed, considering the iron sights. Then again, he had taken only a few deer beyond 75 yards, and for ordinary woods ranges, the .35 was fine. Besides, it was a joy to carry, a mere wand compared to his long-barreled magnum.

Finished at the range, he drove north to the mountain and found the small pull-off where Harry parked. With several inches of fresh snow, it was difficult to locate the barely discernible trail etched into the steep hillside, but when he followed a double set of deer tracks for a while, he was satisfied that he had found it.

The key to Harry's success was simply that he hunted a place that others would either pass by, or, after gauging the angle of the slope, would pass on. Everyone hunted on top or down below, and pressured deer would be moving through or find haven here. Harry had discovered a niche that worked nicely for decades.

JIM'S WIFE WAS PACKING HIS LUNCH the morning of the opener, and when he walked into the kitchen, she did a double take.

"You look as though you've just stepped out of an old hunting calendar," she said.

Jim smiled.

"Thought I'd try the vintage thing this year; old-school deer hunting."

"Kind of like a Civil War reenactor, but for hunting?" she joked.

"Sort of like that, I guess."

She filled the battered silver thermos with coffee and handed it to him.

"As long as you're having fun."

JIM WAS INTENT on taking Harry's route all the way out to Shelf Rock. After a while, the trail became rocky and the hillside steeper, then it eased up, cutting across some small benches below a series of ledges that offered excellent vantage points. At full light, he was only halfway there, but took his time, even after seeing three deer stealing down through a finger of laurel far ahead.

There was no mistaking Shelf Rock: two enormous plates of sandstone had come to rest against each other at a right angle, forming a shelf, of sorts, on the steep hillside. There was a seat of stacked stones at the far end of the shelf that overlooked a progression of ribs on the mountain.

Jim settled in and watched, the rifle across his lap. A steady, frigid wind spitting snow angled in from the northwest, and he raised the collar on the coat, an image in his mind of how – minus the fluorescent orange hat and vest – he could be Harry sitting here a half-century before.

Several does trickled through, but Jim had no antlerless tag for this unit; it was bucks only here. A small 5-point picked its way around him, and Jim watched it intently, but let it pass. He had a sandwich and coffee at midmorning, while being entertained by a large flock of turkeys feeding farther down the slope. He thought of all the hours Harry had probably spent here, how he came to know the girth and tilt of each tree, the shape of every rock and windfall. When he heard some deer coming hard down the mountain, Jim set down his cup and stood up, gripping the rifle.

The last in the group was a nice buck with a drop tine. The buck was moving fast and Jim got off two quick shots, but the buck never flinched. After checking for evidence of a hit, and satisfied that he had missed, he wondered if Harry would have made the shot, and then felt as if he let the spirit of the old deer hunter down.

Jim remained alert all afternoon, and when the hillside fell to shadow, he headed back. He made several brief stands and still-hunted across a brushy flat above the trail, pushing some deer from their beds; the wool outfit was absolutely silent as he eased through the stout laurel.

The dome of the sky ebbed to the palest violet and the leading edge of a leaden cloud bank was aflame with the last rays of the sun. He was not far from his truck, near Harry's final stand, when he saw a doe and the drop-tine buck moving through a thicket. He had only a small window to shoot through, and the gold bead, catching the reflection of the fiery clouds, stood out like a miniature sun against the dark chest of the buck.

A FEW DAYS after butchering the deer, Jim took a package of tenderloins over to Mrs. Lubic. She invited him in for coffee, and they sat at the kitchen table and talked.

"Thanks again for the clothes and the rifle. I was warm all day long, and Harry's rifle brought that buck right down."

"Oh, I'm so glad you could use his things!" she said, her words brimming with emotion.

"Now, let me fill you in on the details," Jim offered.

"Oh, yes!" she said, brightening. "I'd love to hear all about it."

ON HIS WAY home, an icy wind howled down the street, driving him deeper into the depths of Harry's coat. For a single day, he had walked, quite literally, in another hunter's boots, seen and sensed what he might have in the very same woods. It wasn't as much a reenactment or a tribute, he thought, but a folding of time upon itself, a transposition of two hunters seeking deer magic within the frame of the winter hills.

The High Blue Lonesome

He had been hunting for three straight days, and his senses are tuned to the slightest movement and sound, his mind filtering and editing every nuance. The winter woods are a blend of subtle shades, like a faded camouflage shirt, and his eyes strain as he scans the steep slope. He notes the shadow of a raven, the flicking tail of a distant gray squirrel, a wagging fern. Nothing escapes his vigilance.

Suddenly, he spots several deer working toward him less than 70 yards away, and he wonders how they got so near without his notice. He leans against a boulder and raises his binoculars, momentarily losing the position of the deer, then picks up the toss of a tail. Three does browse along, with a fine buck just behind. The roar of his .270 shatters the stillness as the buck falls where it stands.

The hunter attaches his tag to the 10-pointer's ear and ties its front legs between the brow tines of the buck's sweeping antlers. He brings the rope along its gray face, pulls a half-hitch taut around the muzzle and begins the long drag back to his truck on the other side of the mountain.

He could not believe his good fortune in taking this great buck so late in the season, but it wasn't chance alone that brought the deer up through the grape tangles and rocks to his gun. He knew the general location of the buck, and had drawn on it when it came into range during archery season. It never presented a good shot, though, so he eased down and watched as the tall white antlers faded into the fog.

But now, the buck is tied to the end of his drag rope, its wild essence committed to memory, every detail of it picking its way through the woods already playing on an endless reel in his mind.

When he reaches the top of the ridge, most of the adrenaline has worn off and he rests, then decides to seek an easier route down and bears left. The heavy buck slips nicely along the trace of an old woods road bordered by a stone wall where the leaves have buffeted and settled. The raspy sound of the deer sliding over leaves and rocks is amplified by the carcass's hollow cavity. As he brings the buck around a section of broken log, an antler furrows the leaves, and he hears the unmistakable clink of glass. He sees the base of a jar and lifts it intact from the black earth.

The blue-green canning jar has the trademark "Lightning" in raised letters on the front. The glass lid is held with wire bail clamps. He wipes away some moss and dirt and notices something inside. Curious, he breaks the seal and unclamps the lid and takes out a wallet-shaped piece of stiff, leathery hide folded and pinned with a long hatpin. He carefully removes the pin and opens it.

The hide is lined with a thick fabric that together hold several pages of a letter. It is in surprisingly good condition. Written in a delicate script, the black ink has faded to sepia. The afternoon is waning and he has a long drag ahead, but is compelled to read it.

December 20, 1921

To whomever may find this letter:

I had always wanted to see the ocean. I thought we might travel there some day, my husband Tim and I, and see it together as we had talked about. But now that day will never come.

Sometimes on summer afternoons, I would sit on our stone wall and close my eyes and make believe that the winds rushing up from the valley and through the trees were the sounds of waves falling on a shore. And in the spring, when the leaves unfurled and the rain clouds sagged low and the bottomland was layered in mists, I imagined that the broad valley floor was a gentle green sea.

These words are the last I will write from up here at the High Blue Lonesome, as I have fondly come to call our place, and lacking a proper bottle to hold this letter, and a sea to toss it in, I place it instead in a jar and cast it out into the cold tides of winter, with the hope that someday, someone may find it and know our story.

Tim returned safely from The Great War, and we married, looking to start our life together somewhere other than on the farm. We had gone to the city for the work, living in a crowded warren along the river with many others who labored in the ironworks and mines. Soon enough, we found the noisy and sooty city life not to our liking.

Tim hired on at a sawmill 60 miles north, far up in the forested hills. It was a large mill, and most who worked there lived along this winding mountain road. Having had our fill of crowded neighborhoods, we built a small house atop the mountain, at the very end of the road. The elements were more severe up here than in the valley, but the magnificent view and solitude were well worth any inconvenience.

The sawmill work was steady, and we had a mule and a milk cow, Hannah, a flock of red hens and two piglets. It was a wild place, though; one night our spotted pig was carried off by a bear. My garden was my pride and joy, and guarded by our faithful dog, Feather, named so as he was so light on his feet, and would set to flight any wild creature that dared to wander too near.

Sounds carried up to this high point from great distances, and it was easy to gauge the course of the day by the routine sounds of creatures, both wild and domestic. I came to know the songs of certain birds through the seasons and learned the names of flowers and trees, too. On clear nights, the stars were draped low in the sky like strands of diamonds; at times, scores of shooting stars streaked across that black dome.

I became familiar with the many faces and phases of sister moon, and cannot express the variety and beauty of the glorious sunrises and sunsets. Our two years on the mountain were the sweetest of times that anyone could imagine, and I grew to love our mountain as I would a dear friend.

Tim had come from a long line of hunters and, in autumn, carried his double-barrel hammer shotgun to work, sometimes potting squirrels or a rabbit on his way home. Once, he shot a wild turkey, and as I watched him come up the lane it was not hard to imagine him as a frontiersman of the previous century.

One evening in early November, as we prepared to retire for the day, we heard the rapid alarm signal of the bell at White Rock Church. Once outside, we smelled a pungent smoke, and far below could see a bright spot of flame. The sawmill was ablaze, and by the time we got there, it was a raging inferno that had spread to the tall stacks of logs surrounding the mill. It was a bitter cold and windy night, and the heat was so great that we had to stand all the way up on the main road. All attempts to quell the fire were in vain, and we all stood there, arm in arm, and wept, watching our dreams rise and die with the sparks in the fathomless sky.

Without work and a long winter ahead, most of the families moved on. Being that we had no children and had saved a bit of money, we decided to stay the winter with the intent of moving back to my parents' farm in the spring. I had every nook and cranny of the house crammed with jars of vegetables and fruits, and Tim had built a smokehouse and laid up a great store of firewood.

Tim hunted whenever he could, and told of a large buck deer that had eluded him; he hoped for a good tracking snow. I made him a wool mackinaw with a double cape on the shoulders to fend off the cold winds. Soon after, there came an afternoon when the sky promised to bring snow, and he put on his new coat and with his Springfield rifle slung over his shoulder, headed out.

I watched him walk up the lane as icy needles pecked against the windowpanes. My hunter turned and waved, fading then into the graying woods. Tim always returned no later than deep dusk, so I would not worry, but when he did not return that night, I began to fret in earnest.

There had been no snow, but many hours of freezing rain, and the entire mountain appeared to be encased in glass. I thought he might have killed that deer far back in the hills near dusk and would pack it out in the light, or perhaps he made a fire and a camp to stay the night, as it was too treacherous to make his way back through the icy woods. All through the night, branches cracked and treetops crashed, jarring me from my vigilance.

The next morning, I walked partway

out the ridge, calling his name, but only ravens answered. That afternoon, I rode our surefooted mule down the mountain through a maze of fallen trunks, and far out the valley to White Rock Church to seek help.

A group of men returned with me and set out to search. They combed the woods for two days and were joined then by others who came up from the valley.

It was Feather, though, who finally found his master. From what they determined, Tim had shot the buck and was dragging it down through a notch between the rocks and lost his footing, falling to his peril.

I will soon leave here and move back to the farm. I cut a square from the cape of Tim's coat and a like one from the tanned hide of his deer and place this letter between them, my story secure between the hunter and quarry.

I dream sometimes that I am standing at the window, and my hunter is returning home, dragging his deer down the lane along the stone wall. But in my dream, the nearer he comes, the more he fades, until all that remains are leaves blowing across the empty lane.

And know this one last thing: the story of this wild and beautiful place is more than that of wind and trees and rocks and the creatures that dwell here. It also is the forgotten story of those who had lived here a while; a story of lives that came and went, that perhaps someday, in some way, may be carried by a heavenly tide to wash up again on these lofty shores.

Forever here in spirit,
Lorraine Mae Crawford

WITH QUIVERING HANDS, the hunter carefully folds the letter, returns it to the jar and puts it in his pack. He continues on, pulling the buck around a large pile of stones veiled in greenbrier, most likely the foundation of their house. It starts to snow, grainy pellets that gather quickly on the leaves, and by the time he makes it to his truck, it is full dark and snowing heavily.

He finally pulls into the driveway, and sees the silhouette of his wife standing at the picture window, backlit by a fire in the hearth. She comes out onto the porch and into the yard.

He lets down the tailgate and shows her his buck, and as always, she makes a great fuss about his prowess. Together they drag the buck around back and hang it in the walnut tree.

"It was getting late, and the roads were icing up; I was starting to worry," she tells him. "Did you have to drag it far?"

"It was a long way back," he replies. "But now I'm home."

Better Late

IT HAD been light for almost an hour by the time I got to the far side of the Big Field on this, the last day of deer season. The snow started again; big, lacy flakes, rocking and drifting, added to the pristine blanket from the night before. I was late getting in, but in no real hurry.

Normally, I would have already been on stand, but I slept in, ate a leisurely breakfast and took my time getting ready. I had been hunting hard for weeks on end and decided on this last day to kick it back a notch and not let my buck tag burn a hole in my pocket. I stopped often on the long walk across the field to admire the sheer beauty and tranquility of the winter landscape, my thoughts drifting with the slowly falling flakes.

As I neared the woods, several shots rang out from an adjacent hollow. My carefree attitude flew up and away like a window blind suddenly set loose and I snapped to full attention. I was a mile in with another mile to go. This was it, I reminded myself, the last day. Time to get with it and hustle.

I just entered the tree line on a deer trail when I spotted a hunter walking directly toward me. A fellow graybeard, he wasn't carrying a gun and his eyes were locked on mine and he was grinning as if I were a long-lost relative. I didn't know him, but even from a distance I could tell he was eager to talk. And talk he did, loudly and excitedly.

He told me he had dropped off a family

member at a stand down by the creek and that he wasn't hunting because he had killed his buck during archery season. Then, without missing a beat, he launched into a tedious and meandering saga of that hunt. I could tell this was not the first time he told this story, and braced for its telling, resigning myself to this as punishment for being late.

My eyes immediately glazed as he set forth with an analysis of the mast crop of the last several years, shifting then to lessons of woodsmanship imparted by long-departed uncles. There was a lengthy interjection of the tale of a mythical local buck of great proportions, followed by a digression on the finer points of hunting during certain moon phases. Two more shots in rapid succession echoed across the field, jarring me from my self-induced fugue state. I started to look around. He talked on.

I thought his archery odyssey was going to culminate in the killing of the legendary buck that haunted his dreams. Instead, it was a 5-point buck that fell to his arrow, one he said he wished now that he hadn't killed; he should have waited for a day like this, with its classic snow, like those deer seasons of yesteryear.

He said he liked my rifle, wanted to know what caliber it was. I sensed he wanted to talk guns. I know that look and as I turned my head to cringe before answering, I caught a glimpse of two deer, a nice buck and a doe, streaking across the field directly toward us. They swapped ends and bolted back over a rise when the teller of tales quickly shuffled to his right to get a better look.

I sighed heavily; told him I still had a way to go. He said he thought he had seen me before, asked what vehicle I drove. I never offered my name, but I told him I drive a blue F-150. He said he had seen it at the parking area, that his was the red Chevy pickup. He appeared eager to debate the merits of each. I know that look, too, and before he could say another word, I escaped, bidding him well. Daylight was burning, and now I was very late.

THE PROFUSION of fresh tracks on the trails leading toward the thickets looked like the wildly scribbled notes of a mad composer on the staves of a music sheet. As I progressed across the big flat, I kicked up a few deer that were bedded and saw others in flight. It was then I was struck by the realization that there might be a plus side to getting in late.

A lot of deer pushed by the initial wave of hunters might have swung back around from where they came. It's the way of the whitetail to be where hunters are not, and coming in a bit later just might present an unexpected opportunity. It seemed logical to assume some deer were already pushed into deep cover, but fresh sign showed a good many were lurking or bedded in this intermediate area.

It was very quiet and snowing moderately, so visibility was good. These were perfect conditions for still-hunting and I was seeing deer, so I decided to hunt the big flat before heading to my stand and once again slowed my pace.

If there's one thing that captures the true spirit of deer hunting, it's stalking silently through good cover on a snowy day. I was carrying a great little woods rifle, a magnum variant of the bolt-action Remington Model Seven CDL. With its longer and heavier 20-inch magnum-contour barrel, the rifle balances better than the standard model, and best of all, it was chambered for the potent .350 Remington Magnum, a longtime favorite.

I made sure my 2.5-8x scope was set at its lowest power and set out across the flat. Most of the deer were bedded along the ridgeline's sawtooth edge. Often rough and broken, narrow creases along that edge open up and deepen as they continue downslope, becoming ravines. Ridgeline edges bear the brunt of the winds and elements, resulting in numerous windfalls and exposed rocks. Whitetails bed alongside windfalls and just within shallow creases. They can see downhill and also across the flat on top, and in a few bounds are instantly out of sight of approaching danger, from the flat or below.

Late-season whitetails are survivors that really take off when bumped, but that's to be expected after being pushed an entire season. Sometimes, they'll run far out ahead then stop, looking back to see if they're being followed. Then, at the slightest provocation, take off again. I've taken two deer in the snow by dropping far down a sidehill then swinging way out in front. In both instances, they were watching their backtrails, looking for me.

During the late season, a hunter should consider changing up approaches and adapting as the days move along. Weather conditions, food sources and hunter pressure remain prime considerations. Incoming storm fronts always get deer up and moving. Food sources may shift dramatically during this time. Most corn crops have been harvested, mast crops vary widely, and some deer have converted to a diet of browse.

There's usually little hunting pressure on weekdays. A good strategy is to select two or three stands, where you may spend an hour or two, then still-hunt between them. The first stand, for obvious reasons, should be near bedding areas. Deer get up to feed and move every couple of hours, and a good second stand is one along a trail that leads to a food source. The third stand of the day should be a late afternoon stand where deer begin to make their way to agricultural fields or oak flats. The three-stand approach is not only effective, but makes for a more interesting day than one long sit, especially if it's cold.

Sometimes, though, it's fun to just operate on a hunch. During one second-week hunt, I had been still-hunting, when I came to the end of a long, narrow bench and sat on a log to rest. It was midmorning and I hadn't seen a deer yet, but on the next bench below me, I spotted a deer coming my way. The buck popped up over, skirted some pines, and continued on, never noticing me. It was a fork-horn, and I filed this to memory.

A year later, right around the same day and time, I once again still-hunted across that bench and sat to rest on that same log. It was a moment of déjà vu when, within minutes, I saw a buck just below, this time a nice 8-point, and when it came up over the rise exactly where the fork-horn had, I shot him. I'd wager with confidence it was the same buck.

JUST BEFORE noon, I moved to my stand in anticipation of hunters leaving the woods for lunch; many would be leaving for the day, calling it a season. On their way out, they inevitably would stir the pot. I settled in on the steep sidehill just outside the thicket, and it wasn't long before I started seeing deer. They arrived as singles and in twos and threes, and from different directions.

One thing the talkative hunter of that morning had right: there was something special about hunting on a classic snowy day. I thought of other days in the deer woods like this, recalled old photos of dragging deer out in deep snow and of favorite magazine covers featuring deer-hunting scenes. One of those scenes came to life when I spotted the dark forms of five deer running up the hill, then disappearing in the grape tangles. When they re-emerged, I saw that the first two were does, but the other three were bucks. They turned up toward me and when they neared, I saw that the first two bucks were both 8-pointers, but the third was a big, wide-racked bruiser. I focused on him.

I thought they might slow or stop, but they kicked it into overdrive, eager to get into the thicket. I missed the big buck with my first shot, hit a thick grapevine with the second. He stopped, looked around, and at my third shot, bucked wildly and took off on a 70-yard dash, head held low, torpedoing into the thicket and piling up on the rim of a depression.

This monarch was a classic, deep-woods gray ghost. I couldn't imagine the countless miles he had run across these hills and through the heart of this hollow, and fittingly, this one final sprint with the slant of flakes on his face, charging hard into that final realm where the light of his days fades, but burns brightly again as it passes to the hunter.

The 9-pointer was the biggest-racked buck I've ever taken and appeared to be 4½ years old. It was also the third consecutive buck I had taken over 200 pounds. My brother-in-law Dave arrived with the deer cart a couple of hours later. Instead of trying to haul the buck up the steep mountain, we went out the back way, which was farther, through the game lands. As we came through the woods to the road, we stopped to rest and looked back at the setting sun, a peach-colored orb filtering through shimmering veils of snowflakes. Late getting in, late getting out. A great last-day buck. Beyond the gift of the buck, though, it was the snow's mesmerizing motion upon the land that paced the hunter, becoming an ally in the hunt. No matter what the pace of a hunt may be, though, it is never too late to stop and marvel at the singular wonder that is winter in the uplands.

Big Woods Bruin

Northwoods Passages

BLACK BEARS lead secretive lives, moving through the corridors of night while searching for anything edible. Here in Penn's Woods, nature's vast storehouse of diverse natural foods, as well as that provided by agriculture and civilization, offer easy pickings and some bears grow to immense size, like the bruiser in *Big Woods Bruin*. I wanted, however, to capture some element of the bear in this portrait other than its formidable presence.

In the dying light of day, the woods is awash in red light, lending an other-worldly, theatrical setting to the subject. The bear's coat catches and returns light and color like the knapped facets of an obsidian arrowhead. With dusk approaching, this bear may be venturing out into the night, or, it could have been pushed out of its hiding place in a thicket by hunters putting on a final drive.

The mountainous northern regions of Penn's Woods are often referred to as the Big Woods, the Black Forest, and the Northern Tier. It is a place of ravens, black bears and goshawks, where diminutive brook trout fan in the stepped pools of deep, dark hollows.

It is a region of legendary hunting camps where old stories and local tales still linger, a stronghold of traditions and a steadfast hunting heritage.

I have spent much time hunting these northern regions, but what remains foremost in my mind's eye are the long views of the opposing hillsides from across great valleys, drifting rags of fog, some sleet and snow showers, a damp chill that permeates to the marrow.

And suddenly, a bear.

Now I Know the Hunter

Hunt a woods several times and it's fairly easy to become familiar with the general topography and features of the landscape; hunt there long enough, and you may come to sense something deeper, for a woods – like a person – has many subtle characteristics that make it unique. Every woods has an underlying current, a pulse, that is only revealed over time. Once tapped into it, the hunter is transfused with that selfsame lifeblood that flows through every wild heart, every living thing in that forestland. No longer an intruder, he becomes an expression of the land itself: the drifting leaf, the shadow sliding down an oak, the grapevine cinching tighter in the wind. It takes time for a hunter to find this niche.

Last autumn I spent six weeks hunting in various places around Penn's Woods, but I focused on one woodland in particular. It was a place I had hunted before, but no more than a few days each year, and I felt compelled to know it better.

I wanted to know how the wind moves and sounds as it travels through the hollows; I wanted to know the shift and arc of light and shadow throughout the day. I wanted to better understand the temperament and rhythms of this woods on warm Indian summer afternoons, on mornings of fog and drizzle, on frigid days when the wind howls and the snow sweeps in, laying deep on the ridges, or falling softly, decorating trees and vines and weeds with fine lacework. Woods-wise hunters tuck these useful observations away, like cartridges in their loops.

This is a diverse and lovely woods. The crowns of towering oaks are draped with enormous tangles of grapevines. The older vines, where they curl from the earth, are thick as a rut buck's neck. Some ravines are choked with the pervasive tangles, and the lesser trees hunch like captive creatures weighed down by capture nets.

On a topo map, the numerous hollows have the same aimless patterns as insect borings. This may be, in part, why the winds seem so fickle here. Sweeping across the high plateau, they rush down through these deep warrens, dividing, buffeting upwards, rejoining sibling winds, swirling across the flats, eddying on corrugated slopes.

This woods is generally noisy with the steady creak and groan of trees. Many have toppled into the arms of their neighbors, where they bow and saw with the loud and discordant screech of catgut strings. One of the loudest, near a favorite deer stand, whistles and chirps like an elk herd. When the wind is up, I can locate this stand in the dark just by listening for this tree.

Huge logs are scattered about like matchsticks, victims of storms or age, with great spreading root masses taller than a man. The most recent ones are clotted yet, with dirt and rock and sprays of ferns, while the older ones are splayed like desperate skeletal hands.

The zigzag scars of old logging trams are mostly overgrown with birch and hurdles of windfalls, but in some places, they provide easy passage on the steeper sidehills. Dozens of freshets and seeps trickle across the roads, gurgling across the hemlock-filled bottomland to the meandering creek.

From a distance, the creek sounds like blood rushing in the ears; up close, it speaks in whispers and songs. A brook trout fans in a small dark pool, darting under the awning of leaves when I peer over the edge. I wonder if it had done the same when it spotted the buck that made the scrape next to the pool.

The scrape is large and fresh, a rich black canvas sprinkled with rusty hemlock needles. I kneel to study the graying furrows and hoof prints within, reading my itinerary for November.

IT HAS BEEN 20 years since leaf-drop has been this late, and a heavy snow in October has brought down so many limbs and treetops that even the more open spaces are like an obstacle course. The snow melts quickly, and for two days I still-hunt all through the game lands, more an in-season scouting excursion than a real bowhunt. With the leaves still hanging, the windfalls provide good cover when sneak hunting.

Everywhere, clusters of dusty blue grapes lie in profusion among glistening acorns. With food so readily available, the deer don't have to move far to feed. Halfway down a steep, rocky ravine, I lean against a snag and listen to a flock of turkeys below. Just as I turn my head to look back up the hill, a sharp-shinned hawk flares right in my face. I flinch violently, and the hawk circles around me in a tight loop, then weaves away through the grapevines. Was it going to land on me or the snag? Perhaps it mistook the tuft of hair sticking through the hole in the back of my cap for a small bird. The illustrated figure of death wears a dark robe, but for some songbirds, it comes adorned in a feathered tapestry of dark bars and rusty chevrons. As the days slide by, I regain my woods legs and eyes, moving again in synch with the light and wind and the reluctant leaves that continue to fall. I decide to hunt far back in, and follow a tributary that feeds into the stream. I stand for a while in the shadow of an enormous root mass, then continue on. Behind me, I hear, then see, a doe being chased by a terrific buck. They're at least 80 yards up the hollow and, to my amazement, when I give a doe bawl, the 10-point peels away from the doe's trail and comes right down the tributary.

He stops next to the root mass and looks all around. I ease down off the bank and into the water to have a better view – or shot. I call softly and he edges down farther, spring steel in each step, dark eyes searching, ears cupped. Forty yards out and he will come not an inch closer.

He stomps. I wait. Then he turns and continues his chase after the sure thing. This, I decide, is the buck I will concentrate on the rest of the season. Strong winds play havoc for most of the week, and as the leaves continue to fall, the woods opens up, becoming brighter; spaces deepen, all movement more apparent. Deer trails once obscured by successive falling layers of leaves are now more evident. Buck sign is everywhere. With more mature bucks now in the herd, both rubs and scrapes have increased proportionately.

The ensuing days are tests of will and stamina. It's a far way back in, and I can feel the toll of so many early mornings. I set up at promising scrape lines, or sneak hunt. Whenever a lesser buck walks by, I am tempted, but think again of the mass and arc of that 10-point rack and the weighty swagger in the big buck's gait. Hope rises as the rut peaks, but I do not see the big buck again, only his image etched on the back of my eyelids in the fitful sleep of the tired hunter.

On the first day of gun season, the hollow brims with endless curtains of dense fog. Not one deer moves past my stand, and at two o'clock, I gather up my gear and head into the grapevines to another stand. The leaves are wet and silent and I move less than 70 yards when I spot the shape of a big deer as it stands up and starts to sneak through the thicket. It pauses at the crest of the hollow, only its head visible. There is no mistaking his sweeping antlers; it is the buck I have been hunting all month. I try to steady the crosshairs on the patch below its neck, but it's very steep here and I'm standing on a rock that totters when I try to firm up my stance. With the deer sky-lined, I hold my shot, hoping it'll angle down a bit and give me a safe backdrop. Instead, it catches my scent, whirls, and slips away.

At my second stand, I watch deer after deer emerge slowly from the fog, in the way a drawing emerges, stroke by stroke, on paper. In the remaining hours, I pass on more than a dozen deer, confident that I'll get one the next day. I don't want to be dressing out a doe if the buck slips back through.

TUESDAY IS A COMPLETE washout, with torrential rains and more fog, but Wednesday promises to be bright and clear. There are no other vehicles at the parking area, and I set up on a point where several narrow flats wrap around. Not 15 minutes later, I catch movement of something coming around the bend.

At first, I think it's a deer, but it's smaller, and yellowish in color. The coyote pads along and stops to pick up some grapes, continues on a few steps, then gobbles down a few more. Juice with his breakfast. I have only a narrow window for a shot, and when he stops with his forelegs atop a log, my .270 barks.

There, stretched out on the leaves is the most beautiful animal I have ever seen. His slipstream form is built for speed, for travel in the woods, no less than the hawk in the air or trout in the stream. His coat is thick and deep, and largely the color of an aging buck rub, palest yellow, and rusty around the edges, the long black-tipped guard hairs make him appear to be covered with a black frost.

Dark jagged lines of hair delineate fur tracts and run down the front of his forelegs, which is a trait of the eastern coyote. I pull clots of burdock burs from his ruff.

He is the hard hunter.

He has a handsome, intelligent face, the curve of his mouth like a wry smile, with long pristine teeth rimmed by dark lips. The bushy tail is black-tipped with another black spot midway up, like I have often seen on foxes. The feet are surprisingly large, wolfish, the black nails worn to stubs, pads tannin-stained from endless miles on brown oak leaves. He is surely the alpha male of this valley, nearly 5 feet long from tip-of-nose to tip-of-tail, with a deep nail-keg chest and long legs and – I would later learn – a weight of 53 pounds.

I put my palm on the coyote's shoulder, and then, as if this creature were a conduit to something deeper in the earth, I could sense, then feel the true scope of life in this woods. I could see him standing in the goldenrod near the snow-covered field on a brittle winter night, stars like white-hot pinpricks in the indigo heavens, the vapor of his breath billowing after a lively chase, a freshly killed cottontail at his feet.

My hand is warmed in the dense fur, from the heat of his body. Through him, I could feel the humid air of summer nights, hear the rustle of mice in the leaves, owl talk in the hemlocks, the pack yodeling, grinning and yipping in the dark, and see the glint of the moon in their amber eyes.

And in those moments, I knew much more of his days, of sudden storms and fiery red sunsets and the vault of yellow dawns and the grand sweep of the seasons, a glimpse into the hidden folds of the woods that no man ever sees. I understood more about the hunter I am, and the hunter I am not.

A FOOT of fresh snow on the final two days of the season lends the feel of yesteryear when it seemed there was snow every deer season. Abundant sign shows that the deer were eating mostly grapes, and occasionally digging down to snuffle up acorns. At first light, I spot a group of five far down the mountain doing just that, and I shoot a deer that bolts downhill another 75 yards. I take my time dressing out the acorn-fat deer.

I drag the deer uphill a short distance, when a hunter threads his way down the thick, brushy slope, following deer tracks. His face bears an incredulous look.

"Didn't you see a big buck come down through here? I missed him up on top just a little while ago."

"No. It probably sneaked by while I was dressing out my deer."

"He's a real big one," he said, smiling as he continued on.

THE HIDE of the coyote hangs on the wall. To me, it is neither trophy nor novelty, but a memory map. The black line down the back is the rim of the valley, the gray contours around the flank are the point where my deer stand is. Here on the cape is the creek, darker now in winter. The ragged lines that run down the forelegs are tracks of the hunters, coyote and man, that follow the same blood trail far into the hills.

Ursa Minor
SHADES OF BLACK

Years ago, while in New York City delivering some work, I stopped for a quick walk-through at the Guggenheim Museum. On display was an exhibit of paintings by Ad Reinhardt (American, 1913-1967). The paintings were a part of his black square series. From a distance, the large, square paintings appeared to be solid black squares, but upon closer investigation the canvases were divided into smaller black squares that were just slightly different shades of black: reddish-blacks, blue-blacks, green-blacks. Reinhardt's goal was to create non-objective art that was "timeless, spaceless, changeless" with only the most subtle shifting of hues and shades.

The paintings made me think of black bears, not only because of the subtle shades of black in their lustrous coats, but their secretive behavior. For the most part, bears are nocturnal, moving through the night as a black mass moving through blacker shadow, like the shift of hues in Reinhardt's paintings.

Inspired by this connection, I wrote two stories about the secret lives of two different black bears moving through the great black canvas of night as do the fabled constellations Ursa Minor, known as the Little Bear, and Ursa Major, the Great Bear. Black is not only the color of the setting in these stories, but in effect becomes a character, along with a black-phase timber rattler, black vultures, crows, wild turkeys, blackberries and a vintage PRR locomotive. Mostly, we may recognize art in nature, but it is more difficult to discern nature in art: timeless, spaceless, changeless. This, I believe, was part of what Reinhardt was stating.

T HE WORN TRAIL through the rhododendron thicket is more tunnel than path, as if bored by giant worms rather than generations of bears. A dog bear, as some would call such a leggy young bear, pads along this trail, his black form nebulous in the deep shade, except for the glint of ivory grin set above the white chevron on his chest. He travels purposefully, a meal in mind. Where the thicket thins, he leaves the trail, angling through an old burn, past blackened stumps, like a statuary of the bear itself. He swings out of the burn and stops at the edge of a powerline and looks about before crossing.

Dog bear comes upon a wood turtle on the other side. The turtle retracts within its shell. The bear stands on the turtle with its forepaws and pushes down; then steps back. He sniffs at the portals, nibbling at the feet, just out of reach. He licks the shell, his tongue running over the raised geometric relief of the carapace. Frustrated, he sits down and licks his own paw, then flips the turtle over, then back again. The turtle slides down an embankment and the bear loses interest. With dark approaching, he continues down the mountain, the taste of turtle on his lips, but no sweet meat within his pinching gut.

Dog bear walks the thicket between a rail line and the river and stops at a clearing, the site of a derailment two years previous. Greasy, discarded ties lie in profusion. Blackberry canes have sprouted in the opening and between the spaces of the overlapping ties. The canes arc under the weight of ripe fruit. Hungry, but cautious, dog bear listens and tests the air, checking for the scent of a mature bear that had been feeding here. He waits long minutes, keen nose always working the air, ears pricked for any sound. Satisfied that all is safe, he works the canes feverishly, a purple froth gathering in the corners of his mouth. He snuffles down the plump berries into the night, while overhead Perseid meteors flash and die across the great river valley.

Content for now, dog bear rests, sucking in the cool night air that slides down the mountain. Suddenly, his nostrils flare wide and he exhales explosively and bolts from the berry patch to the railroad tracks, running at full tilt between the starlit rails like a phantom locomotive. He crashes through thick tangles and splashes across the shallow river, hiding in a jungle of tall, clattering reeds. Back at the berry patch, an enormous boar bear feasts on the warm, seedy berries. He has a low-slung belly and tree-trunk legs, a true heavyweight, what some might call a "hog bear."

Later that night, dog bear walks up behind a row of cottages along the river. He overturns a grill, licks grease and bits of charred meat from the grate, sniffs at the rubble, then demolishes several birdfeeders, eating all the sunflower seeds within. At another cottage, the owners and their old basset sleep soundly as dog bear finishes a bowl of dog food on the back porch. He discovers a child's pail on the grassy river frontage and munches happily on a trio of crayfish left inside, along with some watermelon rinds left near a dock. He panics – bolting again – when a tire-swing he has loosened from the crotch of a willow tree swings back and thumps him on his rump.

The driving force of his days is a relentless search for food, especially during a period of hyperphagia, or excessive eating, in which he gains weight before hibernation. He is wonderfully equipped to consume a wide variety of foods. He can graze, climb, forage, kill, steal, scavenge, dig, swim and fight for any potential meal. His body is a repository for the diverse bounty of the landscape, and he exploits every opportunity with amazing skill and keen intelligence.

At first light, the forest already dawns hot and humid. He fords the river, crosses a highway and follows a creek up through a deep hollow. He stops at a small shadowy pool. A tall waterfall, now but a narrow, steady stream, plunks musically into the pool. Dog bear drinks noisily, then sits in the water. Polypody ferns dance in the spray of water droplets that spatter off his back. The steaming woods awaken. A wood thrush floats a morning song. A towhee warbles a lingering tremolo. Crane flies loop about, as if moving within an invisible ball. Dog bear laps the gritty water and heads for higher ground.

Farther up the hill he rips apart an old log to its punky core. Black ants frantically evacuate, some carrying eggs, but many of the frantic colony cannot escape his dexterous lips and tongue. Sated, he climbs up between two walls of a towering rock outcropping and comes out onto a mossy ledge where he plops down, front legs stretched before him. He looks intently down the slope at some bobbing silhouettes — wild turkey gobblers moving through some hemlocks — then relaxes. Secure in this cool, rocky bastion, dog bear sleeps.

Farther up the ridge on another sunny ledge, several gravid timber rattlesnakes bask in the sun. They have been at this rookery all summer, not eating, body temperatures warm and stable, ensuring healthy development of the young they will bear live in a few weeks. A black-phase male, nearly four feet long, moves past the congregation of females into the tumble of rocks below. He is the color of summer shadows and moves like dark smoke through the leaves. His is a world of long minutes and careful movement as he mostly waits along logs. He may buzz menacingly, and coil and recoil defensively when startled or annoyed, and can strike faster than the eye can follow, but the rattler is summer's patient hunter, seeking mice, voles, chipmunks and birds.

Five turkey vultures, buoyed by rising thermals, spiral over the hollow. Their huge shadows crisscross over the undulating canopy and as one, they drift towards the open expanse of the river valley. They rock back and forth in what is called contorted flight, where lift is altered between one wing and another.

One, then another, smell the carcass of the dead deer along the train tracks before they see it, even at this altitude. They feed for a while by queuing individuals in an organized manner.

It is not long before other shadows appear

overhead as a group of aggressive black vultures descend and drive the turkey vultures from the carcass. The turkey vultures perch, wings outspread, macabre decorations on the twisted armature of a dead tree like a prehistoric diorama, ghastly and beautiful.

A trio of gobblers, longbeards all, file out of the hemlocks. They are sleek, black and silent, and show a tolerance for each other, far different than their intense rivalries of spring. They scratch through the remnants of the log ripped apart by dog bear, feeding on ants and millipedes and white grubs curling in the sun. One bird, then another, dusts in the pile of exposed dirt near the log. Loosened feathers are strewn about the rust-colored debris. The gobblers move off, stoic lords of the forest's dark folds, anonymous sires of dozens of poults who grow under the care of the secretive hens.

Inky clouds bloom in the western sky, blotting out the sun. No fierce storm is this, with only a mild complaint of thunder. It rains steadily, deliciously, for two hours. The mountains drink. A rivulet of water runs off an overhang, down the spout of a rhododendron leaf and patters between the eyes of the sleeping dog bear. Too lethargic to move back, he turns his head and the heavy drops plunk off his twitching left ear. Dog bear stretches and yawns and licks the water from his nose. The rain ceases and a cool breeze nudges the humidity from the uplands.

A crow gives a series of nasally *aahs*. Another answers with a louder *Awww*! They talk and mutter and are joined by a third. One crow spies a white shape moving nearby, like a small white bird with wings held upward trying to fly. Curious, the crow flies closer and sees that it is the white chevron rising and falling on dog bear's chest. Spoiling for some sport after the invigorating rain, the crow's urgent calls bring others and their raging tirade pries the bear from his hideout. He stands with his ears laid back and when the mob's taunts reach a crescendo, he turns and exits through the back of the fissure and hustles up over the ridge.

Dog bear traverses the old burn again, ranges higher, and emerges into a sea of tossing ferns at the very apogee of the uplands, where a potent wind nudges the secrets of summer shadows aside, making room for the first whisper of autumn. Dog bear moves along quickly, a meal in mind.

Four Months Later

The dead of winter, snowy and frigid. The leafy canopy of August lies brown and tattered beneath the snow. The wild turkey gobblers, barons of this desolate landscape, proceed cautiously to a seep. The timber rattlesnakes hibernate in the depths of the ledges, and the vultures have long moved on. The crows, and higher up, the ravens, will continue to monitor life on the mountain. Dog bear sleeps tucked into a small den within the ledges. He is the wild heart of the mountain itself, beating slowly in its rocky bosom, in this season, in this night, while Ursa Minor, the little bear, pads endlessly through starry thickets.

Ursa Major
ALLEGHENY ELEGY

A STEER SKULL, half-buried in oak leaves, stares out from the hilltop into the broad valley, and far beyond into the black void of a cold and clear November sky. The skull sparkles with an impasto of frost that captures torrents of stars. Cradled between the sweep of its horns is a horned moon, an arc within an arc.

Throughout the night, Leonid meteors crisscross above the Allegheny Plateau, but no eyes are poised to watch them flash and die, save those unseeing sockets of the skull. Like a boulder carried from a distant landscape and deposited by an ancient sheet of retreating ice, the skull is an erratic, a remnant from the tendril of civilization that has crept up the valley floor from the advancing sheet of populations beyond.

On top of the mountain, a shadowy mass ushers silently out of a thicket, fracturing into smaller shapes as it slips down through the piebald birches, then reassembles in the hollow as the complete and immense silhouette of a black bear.

The bear stops and sniffs the skull. He hooks a single claw into the eye socket and presses down, loosing it from the earth. A tenant mouse leaps from its nest in the brain cavity and is quickly snuffed up and swallowed by the bear. The bear steps over the skull and continues down into the hollow to feast on the flood of acorns that fill every cleft and runnel.

The bear feeds for a long time, grinding acorns with his great jaws, as he has nightly for days along this ridgeline. Satiated, he stops gorging, panting heavily; a huge Cheshire grin glistens in the dark.

Far below, a dog barks, then a light flicks on in a milk room. Cows low and shuffle. A vagrant breeze stirs the oak-leaf carpet. The bear raises its nose high, drawing in the cold air deeply and is gone before the plume of that same exhaled breath drifts and rises.

The bear, like the constellation Ursa Major, or Great Bear, is a child of the night, moving endlessly through his universe of starlit fields and trackless forests. Now in the autumn of his 16th year, and at more than 500 pounds, he has survived in the rumpled mountains of this province not only by brute force and terrific power, but mostly as an anonymous shadow slipping through the dense thickets.

IN A SENSE, black bears are born twice; first, while January winds howl, and again in March, when they emerge from the womb of the den into the dazzling world of early spring. And, so it is with Ursa, the last of three cubs to leave the secure den.

Ursa lingers momentarily. The familiar odors of the den rushing up past his nose, dissipating in mountain air alive with birdsong and strange and compelling aromas. He squats in a beam of sunlight, wide-eyed, every sense overloaded, then scrambles along in the shadow of his mother and into the deeper shadows of a hemlock glade and the rest of his life.

Maturing cubs quickly learn what is edible in nature's vast larder. They also learn, that in those fringes where civilization meets wilderness, special treats can be found. In their second summer, they experience the glut of a midsummer night in a sweet-corn patch, and the easy pickings of apple trees weighed down with fruit. They congregate with other bears at the local

dump, gleaning the putrid refuse. One night, the dump is flooded with lights as flashbulbs pop. A man takes pictures from the roof of his '36 Ford while his wife coos at the cubs from inside the coupe.

But danger abounds in the tenuous areas where man meets beast. Once, they were chased and treed by large, fierce dogs. At another farm, shotgun blasts rocked the still night air as they were driven from a corn crib. Ursa learns that man is to be avoided, that he should hide in the thickest cover in remote places while hunters put on noisy drives and rifle shots echo through the hills.

IN HIS FOURTH year, Ursa ranges far into new territory. While plodding

through a broad marsh between a highway and a rail line, an exquisite bouquet of rank meat pulls him through the cattails as if on a leash. He follows his nose to the perimeter of an opening flooded by light.

The light illuminates the stockyard of a small slaughterhouse that belongs to a butcher known as The Swede. His shop is on the edge of a tiny village, and at the close of evening hours, The Swede's three pigtailed and rosy-cheeked daughters come to a pen out back to watch their father feed scraps to bears that he has conditioned to handouts.

Cued by his banging with a cleaver on corrugated tin, the bears enter the stockyard nervously, quickly gobbling the scraps that he lobs at them. Suddenly, the lesser bears bolt from the yard as an enormous boar ambles into the circle of light.

"Make him dance, Papa, make him dance!" the butcher's daughters plead.

The Swede stands on the rung of a stock gate and waves an arm holding a scrap overhead, back and forth, like a metronome. The big bear sits up and begins to sway, following the arc of the meat scrap. The little girls clap in time and the boar, king of the uplands, is reduced to the lowly status of court jester.

Several days later, The Swede invites several neighbors to come over for the show.

Ursa has become part of the opening act, but he gives the big boar a wide berth when it makes its grand entrance.

At the start of the show, the big boar stops, then, in a lightning-fast charge, crashes headlong into the stock gate where the Swede is perched with his daughters, sending them sprawling into the mire. Screaming, they scramble into the shop and bolt the door as the big bear eats the spilled platter of scraps. Mama Swede, holding her whimpering daughters, firmly tells her still-trembling husband that this foolishness is over for good.

Ursa, ever cautious and fearful of the big boar, pads silently up to a flatbed truck parked on the side of the slaughterhouse. A steer's head lay on the tailgate. Ursa grabs it by an ear and takes off, fearing the big boar is after him. He splashes through the marsh, fords a creek and stops on a hilltop with his treasure, deftly peeling a tasty meal from the head, then covers the remains with leaves.

THE YEARS PASS, and summer finds Ursa in the southernmost part of his 70-mile range. He ambles along in the orange glow of a night sky set afire from a steel mill. The monstrous shadow of his form is cast on the side of a factory wall, like an image in a horror movie.

Outside the building are two long benches lined with metal lunch buckets, where men who work the night shift eat while catching the cool breeze that streams down the mountain. It's always lunchtime for Ursa, however, and he pilfers each pail, one at a time, eating the contents. He devours sandwiches of ham and bologna and garlic kielbasa, juicy peaches and bananas, cookies and lunch cakes.

Ursa is caught red-handed by the first worker to appear at the lunch benches. The man stands slack-jawed, face to face with the behemoth, its fur fringed in orange light, as if on fire, a sinister creature from a darker place. The worker tries to yell, but can emit only a hoarse gurgle, then bolts back into the plant while Ursa gently lifts another pail and hustles into the night to finish his lunch.

AN OCTOBER MORNING, and Ursa follows the course of a stream lined by blood-red trees. He stops at a deep crystal pool and stares into the depths at a tiny brook trout fanning in the slow current. The bear's eyes sparkle, and in one mighty leap he dives into the deep pool, the loud concussion of his body hitting the pool startling in the tiny glade. He lunges wildly in a circle, the trout long gone, but he thrashes about, merrily chasing imaginary fish up through the tiered pools, splashing noisily, wildly, then runs full-tilt up the creek, continuing on, up through a fern-covered hillside.

NATIVE AMERICANS believed that the constellation Ursa Major was a great bear being chased across the night sky by three hunters. In autumn, when the constellation rides low in the horizon, they thought the celestial bear to be wounded by the hunters, and its blood caused the trees to change the color of their leaves to red.

The complex social system of the Plains Indians was directly linked to nature by various clans and societies. Most societies were named after animals – The Doves, The Mosquitoes, Wolf, Crow Owners and Elk are but a few.

Some societies were open, while others were secret or elitist. One secret society was the Bear Dreamers – a mysterious, magical cult of Indians who experienced powerful dreams involving bears.

Bear hunters are dreamers, and the dreams of young bear hunters are especially vivid, as bears are steeped in lore and myth.

A teenage hunter, wiry and long-shanked, snakes through a dense thicket, carrying a new .250 Savage. It's drizzling and cold, and milkweed silk clings to the peach fuzz on his face. He climbs a blowdown for a better view, when a drive put on by a neighboring camp passes through the old clear-cut.

He likes the stand and stays there until near quitting time, having spent most of the day admiring his new rifle. He climbs down from his seat on the split trunk, and with this change of eye level, cannot believe his eyes when he sees what appears to be the huge head of a black bear staring at him only 30 yards away.

The bear is laying inside a treetop, and when the young hunter steps closer, the bear bolts out of its hiding place. The bear is so large it appears to move in slow motion. The gun suddenly feels heavy. His knees wobble, and the gun's sights wave crazily, and the shards of his childhood scatter through the brush like splinters from a thick branch as he centers his hurried shot.

He ejects the brass that is the

spent casing of his boyhood, and the next round jacked into the chamber is of a different nature; and in those few seconds, his life has changed forever as myth becomes truth, and his tale would now be inscribed in the ancient annals of the hunt and forever in his dreams.

URSA WALKS ALONG a rail line that wraps around the mountain and stops near a trestle. He feeds on fallen apples from a tree grown from an apple core tossed from the train years before. Down near the river, several hounds sing promises to their master as a raccoon heads up the slope.

The hounds are hot on the scent, and Ursa shuffles off when they get too close. At that instant, a train whistle fractures the air as it rounds the bend and steams across the trestle.

Ursa runs flat out along the rails, the baying hounds just below him, and in the confusion of strobing light and sound, he dashes across the tracks and is struck by the locomotive and thrown from the rails, broken and bleeding. Frightened, he scrambles for the safety of a thicket, but the intense pain, like an unseen tormentor, follows.

The train passes, and the hounds bark treed down by the river. At first light, the sky opens and sheets of rain pound the valley. Ursa struggles to drag his heavy form along the base of a towering escarpment. He is wracked with pain and laps water from the depression of a rock.

Cool air ushers up out of the ground from a large gap between boulders and fills his nostrils, not unlike the earthy air of his birthing den. He crawls into the gap and turns around in a small anteroom. He lies down, then backs up slightly but slides backwards on the wet rock. Too weak to gain purchase, he falls into black space deep into a chamber of the mountain from which he was sprung.

A NIGHT IN early spring, and a rivulet of water flows down through the steer skull, trickling from its sockets like some macabre and tragic fountain. Far below the surface, the bones of the great bear lie upon those of other creatures and others yet from an older time.

Ursa Major, the Great Bear, drifts through a celestial thicket above the Alleghenies.

Starry hunters follow.

The Bog Man

THE PONTIAC'S OLD HOOD had been thrown down the hill long ago, ending upright in a tiny run, and through the engineering inclinations of opportunistic beavers, it became the architectural centerpiece of their dam breast. From there, the chrome Chief Pontiac hood ornament gazed across the pond for decades.

The Bog Man dislodged the hood from the decrepit dam breast, slid it up the steep hillside, strapped it to his deer cart, along with a tire and some other junk, then hauled it to the truck where other spring clean-up volunteers waited.

Back home at his workshop, he removed the ornament from the rusted hood. As he cleaned it up, he thought of all that the noble sentinel had witnessed, including, of course, his own frequent comings and goings.

Only several miles from his home, the vast wetlands not only offered great trapping and hunting, but its primeval features and rugged complexity both nurtured his curiosity and nourished his adventurous nature, and those wild environs eventually became the load-bearing walls that

supported and gave strength to other aspects of his life. Although most believe that people select or title a certain province as their own, the Bog Man thought that with wild places, it was quite the opposite, that it was the land that claimed its citizenry, and he, in that unlikely place, had become a native son.

As a biology teacher, it also was a living classroom. Over time, he had most of the wetlands committed to memory; his topo maps were so heavily penciled with hand-drawn features and notations that they were more like journals than maps. He knew by heart the vast network of sphagnum-lined passages around the acidic tea-water pools, the stand of ancient pines where turkeys roosted, the derelict ponds of beavers, and the progress of their new excavations. At first, the bog seemed a vast and formidable place, but slowly, incrementally, he learned to travel the dank corridors with the stealth and confidence of a bobcat.

He placed the hood ornament on a shelf above his workbench, where it surveyed the big room filled with the accumulated paraphernalia of 40 years in the outdoors. A splendid birch bark canoe hung from the rafters of the high-peaked ceiling, along with a pair of bear-paw snowshoes and two trapper pack baskets. A dense hedgerow of antlers surrounded a large group of framed photographs. Dangling from its chain on a support post was an antique bear trap, pulled from the peat and beautifully preserved.

Tar, his old Lab, grizzled with the hoarfrost of the years, was nestled in the depths of a black leather sofa, appearing at first glance to be a rumpled cushion. The dog whined and twitched, dreaming of forays for wood ducks in the swamp. The Bog Man flicked off the workbench light and sat next to the dog, leaning back into a corner of the sofa, listening to the tongues of flame in the fireplace tell his story…

THERE WAS A DISTANCE between them, an ever-expanding gap that he feared was becoming a chasm that he could never again cross. But this, he knew, was a notion that many fathers with 16-year-old daughters believe.

"She's not 10 anymore," said his wife. "But don't worry, you're still her hero. Why don't you plan a day together? A hike maybe?"

Good idea, he thought. She used to be interested in everything he showed her, and recently he had discovered something she might really enjoy.

A few days later, he was about to knock on her door, but heard her laughing while talking on the phone. He hesitated, then knocked anyway.

"Thought you might want to pull on your boots and take a walk back in, like we used to. But if you're busy, we could go another…"

"Sure," she said, much to his surprise.

"We're going dragon hunting," he said.

"I've seen dragonflies."

"Not dragonflies," he emphasized. "And bring your camera to record the proof."

They followed a circuitous bear trail a long way and stopped at a patch of high-bush blueberries in bloom.

"I remember the day we picked berries here," she said. "And the muffins Mom and I made. We should do that again."

A pileated woodpecker flew across a clearing and alighted upon a riddled snag, then jackhammered the trunk. Bark and woodchips dimpled the water below.

"The excavation holes they make are rectangular," he said. "But the holes of their nesting cavities are perfectly round. I don't know why, though," he said.

"I thought 'The Bog Man' knew everything," she said, smiling.

She hadn't called him that in years, a name she made up for him after he showed her that the bog was not the gloomy or treacherous place many thought, but, instead, a rich and fascinating ecosystem, a relic of time that harbored many unusual plants such as the insect-eating sundew and pitcher plants and Labrador tea.

They walked and talked as life boiled in the great soupy kettle all around them.

Birdsong cascaded from every direction, startled deer splashed away, and the warm, oxygenated air was heavy with fragrances sweet and fresh.

"*And what is so rare ... as a day in June,*" she recited cheerfully.

They stitched a zigzag course around some beaver canals and passed a grassy meadow. He knelt on a mat of moss before a small colony of tiny magenta flowers.

"Here we are," he said. "The dragon's lair."

"What are they?" she asked. "They're so beautiful."

"Rare orchids. Dragon's mouth orchids, or swamp-pink."

As she took pictures, insects buzzed and cloud shadows streamed down through the canopy and across the tree trunks. Their time together burned off like mist in the steaming sun. Time running quickly, too quickly, he thought, but I'll hold this moment for a while. Spring – bright and fresh and maturing – seemed in a hurry to ease into the long, languid days of summer, like a teen rushing headlong into adulthood.

A week later, on Father's Day, she gave him an enlarged photo of the dragon's mouth orchid. On the mat below the photo was an inscription: *To Dad, The Bog Man,* I'll always remember every day, so rare. That was 12 years ago this month, he recalled. The photo still hung on the wall, and every spring since they spent a day together hiking way back in, each treasured as an orchid.

THE ENORMOUS HIDE of a black bear dominated another wall. The swamp was both home and refuge for bears, and he frequently encountered them in all seasons. The best way to hunt them was by putting on drives with a group of friends, and for years he served as captain of a bear crew.

The season he had taken the big bear started out with them bagging a bruin on both the first and second days, but with the forecast of near-blizzard conditions for the next day, they canceled.

By habit, he arose early that morning and was a bit sore from all the drives they had put on and the subsequent hauling of the bears from the swamp; but the flame of the hunt still burned bright. It might have had something to do with the excitement of the approaching storm, or perhaps it was the steely glint of his .358 winking from the gun rack as he walked by with his coffee, but he decided to spend that last day hunting alone.

Several hours later, he was skirting the edge of a rhododendron thicket, moving quietly from one grassy hummock to another, stepping carefully over and between the old lattice of beaver felled trunks. He stopped to study the surface of a frozen pool, and it was like staring into a stained glass window from the outside; the linear network of fallen reeds and twigs like leading, the colors of the leaves beneath the ice now muted; nature sealing off, so artfully, that dark sanctuary within.

It was a nice change of pace to just drift along, with no strict agenda of an organized drive in mind. Deer were out feeding in force, as they do before a storm, and their sheer numbers surprised him. Ever since their population increased, he found far less orchids.

He had ventured deep into the swamp when he spotted a dark, nebulous shape moving in the opposite direction through some spruce. He turned, backtracking silently, then braced against a tree, swallowing hard when a huge bear appeared 75 yards away.

The bear paused on a windfall before crossing an old tram road. The 250-grain Silvertip found its mark, and he quickly levered another round and shot again. The bear did not move from the spot and the swamp was silent. Finally, the earth commenced spinning and his heart beating. And then it started to snow.

The storm began with a prelude of sleet and was immediately followed by a deluge of heavy, wet flakes that progressed to a whiteout.

It took all his strength to push the bear off the log pile, and the driving snow made it difficult to dress out the 400-pound bruin. He marked the spot with fluorescent ribbons then left to round up his crew for the daunting task ahead.

He smiled at the anticipation of first hearing their disbelief, and then the groans and moans and good-natured ribbing he would receive for hunting alone in a snowstorm, and making them leave the comfort of their homes. But they all turned out, and eagerly followed him in.

The bear hide on the wall is like a window into the blackest night, the highlights of the glossy coat sparkling like constellations, and in those depths, he sees a remembered image of those who worked so hard and so late to bring his bear home from the depths of the swamp. As they labored, he scouted for a dry passage ahead, and when he turned back to join them, the glow of their flashlights through the blinding snow resembled, he thought, the torch lights of some primitive tribe from ages before, struggling through that dark place, eager to celebrate the life of the bear.

THE BOG MAN stood before the map on the wall, his gaze coursing old traplines and deer trails, following the easy contours of wide-spaced elevation whorls. He recalled the year when he sent the bundles of coyote pelts to a furrier to have a hooded parka made for his wife, a property assessor, who dreaded the cold. He remembered scrutinizing the color and texture of each pelt, the way an artist might study the layout of color on his palette. In one tract of her coat, he saw again that clear and frigid night when he called in the big male under a sky that rained meteors for hours, distracting him from his vigilance. The coyote came in hard, like a silvery meteor itself, from the blacker depths of the swamp to his position on the hill, kicking up powdery snow that sparkled like diamond dust.

Over the years many others had joined him: birding groups, young turkey hunters, novice trappers, old deer hunting partners, college students. And they all took something back, some memory of this wild place: the hoots of a barred owl, a glimpse of a beaver, wood ducks lifting from the dark water, a nervous mink or a muskrat; or, if they were lucky, a bobcat. And, if they were very observant, they might have noticed the light of an older time in the ever-present antiquity.

The spirit of wild, primitive places runs hard and deep through certain lives, and is carried and shared by those who can harbor such a thing, the way a migrating bird carries something of the wild essence of one place to another.

A Bugle from Afar

HE SAT WAITING on the porch of the lodge, legs propped up on his old Army duffle, his morning coffee steaming in the chill Rocky Mountains air. Stenciled in bold letters on the duffle, McINTYRE CALVIN J, barely legible now after so many years. He had said his goodbyes to coworkers and the ranch owner earlier at breakfast, and was alone except for his cattle dog Blitz, fast asleep, snuggled up against several other bags.

Everything he owned was in the bags; most of everything he loved, in the hills beyond. He found some satisfaction in his ability to still pick up and move on with little fuss, as he had throughout the years, having remained free of the trappings of one who dwells too long in one place.

His was a life defined by the land, how he lived and worked within it, not by what he had built or accumulated. It would be difficult to leave this slice of Colorado though, as there was a certain magic in these mountains that held him here longer than other places. Perhaps it was the elk and the scenery, or his senior position at the ranch, but it was his experience that some indefinable element of the land sometimes reached out, tethering both heart and imagination and there was no choice but to stay a while.

But move he must, as a litany of back ailments and arthritic maladies had advanced to where he had great difficulty walking, and his duties as ranch foreman and elk guide had become too much, even for his wiry frame. At 68 years of age, it was simply time.

Last week, he had sold his sorrel Copper to a friend in Denver. His sister insisted they could trailer the horse back to Pennsylvania, that the stable back home had been vacant too long. But he knew the horse would be a luxury. Besides, his days in a saddle were over.

The dog raised its head and whined, then Cal heard the long, drawn bugle of a bull elk below the lodge, the first of the season. It rose from the blue depths of the shadowed valley, lifted up through the aspens and floated across the horse pasture. It was his favorite sound in the world, and a musical chord that, in its somber peal, reminded him of a fiddle tune he loved, "Ashokan Farewell."

When he saw a dust plume rise from a truck far down the valley, he went inside and washed and dried the mug and hung it in its place on the rack.

"Next cowboy up," he said.

HIS SISTER JEANNIE and her husband Dave helped load Cal's bags, then stood with him, looking down the valley one last time.

"What a view," said Jeannie.

"Sure is," replied Cal, shouldering a tooled leather rifle scabbard.

"I know what's in there," said Dave. "It's your .348. Your elk gun."

"It is," Cal confirmed.

Jeannie sat in the back seat with Blitz. The dog had taken an immediate liking to her.

"Like the old saying goes," she said, "no road is long with good company."

"Thanks," said Cal.

"I was talking to Blitz," she pointed out, crinkling her eyes.

Cal turned and smiled. Jeannie's gray eyes, like his own, like their mother's, were the palest gray of mist above a river, a translucence that cloaked the depth and temperament of the waters beneath.

THE SECLUDED WHITE homestead, bathed in the light of the setting sun, looked warm and inviting after the long journey.

Built at the end of a tree-lined lane and cradled by an amphitheater of wooded hills, the sprawling house, barn, and outbuildings were a masterwork of site planning and design by his father, a noted builder, who fused the fieldstone architecture of the original farm with a compatible country styling.

Cal recalled helping to build the guest cottage one summer under his father's direction. He now would reside there.

"I've got a lot to fix up around here," noted Dave. "My travel schedule has been a bear, and Jeannie is busy at school. At any rate, we'll get to it when we retire in a couple years."

"Don't apologize," Cal replied. "I'll help. I like to pull my weight."

"Now don't go trying to do too much around here, Mr. Ranch Foreman," Jeannie told Cal, fixing a flat, level gaze on him. "I know how you are."

"Oh, I might tinker a bit here and there, to start," he said.

The next morning, Cal finished unpacking, then slipped the Winchester from the scabbard, worked the action and wiped it down.

The Model 71 Deluxe was one of the finest lever guns ever made, a gift from his father when Cal decided to move out West. He had taken a lot of big game with it; moose, mule deer, bears and mountain lions, but mostly elk. If ever a rifle was made to hunt the black timber, it was the Model 71. He still had several boxes of the old 250-grain Silvertips with the grizzly pictured on front.

The rifle scabbard was of bison leather and tooled in a western wildflower motif, a personal project after he graduated from saddlemaker's school in Montana.

He thought about keeping his ranch saddle, the last one he made at the saddlery, but had no need of it, and it became part of the deal when he sold his horse.

CAL AND BLITZ did a thorough walk-through of the property, Cal poking with his cane at rotted boards, crumbling masonry and flaking paint.

He looked around inside the dark barn and stables. Motes of dust drifted through the slatted light stirred by his and the dog's proddings.

It appeared that nature was taking over what man had abandoned. An enormous hornet's nest was built onto a saddle rack, stall doors were encrusted with mud dauber adobes, a black snake's shed skin was hanging from a dilapidated tack cart, a bird nest was built in the loop of a horse collar hanging on the wall.

Cal lifted a tarp, revealing the one-horse antique sleigh they rode in as kids. It was in fair shape, and a good candidate for restoration. He shook a sleigh bell strap and the brass bells jingled merrily. He recalled Dap, their gentle, gray draft horse with his pale spots – like big wet snowflakes – and the long rides up the road through the winter woods.

By noon, he had filled six pages of his leather-bound ranch journal with notes, lists and quick-concept sketches.

JEANNIE LOCATED a physical-therapy clinic for him and, combined with his own therapy plan of getting out in the woods, he made remarkable progress.

It started by taking long walks with

Blitz up the dirt road that led from the homestead far into the hills, then progressed to hiking a network of woodland trails. Several weeks later, he began to explore the deep woods, rediscovering the distant haunts of his youth.

It all came back to him; hollow by hollow, creek by creek, until his mind map was overwritten with new cues and the inevitable changes of a half-century.

He was amazed at the diversity of wildlife and hunting opportunities, vastly different than back in the '60s. He encountered wild turkey flocks, the occasional bobcat and sometimes fishers with their glistening coats.

When he first started deer hunting, the woods were over-browsed and a hunter rarely passed up a spike buck.

The deer herd seemed more balanced now, and several bucks that he had seen were trophy-class. Bear sign was everywhere, especially in the small apple orchard, where they had done extensive damage. Coyotes were abundant, too, and some evenings, while sitting on the big wrap-around porch, Blitz would join in with the howling from some far-off hollow.

Cal replaced his antler-handled cane with a hiking staff. As he grew stronger, the land seemed to rush up to meet him. The mountains here were older, gentler than the Rockies. These were wise old hills, like himself perhaps, having witnessed so much. His spirit was rejuvenated, too, transfused by cold mountain creeks and scented breezes. Ravens beckoned, challenging him on ever farther.

And then he found the elk.

First, he noticed their tracks and the trails they used. Then he discovered wallows, saw where they bedded, spooking them several times in the dark timber, relishing once again the chirps and plaintive whines of herd talk. He, like the elk, had come back to these hills and he formed a powerful kinship with them, a union bound by their shared passage through time and the light and shadow of common ground.

But Cal soon had additional incentive to learn more about the elk; Dave was drawn for a bull permit in this zone.

WITH THE HELP of a couple hired hands, Cal had worked his way down the project list and had the old homestead in tip-top shape. The pasture fence was mended and repainted, masonry repairs were made on the stone springhouse with the old hand pump reinstalled. He built a new chicken coop that Jeannie populated with plump Plymouth Rock hens.

He had painstakingly restored the old sleigh, and refurbished the driving tack. They pruned the orchard trees and laid up a great store of

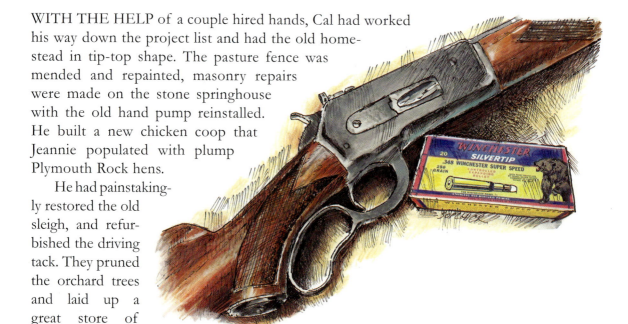

applewood for the smokehouse, which was now in working order.

After the house and outbuildings were painted, they hung a pair of porch swings. The barn and stables were now tight as a drum and immaculate. Jeannie had taken to calling Cal "Boss."

Ahead on his tasks, Cal borrowed the Jeep and took a two-day loop through the elk range. The morning he returned, Cal was surprised to see two visitors sitting on the porch swings with Jeannie and Dave. The strangers wore cowboy hats.

After brief introductions, Jeannie led them all around the side of the house and he noticed that their pickup had Colorado tags. Rounding their truck and trailer, he stopped dead in his tracks when he saw a horse hitched to the porch rail. It pricked its ears and looked at him.

It was Copper, standing in a slice of morning sun, gleaming like a newly minted Denver penny. The horse nickered softly, head alert, nostrils flaring.

Weak in the knees, Cal walked slowly over to the horse, spoke to it softly. The horse quivered when he stroked its neck. He looked into the dark liquid mirror of one eye, at himself and the blue hills behind – what he sometimes imagined was not a reflection at all, but an image that dwelled within the horse, looking outward. For what can a horse possess but the rider and the ground it travels?

"He's here for good, like you," said Jeannie, heading off Cal's questions before he regained his full ability to speak.

"It's our way of saying thanks for all you've done," said Dave, "and that rig on the railing is part of the deal. The horse trailer stays, too."

"That's my ranch saddle," Cal blurted out.

Blitz wove happy figure-eights around and between the horse's legs.

"Copper sure is glad to see you," said Jeannie.

"He sure is," Cal replied. "I missed him."

"I was talking to the dog," she said.

WITHIN THE HOUR, Cal had Copper saddled up. They rode up into the hills with Blitz tagging along.

The horse was eager to stretch its legs and stepped smartly along, then fell into a familiar, rhythmic gait.

Cal sat the horse when he heard the chirps and trills of elk in some timber just above the road. A small group of cows and calves filtered out of the trees, came down through a patch of goldenrod and hustled across the road. A bull bugled up in the dark timber.

Cal knew the mechanics of a bugle well, it was not a single vocalization, but a disparate chord created by two distinct sounds, a simultaneous high whistle and a deep roar, a commanding, ethereal utterance that at once was musical, yet brutish. It was this song that bid him farewell in Colorado, but now heralded his official return to these hills.

The bull muscled through an edge of young aspen, down through the goldenrod and stopped on the road, looking at them, directly between the horse's upright ears, as if held in a gunsight.

The enormous sweep of his beams displayed seven ivory-tipped tines on each side – an Imperial bull, its antlers a visual declaration of raw omnipotence, larger than most bulls he had seen in the wild or on the wall of any lodge.

Another bugle drifted in from afar and the great bull bugled again. Its call was piercingly loud, like standing near a steam whistle. The bull's sides heaved in a chortling finish to its proclamation, and then it was gone, 700 pounds vanished before the echo of its bugle faded.

DAVE AND JEANNIE helped Cal settle the horse into its new quarters.

"Looks like the grandkids will get a sleigh ride when they come up this Christmas," said Jeannie from the seat of the sleigh.

" Dave, why don't you shoot the Winchester tomorrow," Cal suggested. "It's more gun than your 30-30, and you'll need to practice with it a bit."

"I'd like that," said Dave. "I'm ready to do whatever my guide suggests."

Five Months Later

"MORE TO THE LEFT," said Jeannie. "Stop! A little more. Stop! Right there."

Dave and Cal marked the place on the wall of the great room where the shoulder mount of the big Imperial bull would hang.

Dave mounted the hardware and they hung it, then stood back with Jeannie. The cast shadows from the antlers ran far up and across the wall, like the young aspens from which the bull was emerging when Dave shot it.

They stood in silence, the mount evoking emotions and images profound and personal to each.

Jeannie thought of their father and how thrilled he would be to see the majestic mount become the centerpiece of the great room.

Dave relived the moment of that afternoon when the bull fell to Cal's .348. But he would always be struck by the strategies employed by Cal as they closed on the bull time and again, with the bull finally falling into their laps, the result of a final maneuver where it seemed that Cal knew exactly what the bull was going to do, even before the elk did.

The bull was the last Cal would ever hunt. The elk was a symbol of a new beginning, though, a rejuvenation of the spirit, a symbol of new days to come, a reconnection with the land that had called him back home.

Rosetta Stone

THE HOLLOW is like an open book; its sidehills, pages left and right. The sidehill across the hollow is the twin of the one I'm standing on and shares the same snowy blanket. My gaze follows the ridgeline, pausing at the notch where the sun will rise today, as it has every opener of every deer season that I've hunted here, as it has for millennia. The contour of the ridge is as familiar as the face of a loved one.

Pink light washes the stars from the sky and from the vantage point of my deer stand, the dark trees – standing and tilted and fallen – along with charred stumps and black boulders and the scars of old tram roads stand out in stark contrast like jumbled letterforms and fragments of sentences against the background. I find this notion amusing at first because, for many years, I studied typographic design, but then realized I had been subconsciously reading excerpts of nature's text on these hills, trying to piece it together.

Early on, it read as a treatise of complex and marvelous sciences. As the years passed, it seemed more of a drama shrouded in mystery. Later still, the same passages were revealed as splendid prose, artful and extraordinary. Old stories fade, and are replaced by the new. But here, all remain in archive for perusal by those who would wait in these shadowy folds for first light.

IN THE STEEP, narrow gorge, gigantic boulders guard the escarpment on the ridge like sphinxes guarding an Egyptian pharaoh's tomb. Although this isn't the Valley of the Kings, it certainly is a valley of stones. I like to hunt deer in the thick tangles of laurel, easing into the

little anterooms, peeking around boulders. I don't make a sound stepping from stone to stone, but must be careful to test each for balance, so as not to make a grating noise or have it plunk back in place.

I slide around the downhill side of a boulder and glance uphill to see a doe bedded and another feeding nearby. The mast crop is especially bountiful; every cleft brimming with acorns. The standing doe dips her head into the V of a blowdown, eating acorns that have filled this space as if eating from a bowl. Just as I slowly drop to a knee and raise my rifle, the other, larger doe stands and stretches.

At my shot, the deer streaks downhill, disappearing behind a truck-sized boulder. But it doesn't appear from the other side. I find the fat doe piled up behind the boulder and soon have it dressed out and tagged.

I wash my hands in a seep that bubbles up from beneath the boulder and wipe them dry on its rough, sun-warmed surface. As my fingers run over the embossings and debossings on the great stone, I think about how they are like the hieroglyphics on an ancient Egyptian stele. But the inscriptions here are much older. This is the record of countless storms and untold days of freezing and thawing, of floods and fires and the folding and crushing and rising of a violent, unsettled earth hundreds of millions of years ago. But today I read another message in the etched whorls and pocks and calligraphic strokes on this Rosetta Stone. It tells me that the lives of both deer and hunter are but two sparks left over from the cooling cauldron of this valley, each flickering so closely as to be within the same instant.

AMERICAN POET Robert Frost wrote of birches, inspired by the white trees with parchment-like bark and black inscriptions that resemble Frost's own tightly-spaced handwriting. Once, while scouting for a stand for the bear season opener, I hiked up through a dense grove of white birch on a steep, rocky area near the top of the mountain. Finding some promising bear sign, I decided to give it a try the next day.

It was a tough climb in the dark with all my gear, but I was soon settled in. The white birches gleamed brightly against the backdrop of dark clouds, which sputtered rain and sleet. The rain froze on every surface, while sugary snow gathered in the folds on my coat and every crease and crevice on the mountain. I tensed when I heard something running towards me through the laurel and almost fell over backwards when a big, black gobbler catapulted skyward right over me, beating his way up through the whippy branches of the birches in a glassy explosion of ice. In Frost's poem "Birches," he wrote of ice-laden branches shedding their shells: *You'd think the inner dome of heaven had fallen.*

I ALWAYS STOP to examine bear sign, especially the claw

marks on smooth beech bark. As an artist, I like to visualize the bear that inscribed the bark, recreating the scenario in my mind. Black bears will climb beech trees up to the canopy to feed or break off nut-laden branches. In some beech groves, they tend to prefer certain trees as evidenced by a history of old and new claw scars, while leaving others untouched. It makes one wonder if they read the script left by other bears over the years.

Boar bears also leave their bios in the claw marks, bite marks and shredded bark on marker trees along trails, especially preferring trees that lean inwards. A couple of apple trees on an overgrown farm was a favorite hangout for bears, and I found the tracks and a nearby marker tree used by a really big boar. I never saw him, but he left enough clues to inspire some drawings.

THE WOODLANDS ARE inscribed with all manner of writing – each in a different language, yet all part of the same story. Lines of holes drilled by a sapsucker on the hyphen-textured bark of a cherry tree resemble the dot-dash-dot of written Morse code, and the bird's *tap-tap-trrrrrr-tat-tat*, sounds out the same message.

A line of buck rubs are sequential posters, visual signs that describe certain physical properties of their maker. There is a wonderful code of wildness to read in the cuneiform markings on a ruffed grouse's fan. The cursive script of carpenter ant borings under tree bark is the communal doctrine of a worker's society. And the growth rings of a tree trunk section tell the stories of centuries.

Today, volumes of information can be obtained instantaneously, all at the click of a key, swipe of the screen or a voice command. What is written in the natural world does not come as quickly, nor as easily, though. It requires insight and interpretation and becoming fluent in the languages of wild nations. The day will come when that key, that Rosetta Stone, is discovered and the many singular elements written in the hills and hollows will merge. The grand story it will tell, however, will be but a passage in a larger, wild treasury.

Most significant is that if you read between the lines, you also will find something of your own days. Every hunter advances the story of the land, his history bound with those hunters of other ages, their collective role an integral element of nature's narrative.

Oh, Canada!

A FULL MOON, the color of old bone china, eases up through the etched lines of tree branches and sits in the indigo sky. All is quiet except for the distant honking of geese. Soon, their voices become louder, then a line of bold silhouettes passes across the moon's face, black wings rising and falling, occasional soft *hrinks* and louder *ha-ronks*. It seems their voices fly before them, as if they are following some phantom trumpeter.

The clarion calls of Canada geese are oftentimes referred to as "goose music," but I feel it may better be described as "callithumpian," a word one might use to describe a parade of children blowing party horns. All that discordant honking as they fly is a means of communication that maintains the flock's flight integrity; an urging from the ones behind to those in front as a signal to shift positions.

I always stop to watch and listen to the comings and goings of several low-flying local flocks almost every day as they pass right over the central skylight of my second-story studio. Most of the time, they wing along quietly, grunting only minimal directives to each other. While ascending or descending, the conversation is loud and excitable. Geese have a repertoire of more than a dozen calls, but it is the loud cacophony of a big, overhead flock that is the most inspiring to we terrestrials.

The transformative mechanics of a flock's flights is amazing; individual birds gather then

assemble in the air, aligning themselves to create their classic wedge-shaped V, an organic, energy-saving structure, whereby each goose flies slightly higher and to the left or right of the one in front of it, resulting in less wind resistance and an increased amount of free lift.

When flying long distances, the birds occasionally reshuffle, trading places as another bird rotates into the laborious point position. On extended flights, some geese enter a slow-wave sleep state, in which only half of the brain remains awake, while they catch a power nap, much like they do when resting on land or water, one eye peeled. Upon reaching a destination, the flock disassembles, individual birds spilling air, then setting down again.

THE CANADA GOOSE has a great sense of presence; its stout, robust physique exudes power, and at the risk of imposing a too-human attribute, lots of attitude. Ask anyone who has ventured too near a nest and was sent scooting by a protective gander and they would swear his 9-pound body and 5-foot wingspan were twice that.

Certain animals are bound so inextricably to their habitats, it is difficult to consider them apart from it: the goshawk to a deep forest; the beaver to its dam and lodge, the bison to the prairie. So it is that some species have become synonymous with urban and suburban settings. The Canada goose, as an iconic migratory traveler between wide-open spaces and waters, has long been realized as a herald to autumn and spring. In some places, however, non-migratory resident geese are considered year-round messy nuisances and pests, maybe even a symbol for urban sprawl.

I recall a vintage book illustration of country-school children paused on a dirt lane outside their one-room schoolhouse. One of the older boys is pointing out a V of geese flying over the school to the younger children. It's a nostalgic portrayal of rural life from a bygone era, one that illustrates a poignant moment as the young observers paused to wonder and learn something about a wild creature and appreciate a bit of natural beauty. Although those halcyon days are long gone, many places still exist where geese have retained their status as symbols of places wild and free.

Non-migratory geese that are the scourges of office complexes, golf courses, malls, parks and any other place with large grassy areas and water features, are really no different than their wild counterparts. These geese are simply taking advantage of landscaping custom-designed for their lifestyle; one that offers acres of grass, nesting sites, water, a habitat free of predators and shared by creatures that are quite easy to intimidate. The same could be said of many other birds and animals that thrive in suburbia. So it is that the Canada goose today has a dichotomous existence, and depending on who you might talk to, may be loved or despised.

The scientific name for the Canada goose is *Branta canadensis*, loosely translated as "dark goose from Canada." Unlike America and many other nations, Canada, surprisingly, does not have an official national bird. To remedy this, a National Bird Project was started by two prominent Canadian conservation constituencies. A list of the five top birds was compiled from 450 eligible species by 50,000 online voters. Those finalists included the Canada goose, common loon, Canada jay (formerly gray jay), black-capped chickadee and snowy owl.

A panel comprised of ornithologists, conservationists and other experts presented the merits of each species in debate. After much deliberation, it was the Canada jay that came out on top. After two years of much work and fanfare in the press, all that was needed was an official governmental declaration. The Department of Canadian Heritage, however, stated it was not interested in adopting a national bird. Perhaps it will someday, but it might take a while. After all, it took the department 45 years to adopt Canada's maple-leaf flag design.

It would seem from down here in the States, that either the common loon or Canada goose might have been a shoe-in, as both seem, from our perspective, to be the most synonymous with our neighbor in the Great White North. But after the presentations and debates over the five finalists, the Canada goose sadly finished fourth.

WILD CREATURES, once having been regarded only from a purely consumptive viewpoint, have taken on other values as man's relationship with them evolves on both personal and societal levels. Some people have a broad range of experiences with a particular species that changes through time. The Canada goose, long a liaison between various landscapes, has had a wide-ranging relationship with man, ranging from that of a commodity to serving as an iconic species in the collective consciousness of those who watch wild skies and waters. Wild geese continue to be an inspiration to hunters, nature-watchers, artists and writers.

EARLY ON, while the vast majority of geese were still migratory, I hunted them at every opportunity: on farms big and small, out of pit blinds and hidden in fencerows, drifting on waters in a Susquehanna River rollover boat near a spread of hand-carved decoys.

As a goose hunter, the mindset is to invite other geese to join your flock of decoys, an ancient ruse that through the centuries has become an art. On some occasions, it can be a real challenge, but I recall one day when it worked too well as an enormous flock that blotted the sky set right down on top of our cornfield pit blind. They descended in waves, and in such numbers, we could only sit there and smile in the deafening din, the occasional webbed foot stepping through holes in the roof of the blind. We didn't shoot any of those geese as one of the senior hunters said it would ruin that pit for the remainder of the season.

It's one thing to experience the vertigo of thousands of geese rising off a nearby lake, but being at the epicenter of the eruption as they departed felt as if I were about to be carried upwards by the sheer force of that vortex. And then they were gone.

Canada geese make great subjects for nature watchers as most are fairly tolerant of people, but the bonus of watching geese in a wetlands is all the other wildlife species encountered. I've spent much time studying and drawing geese from life; their flight dynamics, how they lift off the water and land. Geese can be quite animated, offering lots of interesting poses as they walk, feed and swim. Once, I located a pair that had nested in the cup of a raised stump near a grassy shoreline that provided lots of material for many pages of studies, from the most aggressive posturing to moments of absolute serenity.

The Canada's graphic combination of white, black and gray tones gives it an elegant, formal appearance. Its white chinstrap can even be seen at longer ranges. The Canada's strong, visual impact makes it a popular subject for many forms of art. Goose motifs abound on apparel and home décor. Vintage goose decoys that have seen some use have become classic examples of American folk art and are highly desirable and often pricey. In my own career, I've worked on dozens of projects that focused on the Canada goose: logos, goose posters, T-shirts, gunner's boxes, magazine covers, book illustrations, murals and fine-art paintings.

Of all those projects that entailed the Canada goose as subject, the most enjoyable was designing an entry for the 10th anniversary of the Pennsylvania Waterfowl Management Stamp in 1992. There were two objectives I wanted to achieve in that design: the first was to use the Canada goose as the featured species, and second, to show an actual place, a wetlands, because the money raised from the sale of the waterfowl stamp and prints was used for waterfowl habitat projects.

While on a scouting trip in Tioga County in Pennsylvania's northern tier, I spent time doing some drawings at a large beaver pond with a lodge. On the far shore, I watched several Canada geese that stayed for a few hours before taking off. Beaver ponds are classic symbols of a natural wetlands in their own right and my ensuing "Beaver Pond Canadas" painting, which grew from that pondside visit, eventually would be selected as the winner from a field of 40 entries.

LARGER THAN LIFE, Canada geese continue to reign as the king of waterfowl, even in the face of ever-expanding sprawl. They continue to halt us in our tracks and force our eyes skyward as they pass, their music washing over, cleansing the land and our spirit with their song of wilderness and freedom.

Autumn Challenge

THE TIDES OF AUTUMN

The piercing bugles of bull elk unquestionably signal autumn's approach and harbor their zeal to get the rut started. But mostly, they telegraph dominance.

There's nothing subtle about the 700-pound bull elk featured prominently in *Autumn Challenge*. I heightened the bull's already imposing presence by having it emerge into the light from dark timber in a high-contrast composition, something the Old Masters did regularly in their 18th century figure paintings.

Autumn in Penn's Woods presents itself mostly through the pageantry of colorful foliage, but I much prefer the days near the end of leaf fall, those chill, overcast days after a rain, when wild-eyed bucks work scrape lines.

The days begin with fog-shrouded ridges where the cries of blue jays carry loud and far. As the deep basins heat up, hawks move from the rising thermals of one spiraling kettle of air to another, trading their way south.

There is a quickening in the pulse of the landscape. Wild turkey flocks gorge on fat grasshoppers and the first white oak acorns and beechnuts that hit the leaf litter. Squirrels and chipmunks enter a manic phase, storing acorns as bears pile on fat.

Watching over all, the warm Hunter's Moon travels at its eternal pace; peaceable, haunting, vigilant, changing places at dawn with a bowhunter perched in his tree.

In a Dark Woods

IT WAS AS IF WALKING in a dream as we filed down through the pines in the gray, predawn light, the dark woods a continuum of that dim world just before wakening. Our footfalls fell softly in the pine straw and no one spoke. Old Jack, our neighbor, led the way on a deer trail, followed by my father and me.

I was now ready for "The Big Time"– as my father called every significant event – hunting for the first time ever with my new .22 rifle. With one hunting season under my belt, I was now expected to step it up a notch. With every step, a powerful emotion boiled up; a feeling anchored in respect, lifted by reverence and a responsibility to do things right; an emotion propelled by a primal purpose keen with expectation, one borne by all hunters as part of a timeless doctrine scribed in blood and illuminated by the love of things wild.

The pines gave way to ancient oaks that bordered the creek and, after much deliberation, my father and I settled into a strategic stand near tilted catwalks of limbs strung together with skeins of grapevines. Leafy squirrel nests dotted the grape tangles and every stump and fallen log was littered with acorn cuttings. This was prime, classic ground. This was The Big Time and I was ready.

WE WENDED OUR WAY up through a maddening maze of mopane trees and thorn-bush, two trackers in front, followed by Tony, our affable professional hunter, and me. It was late afternoon and we were easing in on a herd of hartebeest grazing in a clearing far upslope. We paused in the dark thicket near a waterhole to catch our breath. A blesbok antelope skull grinned up from the depths of the dank water as birds croaked and shrieked and whooped. Before continuing on, one of the trackers pointed out fresh Cape buffalo spoor, urging us to be on high alert at every turn.

I was here as part of a safari to collect representative South African plains game species to be used in dioramas I was designing for a large museum. In all my travels, I had never seen such a tortured, yet beautiful, landscape. The rocky escarpment on top of the mountain was ablaze with fiery light, like an active volcano, but in the shadows below, only a monochromatic palette of color remained: raw umbers and murky olive greens and manganese blue shadows.

The rocky footing was treacherous and a careless stumble could plunge one into a fathomless fissure large enough to swallow a buffalo. Created by erosive torrents running down from the flat-topped mountain during the rainy season, the crevices were like claw marks made by some monstrous mythical creature that used the hillside as a scratching post.

The palpable tension in the air was like an iron tincture of blood on the tongue, and that same emotion from 50 years earlier and half a world away percolated up again.

This was Big Time and this was Africa. I hoped I would be ready.

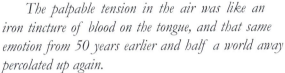

JACK MOVED OUT of sight far up the hollow. He wore a canvas jacket and a greasy red leather cap, red being the safety color in those pre-blaze-orange days. The men carried shotguns, and I, my new Remington .22, a better choice, I thought, for hunting squirrels. I snapped in the clip and chambered a hollow-point. The plan for this first stand would be that my father would shoot any squirrel that was running and I would pot any that was still, or that paused beyond scattergun range.

Nothing moved and it was very quiet, save the murmurings of the creek. I shivered more with anticipation than from the cold, but relaxed when birds began their day. Brown creepers, downy woodpeckers and chickadees gleaned the oaks for insects. A nuthatch spiraled comically down a nearby trunk and the silence was shattered when a pileated woodpecker cackled maniacally and flashed across the hollow.

"That's a Logcock," my father whispered.

"They call it a pileated woodpecker nowadays," I added, taking some pride in that, the year before, I did not know the names of most birds.

My father and I saw the fork-horn buck at the same time. It picked its way down the same deer trail we had and crossed the creek at the tailings of a pool where it stopped, perfectly mirrored, looking right at me. I froze, and after a long minute, it flicked its tail, then continued up the opposite hillside, up through the rocks, halting in a band of sunlight, its sleek gray coat flashing as it turned, then disappearing among the boulders. The sound of claws on rough bark swung my attention back to the hunt as a flash of grizzled silver spiraled around a trunk. I raised the rifle off my knees.

AS WE EASED into position, several warthogs burst across the clearing, and the spooked hartebeest – Africa's fleetest antelope – thundered away, straight up the hillside until they were but a russet smear in the last rays of the sun.

Our disappointment was only momentary, though, as we heard buffalo moving across the slope. We looped down, then up again to head them off. We glassed the thickets, then saw them moving across a small V-shaped notch higher up. I set up the .416 magnum on the shooting sticks, the precarious edge of a fissure at my back, the only point from which to take a shot in the dense thicket. I hoped the recoil would not push me backwards too hard, but Tony was spotting me.

Dozens of bulky black forms streamed by like freight cars, all cows and calves, then there was nothing. I got down off the sticks and continued glassing with Tony.

"Oh well then," said Tony. "Call it a day, I suppose."

"Wait," I said. "I've got something. Higher up to the right, nine o'clock, next to that tall rock pillar."

"Yes," Tony replied. "Good eye; it's a bull!"

All I had seen was the polished curve of one horn. When the bull moved, I was back on the sticks with the big gun.

I SHOULDERED the .22, a Remington 511 Scoremaster bolt-action with a Weaver B4 scope in an N3 side-mount. Throughout the summer, I honed my marksmanship by practicing on hand-drawn squirrel targets.

I enjoyed drawing the squirrels as much as I did hunting them. The big gray had come down the back of the oak and hopped up on a stump, surprising me. It was a long shot and I leveled the rifle and held the crosshairs on its shoulder.

In the moments it takes to get off a shot, the accomplished rifleman should have absolute clarity, relying on confidence born of practice and a complete familiarity with his rifle; and if a live target, a steady observation of its actions. Instead, images of the past year flashed by quicker than the strike of the firing pin on the cartridge.

I could see myself in the thickets of summer, picking blackberries at a quarter per quart to earn the $55 for the rifle. I recalled poring over the pages of gun and hunting articles, and outdoor catalogs; the hours spent studying illustrated wildlife charts and field guides, and watching birds to sharpen observational skills; and dozens of perforated targets tacked to the splintered door that served as the backstop of our rifle range.

The rimfire cracked, and the gray dropped. Walking over to pick up the squirrel, other images of sublime possibilities emerged: a buck lying in the leaves, or a bear or elk, of African game fields and the whickering of zebra and guttural moans of lions at sunset.

Now that would be Big Time.

THE ROUTE OF the bull buffalo was easily determined by the alarm cries and flushing of birds that had settled in for the night. And then he was there, positioned perfectly in that V notch between twisted trees, 70 yards out in that classic pose, looking right at me, through me, head held high, the bores of his nostrils flared wide, in that long, hard, unblinking, unwavering stare of indisputable dominance.

The crosshairs were rock solid against his ebony hide and once again, as 3 pounds of trigger pull diminished, hundreds of images, each a microsecond in duration, reeled past – from that squirrel hunt on that golden October morning through 50 years afield – to this very moment.

The bull died after running 75 yards, without its heart, to a grassy swale. The peal of its death bellow was a proclamation of the passage of a magnificent, wild life.

We sat there a while resting, the pale-yellow full moon reflected from its polished horns.

Tony described to the trackers that the moon was a rock that circled the earth, and they laughed at his foolishness, explaining that it was but a spot of leftover sunlight – and they laughed even harder when he told them the Earth was round.

WE CAME BACK up through the pines late in the afternoon and, this time, I led the way, several squirrels weighing down my game pouch. I spotted the tine of a deer antler sticking out of the pine straw and, giving it a tug, released it from the earth.

"Look here, I said, an old chewed-up shed."

"A what?" asked Jack.

"A shed antler," I said. "This buck dropped this antler here, then the other one someplace else. They grow a new set every year."

Jack laughed telling me, "Never heard of such a thing. Horns just get bigger every year. Bones take a long time to grow."

"I grew a lot since last year," I said.

"You sure did," said my father.

IN THOSE MOMENTS of the hunt, when life and death are at stake, what comes forward may be surprising, because all that has happened before the trigger is pulled, arrow is released, or cast is made is often of greater magnitude than the critical moment at hand.

And, so it is that one hunt may be transposed exactly upon the outline of another. After all, they are – each and every one – The Big Time.

The Tides of Autumn

IN HIS BOOK, *The Outermost House*, author Henry Beston devoted a chapter called "The Headlong Wave" to describe the various sounds and movements of the surf. It is a remarkable treatise of one of the oldest sounds on Earth, each paragraph a poetic wave that washes through the senses. Beston tells us, "The seas are the heart's blood of the Earth. Plucked up and kneaded by the sun and moon, the tides are the systole and diastole of Earth's veins. The rhythm of waves beats in the sea like a pulse in living flesh."

While in the womb, the *thump-whump* of a beating heart is instilled forever in our psyche, as is the rhythm of the tides. Further, I believe that primal cadence stops not at the foaming shores, but continues in the air and winds, through forests and fields, plains and valleys, washing over mountains.

It's been said Earth's atmosphere is simply a less dense form of water, and all terrestrial creatures "swim" through these rarer waters. This is easily realized when walking through a field of tall grass on a windy day or along a tram road on a fogbound morning, when the progression is more akin to swimming than walking. And it's especially believable in autumn,

when leaves spiral and float, and grapevines sway like kelp in the brine. It's when the atmosphere seems charged with the urgency of approaching winter in the same way warm currents shift when pushed by colder waters.

On a windy day, it takes me all morning to climb from the dark abyss of the hemlock bottom to the big oaks on the ridge. Far below, the wind cannonades and booms like wild surf through forested vales. Successive winds, like lines of whitecaps, rush upwards, breaking at the ridge's crest, washing over the mountaintop. Steely clouds stream past, silvery sides flashing like schools of giant bluefins. I drift along, nudged by fickle winds, floating by reefs of laurel.

Finally, the winds cease and I bask in the light on a sun-drenched flat, a castaway washed up on some nameless shore of autumn.

THE RUINS HERE are my Atlantis. They say the mountain farm fell to misfortune and fire even before the Great Depression. Several foundations and stone walls still stand, bedecked in emerald moss, along with a few petrified beams, fenceposts and rails. Nearby, several apple trees still grow, just beyond the margin of a faint pasture line. The trees offer up bright yellow apples; Smokehouse apples I later learned, are a good variety for cider making, and a delicacy to the whitetails I hunt here with my bow.

The farmhouse was built near the lip of the ridge away from the small barn and two outbuildings farther back on the flat mountaintop. It seems an odd layout for such a small farm. The masonry staircases of the farmhouse are built of gray Belgian block. One stairway descends to two small rooms that comprise the root cellar, the other rises 13 steps to what once was the second story. No squeaky stairs in this house. A locust tree provided a handrail. The stairs are rock solid and it's the most unusual stand from which I've ever hunted deer, to stand atop a stairway that suddenly ends.

There's a lot of deer sign at the old homestead. A deer trail winds between the buildings and crosses over the arched doorway separating the root-cellar rooms. The handle of a soup spoon is exposed in a scrape and I pry it from the ground and slip it into a pocket. Another shape at a dumpsite near a wall catches my eye and I use the spoon to dig a small metal figurine of a dog from the soil. To my delight, it's a wire fox terrier, like my wife's dog, Stormy. It's made in Germany and might be linked to the lineage of the farm's residents.

Terry places the figurine on the windowsill among other small antiques. I put the spoon in a catch-all box in my studio. The handle of the spoon shows a design of vines and berries, much like bittersweet, which also might describe the daily struggles on this rough land.

I believe the farmhouse was built near the edge of the ridge not as being advantageous to the farm's layout, but simply for the spectacular view far up the great river valley. Rewards would have been few and far between, scratching out a living in those rocky acres, but sitting on a porch swing at the end of day, watching the undulations of miles of forest rise and fall in the evening light was no less pleasurable than the view of a voyager looking out over bejeweled seas from an upper deck.

What thoughts drifted through the mind of the farmer as he looked far out into the valley from this vantage point? He might have wondered at the temperament of the seas ahead, or if he would be able to steer his family safely through rocky passages.

The woods have reclaimed this mountain farm. The geometric stone foundations erode and tumble, fusing to the rocky spine of the mountain from which they sprang. Are we all on this ocean planet, like the humble farmer, only clinging to these rocks, hoping for the best?

THE TIDES OF AUTUMN

DRIFTING THROUGH the uplands on a warm, drizzly October day without any real plan in mind is akin to beachcombing, an aimless, casual meandering where any real find is a bonus, the luxury of having the time to do so reward enough.

A glade of hickory trees is awash in a surreal golden light, not from the sun, as it is overcast, but from the brilliant intensity of the yellow foliage. The trees glow like huge paper lanterns strung through the canopy of the dim woods.

A lone turkey gobbler treads soundlessly up through the glade. He appears bronze-plated, like a sculpture come alive, prismatic feathers reflecting the yellow light. The gobbler is a study in caution, feeding as he walks. His beard is wide, bristly, graduating from black to gray, like a much-used trim brush. Long, curved spurs jut from legs thick and red as pokeberry stalks. He stands on his toes, head working like a periscope, carefully surveying, scanning the woods for danger, then he hunches, shaking the rain from his feathers like a dog.

Another light seems to emanate from within the magnificent gobbler as it continues up past the dark trunks. It is the incandescence of wildness, a light unlike any other. It can be seen in certain old trees and in the bright parachutes of airborne milkweed seeds, in a raven's feather and the black bead of a chickadee's eye. It's what we seek as surely as the game we hunt, a light we can take back with us and use from time to time to illuminate some passage through the dimmer estuaries of modern life.

LONG AGO, in middle school, I recall having to memorize and recite some lines from Samuel Taylor Coleridge's *The Rime of the Ancient Mariner*. After the Mariner slays the good omen bird, an albatross, their ship is becalmed at sea. "As idle as a painted ship upon a painted ocean." His crew, in their anger, hang the albatross around the Mariner's neck as a shameful punishment.

Becalmed, I sat on a rock, looking down on an endless sea of rhododendron. Nothing moved, not bird nor squirrel nor deer. The only sounds were the creaks and croaks of a sentinel raven. I sat and rested there after a long morning of trying to locate a turkey flock. I climbed higher up the mountain as dark clouds moved in, and put on my rain poncho just as a drenching, cold rain washed the dusty flank of the mountain.

The shower passed quickly, and I moved out into a sunlit clearing to warm up. A group of black boulders steamed in the sunlight, and the wisps of rising vapor were not unlike the spectral crew that stood the deck of the mariner's vessel under a bloody sun, no bigger than the moon.

Later, I broke up a flock, and called in a jake. I carried him back, on a tote slung around my neck and shoulder. But unlike the Mariner, who bore his burden in shame, I carried the jake proudly, thankfully, as a gift from the coppery hills.

October Solitaire

THE RUMPLED TERRAIN of this woodland is like a hand laid flat, palm down, fingers spread wide. The four hollows between the fingers harbor wild turkeys, squirrels, deer and a good population of ruffed grouse. It's a chilly day, the sky is dark and it drizzles off and on. But that's to my liking; the birds always seem to sit a bit tighter on these days.

I inhale a deep breath of country air, exhaling vapor that drifts and rises with the moist breath of the living woods, then close the breech of my sleek 28-gauge Parker on a brace of 8s and slip into the hollow. Zigzagging through the diverse cover, I come upon a recent windfall. It's a tree I know well, a huge, ancient white oak; its outstretched arms having taken down several lesser trees with it. The wreckage is like the shattered hull and splintered masts of a great wooden sailing ship that crashed onto rocks during a storm. Most of the grapevine rigging has been ripped loose, dangling from the branches. In other places, it is pulled taut, pinned by the fallen oak's crushing weight. At first, I'm a bit sad, but great oaks like this never stop giving; they continue as a vital element of the forest, even in their demise.

The windfall looks "birdy," and when a grouse suddenly roars out, I shoot too quickly and then miss with the second barrel as the bird flies straight up the hollow. I'm confident I'll flush it again, but don't. This is a hollow of humility.

In the middle of the second hollow, are huge boulders that form the knuckle of the second finger. One car-sized boulder is balanced upon another smaller boulder that has broken apart, making the one on top appear as if it were stranded there. The boulders are a dark gray-green and covered with a variety of lichens and mosses with minute textures, beautiful colors and intricate patterns that even the richest decorous embroidery couldn't top. The boulders lay in repose, like bored royalty, cloaked in all their finery, watching for centuries the procession of visitors who pass through this sylvan court. Look there, that jester comes again, chasing birds in the rain.

There are always birds in the third hollow, hung with great curtains of grapevines. The only sound is water gurgling in the leaf-choked gullet of a small run. Up near the source of the run, a grouse flies straightaway, as if on a snapline, toward some pines. This time I am patient and drop the bird neatly.

I hunt every inch of the fourth hollow, but can't raise a bird. I sit next to a tree trunk on a raised root to rest. Sitting here, I'm reminded of a painting by the renowned Pennsylvania artist Andrew Wyeth. His painting is simply titled *Seated by a Tree*, and depicts the artist's model, Helga, in a dark coat, brooding in the tree's shadow. Elaborating on the lone figure in his painting, Wyeth once said: "I think anything like that – which is contemplative, silent, shows a person alone – people always think is sad. Is it because we've lost the art of being alone?" I believe the solitary hunter understands the nature of Wyeth's commentary.

IN THE MEMORY of every hunter there exists certain images, or a series of images so powerful they require little effort to recall. They come to mind with every detail revealed, unchanging as time goes by. One of mine concerns a brace of grouse.

A cold front roars into the uplands, pushing leaden, wintry clouds before it. The cloud cover causes the afternoon to grow dark earlier, and darker yet in the thick second-growth where I'm hunting.

As I make my way through the dense cover, I'm drawn to a light area, toward a small clearing of ferns, the color of summer deer. Tall, jagged stumps protrude from the ferns like a wolf's open maw as the howling wind drives leaves across the clearing. Branches click and snap and the ferns toss wildly – all is violent motion, ominous and beautiful. Then, in my mind, everything slows when, yards away, two grouse explode from cover. One is a brown phase, the other a silver-tailed cock. I never hear them or the sound of my shot, but the silver bird cartwheels into the ferns.

At one time I considered a painting that scene, but doing so would ruin it for me. The unforgettable beauty of that moment was the wondrous motion of wind, ferns, branches and the flight of the birds, with the hunter standing within the eye of this swirling, tornadic scene. Freezing this moment into a single, unmoving image of paint on canvas would destroy its magic. Some things are best left alone.

THIS IS NOT YOUR classic grouse covert as portrayed in idyllic sporting prints. A few isolated acres below the old farm is a rough-and-ugly bit of ground. It is a tangled obstacle course of vines, weeds and thornapples with hummocks of black, spongy ground and a pair of braided serpentine runs. It has more the character of woodcock cover, although I have only seen one here. Part of it is an old farm dump. Out of curiosity, I rake at its surface with a stick, exposing broken cobalt bottles of medicinals from another era, the tongue from a clodhopper shoe, rotted barrel staves. Even a cow's skull stares up at me with a silly bovine grin.

In the very center of this acreage is a great clot of violet and crimson briars. I'm going to regret forgetting my shooting gloves. A cottontail pops out from under some old black boards by the foundation of a springhouse and tumbles at my shot. Its limp body is supple and feels like a half-filled hot-water bottle. It smells vaguely of the mint that grows here. I bury my cold fingertips in its soft fur for a few moments before dressing it out.

Farther on, a grouse takes out, towering up, white breast and silvery underwings flashing against a dark pine makes for an easy shot. It puffs and tumbles through the air and plops into a blowdown. As I reach for it, a trinkle of blood from a thorn scratch runs down my wrist, off the tip of my finger and onto the lemony breast of the bird.

Sometimes I sense that it takes a few moments for the life of a bird to leave its body, unlike a rabbit. I can still feel the keen, wild edge of the grouse's life, a roll of drumming log thunder that continues within its breast, a vibration that fades now in my hand. I wonder if this is what the mantling hawk feels in the clutch of its talons. Does the quivering bird reinforce to the hawk that what it has done was done right? Does it reinforce to me that what I have done was done right? Is right? I think so, on all counts.

THE EARTH GIVES up its child reluctantly, holding it fast until the last second when it is set loose in thunderous flight away from danger. But the grouse is not a bird of the air. It's a short-distance flyer, not like a duck, which is designed for long, sustained flight. To a grouse, the air is the quickest escape corridor to return to the safety of the forest floor. To the wing-shooter, those few seconds of flight also are a vital part of his life, where he, too, is set free from his own earthly tethers for a few unimaginable moments of absolute freedom.

Alive or dead, the bird will return to Earth again. Alive or dead, it will have further delineated the success or failure of its flight gambit, for the benefit of the species. Alive or dead, it will have afforded the hunter a better understanding of his love for a wild thing, and, ultimately, the greater Earth. And this is to the benefit of all.

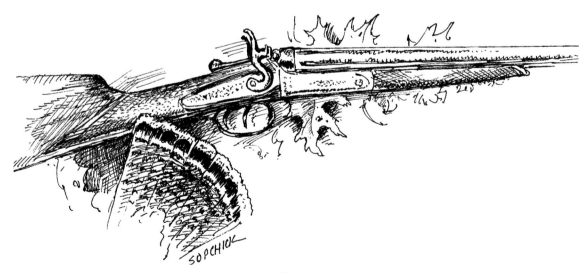

The Light of Older Days

I DRAG THE BUCK up the faint scar of a logging road onto a narrow flat, where I'll wait for my hunting partners to swing by with the deer cart. They wouldn't get back in here for several hours.

I relax with a cup of coffee, admiring the buck and letting the sights and sounds of the deep woods wash over me. The buck is an especially handsome animal, with a rich chestnut coat that made him stand out against the somber November woods.

I run my thumb over the beading above an antler burr. These bumps, or "pearls," as scientists call them, are indicators of nutrition quality. The deep, dense pearling on this buck suggests that good nutrition was available during antler growth.

I read the worn, bony braille as a tactile footnote in the deer's life. I could see him in the light of the yellow Hunter's Moon, rubbing a sapling, his neck swollen, eyes rolled, showing the white as he grates the tree, 180 pounds of geared-up attitude at the cusp of the rut. Nature abounds with endless examples of science meeting art.

Gray-blue cloud shadows flow across the opposite hillside of the broad, deep hollow, slowly rising then falling with the undulating terrain, like a pod of migrating whales. It is windy up high, but down here in the hollow all is still, peaceful. I can smell the disrupted leaf litter and broken ferns, the black, furrowed earth where I dragged the deer and the pungent, eviscerated cavity of the buck.

As I look over my buck, I feel my hunter's senses shift. There is a noted hitch in my very being, like folding the blade of a lockback knife. I become aware of the enormity, the presence, of the forest that surrounds me, of my place within it and that of the deer and now, this union. Through the deer's harvest, I am reconnected to the light of older days and to others who have hunted here.

ONCE, I WAS ASKED to do a presentation on approaches shared by both artists and writers. One common thread I spoke about also relates directly to hunting.

I showed the audience a painting in progress, where the artist first takes a single earthy color, an umber perhaps, and develops light and shadow, the tonal atmosphere upon which colors and detail are later developed. This is called the underpainting, and in many works of art, the viewer can still see evidence of this initial foundation. It lends both visual strength and mystery to the finished work. Writers may use a similar approach whereby another, or secondary theme or tone simmers beneath the surface, or echoes throughout, adding depth.

So, it may be for the hunter, too. Can we identify what exists beyond the obvious? Can we sense those ancient undercurrents that lie beneath the leaf litter, that resonate from within the land?

THE TIDES OF AUTUMN

I REVEL in the ancient undertones and timeless themes that reverberate as echoes of the past in the hills and hollows. I delight in simple, primal elements, the pure, driving forces of the hunt, the interplay of light and shadow, the magic of bird flight, the dynamics of rain and snow, and how solitude reveals the true nature of the hunter.

Earlier in the season, I picked up a broken shard of shale that caught my eye. On it is a detailed fossil relief of seed ferns that grew in the carboniferous coal forest that was here some 300 million years ago. It is like a Post-It note that traveled across an unimaginable span of time, intended for my eyes.

The cryptic message is a reminder that older forces are still at work here, that the wild, primal nature of that prehistoric forest, although vastly different in form today, still is present. Every hunter who has ever lived is passing through the brief, latter part of that timeframe, and by the very nature of his dealings with life and death, carries that untamed nature of the ancient wild in his heart. It is what brings him back to the fields and forests every year, what helps to define him all his days.

I HAVE HUNTED along many creeks that run through hemlock bottoms, and all one has to do to shed the frenetic pace of modern life that sets the blood to boiling is to sit at such a streamside for a while near a small waterfall. Within minutes, one's own blood will synch with the calming music of the waters.

It may be the dark, primitive backdrop of the hemlocks and the steady echo of the falling water chugging like a slow drumbeat in the cavity behind the falls, but whenever I hunt along the braided creek below my deer stand and sit beside one such picturesque pool, I think of the native hunters of three centuries earlier.

Research suggests they hunted deer, turkey, bear and elk here. I like to think they stopped occasionally to rest at this pool, the peaceful water music as mesmerizing then, as now. I also can imagine the progression of other hunters through the ages pausing here to rest and listen.

Decades pass. A father and a son from a hardscrabble farm at the other end of the hollow stop to sit on the big rock near the pool. The boy carries his father's double-barrel hammer shotgun. The father lays the big gobbler slung over his shoulder. He opens the bird's crop and shows his son the chestnuts, fox grapes and bits of plants within. He is proud of his boy who kept up all day, and remained motionless when they saw the trio of autumn longbeards. He plucks a feather from the gobbler's wing and slides it behind the boy's hatband. Decades pass.

Two hunters clad in red-and-black-checked wool and high leather boots that lace at the knees pull a spike buck tied to a pole between them. They stop to get a drink of cold water before continuing the long drag ahead. When they slide the deer through the riffles at the tail of the pool, they pause briefly as the water runs through the buck's cavity. The red bloom in the water dilutes as it washes downstream and the hunters head upstream, their red coats fading into the shadowy hemlocks.

A half-century later, a solitary hunter in a new, waterproof blaze-orange coat hunts through the hemlock bottom during a snowstorm, stopping to admire the dark waters of the pool dotted by rocks wearing high, white turbans of wet snow. He sees the fresh tracks where a lone deer has just crossed, and takes up the trail. The hunter is young and strong and heads straight up the steep hillside. The day is new, the snow, wild and invigorating. He scales the steep bank in two quick steps, hot on the trail.

Four decades pass. A modern day, camo-clad hunter on an early November hunt carries a crossbow, face painted in earthy hues. He follows a scrape line along the creek and stops to watch a mosaic mat of colorful leaves spin slowly in the pool. There is a good deer crossing here. He looks at the deep muddy trail that scales the steep embankment and remembers when he took up a track here during a snowstorm and killed a buck bedded down in the slashings high above.

See your own reflection in the pool. Yours is but one of many. The murmurings of the waters are like voices from the past. Listen closely and the waters will whisper old stories. Your story is there, too. The hemlocks lean in, listening as they always do, a solemn audience nodding approval in the autumn breeze.

IN THE NEXT HOLLOW over is a large, crumbled foundation and wall of a farm from the mid-1870s. I always stop there and visit whenever I still-hunt through. A red fox bolts up the hollow as I approach. Upon reaching the stone wall, I see his tracks atop it in the light skim of snow from earlier that morning. I notice where he lay on the wall, a tenement for chipmunks, and where he jumped to the ground at my approach.

The stonework here is covered with a green moss so brilliant that it appears fabricated. Stout grapevines hang in profusion from towering oaks, and the slightest trickle of a spring still bubbles just down the slope.

It's a good place to sit and enjoy lunch entertained by gray squirrels performing high-wire acts in the network of vines, and scores of winter robins bickering and feasting on the grapes. It is a hauntingly beautiful setting and I wonder at the resilience and grit of those who had lived here. In a way, I feel as if I am invited in to sit, rest, and dine in what might have been the kitchen.

At the top of the hollow, just up from the foundation, are several American chestnut trees. These trees come from old root systems, which are not affected by the blight fungus that killed billions of chestnut trees in the early 1900s. Eventually, these chestnuts will die of the blight, but science has responded, especially The American Chestnut Foundation, which has spearheaded an effort to produce a blight-resistant tree.

THE TIDES OF AUTUMN

The old farm foundation will continue to crumble, but someday on the ridge above, healthy, stalwart chestnuts will tower again and it will be a new day.

FAR DOWN THE HOLLOW, I stop to sit on a sloped embankment near the creek. The sun feels good on my face and I lean back on an elbow and watch a mixed flock of winter birds work through. A large, rusted hand-forged hook protrudes from the leaves near my elbow. I pull on it with some effort and lift a short, heavy-linked chain with another hook at the other end. I determine it was a logging chain, probably forgotten here more than a century ago.

Recently, several areas where I hunt were logged extensively, and it wasn't long before the deer utilized the regenerating thickets as bedding areas and escape cover. Their former patterns changed significantly and we had to discover new vantage points to adapt to these changes. It took a couple of seasons, but it really paid off.

The chain hangs on my studio wall along with an old two-man crosscut saw and a mule shoe. I imagine that one hook of the chain is fastened firmly to the past, and I have only to pull on the other to drag old images from the woods.

WHILE HUNTING, and in my work, I have always strived to look beyond the obvious. That one dictum has opened worlds for me, and I have never spent a day afield that was boring. It makes one look deeper, to become a practiced and passionate observer, and that, in turn, drives a search for knowledge and expertise as the learning curve arcs ever skyward. We hunt to understand.

Nature offers up many signs, symbols and cues. Things once hidden, become evident, mysteries unravel. It requires an immersive approach, but soon, one may feel the collective, living pulse of the woods, hear the land inhale and exhale.

I WILL REMEMBER the beauty of the deer at the end of my drag rope this day, but also the sight of yellow morning light sliding down the oak trunks as the sun gained purchase. I will remember the polished walnut of the rifle I restocked, but also the knots, moss and acorn cuttings on the log I sat on at my favorite deer stand.

From earlier in the fall, I'll never forget the enormous, rut-crazed 12-point buck chasing a doe down a sidehill along with five other bucks. When the big buck slowed momentarily at 10 yards, I buried a bolt from my crossbow deep into the edge of an oak as I led him. Someday, perhaps, another hunter stepping over that fallen oak will see the exposed antique broadhead, and wonder.

As part of a perpetual wild continuum, the light of a hunter's days still shines after his own shadow has grown long and fades. Look closely, see the images of all the fine hunters and yourself in the underpainting. As long as there are woods, it will always be there.

Far-Off Fields

PETE SAT AT THE kitchen table, loading a clip for his .22, as his mother nestled the last of several dozen cabbage rolls into a big broiler. He and his best friend Sonny would have gone hunting early that morning, since it was Saturday. But after losing a tough Friday night football game and still feeling sore and tired, they decided to wait until after lunch before heading out.

His mother poured two quart-jars of stewed tomatoes over the cabbage rolls and set the broiler in the oven. Still holding the coolness of the root cellar, Pete pressed one of the empty jars against the corner of his eye.

"That eye's still really puffy," his mother told Pete. "Are you sure you want to go out today?"

"I'm sure. Now I won't have to squint when I'm aiming."

"Why don't you take Easy along? I think he wants to go."

"All he does is follow us until we take a break to eat, then after he gets his share, he heads for home," Pete complained. "He's no hunter."

"Well, take him along anyway. He's getting a little paunchy."

"All right, but I wish he'd scare up a rabbit or something at least once in a while."

Easy, their enormous black-and-white dog, quivered, not with the anticipation of hunting, but with the prospect of some morsel falling to the floor. The shaggy beast was a stray that had followed Pete home from school several years earlier. He was named Easy by Pete's father, who found great humor in the vagabond pup that had lucked his way onto Easy Street.

Pete buried the remaining cartridges into his pocket, then wrapped a scarf around his neck and tucked the ends into his canvas vest. He yanked his watch hat down tight and folded the front back up. It was cold and blustery, with the promise of snow.

His mother stashed a bag of sandwiches and some peanut butter cookies into the back of his vest.

"There's an extra sandwich in there for Easy," she said. "And remember to trade Sonny squirrels for rabbits. His grandpa likes squirrel and I could use some rabbits."

OUT IN THE FARMYARD, Pete slipped the clip into the rifle, chambered a round, and checked the safety. Long tapering clouds streamed south, like a pod of gray whales riding a current. Whenever a cloud breached, a great bar of yellow light would appear until the gap closed.

The wind nudged him far up through a swale of goldenrod. Pete knelt in the weeds to tighten the lace of his high-topped boot. Easy shouldered up beside him, and he studied the dog's smiling face, raking some beggar-ticks from his silky ears. From that low angle in the weeds, Pete spotted the dark, shiny "button" of a rabbit's unblinking eye and then saw its outline. He raised the rifle and fired, the peal of the shot, a long *k-e-e-e-c-r*, echoed off the pines.

Easy showed no interest as Pete gutted the rabbit.

"That's one for Mom. Now let's get a couple more."

They came out onto the grassy lane, where Sonny sat waiting on a decrepit hay wagon.

"Wow, look at that shiner!" Sonny joked. "Did you get the number of the truck that hit you?"

"Nope. After that tackle, I don't remember much, except that I had fumbled and they scored," Pete recalled. "Hey, how about those new face protector bars some of their guys had on their helmets?"

"I guess they're okay if you got a movie star mug and want to save it," Sonny replied. "That wouldn't help you any, though."

THEY SET OUT through the tall oaks with no plan in mind; there was no room for any sort of organized effort in their afternoon of absolute freedom. As they walked along, Pete shot a big maize-colored fox squirrel from a stump and Sonny missed a gray that spiraled wildly around the trunk of a hickory. He reloaded the single-shot 16-gauge and they walked down to an old homestead.

Easy unknowingly panicked a rabbit that squirted out from the foundation of a collapsed springhouse, and Sonny tumbled it neatly as it ran straight away. Pete swapped him the squirrel for the rabbit.

Easy slurped the runoff as the boys palmed and drank the clear, cold water from the bubbling spring. They always stopped here for a drink while picking berries or hunting, sensing a kinship with the family that had once farmed here.

The wind had died, and it was very quiet, except for the spring. The clouds had thickened and blended as a seamless case-colored expanse. Whispers of sleet dimpled the water.

"Time for a sandwich," said Pete.

They traded their second sandwiches, ham for beef, although Easy would have no part in it, wolfing his down, then begging for a cookie.

Easy perked his ears in the direction of the wooded hollow below, then they heard the dull thumping, too. They followed an old barbed-wire fence that wrapped around the sidehill, and when they stopped to listen, the thudding became louder and more frantic, followed by a guttural bawling.

"It's a lost calf somewhere," Sonny said.

"No, it ain't," Pete interrupted. "Look there."

He pointed farther up the fence line where a big buck stood splay-legged.

"He's tangled up in that fence."

The buck was near exhaustion. His once lustrous coat was gritty with mud and leaf chaff and lathered with strings of spittle. His heaving flanks pumped and hot puffs of vapor rolled from its gaping mouth. Yards of wire were wrapped around his huge pale antlers, and his right foreleg was raised from the ground, snared in the twisted strands.

The buck lunged away desperately, dragging a post, side-hopping and skidding in the pocked mire, straining against the extreme end of its tether toward the thicket. His eyes rolled back showing white.

The boys led Easy out of sight around the sidehill and told him to stay, not wanting to panic the deer further, even though the dog was only mildly curious.

"We have to get him loose somehow," Pete said. "I wonder how long he's been like that?"

"A good while," whispered Sonny. "But he still has some spark left. Sort of looks like you did after yesterday's game."

There were not many deer in the area, and the buck was the biggest they had ever seen. It was long-legged and thick-necked, with a deep, powerful chest and tall, white antlers.

"We have to get him on the ground," Pete said. "Then, work on that wire."

"Do you have that fancy knife with you, the one with the cutters?"

"Right here on my belt," Sonny replied proudly.

Lacking a rope, they cut several long pieces of supple grapevine. Using a long stick, they snaked one length under the buck, then back and around again, and then dropped an end through the loop. Pete raised the loop slowly until it was above the hocks, then Sonny pulled, cinching the back legs together. They brought a second vine across its neck, pulled the buck's head around a trunk, then tied it off.

Pete moved in and draped his wool scarf over the buck's eyes, which calmed the deer a little. Sonny pulled the back legs toward him, as Pete leaned in against the buck and eased it to the ground, pinning it. Bound as it was, the buck could not rise or flail. It struggled in fitful bursts, but with the weight of two strapping football players on it, it resigned itself to fate, and even

began to breathe a little more slowly.

Ever so carefully, the boys worked the foreleg free. The leg was not broken, and bleeding only slightly where the wire had sliced in. Pete bound the forelegs together with his braided belt. Sonny began cutting the wires on each side of the antlers. As he did, Pete studied the buck.

He had never touched a live deer before, and with his palm he felt the big heart beating beneath rib and hide, and it was as if all the wildness of the land was being pumped up from the black soil, up through the heart of the deer and transfused into his own and back again, the wildness of those shared acres, the same life's-blood for both man and beast.

He wondered about all the deer had seen: frozen fields under the glare of a Hunger Moon, hazy summer hollows, the constant tides of dark and dawn. What did the buck see now in that black void beneath the scarf? Was it an image of freedom? He also wondered about all the wild smells the buck sucked in through its flaring nostrils; the mint that sprouted by the springhouse; the acorns, which he could not smell; or maybe even his own passage through these same fields. Did the buck smell the snow that was coming, as Pete now could? Did all things burn brighter for this creature, brighter than what he could ever imagine?

Sonny unraveled most of the wire, except for one tough strand at the base of the buck's antlers that curled backward, like an antenna.

Pete reached around the tree and pulled his scarf off, then untied the buck's legs and backed away. The buck stood on wobbly legs and stumbled forward, much like it probably did when it was a newborn fawn. Then he bolted for the thicket.

The boys watched as the buck shook like a wet dog. A short time later, they saw his white tail flare as he gathered his former grace and sliced up through the woods.

THE TRIO CONTINUED ON through the woods. Snow squalls marked the furrowed field in a striped pattern. As the hunters neared the edge of a field, Sonny stopped abruptly.

"Cockbird!" he said excitedly, pointing with his chin to a huge, dense mass of greenbrier.

Pete spotted the vibrant white ring on the pheasant's neck. Pheasants were rare on these upland farms, and this rooster was crouched low, belly to the leaves, safe in its thorny fortress.

They advanced on its hiding place; but the bird wouldn't budge.

"Get in there and kick it out, buddy," Sonny coaxed.

"Setting that buck loose was probably easier," replied Pete. "Besides, I think you can pot it through that little opening with my rifle."

"Aw, that's not very sporting," Sonny said.

"I have an idea," Pete said, taking a last cookie from his pocket. "C'mon Easy. C'mere, boy."

The big dog lumbered over, his pace quickening when he scented the cookie. Pete gave him half of it and the dog sat back on its haunches, one paw raised, eyes riveted on the remaining portion.

"Get ready, Sonny."

Pete flipped the cookie into the greenbrier and Easy nosed in after it, belly crawling. The unnerved rooster slipped out the back, then launched, banking wildly to the left. Sonny shot behind, peppering its tail, and the pheasant flew on, alternately flapping and gliding far across the field.

A short time later, Sonny had to get home.

"Let's swap guns, you might run into another bird," Sonny suggested.

THE STORM FRONT HAD MOVED ON, and Pete crossed the field, walking from brilliant sunlight into blue shadow, as if crossing an imaginary line separating autumn and winter. He eased into a border of sumac and milkweeds, hoping to kick out a rabbit. Something flashed ahead, and then the same cockbird erupted from the weeds, screeching like a feverishly worked pump handle, its satiny harlequin costume aglow in the red light. It angled into level flight, gaining speed and momentum, then plummeted, thudding hard into the weeds. Pete broke open the gun, marking the spot through the milkweed silk and coppery feathers that drifted through the rising gun smoke.

He walked back out into the field and sat on some sun-washed rocks admiring the rooster beside him. Easy turned circles in the foxtails then plopped down at his master's feet. Everything smelled fresh and clean, and Pete leaned back and inhaled deeply, watching scores of crows passing high overhead, flying slowly to roost. They talked as they flew, *Aw, aa, ot, ca*. They were black and sharp against the pale sky, like paper cutouts laced on a string. Their unhurried flight was mesmerizing, as if they were reluctant for the day to end.

Pete sat up then and spotted a doe cutting across the corner of the field, followed closely by a buck, a wire on its antlers springing with each step.

As he walked through his yard with Easy, the dog, for the first time that day, took the lead. Once inside, he was immediately enveloped in the aroma of cabbage. When he plopped the pheasant and rabbits onto the cutting block, his mother turned from the stove.

"You're just in time for supper," she said. "Rabbits and a pheasant, too! Looks like you had a good day."

"It was a great day, definitely better than yesterday," he said, glancing out through the steamy window, watching the last light of day fade, the far-off fields ready for winter, and he for whatever the world might bring his way.

Nexus

A COUPLE BOYHOOD FRIENDS and I were standing at the head of a long, deep ravine on land owned by family of one of the boys. The ravine had been used as a dump by both a long-gone mining company and a brickyard and was full of sandstone, timbers and broken bricks. But it was a great place to shoot our slingshots and I had brought along a bucket of slag pellets to share.

After a couple hours of accuracy and distance contests, my friends went home, but I stayed on and just sat there a while, before taking one last shot. The slag ammo was gone, but I retrieved a marble from a pocket. But this was no ordinary agate, it was my "lucky" marble. Back then, kids carried odd things, for show or to trade: brightly-dyed rabbits' feet on gold chains, whistles, Army soldiers, tiny compasses and the like. Among those trinkets, one bauble always was designated as being lucky, giving it greater value in a trade.

My lucky marble had been carefully selected from a big jar of marbles, chosen because of its unusual colors: burnt sienna, cream white, mint green, pale blue and turquoise. Despite my feelings for it, I impulsively pinched it into the slingshot pouch, raised it at a high angle and loosed it into forever.

Some 30 years later, on an October visit back home, I spent a morning hunting on my boyhood hill. I missed a grouse at the old orchard on top, but killed a rabbit at the edge of the powerline. On my way back, halfway down a steep sidehill, I dug my boot heels in and plopped down to take a break. A glint of color near my boot caught my eye. It was a marble. I plucked it from the clay and wiped it off, recognizing immediately it was my lucky marble.

I couldn't fathom the odds of ever seeing that marble again. It brought back memories of that hot summer day and of us sitting in the shade of an elderberry jungle sharing tales of an anaconda-sized black snake that lived in the ravine. I could almost hear the dull *thwap* of the heavy slag pellets hitting the black mine timbers and taste the tinny water from my canteen. I don't know why, but I had no regrets after shooting away my lucky marble that day, nor did I know why I did. Maybe it was just a way of discarding a childhood thing and moving on.

I thought of tossing it into the ravine, but instead put it in my pocket. Everyone can use a little luck now and then. And when it comes to hunting and the outdoors, coincidences, inexplicable alignments and moments of déjà vu are not uncommon. Perhaps trajectories of so much life in motion present greater opportunities for some elements to intersect. At any rate, this nexus is part and parcel of the landscape we hunt – magical, mystical, mythical.

I ONCE WROTE an upland-bird-hunting fiction piece called *New Blood*. In short, the main character, a bird hunter, stops at a yard sale and buys a canvas Filson bird hunting vest. In one of the vest pockets, he discovers a map left by its deceased former owner disclosing three prime grouse coverts. Taking advantage of his good fortune, the bird hunter finds these classic coverts and discovers that they are productive. At each, though, he encounters another hunter, and at the last, meets an old man wearing a Filson vest. The reader is left wondering whether the other hunters and the old man at the last covert are a spirit that had guided the bird hunter to the beloved coverts, infusing "new blood."

I did an illustration of a classic Filson vest as part of the suite of illustrations for the article and was going to include the story as a selection to be included in this book, but what I am about to relate is true, and far more extraordinary.

Months after *New Blood* was published, I received a letter from a reader inquiring if I could send a copy of that story to him; he had misplaced his. He explained that the story was especially meaningful to him, because his best friend and long-time grouse hunting buddy, who had recently passed on, had worn the same Filson bird hunting vest illustrated in that story.

Touched by his request, I signed the magazine article, found the original artwork of the vest and slipped both into an envelope. That same morning, I received a call to fly out west the next day to attend an important meeting. I had to bring along several architectural drawings and somehow, in my haste, the letter got buried under a stack of drawings. I ended up staying in my Midwest studios for six weeks and completely forgot about this letter.

Some months later, I discovered it under the stack and felt embarrassed mailing it after so much time had passed. But I did.

I received an email from the reader a few days later noting that he had just opened the envelope and was thrilled with the original sketch of the vest. But what he really wanted me to know was that before arriving at work that morning, he had already been thinking of his friend, and when he opened my envelope, and took out the sketch, its sentimental value really hit home – it came on the one-year anniversary of his friend's passing.

THE TIDES OF AUTUMN

ON MY WAY to western Pennsylvania for a week of deer and turkey hunting with family, I stopped for a couple of hours to do a little still-hunting and to visit my late father's deer stand.

I parked my truck at the gate, jumped out and stretched. It had been a long drive. Looking around, I inhaled deeply. Those minutes just before going afield are a favorite part of my hunt, when it seems autumn's progression, muscling through these uplands, invites me to move within its slipstream.

While gathering my gear, I saw that I had stepped on a pocket watch when I got down out of the truck. Pressed into the ground, I yanked it free by its chain. It was an everyday field watch, nothing fancy. Still, I set it on the front seat floor mat, planning to clean it later and see if it would work.

The day was very warm and nothing was moving. After a long trek, I was back down the mountain, seated on a log at Dad's stand, which is only a couple hundred yards from the truck. The sun was slanting in hard. Half asleep, images drifted by of all the wonderful days we had spent on these oak flats. Soon, I dozed off.

I was awakened by a slight shifting in the landscape, that strange, almost otherworldly energy in the air that hunters sometimes experience. It's not just a sudden quickening preceding an impending weather front. It's more like a switch had been thrown, provoking a pervasive restlessness across the hills, a signal to stand and start moving in step with the season. Dark slashes of gray clouds, like the wispy marks of a wet broom on concrete, swept across the western sky. I stood up and turned towards the powerline 50 yards away, edgy and eager to get back on the road for the final hour of my trip.

"Okay, Dad," I said, "I'm heading out."

But I was not the only one being stirred into motion. A big, gray rut buck was nosing slowly along a wall of greenbrier, his head bent to the ground like someone searching the leaves for something he had dropped.

The buck was only a 6-point, but his rack was high and wide, and when he stopped at 37 yards, I sent a fixed-blade broadhead tight behind his shoulder. He jumped a few steps, stopped, then walked to the powerline and stood there. Whenever I shoot a deer, I always glance at my watch and I saw that the shot was at exactly 2:12.

I watched him through binoculars and saw that he was bleeding profusely from the exit wound. I waited for him to wobble and fall, but he never faltered. Then he took a few more steps and melted into the tall weeds and grasses on the powerline.

A half-hour later, I gathered my gear and walked up to where he had stood. A placemat-sized puddle of bubbly blood in the leaves gave me great confidence. My arrow had gone on, into a knoll covered with dense clots of greenbrier. I'd look for it later. I followed blood into the powerline, where I am sure the buck had died, and there the blood quit, like a faucet turning off. Not a single drop more.

I searched for another hour and called my brother-in-law, Dave. I didn't want my sister and him to worry if I was late. Dave drove down and we looked together until dark, then decided to back out.

Sun streamed down the powerline the next morning as we continued the search. We looked hard for another hour and still found no other sign. Then we did a directional line of flight search. Dave spotted him piled up in a dense thicket 60 yards from my truck. I dressed and tagged the buck and we loaded him up.

We figured that when the buck walked out onto the powerline, he must have stopped again, maybe to lie down. But when I came up, he took off on one of those last-mad-death-sprints down through the woods, right past my truck and into the thicket.

Later, after lunch, Dave cleaned off the face of the pocket watch. He tried to wind it, but the hands were frozen in place.

"What time did you shoot that buck?" he asked.

"Exactly 2:12."

"When?"

"2:12."

He turned the watch by its chain toward me.

"Read the time."

A Reluctant Passage

I HANG A new wildlife calendar on the wall of my hunting room. With hunting season mostly over, it's time to put my gear back in its proper place. One table is heaped with clothes, the other with contents of pockets and packs. I begin to clean and sort, making good progress until I empty my bowhunting pack and a big, leathery black oak leaf falls out. I hold it by its stem, examining the raised network of delicate veining. Its satiny surface reflects a blurred image of my face, as if I were held within the autumn just passed.

It's hard for me to let go of autumn, especially now, in the autumn of my own days afield. The hunter lives in autumn. His hunting spirit lingers there, coursing hills and hollows, fields and ridgelines. His heart beats strongest then, surging full bore through his veins at the promise shown in fresh buck scrapes or the track of a black bear, charging the vessels of his spirit, sustaining him until nourished again by mountain air.

Solitary winter hunts are like re-reading a book. They can be enjoyable and some elements may have been overlooked, but the element of discovery is mostly gone and the storyline is unchanged. The woods shrink in the intimacy of winter. In autumn, each hollow, field and woodlot seem a place unto itself, but a blanket of snow unites all those provinces, and the landscape becomes smaller.

I'm not done with autumn yet. I want to linger in the wooded hollow below the old farm again. A hollow bordered by goldenrod and populated by ancient white oaks contorted with age and decked out in russet leaves, where oily yellow acorns lay on deer trails, browning in the sallow light. A hollow where freshly made buck rubs and scrapes declare through visual and complex chemical markers their maker's omnipotence.

I want to sit for one more hour in that hollow with my bow, just before dusk when the lower reaches of rocks and trunks blend into a single, graying mass as the tops of the trees ignite in the fiery light of the setting sun. It is an enchanted time when the breeze dies and the thermals reverse and the hollow begins to fill with cold air. This is what hunters call the magic hour, when deer seem to suddenly appear, revealed only by the white flash of a twitching tail, antler tine, or flick of an ear.

I remember a doe running, not in alarm, but in the stop-and-go hustle of the rut, her ears back, eyes flashing white as she turns them hard in the sockets to catch a glimpse of her pursuer. The rack of the buck glows like palest jade in the waning light. He grunts loudly, steadily, oblivious to my calls. The pair flow over the broken ground, weaving through deadfalls, over logs and around rocks in an amazing display of dexterity and grace no less marvelous than that of a Cooper's hawk threading its way through veils of grapevines in pursuit of prey.

PUTTING MY TURKEY calls into a bin, I think of Grapevine Hollow. Let me walk once again, if only for a while, on that misty rain-soaked hillside, thick with grapevines and hickory. In November, after leaf fall, the riotous palette of October is reduced to only a few somber colors upon a neutral background. Grape clusters lay scattered everywhere, many still hanging in the matted canopy of vines. Soft blue-violet clusters, the same hue as the distant hills.

Seven gobblers, beetle-black and shiny, materialize from the mists. Their long, two-tone beards droop like old, frayed rope. They are here to sample the grapes – expert connoisseurs of autumn's finest. There is a formality in their manner and distinguished garb, like stoic elders of some secret society who have set themselves apart from the flocks of younger birds, away from the piping and whistling of mixed flocks feeding pell-mell across the oak flats.

The gobblers stop when one member raises its head high and double-putts loudly. Somehow the bird had spotted me watching through binoculars. In the next instant they launch downhill, great barred wings fanning the mists. Once clear of the treetops they lock their wings and sail far down the hollow and regroup. Soon they will continue their work of sampling yet another wild vineyard.

Before I put the last call away, I stroke a cascade of yelps from a box call made of Pennsylvania locust. Five months until spring gobbler season. The gobblers will be transformed entirely then. They will strut and display through the hardwoods and along the tram roads like colorful floats in a parade, loudly proclaiming their presence, a far cry from what might be the wariest of autumn's creatures.

LOOKING DOWN THE long slope, there appears to be a cloud of blue smoke wafting through the woods. It's only the pale, dense canopy of a crabapple thicket. There is always a grouse or two there, and I head down. I flush one bird, missing it. The umbrella of thorny branches is so densely intertwined I don't know how a grouse can bust through it without injury.

I pick up a crabapple, sticky and resinous, and inhale its tart perfume. As autumn progresses, the sweet fragrance of the crab thicket of early October takes on a pungent mustiness, reminding me of an apple bin we had in our canning room from when I was a boy. Once, a few days after a heavy, early November snowfall, I hunted a crab thicket and flushed six grouse from one smallish crab tree. One after the other, they rocketed out, snow flying in the blinding light and, somehow, I dropped the last one. It was one of the most unforgettable moments in all my days outdoors.

The crab thicket is a safe haven, kind of like a coral reef, sanctuary from great horned owls that always nest in the white pines at the head of the hollow. Doves and songbirds seek shelter from storms here and rabbits and deer head deep into the interior when pushed.

After wiping down my 115-year-old double-barrel hammer gun, I close the action and place it into the safe. The old gun has another page added to its long history, begun in English shooting fields, continuing on an autumn day in a crab thicket in Penn's Woods.

AS I TRANSFER the potent .350 magnum cartridges from the belt pouch to their designated box for storage, I'm reminded of bears, but more of the bear country of the Big Woods.

The narrow flat where I sit is little more than a pouting lip that wraps around the face of the mountain, the chin below the lip a rocky, near vertical 40-foot cliff. It is very quiet. The only sounds are far-off raven-speak, and closer, the mutterings of porcupines in their den just below the rim. I'm up here for the view as much as the hope a bear will amble by. This is a distant, isolated stand, difficult to reach, climbing over rocky slides and pushing through two laurel jungles. There's a lot of bear sign here; it's the sort of place a bear might seek after being pushed by the hunters far below.

My seat is a mossy, square rock 25 yards from the edge of the cliff. Within the space of a few hours, it rains, snows and sleets. Wild vapors, tattered and torn, drift through the great valley like aimless spirits. Fog peeps up over the flat and slides down again. Chilled to the bone by the damp air, I decide to loop up the mountain to warm up.

On my way back down, I come around a tree and reach down to move a branch that blocks my way. The branch slips from my hand and plops onto the leaves, and at that moment, I look up

hulking black shape of a bear pop up over the cliff in front of my seat. Before I straighten up, it ducks back down and sprints along the rim. I can only see the very top of its back, and then it cuts across the far corner of the flat. In my scope, I see tree…tree…tree… Then, a flash of black, followed by a deeper black of the hole in the laurel that swallows the bear. It's gone. The only bear I have ever seen in 35 years of bear hunting has vanished.

What will never vanish is an image of the split-second when the bear's eyes met mine. Upon killing that bear I would have possessed it as a result of woodsmanship and luck, a physical memento of a goal achieved. But I am satisfied to possess that magical instant of our meeting on that high mountain bench.

THE HUNTING ROOM is in order, guns cleaned and locked up. Camo clothes back on hangers, gloves paired, hats stacked on the wire racks. I flip through the months of the calendar. 303 days until October. I shut and lock the door of the gun safe, turn off the lights and reluctantly close the door to the hunting room. I think of the woods advancing to winter, and the hunter, that reluctant child of autumn.

Dogwood Dandy

THE SULTAN OF SPRING

AN UNUSUAL ASPECT of this painting is that it isn't painted with acrylic or oil, but with hard pastels on a fine-grit German-made sandpaper. The vibrancy of pastel pigments was perfect to simulate the chromatic cascades of colors that wild-turkey feathers reflect.

Birds don't show attitude through facial expressions in the way mammals do, but more through movements and posturing, while displaying and positioning various feather tracts. Watch a gobbler move toward a hen and you may get to see nature's master shape-shifter at work.

He may enter a field sleek and wary, then stands upright, feathers tightly compressed, surveying for danger. He then proceeds, tail-fan opening and closing, umbrella-like, lifting then dropping in a half-strut display. His breast expands, the feathers louver up, and in a sudden motion his red, white and blue head is thrust forward as he gobbles mightily. The gobbler relaxes momentarily then inflates to full strut, chestnut-colored tail fanned fully in an arc held upright, facing toward the hen. He steps slowly, then advances quickly, great barred wings dragging as he spits and drums.

He is a feathered ornament, a rhinestone bauble, an ornate float in the grand parade of spring. As you sit and watch him down the barrel of your gun do not become mesmerized. And don't move!

Aubade

THE MISTY WOODS lies pale and broken, weary from the relentless storms of a brutal and vandalous winter. The carpet of leaves has been compressed into thin and ragged mats by a sea of snow and ice and a gentle breeze lifts only the tips of leaves from the wind-enameled earth. Powerful winter gales have rolled the land upon itself, driving the crumbled detritus of the uplands into every crack and crevice. All the varied hues of the forest are reduced to a nameless monochrome; even the gray squirrel's acorn-shiny, salt-and-pepper coat appears dull and faded. Sun-bleached windfalls lie tilted and scattered like long bones cracked and sucked clean by some great predator. But in this sere and tattered landscape, a wondrous refrain, older than the land itself, sings of life and of life to come.

Clear water percolates upwards, trickling and gurgling from every pore on the skin of the mountains. The snows of violent winter storms have been stored and filtered and now are released gently as cold, sweet water. Water, ever-moving, life-giving rivulets building, now flowing, feeding fugitive runs and familiar creeks and on to famous rivers.

A recipe for spring might read: Take one freeze-dried mountain, add water, heat and sunshine, then stand back.

Water music plays in constant refrain to the

manic surge of myriad lifeforms bursting forth, each adding its own unique song to the ever-expanding chorus. Nature steps forth boldly, and the earnest songs of courtship, demarcation, dominance and even joy ring through the uplands.

Rising above all other voices is one morning serenade, one aubade that rolls upon the land like thunder before a warm spring rain – the gobble of the wild turkey. All of this is realized by the spring turkey hunter who replicates crow calls, owl hoots, turkey yelps, clucks and purrs and sometimes steals the thunder of the gobbler himself. Although these calls are meant to locate or lure a gobbler within shotgun range, I believe there is another reason that the hunter adds to the tumult – it's his way of joining the sylvan choruses, another wild voice speaking the language of the land, rising with the crescendo, proclaiming his own joy at being alive.

A CROW FLIES low over the freshly plowed field, its dark blue shadow growing larger and less distinct as it gains altitude. It's heading to the woods to join a crow riot taking place not far from where I sit along a tram road.

The crow passes overhead, its shadow dappling the branches of the big white oak I'm sitting against. I can't determine the source of the mob's wrath, and I'm too tired to sneak up the road to find out. Several grueling days of gobbler hunting on these steep, rocky mountains has worn me down, and I'm resting here, fiddling with a new slate call, before heading back to my truck. The clucks sound clear and sharp, but I need to improve the vigor of the yelps. I decide to call it quits for the day and take the tram road down to the field.

I take only a few steps and look over a rise on the road when a big longbeard launches, his red legs scissoring up beneath him like landing gear. He had to be coming into my calling, and I broke a basic rule by not watching for a bird that might be coming in silent.

Two days later, I locate a gobbler tucked away at the head of a hollow at the end of a big pine woods. My goal is to coax him to the rim of the hollow, where I'll be waiting near the field's edge.

Although well after daybreak, it's still gray and drizzly, and the gobbler should be getting hoarse by now as he has unleashed tirade upon tirade of commanding gobbles since flying down. I can't figure out why he's hung up. Usually, when a gobbler gets in with hens, he might continue to gobble occasionally. But this bird sounded alone and frustrated. Some hen yelps from the pine woods really get him fired up again. Then he moves deeper into the woods and clams up.

After a while, I walk down and discover an old property-division wire fence that runs far into the woods. Fences are baffling, insurmountable barriers to some turkeys and the bane of a turkey hunter if he happens to be on the wrong side. In effect, they might as well be the Great Wall of China. I once watched a trio of jakes forced up-against a wire fence go berserk: feathers flying, legs scrambling, wings flapping. For some birds, fences are an everyday obstacle and they have no qualms about going under, weaving through or flying over. Others may follow them a distance until they find a place where they feel comfortable crossing over.

Ominous clouds find me far back in new territory. As I hurry along a woods road, looking for a place to put on my military rain poncho, I trip on something protruding from the ground, but when I look back I see that it's an old twisted horseshoe. I remove it from the earth with much difficulty, then hunker down in a windfall as an inky sky scuttles impossibly low and lightning crashes across the big flat. The air is warm and sweet, like the breath of a baby asleep on your shoulder. A grouse drums nearby that prolongs the tailings of each peal of thunder.

The rain doesn't sweep down the valley, but bursts straight down with terrific force. I'm dry under the big poncho and hold the 'shoe out, turning and rubbing it as it washes clean. I put the 'shoe in my pack, feeling lucky to be out here in the heart of spring.

Later, I hang it in my studio; a friend points out that it's not a horseshoe, but a mule-shoe, which is longer and narrower. He also notes that I have it hanging upside down. It should be hung with the U-shape up, like the letter, to hold in the luck.

ENGLISH SCHOLAR and writer Edward Fitzgerald is best known for his 1859 translation of *The Rubaiyat*, written by Persian mathematician Omar Khayyam 900 years ago. The first quatrain of this work is something every turkey hunter will immediately recognize as a familiar occurrence in the turkey woods:

> *Wake! For the Sun, who behind yon Eastern Height,*
> *Has chased the Session of the Stars from Night:*
> *And to the field of Heav'n ascending,*
> *Strikes the Sultan's Turret with a Shaft of Light.*

This is exactly what happened at first light when the sun lit up the oaks and the Sultan of the Big Flat, a big longbeard I had roosted there, gobbled at my soft yelps, then flew down and ran right down the pipe of my 12-gauge and into an outgoing load of magnum 5s.

Maybe I owed it to my lucky mule-shoe, but my fortune and the weather had taken a turn for the better.

Whenever I have a gobbler on the ground, I spend a lot of time admiring what I consider to be one of the most beautiful fowl in the world.

To some, a turkey is just a turkey, whether domestic or wild. But comparing a sleek wild gobbler to his meaty, domestic counterpart is like comparing a Ferrari to a Zamboni. At one moment, he snakes along, reptilian-like, sleek and dark as he seeks a hen. In the next, unsure, he half-struts, expanding like an accordion bellows, tail fanning and collapsing. Then he goes into full strut, becoming a great and ornate disco ball stepping along with his great barred wings dragging and vibrating in the leaf litter. Displaying in the sun, glistening with myriad iridescence, his red, white and blue head and magnificent fanned tail display his temperament.

Holding a single breast feather and turning it slowly in the light, I can see many colors: copper, cadmium orange, yellow-bronze, a highly chromatic yellow-green, pale red-violet, burnt sienna, and a black that also returns shades of blue and violet. I twist it slightly and these prisms move and cascade. Considering that a gobbler has 6,000 feathers distributed within various tracts, he becomes one of nature's grandest visual spectacles.

A gobbler facing off against an adversary, or even while bullying a decoy, is a formidable combatant; circling, measuring, looking for an opening, strategizing attacks and counterattacks. The wild turkey is the juggernaut of spring, his gobble a thunderous, singular proclamation representing all things wild that life has started anew in these greening hills.

The Bones of Spring

YEARS AGO, I MADE a turkey call from the wing bones of a hen turkey. With a wood-burning tool, I etched a line of turkey tracks along the length of the call, a symbolic path for a gobbler to follow to the source of the sweet yelps. With artist's ink, I then stained the call a pale olive green. For a lanyard, I used a length of old leather bootlace.

Inspired by the same muse that directed ancient hunters to adorn their tools of the hunt, I laced the leather through three buttons made of deer antler, and a single spur from a gobbler. With thread, I tied on several breast feathers from a jake and a tailfeather clipping from a cock grouse. As a final touch, I threaded on a small snail shell.

With these totem objects, the tribal-like call was complete. Now accompanying the voice of the hen turkey were the spirits of other creatures. The gobbler would be reassured by the familiar presence of the deer and the sound of the drumming grouse, and if he did not find the hen quickly, a jake or rival gobbler certainly would. The snail shell would remind me to always move slowly. I felt a certain magic in the call, and practiced with it throughout the winter.

I like the sound of a wingbone call in the woods. It has a musical ring, a resonance that lingers like the peal of a distant bell. On the first day of the season, I raised the attention of a gobbler that at first gobbled mightily, but soon lost interest, probably falling into the company of some hens. Promises from afar can't compete with soft clucks nearby. On the second day, I hunted different woods, but the scenario was the same.

The third morning, I was back on familiar ground in one of my favorite haunts, a mature woods below some charcoal flats. At midmorning, I set up against a tumbled stone wall atop a slight rise. Liquid yelps from my wingbone spilled down the mountain and a gobbler answered from below.

With every run of yelps, he gobbled. Then, off to my left, I spotted a hen hopping up over a section of the wall and headed downhill. Not long after, the gobbling stopped. He knew my location, so I decided to wait. Perhaps after the hen left, he'd come a-calling.

Two hours later, he came in silently, but from behind me. He was on my off shoulder and stood atop the wall, looking around. If I moved an inch, he would see me. If I breathed, he would see me. If I blinked, he would be gone. I became part of the tree, my spine laminated to the bark, my legs planted like roots, my camouflaged gun barrel perfectly still, little more than a fallen branch. He saw me anyway, and ran down a ravine.

Soon after, I heard a distant gobble from around the mountain. The morning was fading fast, but if I could get over there quickly, I'd have time to work him. I followed the flat around, then climbed diagonally across a broad expanse of rocks and through a patch of greenbrier. I took a deer trail through some laurel and came out above the bird. When I reached for my call, it was gone.

I quickly checked my pockets as I sometimes remove calls from around my neck when I'm walking, because I don't like them swinging about. No luck. I spent the remainder of the morning looking for it. The old leather lanyard probably got snagged and broke, and the call must have fallen in one of the countless nooks or crannies in the rocks. I coursed back and forth, trying to recall my original path, but it was difficult. I searched high and low, but to no avail. No doubt the call now lay somewhere in the rocks, in the secret ward of mice who would gnaw at it as they would any other bone.

The bones of the hen from which I made the call had returned, in a roundabout way, to the very mountain where she once lived. It was a rendition of her voice that called in the gobbler: a voice silenced in autumn that sang again in spring. Later, sitting on the stone wall, I recalled the beautiful autumn afternoon when I lured the hen to my gun with a series of *kee-kee* runs, which, ironically, also is known as a lost call.

I AM A CHILD OF AUTUMN, born in October, with a strong allegiance to the fall as if it were a country more than a season. Most hunters find scouting for gobblers before the green-up to be enjoyable, especially after a long winter. For me, though, a stalwart citizen of autumns past, there is a sense of melancholy to the early spring landscape. Even though I appreciate the signs of resurging life, I find that the remains of autumn draw me back more to that time than the season to come.

I see a line of old buck rubs, and remember when they were newly made, sticky to the touch, and how they fairly glowed in the dim light of an October morning. Soon these saplings will bear only a brownish scar, not unlike a person with a skinned shin that has healed.

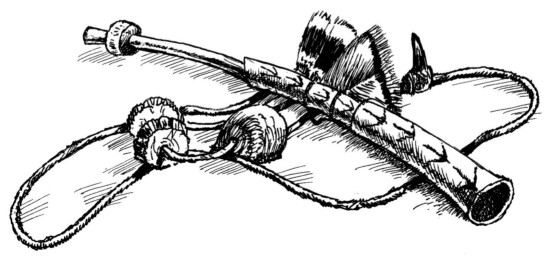

Nearby, I find the skeleton of a deer scattered about, a section of its hide enameled to the ground by winter storms. Spring beauties grow up through the trellis of its ribcage. Autumn's thick carpet of oak leaves, once a rich, glossy brown, like a deer's hide, is now a continuous pale and threadbare mat. Where the wind reveals the ground are fragments of acorn hulls. A small hornet's nest hangs in shards within a witch hazel shrub.

Strewn in the goldenrod beside an old tram road, I find some breast feathers from a hen turkey. I pick up a tail-feather and preen it between my fingers. It is gritty and wet. What predator ambushed this hen during the winter? Perhaps a bobcat or coyote waiting at the curve of the road, crouching behind the root mass of this windfall. Or maybe the predator dashed across the road, driving the turkey into the tall goldenrod, where she might have hung up for one fatal second.

Farther up the mountain, an old familiar white oak has finally fallen, the gnarled branches of one limb look like a great bony hand laying palm up. I remember seeing this mighty tree for the first time decades ago, and how it stood out like royalty among the others at the edge of the clearing, its regalia of copper and brass leaves shining in the morning sun. I used to go out of my way to visit the oak, to watch for squirrels in its branches, or post nearby for deer or turkeys that would come for its acorns. Sometimes I would lean against it, watching the hollow below, watching as it had for so many years.

Like some pseudo-shaman, I can see in these bones of spring, the flames of an autumn past flickering yet, but fading, soon to be extinguished by spring rains.

EACH YEAR, THE WOODS are like a house torn down to its framework and then rebuilt, cell upon cell, leaf upon leaf, scarcely changing to our eyes from one spring to the next. I cling tightly to the vestiges of autumn until that house is fully rebuilt, and only then do I let go. The rebuilding is a wondrous process to witness, and spring turkey hunters know it well. It begins with light, then water, and it is water in the form of rivulets and cleansing rains that washes autumn from the uplands.

Numerous freshets up here swell and gather momentum, crisscrossing as braided runs, merging with others on an upland plateau, forming there into a single, vigorous mountain stream. From there, the brimming pool cascades over a stretch of rocks in an agony of white, and as the hollow narrows and the slope falls away, the water gathers again in a succession of deeper pools, bursting out of tight chutes, rushing ever downward through rocky flumes, rushing then in the deepest and most level part of the hollow. Eddies swirl, turning back in dark, languid pools before joining the nation of waters that is the river.

Aside from the water music, spring is heralded by myriad voices: frogs and red-winged blackbirds, droning flies and towhees. Every creature capable of making a sound adds to the rising tumult that proclaims the tide has turned. It is the gobble of the wild turkey, though, that says it best and loudest, his only competition the roll of thunder echoing down in the valley. Although I have heard gobbling in all seasons, it is the gobbler's declarations in spring that speak for the rocks and trees and soil, the silent land itself exalts the miracle of renewal through those booming gobbles.

HERE IN THESE WOODS, the current of yesteryear flows just below the surface and ushers from the pores of the mountain as surely as spring runoff. When I drift across the charcoal flats, I can imagine the woodcutters and charcoal colliers toiling there. It is back-breaking work, as an ever-expanding, smoking wound opens in the dark forest as acre upon acre of hardwoods are felled to make charcoal to fuel the iron furnaces down in the valley. I can hear the steady chunk of axes and saws and crashing trees and the clink of chains as mules pull the logs down the slick drag roads.

Cut and stacked into large domes, the hardwoods are converted to charcoal through a precisely controlled burning. Even now, I can almost smell the smoke, that constant smoke wafting throughout the uplands, week after week, until it seemed to permeate the soot-covered souls of the workers themselves. Traces of black grit remain 150 years later, as it does in caves and pits from the fires of earlier people 14,000 years before.

The mossy stone fences speak, too, of a time when the woods were settled and subdivided by hopeful mountain farmers, when long fences defined property lines, protected crops and corralled livestock. I can see that gobbler yet, charcoal black, standing atop that lichen-covered fence, a fence that can neither confine nor shut out any wild creature, a monument now that harbors only old dreams of a people long gone.

AS THE YEARS PASS, I have acquired a different perspective of the spring turkey hunt. The gobbler that always has loomed so large in my thoughts and dreams has now shrunk in relation to the land, or perhaps it is that the landscape's persona has swelled in true proportion to the bird. Turkey hunting is very exciting, but now it is the recollection of other elements within the landscape – all those things surrounding the gobbler – that I treasure most.

I FOUND THE BLEACHED carapace of a turtle shell, and I'm thinking of making an old-fashioned slate call with it. I have a piece of slate with a tiny fern fossil embossed on one side that I can glue into the shell, which will act as a sound chamber. To be safe, I'll paint the white shell olive green, so it doesn't resemble the white head of a gobbler. I'll whittle a laurel peg to use as a striker, and with it will summon old music from the slate, turkey music from an older time, a voice from the past that will echo.

The Callmaker

FORD PARKED his truck up on the hard road, deciding to retrace his old route to Spencer's farm, the one he often took as a boy living just over the hill. He cut down through the woods, where a few reefs of snow remained, then came out onto a dirt lane that he followed until he found an old deer trail that wound down through a field of goldenrod. The trail diverged then, at a small, wild orchard overlooking the farm.

The damp February air held the briny odor of dying winter. In the mist-shrouded bottomland, the farm had the two-dimensional appearance of stage scenery. The gabled roof of the farmhouse protruded sharply, and only the crowns of some black willows etched the sky. A crow jerked across the hollow like a paper cutout on a string. The gray sky – the canvas backdrop of this upland stage – tore silently, flooding the hillside with light. Ford stood in the warmth until the seam mended and then went on.

The farmhouse was colder inside than out, and in short order, he had a fire roaring in the woodstove. Ford prodded the flames with a poker, then made some coffee. He was considering buying a camp up north when the farm came up for sale. The house was run down, and he had spent countless hours restoring it. The farm had been owned by a man named Maitlin, although everyone called it Spencer's farm, after Alvin Spencer, a tenant from North Carolina.

Spencer and his wife, Milly, had spent most of their lives on a circuitous migration north, putting down stakes every few years, then moving on. The farm was secluded, grown wild even back then, with a budding turkey population. This suited Spencer just fine, because he was first and foremost a turkey hunter, one of a long line of celebrated turkey hunters from the backwoods of the Carolina Piedmont.

Ford recalled the summer he met Alvin Spencer.

Spencer worked with Ford's father at the gravel quarry and asked him to send his boy over to shoot some woodchucks wreaking havoc on Milly's garden. While coming down through the orchard, Ford heard the strident yelps of a hen turkey, then saw a smiling Alvin Spencer sitting on the porch, fanning a box call, greeting him with all manner of turkey talk.

"I like it you come early, son," said Spencer, translating his turkey talk. "It's what I was tellin' you while you was comin' down the hill.

"Hey, neighbor, come on down here now; I been waitin' on you," Spencer said, continuing his translation. "There's much to do today."

"You really said that?" Ford asked.

"Jest a bit of friendly flock talk," Spencer replied. "Listen now."

The elfin man stroked and plucked the call. It sounded exactly like a flock of turkeys, one voice running into another, contented purrs and perts, whines and soft clucks, and liquid yelps, over and again, ending with some sharp alarm putts. Then Spencer took off his cap and beat it against his legs like a turkey taking flight.

"I walk along with 'em up here," he said, pointing to his head. "I seen 'em scratchin' and pickin' up akerns and such. Then one sees a man, and they all get nervous. Oh, they are nervous creatures!

"They spy somethin' in the shadders – maybe yerself settin' there with this gun and – *whump, whump, whump* – off they go! If a caller's gonna talk proper turkey, he got to believe in what he's sayin'. No gobbledygook. Hey, that's a joke – gobbledygook. Get it?"

As they walked to the garden, Ford found it curious that Spencer looked much like a turkey. He was bald and long-necked, with ruddy cheeks and a pointy nose. He walked like a turkey, too, round-shouldered, with a hurry-up-and-wait cadence.

At noon, Ford returned to the farmhouse with a brace of chucks and handed them to Spencer's wife.

"Oh my, they're hogs!" she exclaimed. "And cabbage fat! I fixed y'all some lemonade and sandwiches. Alvin's out in the shed."

The aroma of freshly sawn cedar wafted from the open shed door. Spencer sat at a workbench, sanding a turkey call. The shed was like a small museum that housed a collection of artifacts recovered from the digs of some ancient hunting culture. Turkey calls of every shape and design hung in chaos from pegboards. There were calls made from the shells of turtles and coconuts and cow-horns, and dozens of box calls fashioned from combinations of wood, both domestic and exotic.

On a shelf were rows of slate calls and coffee cans full of strikers. Scrimshawed wingbone yelpers dangled from beaded and feathered lanyards. Several turkey-spur necklaces hung among the calls. Chorus lines of turkey legs strung onto wire crisscrossed the ceiling, and one entire wall was plastered with spread turkey fans and cupped wings.

"Think you could teach me to call like you?" asked Ford. "I have a box call at home, but it doesn't sound like yours."

"Let me see your hands," Spencer asked.

He studied Ford's palms with the discerning eye of a fortune-teller.

"A caller, a *real* caller, got to have a call made for his hand and tuned for the turkey's ear," he explained. "Store-bought will work, but a caller's got to find his own voice. Only way is to make yer own. Here now, try this'n. You got big paws and this'n might fit."

Ford stroked the call as best he could.

"Well, it'll do," Spencer said. "Y'all sound like a schoolboy recitin' from a paper, though. But we got all summer to work on that now, don't we?"

BY SUMMER'S END, under the tutelage of the maestro, Ford had made steady progress with a variety of calls.

"When you practice, don't look at the call. Look yonder, where the bird is," Spencer advised. "A fiddler don't look at his fiddle. He's studyin' the faces in the crowd, getting 'em fired up. Y'all got to do the same.

"They's a whole flock of turkeys lives in a box call, and each lives at its own sweet spot here on the ridges on each side. They's lost youngins peepin' for their momma, and big ol' gobblers, and dumb jakes, and mama hens, and jennies whisperin' love talk to gobblers that would get themselves kilt to hear such sweetness.

"The trough is like this deep holler where the farm sets," Spencer explained. "When the paddle is stroked, the sound gathers up in the holler and rolls out across the woods. Now it's time I show you how to build your own box call, the way it was taught me.

"First, you got to start with the right wood," Spencer noted. "They's all kinds of woods, but I got somethin' special here."

Spencer carefully unwrapped a blank of wood from a quilt.

"American chestnut, 150 years old, from my granddaddy's west Carolina furniture shop; ain't no more chestnut like this," Spencer declared. "The longbox pattern I use was first cut by my great-granddaddy, Earl Thomas Spencer. Down Carolina way, it's still called a Spencer pattern. The key to a good call is the paddle. I like a heavy paddle, 'cause you must have control. You got to have weight to draw those notes up out of the box. Light paddles can't do it. Sometimes, I'll even dovetail a piece of slate in the belly of the paddle."

They built a call just over a foot in length that fit Ford's hand exactly. Spencer created a unique paddle that terminated in a carved breast feather, and affixed a long turkey spur on top for added control. Behind the trough, he hollowed out a small trunk with a brass lid to hold a disk of chalk. Milly stitched a beautiful call holster from doeskin, with fringes and delicate beadwork.

Ford ran a series of yelps that rang with the clarity of vesper bells, floating up the hollow, fading in the pines.

"Special, ain't it?" said the callmaker, smiling.

That autumn, Ford called in a jake to Spencer's gun. The next day, Spencer returned the favor, reeling in a long-spurred gobbler, with a combination of deep clucks and raspy yelps so convincing they seemed to Ford to be the secret doctrine of the longbeard society itself.

The litmus test for the new call would be a spring gobbler, and come February, Ford was bursting like a catkin bud. His enthusiasm waned, though, when he learned that Alvin and Milly had decided to move back to Carolina. Milly's health was poor, and living in the damp hollow, where cold air settled, only aggravated her arthritis. Ford took a gobbler that spring with his new call and enclosed a single breast feather in his letter to Spencer.

Months passed before he received a reply, which noted that Milly had passed on. After that, he lost touch with the callmaker.

FORD FINISHED HIS COFFEE, amazed that 21 years had passed so quickly. He had become a dedicated turkey hunter and student of the wild turkey, making and collecting turkey calls as a hobby. Last year, though, his beloved Spencer box call was shattered in a fall while he traversed a boulder field. He painstakingly glued it back together, but the resonance was gone, and he relegated it to the mantle. He copied the pattern, but could not recreate the magical tones.

Ford went upstairs to finish a few remaining jobs. While sweeping out a small bedroom closet a pleasant smell jarred his senses: it was the singular aroma of cedar, and reminded him of Spencer's turkey shanty. The closet was cedar-lined, and one board, one he hadn't noticed before, caught his attention. It was a different than the red cedar and was tacked in place with different nails. Ford removed it with a pry bar and saw that it was American chestnut, of the same hue that Spencer had unwrapped from the blanket.

A few days later, he had fashioned an exact reproduction of the Spencer call from the chestnut plank, and to his delight, it rang with the same flawless tones.

On the first day of spring gobbler season, an old gobbler that had foiled Ford the previous year almost tripped over its long beard as it came running in to the lovely yelps.

AT THE PROMPTING of his friends and wife, Ford entered a turkey-calling contest at the local sportsmen's show. It was bigger than he imagined, with a large audience and a long line of seasoned competitors.

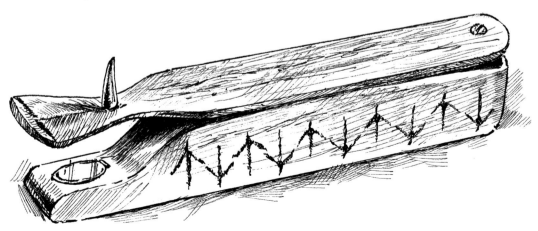

He drew the call from his holster and strode across the stage to the camo curtain separating contestants from the judges. Ford, much to his surprise, scored well in the preliminary round.

The final round concluded with a caller's choice. When his turn arrived, Ford looked beyond the crowd and lights and banners, stepping outside the moment, and in that place, watched a mixed flock of turkeys work the oak flat above the farm. He walked and talked with them. Each time he stroked the paddle, genuine turkey talk flowed from the call and streamed across the stage, filling the auditorium with its rich wildness. His declarations were pure avian, beyond the rote of practiced inflections bent to please a judge's ear.

Ford climbed the stage one last time then, hefting the box-calling trophy. He shook hands with the line of judges, and when the oldest judge grasped his hand, Ford got weak in the knees – it was Alvin Spencer.

"If I warn't an old hermit gobbler myself, I'd a flew right over that curtain to join your flock," Spencer declared. "I never heerd talk the likes of that, son."

"I have," said Ford.

It was then the callmaker recognized Ford and shook his hand even harder.

A Hallmark Season

THE 50-YEAR ANNIVERSARY of Pennsylvania's spring gobbler hunt was special for many reasons, but none meant more to me than the milestone it represented to those senior hunters who hunted turkeys every one of those springs.

That distinction made the 2018 season a pinnacle from which I could see that great expanse of places and people and certain gobblers stretching all the way back to the morning's gray horizon on the inaugural opener.

Nostalgic memories of hunts past are often like sepia-toned antique photos with thin, worn edges, but recollections of spring hunts, when life surges in the hills and sounds ring loud and clear across the greening landscape, remain clear and sharp. Those moments, fresh as ever, usher up to my place at this vantage point in time like thunderous gobbles from afar.

Reviewing all of them, though, I felt the 50th spring hunt was my all-time favorite.

First, though, it is important to reveal the armature upon which this lifelong pursuit was built.

First Day
Monday, May 6, 1968

IT WAS COLD and foggy on the mountaintop as I waited in the dark, with only the whisper of a fine drizzle against my hand-painted camo outfit. Everything I had read about locating a gobbler suggested listening from a high elevation, and this was the highest mountain around. It was a long way up, but no real test for 17-year-old legs driven by the anticipation of a new outdoor experience.

THE SULTAN OF SPRING

It seemed I waited forever for first light, shivering slightly in the mid-30-degree air as I cooled off from the long climb. I tucked my Olt crow call on its lanyard beneath my jacket to keep it dry.

In one inner pocket, I carried an Olt F-6 turkey scratch call that produced a nice rendition of hen yelps and clucks, like those on my 45 rpm instructional record. Bought in a hardware store, it worked by scraping one of the cedar edges against a chalked wooden dowel or the gun stock's comb. In another pocket, I carried a small peg-and-slate call.

Finally, I could make out the etched lines of branches against the sky as night eased imperceptibly to day and the woods emerged, gray and primeval. I was nervous, hesitant to break the silence, feeling like a student selected without warning to read aloud in front of the class.

Spicules of moisture moved within the thinner fog. No bird sang. I hedged some more, listening hard for a gobble. Then, it was time to move boldly. I would get the day rolling like the crows that awakened me every morning with their raucous reveille. I rolled out a series of spirited, throaty caws until a single gobble far down the steep slope compelled me to stop.

Setting up against a big oak, I began yelping with the cedar scratch call, but the dowel had dampened; all I could muster were scraping sounds and clicks. Switching to the peg-and-slate, I sent out several strings of yelps that sounded sweet and clear in the waterlogged air. A fierce double-gobble, followed by another, set my hands to shaking. Gaining confidence, I called louder and with emotion. He gobbled again.

I waited two hours in the intensifying drizzle, clucking occasionally, but never heard the

gobbler again. I would have waited longer, but the slate-and-peg was now wet and useless, and the wind had picked up. I left the woods satisfied, though, having learned that calling was like reading aloud, that you have to recite it like you wrote it. Don't just make turkey sounds; tell him something.

In the way the identifying marks on the barrel and receiver of my Winchester Model 12 were made by striking punches with a hammer, so, too, were the gobbles of that morning like hammer blows ringing across the mountaintop, marking the steely frame of the hunter within, forever distinguishing me as one of that order of hunters who would forever celebrate the spring hunt. And so, it began.

2018 Opener

I STILL CARRY my old Olt crow call on a lanyard around my neck and, in my pocket, the small peg-and-slate call. I have a diaphragm call clipped to the bill of my cap with which I do most of my calling. A few other calls and the rest of my gear are stashed in my turkey-hunting possibles bag, a compromise to wearing turkey hunting vests with every pocket filled with some redundant call or contrivance I don't need. I never could remember which pocket contained what, but that might be a sign of age.

After my first calling location failed to produce a gobble, I moved to another a half-mile distant. A trio of gobblers cut loose immediately, but began moving away. From the sound of their gobbles, I determined they weren't jakes, but adult toms. I couldn't entice them back, so I cut across a field and got way out in front of them.

I set up quickly at the edge of some choppings and open woods, then called. When they gobbled, I shut up. They were coming right toward me through the thicket, instead of the open woods, following a deer trail single file with the sun at their backs. At 35 yards, they gobbled, but I couldn't shoot without possibly wounding the birds behind the lead tom. On they came and then, in the next instant, exploded up through the brush, sailing far down into the hollow.

I sat there a long time before I began calling again, softly at first, then building. Suddenly, a single gobble fractured the air from another brushy hollow, this time to my right. I repositioned to the other side of the tree, gun up, not moving. He was down over the hill and I couldn't see him, but he was coming up through a slot between two thickets.

The unmistakable beating, flogging and slapping of wings and some coarse clucks jarred me. Again, there was a buffeting of wings and a shuffling in the leaves, distinct whumps, then the gobbler launched and I watched in disbelief as he skimmed the treetops and set his wings. Sitting tight, gun still up, I figured his path had converged with another incoming gobbler and they'd mixed it up. I waited for the dominant bird to show.

I clucked and purred. Nothing. Perhaps it was a predator, maybe a bobcat tried to ambush the gobbler. I called softly a few more times over the next hour and the first day was done.

Long-Distance Longbeard

AMONG THE FIRST birdsongs of the day, an eastern towhee warbled, *Drink your tea-ee-ee-ee*, several times, a beautiful, lilting refrain to welcome a new day, but it wasn't the song I was listening for from my position on the rocky ridgeline.

Next, a raven gurgled, then uttered bursts of *Quork! Quork! Quork!* The ventriloquial echoes deep in the hollow made it difficult to discern its location, but the raven's commands seemed to cue other birds to add their voices and soon the great hollow brimmed with birdsong.

Joining the chorus were two gobblers far down below. They seemed fired up and carried on for quite a while. I thought another turkey hunter might be working them. I waited for the sound of an impending shot, but none came.

They quit gobbling and I moved farther along the ridge, sitting on a mossy, seat-sized rock and listened some more, yelping occasionally with my mouth call. A short time later, the gobblers opened up again, gobbling furiously.

Considering the distance, I didn't want to go down to them, because I had a hard time hiking downhill from a leg injury, and the rocky terrain made it even tougher. I hobbled down over the lip of the ridge anyway and set up in a stand of hemlocks. It was open and shadowy and I could see far.

It was then I remembered a gobbler I called up almost to the top of a mountain from way down in the valley floor some 30 years earlier. I didn't get that bird, because I was busted as I started moving down to him, thinking there was no way he would come up an entire mountainside.

If I could entice a gobbler all the way up a rock-strewn mountain back then, it might work now, I reasoned. I dug out a flexible rubber tube call – raspy and loud – from my possibles bag and spilled a series of boss hen yelps down the mountain.

The gobblers exploded with excitement.

We traded long-distance calls for a long while, but no one was making a move. Finally, I moved down the steep slope and called with my slate-and-peg. Again, I got an answer, but now it seemed to be coming from a single bird.

I edged down onto an old tram road slicing straight downhill that was much easier to negotiate than broken ground. The gobbler was still far off and I wanted to get directly above him and switch to a mouth call.

I slid over a blowdown on the tram and sat up against an embankment to rest. Suddenly, a gobble erupted right below me. I got my shotgun up, but I was out in the open. I pushed my back into the embankment hoping my camo would work, and when he popped up onto the tram, I would shoot.

Instead of jumping up onto the tram, though, the eager gobbler fluttered across it, winging up onto the high, steep embankment on the other side and was hidden behind a blowdown.

He was headed up fast for the hen on top. I tried to swing my gun onto him, but he saw me and took off running, then launched.

You can teach an old dog new tricks, but sometimes they forget the ones they learned a long time ago. When a long-distance gobbler responds, he's telling you he's heard and knows where you are, and he's inviting you to come to him as nature dictates. Stay put for a while. Be reluctant. This creates tension, and tension triggers action. Moving and calling toward the gobbler tells him you're on your way. If he commits by closing the distance even slightly, get ready. Distances you determine as too

far, or mountains too steep or rocky mean little to a dedicated longbeard. He can be there in a heartbeat.

Around the Bend

HALFWAY DOWN THE WOODS road to a large field, I realized I had forgotten my decoys. But it was early, so I returned to my truck to get them.

It was full light as I began walking around the bend into the field and I glanced up to my left and spotted a strutter several hundred yards away displaying for a trio of hens. I stepped backward slowly to where I could just see them.

They were all moving away from me. But just before they disappeared over a rise, the hens filed back into the woods in succession, leaving the gobbler alone in the field. Now was my opportunity. I moved back a bit farther behind a big log, resting the forearm of my shotgun over it. I yelped and clucked and he answered immediately. I yelped again and he double gobbled, now closer. All I had to do was wait.

Instead of cautiously stepping out, looking for the hen, I was shocked when the big, black gobbler came steaming round that bend like a locomotive, white head held low, beard swinging.

He was farther out than I thought he'd be, but in range.

I moved my gun ever so slightly, like a minute hand on a wall clock, and before I could putt or cluck loudly to stop him, he rocketed off, just as I shot and I missed him completely.

I wondered if I would have gotten him with my old pump gun as I studied my specialized turkey gun with the vertical pistol grip and red-dot sight.

The Last Day

THE DAY WAS WARM and the gobbling I heard at first light ended quickly after sunrise. I hunted several hollows until noon, then decided to hunt back to my truck, which was a long way off. I stopped in a hedgerow to do some calling and watch the fields below that stretched far away into the blue hills.

As white clouds drifted, life boiled all around me. Cardinals sang, red-winged blackbirds scolded, a bluebird landed on a nearby snag, repeating its peppery *tu-a-wee* song over and over again, then flew away. A big woodchuck stood up 10 yards away, surveying the fields I, too, watched.

I rolled out some loud yelps with my tube call, but there was no response. It seemed as if a page had turned. The sun was hot on my face, leaching out the remnants of cold, early mornings. The season is done and I am tired, but a "good tired," as some might say.

A lone hen slips out of the woods below and wades into a large swath of tall grasses nourished by a seep. By now, she might have been incubating a full clutch of eggs. Maybe

THE SULTAN OF SPRING

she was taking a short break to drink and feed.

With binoculars, I watched the precise darting of her pale blue head as she fed feverishly on insects. Dandelion seed heads rose and floated away in her wake. Sleek and shining, her bronze feathers reflected the cerulean sky and green grasses, then muted brown again as she returned to the folds of the shadowy woods.

I pictured her back at her nest, sitting on her eggs. It was as if she transported the sun's rays from field to forest. Insect life ignited by the sun, now a protein fuel in her crop, transferred over time as heat to the precocial lives developing within the shells, lives that will amazingly, in another few weeks, be traversing forest and field with her, flying up to roost, flourishing in the wonder of summer, cradled in the aching beauty of these uplands.

The gobbler, nature's bold warrior in his plated iridescent armor, is the focus of the hunt, but it is the hen that embodies the season.

On my way back across the field, I pick up a long, barred turkey feather, a gobbler's primary feather as told by the tip that is worn from dragging it while he struts. I twirl it between my fingers as I walk and use it to flick gnats from my face. I think about that brief, six-day season 50 years ago, and the exponential growth in wild turkey conservation and the tidal wave of industries that followed. Who could have ever imagined?

Beyond the obvious genesis of this grand pursuit, the armature upon which it was built remains the same. It is a celebration of the rites of spring, of being alive; a time to recharge the spirit as proclaimed each morning by the gobbler; a time to wander the hills and to wonder at the promise of life to come harbored in pale, speckled eggs.

Spring Anthem

PERCHED ABOVE the hollow, the ridge's towering sandstone escarpment has the shape of a deer's jawbone. A turkey hunter, bent with age, silently eases down through a narrow gap between two of its boulder teeth and sits against a tree near the edge of a narrow bench. He waits for the rattling and crackling in his lungs to stop, then listens.

A dense fog fills the hollow. Somewhere on the hollow's opposite hillside is a wild turkey gobbler. Of that he is certain, because he roosted him there the evening before.

While staring into the void, a tune his daughter learned in grade school many years ago runs through his mind. She had drawn for him a turkey by tracing the outline of her hand and her teacher glued a copy of the song beneath the bird:

Spread your wings, Mr. Turkey,
Stretch your neck high and tall,
Talk to me, Mr. Turkey,
Tell me anything at all.

He fishes in a vest pocket for a slate pot call he made. A skilled craftsman, he could make or fix just about anything. His gun, a single-shot, hammerless 16-gauge, was salvaged from a mountainous scrap-pile at the steel mill that once employed him. The gun's barrel was free of dents and the action was tight, with traces of case hardening. All it needed was a new buttstock, and who couldn't whittle one of those? He shaped one from a piece of fancy walnut and made a matching forend. After successive layers of a special blend of stock oil were hand-rubbed into the grain enlivening the figuring and color, the depths of the wood rippled, like shadows on the bed of a mountain stream. He thought about re-bluing it, but after removing the rust, he liked the pewtery patina.

Oh my, how he loved to call turkeys. That was the fun part. You could keep all that walking, he thought. Make the gobbler walk to you. They were made for walking. Long, stout armored legs and toes with wide claws for raking heavy wet leaves, skid-proof soles for holding onto roost branches and slippery slopes.

Let him walk, the man thought. Just tell him what he wants to hear. White lies. Sweet

nothings. Or yell at him real good to get over here, the way his mom used to when dinner was ready. His brother and he always came running.

The man floats a few soft tree calls, like a musician warming up. He works the slate call slowly, with feeling, the way a practiced violinist bows the music up from the chambered heart of the violin.

He dislikes bad calling. There is no excuse for it. No stiff, mechanical yelps, or flat-sounding, sloppy honks of fluttering latex. No nails-on-blackboard screeches.

His calls are the crisp, avian utterances of the hen herself. Slate is old, part of the hills, and the primal music of the hills is held within it until the skilled stroke guiding the striker plucks and pulls that old music out.

Again and again, lovely yelps cascade down through the mist and float up through the hollow, then shift to strident clucks – the lonely hen inquiring.

More yelps follow; a trifle urgent this time.

Talk to me, Mr. Turkey, his daughter's voice sings.

Tell me anything at all, whispers the hunter.

Across the hollow, a gobbler walks anxiously along a white pine's bough, like a gymnast on a balance beam. He raises and lowers the louvered plating of his feathers and partially fans his tail several times. His beard is like a fuse attached to a bomb inside his breast.

Finally, the yelping from across the hollow prompts him to fire off several booming gobbles.

When the fog dissipates, the gobbler pitches out of the pine, gliding through the hardwoods and alights on the opposing hillside. Standing on tiptoes, he flaps his wings several times then folds them, the black barring on his wings aligning perfectly like sentences on a sheet of paper, a script yet to play out this day, written in another time.

The hunter unclips an old ballpoint pen from his shirt-pocket and disassembles it, placing everything but the tip back in his pocket. He uses the tubular tip expertly like a wingbone yelper. He moistens the point and with cupped hands in front – one restricting air, the other directing sound – he sends out a practiced series of clear, high-pitched yelps, then with a slight shifting of his hands, it becomes the voice of a different hen.

The gobbler shouts back three times.

Gobbles follow yelps, back and forth, sometimes overlapping. The gobbler is waiting for the hens, the hunter for the gobbler. Long minutes of silence ensue.

Then, a sudden throaty tirade of escalading yelps, clucks and perts motivate the gobbler, and he is on his way. He walks straight uphill, then swings far around a patch of laurel in a long J-hook and heads back on the high bench where he believes the hens are.

With gun already up, the hunter presses a mouth call in place with his tongue. The sun continues to add clarity to the thinning mist.

Far out on his left, he spots the black form of an advancing longbeard, its head a white orb thrusting fore and aft as it steps. The gobbler stops occasionally, standing on tiptoes, searching, then half-strutting, uncertain, hesitant.

At first, it was only a distant rumble, but now the loud clattering, clanking and screeching of a freight train out in the valley rolls like thunder up into the perpendicular hollow, which holds sound like an amphitheater.

The hunter's heart thuds in time with the click-and-clack of the speeding freight. At this odd moment, he starts thinking how the many days of his life, like a long line of railcars coupled together, have seemed to be rushing by lately.

As the train's disturbance fades, he hears the gobbler drumming and then spots him strutting, behind a windfall.

There is no shot as the gobbler follows the length of a fallen trunk, and his daughter's singing returns, urging the gobbler for more cooperation.

Stretch your neck high and tall,
Talk to me, Mr. Turkey,
Tell me anything at all."

The longbeard's sudden gobble at 16 yards is startling. When the gobbler sees him, its head periscopes up, a jolt of alarm in its dark eyes.

At his shot, the great bird collapses. Its powerful wings, seeking air, beat a final tattoo against the leaves, the piston-like legs scissor, unable to launch, its fan folding and unfolding, flopping left and right, rudder-like, as if it were flying. The gobbler is already dead. Its lingering movements driven by instinct. It lies still now, a creature of spring, born of the leaf litter, and returned there now.

The hunter reassembles his pen and fills out his tag, taking a few moments to admire the cascading metallic hues of the gobbler's feathers as the bird lay in the sun. He holds the beard along the gunstock's comb and sees it is 10 inches long, confirmed by a premeasured tiny knothole on the stock. He tests the sharp point of a long, curved spur with a fingertip.

With the gobbler slung over a shoulder, he hikes back up through the space between the boulders, humming that grade-school tune – his turkey hunting anthem – happy to be alive on this bright and shining spring morning, as all turkey hunters are.

A Little Help

TREAD LIGHTLY. It is a fragile world we step into each day, a complex continuum where each element is affected by the progress of another. Form unto form, force unto force, even the slightest influence may compound dramatically, spanning distance and time.

Step boldly. It is a resilient world that awaits each passage, each form contending with the wake of another. In spring, the vagaries of the wind and the wild rise like a wave that washes over the greening uplands. The world grows keen on whim, is strengthened by chance. Miraculously, order reigns.

YAP-YURRRRRR, *Yap-yurrrrrrr*! A fox barks as he does every morning when the false dawn creeps in the western sky. His mate, back at the den with a litter, hears him, as does a wild turkey on roost that responds, gobbling mightily.

The fox takes a tram road down the mountain. Halfway down, he encounters a turkey hunter rounding a bend. The hunter never sees nor hears the fleeing fox, but plods along, a long way yet to climb. A blush rises in the hunter's cheeks and in the eastern sky as hunter and sun labor to ascend the same ridge.

The fox weaves his way through a blackberry patch in the river bottom. The damp, alluvial earth is redolent with the sweet scent of rabbit. Patiently, the fox unravels the cottontail's trail, then inches forward. With vertical pupils open wide, and ears pricked forward, he scans the immediate cover. His wet nostrils quiver, drinking in molecules of rabbit. So close now. His forepaw raises like a pointing dog.

The rabbit blinks and the chase is on. It squirts through a slot in an exposed root mass and streaks down a reedy aisle. The fox is right behind the pulsing puff of the rabbit's tail, the white tip of his own glorious brush whipping as he zigzags through the brakes. The rabbit arcs through deep cover, gaining a few yards, but the fox bisects that radius expertly, and in a sudden rush, pins the rabbit to the ground. Its quavering scream rolls across the river, then muffles and quits. Without resting, the fox picks up the rabbit, and with his pointy ears pinned back, turns uphill to the den.

A BOAR RACCOON hears the tread of the approaching fox and shuffles up the tilted trunk of a windfall. The 'coon watches the fox pass beneath, then follows a mossy drainage gut to a wetlands bordering the river. The marsh is usually flooded, with grassy hummocks sticking out of the water here and there, but this year it is mostly grass. Even with recent rains, the marsh is still recovering from a late-winter drought.

The 'coon follows the slick drag trail of a beaver, and its nostrils flare at the pungent scent left by a muskrat. The 'coon flushes a nesting mallard hen from atop a stump, and finds a clutch of eight pale-buff eggs cupped neatly there.

After eating the eggs, the raccoon waddles through a copse of towering sycamores. It climbs the tallest, and curls up in the abandoned penthouse nest of a great blue heron. The 'coon falls asleep just as the mountaintop across the valley is washed with yellow light.

With their nest destroyed, the mallard hen and her mate fly downriver. They set down in a sheltered cove, but are immediately driven off by another mallard drake defending that nesting area. The pair circles back upriver, beyond their original site, and veers into a wide, weedy hollow that crosses a road, ending as a deeply dished bowl.

The ducks course low, round and round, above the weathered ruins of an old farm near a tributary creek. The hen spies the glint of water from a trickling spring. They set down in what was once the farmyard, where decades before, domestic ducks waddled about. The hen surveys the deep pockets of weeds for a place to re-nest.

SEVERAL CHICKADEES flit among last year's goldenrod, hanging like acrobats as they glean the withered stalks. When the mallards sweep above the weed-tops on whistling wings, the chickadees shift into the edge of the woods. A hairy woodpecker joins them and works a decayed stub. Nearby, a white-breasted nuthatch spirals headfirst down a black cherry trunk.

The birds filter deeper through curtains of grapevines. They are a noisy lot, talking constantly: *Dee-dee-dee. Peek! Peek! Yank! Yank!* Bits of bark sprinkle down through the rigging, peppering the leaves.

From the deep shadows of a white pine, crimson eyes watch the lively troupe. A female Cooper's hawk lets loose her perch and glides like a gray wedge through the grapevines, plucking the woodpecker neatly from a tree. She lands next to a puddle and then holds the woodpecker underwater, drowning it.

In short order, the hungry hawk mantles and plucks her prey, then devours most of its breast. A blue jay first sees the reflection of the hawk in the puddle and then the hawk itself. The jay shrieks an alarm, and two others quickly hail its call. The screaming jays triangulate on their archenemy. At first, the hawk ignores her tormentors, but when several crows pile in, the hawk flies away, the crows in pursuit.

The hawk pumps hard across a flat, but is met head-on by more crows pouring over a rise. The Coop flares sharply, tucks her wings, and dives through a portal into a hemlock fortress, losing the mob. She swoops down, then climbs swiftly, up through strobes of laddered light, and lands. She wipes her bill back and forth across a limb, then ruffles and preens her feathers.

ONE OF THE PURSUING crows lifts on an updraft, facing into the facade of a steep sandstone escarpment. Near the top, it kites in the wind when it spots a pair of yellow-green eyes in the shadows. The din starts anew as the mob regroups, and a bobcat is pried from his niche in the rocks by the diving marauders. The bobcat pads along a shadowy bear trail bored like a tunnel through the rhododendron. The crows lose interest and disperse.

The cat angles up the mountain, then crosses an open woods and stops to lap water at a tiny, crystalline pool. Farther on, the bobcat crouches at the lip of a deep hollow when he hears turkeys clucking just below. He waits, motionless, just another tan stone among others.

His muscles bunch when a large hen emerges from the thinning laurel, pecking at the duff only a few yards away. Cat and bird launch skyward, and a single claw on the cat's raking paw snags the claw on the turkey's hind toe. For a fraction of a second, gravity seems suspended as life and death hang in the air. Then the bobcat falls, dropping down through the springy limbs of a laurel shrub, landing awkwardly in an un-catlike heap.

Three hens rise above the trees and glide across the hollow. With much commotion, they land in a birch thicket, where two yearling does are bedded. The deer spook and bound away.

A gobbler, walking from the edge of an old, grassy field into deeper woods, stops when the deer trot by. He turns and walks quickly back to the edge of the field, where he stands on tiptoes and looks around. Nothing follows the deer.

When the hens begin to cluck and yelp, he gobbles. Earlier, the gobbler had heard another hen near a rockpile out in the middle of the field, but when he didn't see her, he turned and walked off.

Below, the trio of hens files out into the field. They spot the lone hen clucking and purring near the rockpile. The lonesome gobbler sees them and double-gobbles. He strides into the field, eager to join them.

He walks and struts across the field from a distance, resembling a black umbrella held horizontally, opening and closing. When the noisy hens join their sister near the rockpile, the gobbler strides along quickly, leaving a dark green line in the silvery grass. He pulls up at 10 yards and displays.

His long beard is bejeweled with dewdrops, and when he turns into the sun, his feathers gleam like a suit of gilded chain mail. Sunlight glares from the flat plane of his chestnut-colored fan. He pirouettes so his fan is always fully displayed to the hens. He spits and drums several times in succession. When the deer cut across the field, his head raises up, and a shotgun blast shatters the silence, echoing.

The turkey hunter jumps out of the rockpile and brush, and on wobbly legs hustles over to the gobbler. He kneels beside the bird and watches the hens and deer disappear into the far woods.

He had been hunting the gobbler for three straight mornings, but the longbeard always hung up or went off with hens. This morning, he brought a decoy and set up in the rock pile. He heard the gobbler behind him, and was disappointed that it could not see the decoy. Luckily, just when the gobbler was moving off, the hens came into the field, and the gobbler couldn't resist.

The hunter takes the long tram road down the mountain. Even though he is tired, and the turkey is heavy, he walks with a spring in his step.

All he needed, he thought, was a little help.

Grandpa's Woolrich

Rural Route

PENNSYLVANIA has a quarter-million miles of roads of all types, from super-highways to single-lane dirt roads that wind through the hills and boondocks. Add to that thousands of miles of utilitarian logging, or tram roads, from bygone eras, and it's safe to say Penn's Woods is covered with a vast, complex web of byways.

I've always enjoyed those less-traveled routes through small towns, villages and farm country. This painting, *Grandpa's Woolrich*, depicts an iconic figure sometimes encountered when traveling rural routes, the scarecrow. This one is a hunter scarecrow that some children made from an old coat hanging in the barn. They carved a pumpkin for its head, then tied the scarecrow to a wooden fence rail and stood it upright in a woodchuck hole. With broomstick gun in hand, the vigilant hunter watches over the fields of old-style corn shocks.

In late afternoon, a Hunter's Moon rises and a small buck ventures out and nibbles at some straw protruding from the scarecrow's elbow. There will be a heavy frost this night, and other deer will leave the wooded hills for the Big Field.

With Halloween fast approaching, bonfires, hayrides, and other festivities lay ahead for those who celebrate the harvest. Soon enough, snow will be dusting the scarecrow's shoulders, yet he'll be warm in his Woolrich, watching the fields for the comings and goings of deer and those who drive by the farm out on the hard road.

Poke Salad Days

LAST SPRING, A POKEWEED plant sprouted just outside our bedroom window in my wife's small, formal garden. It quickly overshadowed the irises, coneflowers and heather, even the rapidly growing yarrow. A month later, it dominated the small space like a wild, unruly rock star standing among the conservative perennials.

Just as I was about to sever the stalk and yank out the roots, Terry said, "Wait; let it stay."

"Are you sure?" I asked. "This plant will be the size of a beach umbrella by the end of summer. The birds will eat the berries and deposit seeds in their droppings; it will stain the deck purple. Next spring, I'll be digging pokeweed out of the hedges. This stuff spreads quickly. The seeds can sprout years later."

"I like it," she said. "It's different."

The pokeweed invader flourished in the unrelenting sun, completely unaffected by the drought. By late August, it was 8 feet tall, with an equally broad span. The pokeweed shaded the window better than an awning, and many times I awakened at first light to catbirds and mockingbirds gobbling up the indigo berries and chasing one another through the maze of pink stalks.

This icon of summer reminded me of summers past, those salad days of youth, and of long journeys on the endless network of dirt roads that led from the edge of town, through farmland and high into the uplands, deep into the heart of summer.

DURING A HEAT WAVE in the early '60s, two friends and I set out to find the spot with the coolest shade. It was my father's idea, a way for him to get a relaxing day off, free from kids whining about the heat.

Our search begins under the elms bordering the ballfield, but heat wafts in from the baked yellow clay field and is trapped under the trees. We try the grassy lawn in the shade of the school building that's always in shadow, but we decide that no good shade would be found in town, so we pack our rucksacks and head for the cool, green hills.

We seek relief in the crabapple woods, but here the canopy is low and thin, so we follow a favorite creek west of town. The creek is wide and rocky and only ankle-deep. We splash far upstream, the white-rubber trim on our black high-top sneakers washing clean in the gritty bottom.

The tributary tapers, narrowing into small pools where the water barely trickles over the rocks. Crane flies loop above dank eddies. It's a little cooler here, where the oaks arc high overhead, cooler than any place in town. But we just aren't satisfied, and continue up the mountain.

After clawing our way up through the thick tangles to a dirt road, we're sent back into the brush by an approaching pickup truck billowing plumes of dust behind.

Time for lunch on a mossy log at roadside. We carry Army canteens on webbed belts, and drink most of our water trying to wash down clots of peanut-butter sandwiches. While we eat, cicadas buzz and a woodchuck scrambles across the road, diving into a patch of Turk's cap lilies.

As we pour the remaining water from our canteens over our heads, the pickup returns down the hill, coating us with yellow dust. Each of us carries a walking stick, mine fashioned from a perfectly straight crab sapling. It has a leather thong looped through a hole in the top, is carved with my initials and decorated in green and yellow stripes. Streaks of water and sweat stripe our faces and arms, and we plod on like some wild and rare painted tribe of nomads.

Farm country lies just ahead, great expanses of brilliant fields where the corn sighs, and fields of goldenrod, Queen Anne's lace and thistle are alive with bees and butterflies. We walk gingerly past a farm when, on cue, a shaggy red dog roars down the lane. We run madly, then climb a willow tree, sitting there a few minutes until the panting beast heads back home to his water dish. No one speaks; we have been chased by this dog before.

We know the limits and temperament of every dog in our territory. Farm dogs never pose much of a problem, because there is usually a tree nearby. But we fear city dogs since most are bored and overzealous in the defense of their small territories. Country dogs know how big the world is, and their noses possess an extensive lexicon of smells. City dogs are limited in all regards, and overreact to everything.

LIKE A MALLEABLE ALLOY, the sere landscape tempers to a noticeable red color in July's forge, then is hammered, blow by blow, day by day, on the broad anvil of summer until the decorous frills of spring are pounded out.

Holsteins rest under a copse of locust trees, unmoving, like painted plywood cutouts. There is no birdsong. Heat rises in waves from the road. All is still, except for the barn swallows that follow our progress. We drag along, then brighten a bit, stopping to gorge on blackberries from a roadside patch. The juicy berries taste like tart, hot pie filling. My pals complain when I carefully fill my canteen, one berry at a time, but I know it'll be worth it later.

Past the last mountain farm, the road continues on into the forest. We stop at the edge of the woods at an ancient trough, a V of mossy boards lined with tin. The water trough brims with cold, eternal spring water, streaming at a quarter-measure from the old pipe. We drink deeply until our sides hurt, then submerge our heads in a contest to find out who can hold his breath the longest. When we glance at each other under the water, we start laughing and come up choking and gasping in a spray of bubbles. Soaked to the bone, we fill our canteens and continue on.

Catbirds follow and scream from the dark thicket. In the fine dust of the road are delicate beetle tracks like the faint scars of stitches on delicate skin. More obvious are the tracks of raccoons, deer, songbirds, foxes, rabbits and the serpentine twining of a snake. Deer flies and gnats descend on us like dive bombers. Dragonflies buzz by, sounding like the baseball cards we placed in the spokes of our bikes. At a turn near an old burn, a huge black snake slithers out of some ferns, and seems to take forever to cross the road.

Farther on, a doe stands up just off the road, her liquid eyes fixed on us. She stands still, like a perfect copper statue, newly struck, monumental, shimmering. I am startled when she lifts her tail and sails away, and startled again when two fawns rise and do the same.

The road climbs sharply, becomes rutted and rocky. Our worn sneakers squish and slip on the sandstone. Several yellow swallowtail butterflies cluster in a group on the road. We lie down slowly to watch them at their eye level.

There must be water just under the ground here as the ground is gritty and damp in this heavy shade. It leeches the heat from our bodies.

"This is it!" I declare. "This is the place with the best shade."

WE CLIMB HIGHER, all the way to a fern-covered powerline. This is as far as we have ever hiked. From here, the river valley gorge looms invitingly beyond, but we're already miles from home. I stand transfixed by the depth of the blue shadows of the opposing mountain. This is serious country, and I feel I am standing at the near edge of the rest of my life.

On our way back down, we are drenched by a sudden, brief thunderstorm that, like a country dog, has a bark worse than its bite. Towhees sing their rain song in the shadows. A family of young grouse whirr out, one after the other, each peeping nervously before takeoff.

The humidity rises, and the sun bears down again. Lightshot mists rise from the fields. Indigo buntings flash blue, a much different blue than the pale azure chicory flowers. Goldfinches flit like yellow sparks before us, launching from and alighting on the stalks of bull thistle and teasel.

With a long way yet to go, we take a more direct route, a long path in the woods that follows a steep ridge. We walk quietly, Indian file, several yards apart – something hunters do even to this day.

It seems an ancient thing, walking like this. This is the progression used on a game trail, on the sharp spine of a ridge, or when breaking a heavy snow trail. There must be a safe distance between, so as not to jab your fellow traveler with lance or bow, and not bump into him if he stops suddenly after spotting danger or game ahead. You must be able to read his body language or catch a slight hand signal. Also, walking in file, three can walk as silently as one. All these simple, wondrous, forgotten practices, these hard-earned lessons basic to human survival, where are they now? Some live on only with hunters.

It is late afternoon, and raindrops spatter from the canopy as an unseen squirrel runs along a treetop sidewalk. Chipmunks chirp at our progress, and down near the creek, the liquid song of a wood thrush trickles through the hollow. We come down out of the woods into a field where waves of fireflies rise and blink. Beyond is our neighborhood.

THAT EVENING I sit on the steps of our big painted porch while my parents creak to and fro on the swing. My sister and her friends catch fireflies in the yard, while I eat vanilla ice cream sprinkled with blackberries. Down the valley, heat lightning flashes in the bellies of clouds.

A cool breeze descends the mountain and washes through the neighborhood. It is a breeze from some high, wild place, maybe all the way from the big woods beyond the powerline. On that breeze are images of all things wild, and I see them in detail as they flash by: ferns and feathers; fur and flowers; black earth and rank puddles; turtles and mossy logs; pines and pokeweed, and myriad other things I have seen this day for which I have no name. It is all here now, on my porch, carried on this sweet summer breeze.

I stare up into the woods, into shadows within shadows, and wonder what deer do on summer nights.

Tram Road

JACK WAS BORN in 1896, in the last clapboard house where the good road stopped and a woods road that climbed far into the uplands started. He called it a tram road.

In country-speak, a tram road, skid road or old logging road all are used to describe a road that was a vestige of a former logging operation. Some logging operations used specially-built, small, steam-locomotives, or trams, that ran on narrow-gauge wooden and iron rails to haul timber out of the woods. Thrown into this mix are ordinary woods or wagon roads, which were used more for travel than industry.

In 1910, Jack worked at the general store down in the valley. One of his main duties was to drive the store's mule-team mercantile wagon on a long circuitous route selling, trading and delivering goods at mountain farms and cabins far up in the hills.

Jack was our next-door neighbor and a hunting mentor to my father and me. One September day – two years before he passed – he took me on a history tour of his backwoods route. Although my father and I had hunted up here several times, it wasn't until this day with Jack that I really paid attention to the stone walls and tumbled foundations veiled with greenbrier and grape tangles. It explained the errant apple and pear trees and clusters of daffodils and tea rose bushes I'd often encounter. At each foundation, he would recall with startling clarity the names of each family, what they bought or traded for, even where the father worked.

By the start of the Great War, most of the families had moved on from eking out a living up in the hills in favor of the burgeoning iron industry in town. It was easy to visualize one of Jack's trips from his detailed depictions:

THE DRAFTY CABINS were built of rough-cut boards and stone and didn't appear on any deed or county record. Out back, a hog may be found, along with a mule or cow. A scarecrow stands watch in a well-tended garden while a lean hound lays in a worn depression under the porch. Several chickens scratch around the exposed roots of trees. They are as wild and wary as jungle fowl but don't last long; too many hooked beaks, talons and curved fangs in these woods.

A hawkish-looking young man drives his mule team up the rutted lane, the clinking and clanking of assorted wares announcing his progress. A noisy group of children and dogs that had intercepted him farther down the hollow adds to the din. Lots of teasing and laughter, towheaded youngsters shouldering wildly to get in line to get the free treat of store candy. Only one piece each now.

A fragile economy in these woods. Budgets carved in stone. The wet stub of a pencil ciphering on a chit, to be paid after berry season. For the oldest boy, six more traps, he's done well with bounty money. A small keg of nails as ordered. A hardly-used washboard only a dime, would you take the old one in half trade? At every stop the men examine a new Winchester M97 pump shotgun, a 16-gauge takedown model. Twenty-five dollars, but you can pay over time.

Waves and final goodbyes shouted out to him from the children, as if their farewells were tangible objects he could take back with him. He did.

BACK THEN, there was a big sawmill operation up here and Jack showed me the shrunken, still-moldering piles of sawdust and the petrified millworks thick with poison ivy vines and blackberry canes. For years after, I killed lots of grouse and big "woods" rabbits around the sawmill works. Stopping at a turn on the tram road, Jack told of an autumn when he was squirrel hunting at this spot when a wave of gray squirrels numbering in the hundreds were moving through the woods as a migrating mass. And it was here, too, where he killed the one and only buck he would ever kill. Deer were scarce then and he shot the 7-point with a .30-40 Krag he had sporterized.

On our way back down at the end of the day, we stopped at the edge of a deep, oak-filled hollow. Jack reflected on how quiet it was here when the hollow was full of hemlocks, before the drone of planes, trucks and chainsaws.

The only thing he disliked about his route was the stretch of rock we were standing on, a

20-yard-long, ribbed hump of exposed rock that spanned the road. Two parallel green lines running the length of the rock are grooves etched by wagon wheels that have since filled with moss. At times, a seasonal seep ran out onto the rock and it would become slippery. The mules would get nervous and he always feared that the wagon would slide off and tumble into the hollow.

I always think of Jack when I hunt here, and swear at times that I can hear the rhythmic chink of mules plodding in their traces and the laughter of children in the buffeting leaves racing up the chute of the old tram road.

LONG AFTER JACK'S PASSING, I took a fork at a high stretch of the tram road that went way back in. It grew very faint and that is where I discovered an isolated homestead. I noticed the sawed-off end of a weathered plank sticking out of the leaves. I pried it from the earth and flipped it over. It was a "no trespassing" sign without a space between the words, so it appeared as one long word – NOTRESSPASSING. The sign painter, wanting to get the message across as boldly as possible, had more letters than board, though had he not added the extra S, misspelling trespassing, there would have been enough room for a space between the words. I liked the sign with its folksy block letters and considered taking it back with me to hang in the studio, but then set it back in place. I was already a trespasser and didn't want to be a thief as well.

A bit farther on, the road faded entirely at a narrow, crescent-shaped flat bordered by stone walls. A tumbled foundation showed the footprint of a house. Rather than being a trespasser, I had that warm and comfortable feeling one has when they arrive back home. Looking around, there's an immediate sense of belonging one gets from this place, perhaps from the way it is held within the cradle of old oaks, or the terraced topography that lies before it.

I START THE morning of a recent fall turkey hunt up here on the homestead flat by sipping some hot tea while sitting on a large rock. A light, translucent frost coats everything, but the sun is already flooding the flat. A gray squirrel hops along the top of a stone wall, spots me, then jumps down the other side. The wall is striped white and green as the sun burns off the rime, revealing the dark, mossy sandstone. Where the vertical shadows from the trees fall on the wall, it remains

frosty white, but as the sun shifts the white striping becomes narrower, then disappears altogether.

A greenish-white stone set in the wall catches my eye. I remove it and am surprised to see that it is a perfect circular disc. I can't fathom what kind of stone it is, but it's much grainier and softer than sandstone. Finally, I decide that it's not a stone at all, but several inches of mortar that had hardened in the bottom of a bucket, was knocked out, then placed in the wall. I set it back into its place, where it belonged.

Without this single stone, the wall would have always remained, but would never be the same. It takes the odd stone to make a wall, or life, interesting.

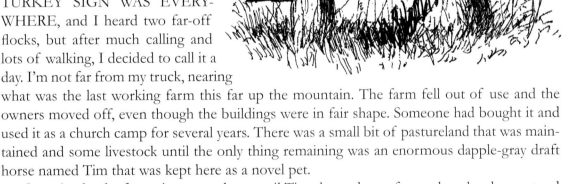

TURKEY SIGN WAS EVERYWHERE, and I heard two far-off flocks, but after much calling and lots of walking, I decided to call it a day. I'm not far from my truck, nearing what was the last working farm this far up the mountain. The farm fell out of use and the owners moved off, even though the buildings were in fair shape. Someone had bought it and used it as a church camp for several years. There was a small bit of pastureland that was maintained and some livestock until the only thing remaining was an enormous dapple-gray draft horse named Tim that was kept here as a novel pet.

Stopping by the fence, it was not long until Tim clopped over from where he always stood by the barn. I fed him a few apples from my pocket that I had gathered up near the homestead. Like all polite country folks, he nodded politely as I talked. I enjoyed the hollow chomping sounds he made, like rocks falling below in some great underground vault. His big, dark eyes reflected in curved panorama the solemn, still woods and me. His nostrils flared with the slow, measured bellowing of his great lungs and I wondered if he ever knew loneliness.

The horse had been here for years and was well-cared for, but then he, too, was gone. He was the last domestic creature left in these uplands, a province that stood mightily in the face of historic, brutal storms that swept in from the west, a landscape often fogbound, where snows lay deeper and winds blew harder. All of it now given back to the wild in the form of public land.

In the vagrant archaeology of stone walls and temporal plantings, in the old scars of roads where mules and mountain dwellers once trod, some element of that experience remains that always can be taken back, inspiring the traveler of these tram roads to face, head on, any difficult passage.

Rural Route

OCTOBER IS the funnel through which the bounty of the year pours, sustaining us during the long winter months ahead. It is a time of harvest, a time to hunt, a time to relish the pageantry of colors on the hills, to enjoy the celebrative air along rural routes and farms and in small towns.

In the old Roman calendar, October was the eighth month of the year, its name derived from the Latin word *octo*, meaning eight. It is now the tenth month of the year, the name carried over to our modern Gregorian calendar. Another element of October, steeped in antiquity, peaks around the third week as a meteor shower, the Orionids. This annual event is made visible as Earth passes through the stream of debris of Comet Halley. The constellation Orion, the hunter, is the radiant point of the Orionids, and I like to think that the meteors which originate from that point are the hunter's streaking arrows shot from his bow.

It is the full moon, or full moons – as there may be more than one – of October that steal the show, however. Sometimes, the big, warm Harvest Moon may fall on October 1, and the second full moon of the month, the Hunter's Moon, also known as the Blood Moon, may occur on October 31, Halloween! This drives bowhunters who obsess about moon phases to the very edge.

October is the least cloudy month of the year. What's the need for a dazzling thunderhead or streaky cirrus brushstrokes when the hills rage crimson and yellow? Nature's great warehouses of seeds, nuts and fruits and all her wildlife nurseries have burst at the seams, and are now distributed upon the land. Turkey poults stand tall and wild-eyed, legs and wings made strong from the protein-rich insect diet of summer fields. Flocks join others, and like a great harvester machine, the big fall flocks rake the sidehills and flats for anything edible that is uncovered beneath the leaf litter.

While the turkey flocks work the slopes, small bands of chickadees glean tree trunks and vines, seeking cocoons and spiders, poking holes in goldenrod galls, hammering seeds. It is always a delight when a lonely mountain hollow suddenly brims with life when they appear, vocalizing continually in their complex language while feeding in close proximity to each other, as if all are tethered by an invisible thread.

Manic gray squirrels go into a higher gear, working the oak groves feverishly as do black bears among the beeches. Whitetails, too, feed heavily on the mast crop, especially white oak acorns, which are rapidly converted to fat. The woodchuck waddles through autumn fields, still foraging, his nickname, "pasture grizzly," is quite appropriate as his portly shape and grizzled coat resemble that of a bear traversing an expanse of tundra.

Summer bachelor groups of whitetail bucks disband, sparring with a bit more intensity as the days grow shorter and testosterone levels rise. They make dozens of rubs, and scrape lines begin to appear on woods roads. The period of heavy rutting activity is just around the corner and there is no greater visual expression of the richness of the land than a mature whitetail buck in prime condition just before the rut.

Tendrils of frost creep along damp, low-lying thickets where migrating woodcock alight, to rest and feed, while under the Hunter's Moon a grouse may be heard drumming. Woolly bear caterpillars, larvae of the Isabella tiger moth, inch along everywhere, but the length of theirs black and brown bands are not indicators, as country lore suggests, of the severity of the winter ahead. Neither is the height of now visible hornets' nests a predictor of the severity of the upcoming winter; the rural axiom being that the higher the nest, the deeper the snows will be.

The masses of spring tremble and surge in response to increasing light, warmth and water, but the multitudes of autumn move with a different urgency, spurred on by shorter, chillier days. Everything moves at a quickened pace along these ancient courses, and there are no finer or renowned avenues than the rural routes of Penn's Woods in October.

OF ALL THE images one may hold from autumns' past, among hundreds, I can quickly produce one that reigns above all others in my experience as that singular image that captures the very essence of the season, and somehow, something greater.

A chill morning in late October, and I had been still-hunting for deer with my bow, drifting across flats, skirting the borders of bedding thickets, poised along scrape lines. The air warmed as westerly zephyrs stirred the ridgeline. At mid-morning, I came up through some hemlocks then walked across one of my favorite flats populated by tall oaks.

There are stretches of time in the natural world, much of it determined by the weather, when a certain tempo, a collective rhythm can be recognized. The wise still-hunter should, from time to time, determine what that tempo is and pace his movements to that which surrounds him. When I reached the end of the oak flat, I sat on the ground, my back against a log to reset my internal switch.

The sky, peeking through the gaps in the branches, was a stunning and brilliant blue. Not a single cloud drifted. I lazed in the leaves, legs outstretched, then I heard a clattering, a chattering, that started far up the hollow and began moving toward me, getting louder, a long, slow tidal wave washing downhill.

It seemed that the dense canopy of oak leaves had all begun to fall on the gentle, but sustained cusp of the wind. The sheer volume and expanse of it was unlike anything I had ever seen or heard. It was mesmerizing, hypnotic, the entire leafy ceiling tumbling, spiraling, tens upon tens of thousands, louder now, spreading across the flat, big oak leaves and poplars striking the trunks and ground stiffly, yet all at that same slow and steady speed, minute-upon-minute, an entire seasonal event happening all at once.

When it slowed, I expected to see not a single leaf remaining, but there were plenty more. When I stood, heaps of leaves fell from my shoulders, hat and legs, from my bow and quiver. Immersed in autumn, I rose as if buried there, shedding leaves, sprouted from the earth, a citizen of autumn, which, being born in October, I surely am.

A HALLOWEEN grouse hunt today, and fittingly, on the gentle slopes of the mountain it drizzles and mists swirl. The air is warm and redolent with the sweet aroma of autumn's wine: a blend of fox grapes, derelict apple trees and the heady, complex spice of leaf litter, aged within ancient white oaks.

In contrast to the gaudy hues found here earlier this month, these uplands have become a watercolor painted with a limited palette of somber shades, as is the old, rainy-day double-gun I carry and the robust cock grouse in my game pouch. These subtle hues of olive and umber tree trunks, fire-charred stumps, maroon grapevines and mossy stone foundations are more to my liking.

There is no sky, only an extension of mists rising into a muted nothingness. Although it is early afternoon, the light is the same as it was this morning, time stalled in a timeless image where I am bound as in a dream, a lone figure in a subdued and melancholic painting and I think should I walk too far in any direction, I will run into the frame that holds this composition.

I have heard more grouse drumming today than any spring day in memory, but autumnal drumming is not a beckoning for female company. As young grouse disperse in the fall, they will invariably appear in the established territories of mature males who drum as a proclamation to previously claimed provinces.

The drumming imparts a ghostly air to the woods, ventriloquist voices calling from several directions. I have a hard time pinpointing their locations and my course becomes haphazard, without plan. When I arrive at a spot from where I thought a grouse was drumming, I don't flush a bird, but am immediately lured to another hollow, higher bench or distant thicket. For more than an hour I beckon foolishly to these spectral drummers. Later, surprisingly, I wrestle out of a dense tangle onto the dirt road above my truck.

Sipping some coffee, I'm reluctant to leave. A warning roll of thunder from a distant front rumbles up the hollow. I drink in the heady aroma of the soggy woods. It is very quiet, except for the occasional splat of a heavy rain droplet hitting the leaves. The dirt road is part of the frame that separates this enchanting covert from the rest of the world. I am not ready to return from October's grand gallery where the artful, primal proceedings of the hunt are temporarily on display.

A grouse drums from the far side of a nearby thicket. But then it sounds like it's coming from deeper in the woods, higher up, near the pines. I slip two shells into the double and snap it shut, wondering if, when grouse hunters die, their spirits live on, hunting phantom birds in woods like these.

AFTER A MORNING of hawk-watching, my wife and I take the long way back home, driving through some small villages and farms looking for a roadside stand to buy some pumpkins. At one farm, we pull in front of a white-washed stand with produce that spills across a short section of lawn and onto a big, wide porch.

Terry's famed autumn displays require pumpkins with great character, only those retaining much of the curled vine remaining on the stem being worthy. The pumpkins here are exceptional, and the farmer's grandson loads more than a dozen of various sizes into the truck along with a box of carbuncled gourds. My interest is focused on the display of goods on the plank-and-cinderblock shelves; jars of pickles, relishes, apple butter, jams and a row of several freshly baked pies. I immediately snag a loaf of raisin bread and two pies, one apple, one peach.

Farther up the road, I ease into a shady roadside pull-off. I fish out a camp knife from the console and with the spoon and knife utensils we alternate, sharing some of the peach pie. Beneath the flaky, cinnamon-sprinkled crust, the filling is warm and sweet, and the surprise ingredient of blueberries provide a touch of tartness.

Yellow fields of corn, as far as the eye can see, toss in the breeze. Doves teeter on wires, a groundhog scurries across the road. Yellow leaves land on the truck's windshield, littering the pull-off. For a time, the rural routes of Penn's Woods are paved in gold. Don't miss out, as you will be the richer for it.

The Qualified Buyer

A TRIO OF TURKEY VULTURES circled above a sprawling outdoor flea market. Smells and sounds carried easily up to them: a vendor selling barrel kraut and sausages, the frenzied scraping and tapping of a man in bib overalls performing a washboard solo, the smoky haze from a chicken barbeque sold at a tent called the "Chicken Shack." The vultures wheeled like silhouettes suspended from a mobile until a lost balloon drifted too near and they filed away to seek another thermal.

Cradled within a picturesque setting of forested blue hills and farms, the Crowfoot Valley Flea Market draws visitors from near and far. Volunteer firehouse members sell tickets in a perpetual raffle as children pose for pictures behind the wheel of a vintage pumper truck. The strident drone of cicadas harmonizes with the folksy tunes of an autoharp duet played by two old women wearing long calico dresses.

The most popular attraction is at the market's hub, where visitors partake in the diverse offerings from a caravan of food vendors surrounding a circular dining pavilion.

Down-county tourists parade designer dogs, drawn to this backcountry setting at the chance to discover some primitive collectible, or procuring items made by local artisans.

Also cruising the rows are hunters in camo T-shirts and logo ball caps with wraparound sunglasses perched on the brim, eyes peeled for an antique turkey call with some old magic still within, or partial boxes of ammunition to be had at a bargain. Announcements crackle like old-time radio broadcasts over an aging loudspeaker system, the tail end of each returned as an echo by the woods:

"Get it now while the sugar is good! Crowfoot Valley sweet corn, picked just this morning right down the road at Stutzman's farm. Peaches and Cream, or Butter and Sugar. Ready to go or eat it here. At the food court…food court."

"Genuine folk-art husk dolls and handmade brooms, by Annie and Tom Spahr. Vendor spaces 73 and 74 … and 74."

"Something for everyone…for everyone."

ON A BEAUTIFUL, late August day, Drew had rolled back the roof of his Jeep and removed the doors before an excursion to mark on a map promising farms at which to later ask permission to hunt and game lands parking spots. He noticed the flea market signs at several crossroads and didn't consider going, until he came over a rise and was caught in a web of delectable aromas.

Ravenous from the morning's scouting trip, he made a lap around the food court hub, settling on a breakfast sandwich of scrambled eggs, country ham, smoked cheese and fried onions. After eating, he removed his sunglasses from his cap brim, put them on and walked through the crowd, sipping his coffee.

From the snippets of conversation he overheard, it was apparent the flea market was a popular weekend gathering spot for locals. Now a local himself, having recently moved to Crowfoot Valley with his wife and young daughter, next weekend he would make it a family outing. He glanced up at some vultures backlit by the sun and followed their enormous shadows to a row of shaded yard-sale spaces near the woods.

The crowd had thinned there, and he set his coffee cup down on the corner of two long tables covered in white canvas. He wiped his sunglasses, then placed them back on his cap brim. The vendor, an old gentleman, eyed the cup. Drew quickly picked it up, drained it, and tossed it in a trash barrel.

Drew's heart leapt at the neat, impressive display of vintage archery gear and accessories, as traditional bowhunting was something he wanted to explore. Inundated with ever-expanding technological advances in his consulting work, hunting with his high-tech compound bows had lost a bit of luster.

"Pick up anything you want, and don't be afraid to ask questions," offered the vendor.

Drew scrutinized several orange-and-black-crested cedar arrows with Bear Razorheads. He held one up, examining the design of the broadhead closely, ran a finger alongside an edge, then returned it to its place. When he reached for a leather armguard, the old man stopped him.

"Whoa, whoa, young man! You're leaving a pretty good blood trail there!"

Drew looked down at a line of crimson drops spattered on the white canvas. He stepped back and wiped his forefinger on his jeans.

"I'm sorry," he said. "I must have cut myself somehow. I didn't even feel it."

"Here you go," said the old

man, handing him a Band-Aid from his change box.

"Thanks," Drew replied, wrapping it around his finger. "They sure are sharp."

"Surgical, like a scalpel. That's how I keep them."

"I've been thinking about going the traditional route," said Drew. "You really have a nice collection here."

The old man frowned.

"Thanks, but it's not a collection. This is my personal gear and it's meant to be used, not stuck up on a wall or shelf. I won't sell anything if it's not going to be used. You want to collect something, go buy a teapot."

Drew smiled. A seller with principles.

The old man took a recurve bow from a rack, strung it and handed it to him. "Here's a good place to begin. Start with something old and honorable. Back in '68 it was called *The Everyman's Bow*. It's a 45-pound, 58-inch Bear Grizzly with a 28-inch draw. We're the same size so it should fit you well."

The bow was a laminate of glass and wood, dull green and brown, like the faded greens of late summer that precede the umbers of deep autumn. It was light and lively, with the same grace and beauty as that of a fine double shotgun. Drew held the bow up and looked beyond the arrow rest and, in that instant, images of deer and autumn woodlands flashed by, grainy and faded, like an old home movie.

"It's a beauty," said Drew. "Exactly what I had in mind."

"Well, if you're serious, do it right. Take the bow and stringer and a couple field tips along today. See what you can do. And I have a couple of books for you, too. Read them. By the way, I'm Ed Holt," he said, shaking Drew's hand.

"Drew McGinnis. Mr. Holt, I didn't bring much cash along. I…"

"I'm not concerned about money right now," said Mr. Holt. "I trust you. Stop back next week at the end of the day. I'm going to put some gear together for you. We'll get you set up and shooting proper in no time, right down here by the woods. See if it appeals to you before you commit."

After exchanging numbers, Drew leafed through one of the books, Maurice Thompson's 1879 classic, *The Witchery of Archery*.

"Witchery, huh?"

"The first book written in English about hunting with a bow," said Mr. Holt. "Once the Witch of Stick and String casts her spell, you'll be held by her magic all your days."

Driving back home through the accordant landscape of Crowfoot Valley, Drew felt a deep connection with the harmonious blend of natural environs, farms and rural commerce. Here, he and his wife Yelena found the balance they had always envisioned. With both of them working from home, it freed up time to enjoy other pursuits.

DREW SET a bag of Chicken Shack

takeout dinners and another with ears of sweet corn on the long plank table. Sitting motionless in a wedge of sunlight, Raven, his wife's black cat stared at him, the silver star it wore on its collar glinting in the yellow light.

"Hey, Raven, hey kitty," coaxed Drew. The cat dashed away as he spoke. Five years now, and it still hadn't warmed up to him.

He looked out the kitchen window and spotted Yelena and his daughter Ayla in the garden. When he went out back, Yelena stood up, a basket of zucchinis on her hip, red hair ablaze in the slant of light, befitting her name, which means "ray of sun."

Three-year-old Ayla ran up to him.

"Here, Daddy!" she said excitedly, handing him a single cherry tomato.

He popped it in his mouth and scooped her up. Ayla, which means "moon glow," was born during October's full Hunter's Moon.

While they ate their chicken dinners, Drew described the market and the traditional archery gear he discovered at Holt's space.

"I remember you saying you were interested in that," said Yelena.

After dinner, Drew brought the bow and books in, along with a kitchen broom with a crooked sapling handle. He handed another bag to Yelena.

"Corn husk dolls!" she said with a huge smile. "Look Ayla, it's you and me!"

The primitive dolls, one large, one small, had reminded Drew of them.

"I love the handmade broom, too." said Yelena. "I can't wait to see what we can find next weekend."

DREW AND AYLA enjoyed an ice cream treat while Yelena finished browsing the rest of the flea market. He took them back home and returned just as the vendors were packing up. Holt was waiting for him.

"I have a bow quiver, a field quiver, three field arrows, six Razorhead arrows, an armguard, shooting tabs and a glove if you prefer," said Holt. "And here's a tackle box with all kinds of accessories and tools, too. Now let's get you shooting."

They met for a few sessions in early September, and under Holt's expert tutelage, Drew showed he was a quick study with a natural talent for traditional shooting. In the ensuing weeks, he practiced endlessly, until muscle and bone laminated to glass and wood, and the arrows seemed to fly on target through their own accord.

Drew and Yelena had blocked out a five-week hiatus, a reprieve from months of hard work, both on their old stone home and businesses. Yelena and Ayla drove across the state to visit her parents and would return just before Ayla's birthday; and with archery season right around the corner, Drew could fine tune his shooting skills.

HE HUNTED HARD every day, mostly still-hunting, sometimes posting at the corners of cornfields and food-plots or drifting through woodlots. His approach was fluid, a freelancer in the forest. He saw plenty of deer, but none had offered a shot.

One evening, while Drew was sitting at the table waxing his bowstring, Raven jumped up onto Yelena's chair across from him. The cat peeked up over the edge of the table, those fathomless jade eyes, the same color as Yelena's, fixed on his.

"Getting lonely, Raven? Sure is quiet around here."

The cat meowed and slipped from the chair, like ink spilled into shadow.

DREW STOPPED BY the flea market after a Saturday morning hunt to visit with Mr. Holt and report on his progress.

"Tell you what," said Holt. "I'm going to write down directions to a place where I think you might have some luck. It's a tidy little farm with an apple orchard.

"Look for a bright red barn at the crest of the hill and a white house right across the road.

"Ask permission. I missed a really big buck in that orchard one time. Buck fever. A wild shot. One of those you wish you could get another crack at."

"Thanks for the tip," said Drew. "By the way, could you send me a bill for what I owe?"

"I didn't get to it yet, but now I'll expect some backstrap, too."

Drew stopped at the hilltop farm on his way home. At first, he thought Holt was mistaken, as the barn was collapsed in on itself and the white house, which appeared abandoned, was a weathered gray clapboard with curled shingles. From inside he could hear the twanging of a stringed instrument accompanied by singing. He waited until it stopped, then knocked.

An old woman answered the door. Seated in a wingchair was her twin, an autoharp on her lap. On the table next to her was a big wooden bowl full of bright red apples.

"Sorry to bother you," Drew said. "A friend, Ed Holt, thought that I might get permission to hunt here."

"Have him come in, Lureen," said her sister.

"Used to be a Holt lived 'round here, wasn't there, Velma?" asked Lureen.

"Back when we was kids, I believe," said Velma. "But go on and hunt all you want. Those deer eat up all our nice red apples. Here, take one along. We give them out for Halloween."

"Before you go, though, take a listen," said Lureen. "It's called *The Blackest Crow*."

Their performance was loud in the sparsely furnished parlor. The spidery strains of the autoharp resonated deep within his chest as the windowpanes vibrated in their old frames. He complimented and thanked them, then left.

Throughout the night, the old folk tune's beautiful, haunting melody played again and again in his head, and he dreamed he was a crow coursing above Crowfoot Valley, searching, hunting for something.

Drew thought of how Yelena loved Halloween, and the celebrative spirit of the harvest. It inspired him to spend a day decorating the yard and porch with dozens of pumpkins, gourds, cornstalks and potted mums. He fashioned a scarecrow clad in camo holding a stick bow, propped it up in the front yard and perched an old crow decoy on its shoulder.

LATER IN THE WEEK, he eased into the orchard for a late afternoon hunt. It was overgrown with weeds and the apple trees were wild and broken, with only a few wizened and spotted fruits. The weary trees hadn't seen a red apple in years.

It did not take long, just one of those lucky hunts that happens sometimes. He followed a deer trail to where the orchard blended with the encroaching woods and set up near a fresh scrape.

A half-hour later, a big, gray buck ghosted beneath an apple tree and began to work an overhanging branch, and in one smooth and practiced motion, Drew sent an orange-and-black-crested cedar shaft – topped with a Razorhead – through its chest.

The evening was very warm, so he butchered the deer and wrapped it for the freezer. It was after midnight when he collapsed onto the old leather sofa, nodding, watching a furry white moth flutter around a light on the table before him. He swiped at an insect that had tickled the back of his neck, then again at his cheek, sucking his breath in hard when Raven's whiskers brushed against his cheek again. The cat purred and slid down from the back of the sofa and onto his lap. Together they watched the moth.

THE 11-POINT RACK had lots of mass and a 21-inch spread. He cleaned and boiled the skull for a European mount, finishing in late afternoon. When he saw Yelena's car coming up the drive, he tucked Raven under his arm and went out on the porch to greet them.

"You grew a beard!" she yelled. "I like it! And who's your buddy there?"

Drew grilled tenderloins for dinner and they dined outside, talking for hours until the Hunter's Moon climbed above the dark pines surrounding their yard.

The next day, Yelena and Ayla were going to a Halloween party for kids at the firehouse. Yelena was dressed as a witch, and Ayla as her black cat.

"You guys look great!" said Drew. "See you later for birthday cake."

It was also the last day of the flea-market season. Holt had never sent him a bill and Drew wanted to settle up, remembering to bring some backstrap in a small cooler.

When he got to Holt's space it was vacant. He called the number Holt had given him, but it was out of service. Bewildered, he went up to the manager's office and asked if he could get the contact information of a vendor to whom he owed some money.

"Sure thing," she said. "What's the name?"

"Ed Holt."

The manager scrolled through her vendor file several times. "I don't have any record of a Holt," she said. "Was there someone else with him? Another name?"

"No, just him. Could you look again? He had vendor spaces 237 and 238."

The manager, growing uneasy, searched other files. "Sorry, but I can't find anything. Anyway, our spaces end at 236."

Before he could lobby for another search, she cut him off.

"It's not rocket science. No Holt, no receipt, no such spaces."

Once outside, Drew reeled, the pillars of

logic and reason toppling like a line of dominoes. He felt panicky, then detached, as if floating in a vacuum.

Back home, he sought the comforting reality of his family. Ayla blew out the candles on her cake, the cat rubbed against his leg, Yelena swept the floor. He picked up the bow, the bloodied arrow still in the quiver. He touched the skull mount of his buck Yelena had placed on the deep windowsill of their bedroom window.

All of it, real.

In the middle of the night he was awakened when the cat jumped onto the bed and curled up between them. The antlers, backlit by the full moon, cast a large shadow of long crooked fingers onto the wall. The Witch of Stick and String, he thought, recalling Holt's words.

And then he knew, or dreamed that he knew.

An errant arrow loosed long ago by a kindred spirit had come to land in the present. He had been chosen by blood and fortune to be the conduit between two dimensions, a conveyance enlisted to fulfill the wish of a hunter long gone at another chance to release that shaft again in that same Crowfoot Valley orchard.

Drew exhaled deeply, breathed steadily, then slept.

Yelena, her back turned toward his, opened one eye and smiled. The silver star on the cat's collar twinkled as it purred, catching the light and magic of the Hunter's Moon.

Anonymous

COBB WAS AWAKENED by the resonant chug of a motor and crunching gravel at the end of his drive. A small figure in a blaze-orange coat ran past the window. Head down, fighting the wet chill of a November rain, he placed a plastic-wrapped newspaper on the threshold, and dashed by again.

Four o'clock. Cobb rose and watched the taillights of the patchworked truck dip over the hill. He retrieved the paper, went to the kitchen, and made some coffee. He couldn't remember a time in the 21 years they had lived up here in the woods when Skip Yoder had failed to deliver a paper. Whenever it rained or snowed, he always delivered to the doorstep instead of putting it in the box out on the road. Now, his two boys helped out on the long route.

The Yoders were a large clan, and like those families from an older time, each worked some odd job or another as soon as they were able. They were not prosperous, but made their way by working two jobs and supporting each other, surviving through collective effort.

In recent years, most of them had moved on. Skip had worked at a cousin's garage, but when that closed, he split his time doing part-time jobs. Cobb imagined that with the boys and a younger girl at home, it was a struggle.

Whenever Skip came to collect for the paper, Cobb would try to strike up a conversation with him, but like most of the Yoders, Skip was shy and spoke little. Cobb knew Skip was a hunter, but not even the mention of acorn crops or deer or the size of turkey poults could get him going. Cobb hadn't spoken to Skip for months, ever since the newspaper company began to bill by mail, instead of having carriers collect.

The rain eased to a drizzle. Cobb went out to his shop where he kept his hunting gear and got dressed. It was the last day of turkey season, and on his way out, he walked past several birdfeeders he was making for his wife Suse.

He smiled at the light manner of this work. Cobb was a master furniture maker and widely noted for his skill, specializing in reproductions of 18th century furniture: Windsor chairs for fine colonial estates; blanket chests for a gallery in Lancaster; important restoration work for discriminating collectors and museums.

At one time, he had a shop and showroom in Chester County, but the work all but consumed him until he and Suse moved north to a lovely rural farmland at the base of the Kittatinny range. After much searching, they found this place tucked partway up a gravel road.

Suse was a serious birder, and Hawk Mountain wasn't far away. With just the two of them, they really didn't need much, and every fall Cobb declared himself semi-retired and spent most of his time hunting.

COBB HEADED UP the mountain to a hollow thick with grapevines where fall flocks often came to feed. He hunkered down along a windfall and listened. Thanksgiving would be here in several weeks, and only wild turkey would suffice for traditionalists like Suse and he.

He could taste it now, the delicious wild meat complemented by chestnut stuffing and gravy. Suse always gathered enough native American chestnuts to make the stuffing. And there would be candied yams and pumpkin pie made fresh from her garden.

He was getting ahead of himself here, thought Cobb. He hadn't heard a bird fly down or a distant cluck or yelp. They just might yet be dining on store-bought.

Cobb cut across the face of the mountain by taking a deer trail through a long, dense reef of laurel above a creek. In the center of the laurel patch was an oval clearing about 50 yards long, where he had taken numerous deer over the years. No one came in here because the laurel was thought to be solid, and in all the years that he hunted here, no one put on a drive. The trick was to get in position very early; come in too late and you would just be pushing deer out.

He stirred from his reverie when two does and a big buck ghosted along the far edge of the clearing. A quilt of fog slid down over the mountain, and at first, all he saw were the white markings around muzzles and eyes, the flick of a white tail, and a high, pale rack. He had to look hard to make out the slightly darker grays that were the bodies of the deer.

Cobb continued through the laurel to more-open woods, out to an outcropping of rock the sidehill wrapped around. This is where Skip Yoder and his kids posted for deer. Cobb saw them here whenever he dragged a deer up the tram road past their stand. It was a good place to post on the first day, with a commanding view all around.

He recalled how the Yoders walked slowly back and forth and around the boulder, stiff-legged and poker-faced, as if they had been assigned to guard the rock itself. Like elfin sentinels on a miniature castle, one Yoder, then another, perched atop the battlement, a single rifle of military vintage among them, carefully changing hands between the young hunters at the precise stroke of the hour.

The drizzle gave way to powdery snow that quickly gathered in the folds of his coat. Cobb sat under the overhanging rock and watched the somber brown woods brighten, reminding him of Suse sprinkling powdered sugar on walnut breads.

Cobb grew excited when he heard the falsetto piping of turkey voices. The flock was headed his way, and he tucked in tight against the side of the rock and waited, motionless as a bobcat. It was a large flock and feeding in earnest; leafy duff raked back noisily, serpentine necks darting to snatch up the exposed acorns. He would be patient, get a good break on the flock, and call them back in.

That was his plan until the pale head of a turkey popped up above his silver shotgun bead. Cobb cocked the hammer on the black-powder shotgun and took the sure thing. At his shot, turkeys erupted everywhere, and he could hear them slap up through the whippy branches of the canopy, flapping and gliding, plopping down far across the hollow. If the Yoders were here, he could've called in birds for all of them, he thought.

Cobb was surprised at the size of the gobbler that lay on the tapestry of leaves. At more than 20 pounds, this was the largest gobbler he had ever taken. He slipped and slid up to the crest of the hill, his balance off kilter from the heft of the gobbler.

COBB READ SUSE'S note on the table. She had driven to Allentown to settle on her recently deceased uncle's small estate. Cobb plucked the turkey and burned the downy feathers off with a torch, then put the turkey in a tub of water on the porch to soak.

Next, he cleaned his flintlock fowling piece, then removed a flintlock longrifle from the cabinet. It was a magnificent rifle, built by a friend who patterned it after an original Lebanon County rifle made by a relative more than two centuries earlier. Cobb had swapped him a Windsor settee for it. Cobb shouldered the rifle and thought of the buck he had seen earlier, of its eight tines, long and shaped like saber blades.

He finished putting the final touches on the birdfeeders and strung a wire between two trees on which to hang them. Suse would start feeding birds on Thanksgiving, after more bears had gone into hibernation. He was fastening the feeders to the wire when Suse pulled in.

"You better call the newspaper," she said, peering into the tub. "Someone killed a pterodactyl."

"That's Thankgiving dinner," said Cobb.

"That big bird? For just you and me? There weren't any little tender poults in the flock!"

"It was the gobbler's fault," said Cobb. "He lined himself up with my gun barrel and that was it. I bet I can eat that bird by the end of deer season. Hot turkey sandwiches, turkey salad, turkey and biscuits, turkey chili. Bring it on."

"I gave all of Uncle Cal's things to charity, except for this box of photos and two guns rolled up in that sleeping bag," said Suse.

Cobb examined the guns. He recognized the M94 .30-30 rifle with its pistol grip stock and long barrel. For all its age, the gun was in excellent condition. The other was a featherweight Model 70 in .257 Roberts. It was a sweet little gun, and he recalled making the special short stock of highly-figured walnut for her uncle who was a small man. Although he was thrilled with Cobb's work, he went back to using his M94 carbine, afraid to scratch the beautiful wood. Cobb put the guns away then walked out and got the mail.

Back inside, he opened the bill from the newspaper company. Under the amount due was a blank line with *Tip for Good Service* printed beneath. Cobb always added a generous tip, but now had a different idea.

COBB CALLED THE outdoor columnist of the local paper and told him his plan.

"Now let me get this straight," said the writer. "Instead of a tip, you want to give your carrier two rifles."

"That's right." said Cobb. "This family has one gun between the three of them. I have no use for these rifles. I'm a blackpowder hunter, always will be. If I tried to give these guns to Yoder, he wouldn't take them. You know, too proud. But if the newspaper somehow gave the guns to him as a reward for longtime service as a bonus, then it would be different. Just so long as I remain anonymous."

"This is great," said the writer. "I'll find a way to get it done."

THE FIRST DAY OF DEER season started with snow that changed to freezing rain. It would be tough going in the woods, and Suse was surprised to see that Cobb was heading out so late.

"Don't forget your turkey sandwiches on the counter," she said.

"Oh, boy, more turkey," he said, pretending to swallow hard.

COBB GOT TO THE laurel patch an hour later, zigzagging slowly through the cover, skirting the clearing inside. When he was almost through to the open woods, he heard two quick shots farther out the mountain. He took the trail past the big rock where Skip Yoder was showing his boys how to dress out the deer.

"Now that's a dandy buck," said Cobb.

Skip looked up and smiled. "They did good."

"I got him with my new rifle," said the red-cheeked youngster. "I hit him hard and my brother put him down for keeps with his new gun."

"It's our first deer," said the other boy. "But he shot first, so he tags it."

"Now that's teamwork," said Cobb. "Before you start dragging that buck, you're gonna need some energy. How'd you men like a couple of sandwiches?"

The Yoders thanked him, and Cobb continued on.

AS HE WALKED AWAY, he reveled in the tone of excitement in their voices, the bloom of legend as they repeated to each other what each already knew, and would never forget. Indeed, they had become guardians of that rock, thought Cobb, for now it was a hallowed monument to a brotherly bond.

Cobb walked until he could no longer hear their voices, beyond the cast of the sublime light of gracious anonymity, deep into the graying woods.

The Potato Fires

FRANK SELECTED a half-dozen large potatoes from the bin in the root cellar, slipped them into the game pouch of his canvas coat, then went upstairs to the kitchen. He poured salt and pepper onto a torn corner of newspaper, folded it several times, and put it in a pocket along with two kitchen matches.

His mother was sitting next to the woodstove, like she did every evening, reading and drinking her tea, waiting for his father to return home from the second shift at the rail yard.

"Where you going, Frankie?" she asked.

"Out back to make a fire. I'll have a baked potato for Pop when he gets home. Want me to bring one for you?"

"No thanks, that's too late for me to eat anything. You go on now."

Their yellow dog whined and circled at the door.

"Look, Lucky's waitin' on you."

Frank stood on the porch, inhaling the crisp March air, and watched his dog lope across the yard, resembling a small, pale wolf in the brilliant moonlight. It had been a snowy winter, and he could hear freshets of water rushing down the mountain. Scattered choruses of spring peepers trilled in the bottomland. The lonely whistle of a train rounding the curve in the river valley signaled it was 9 o'clock.

From the shed, he took a garden spade and a blackened hubcap attached to a chain. He dug a shallow pit at the edge of the field, then brought over a sling of kindling and cord wood from the woodshed. He put the hubcap in the pit and laid a latticed framework of wood on it, placing the potatoes in the spaces between, then stacked on more wood. In a few minutes, flames danced and crackled.

Frank heard his best friend Lewis scuffing along in the leaves before he saw him.

"Figures you'd show up when all the work's done," Frank quipped.

"You got room for these?" asked Lewis as he produced a pair of small, rubbery potatoes, their eyes so long they looked like tentacles on some primitive ocean creature.

Frank laughed at the sorry-looking spuds, tossed one to Lucky who mouthed it and quickly dropped it, and threw the other into the hedgerow, which the dog retrieved and dropped next to the first.

"We're at the bottom of the bin this time of year," said Lewis.

"That's okay. I already had an extra one in there for you."

Now in their junior year of high school, they had been friends since childhood, as much out of necessity than anything, theirs being the last houses on the long dead-end road that led out of town. Lewis had been stricken by polio when he was a child, but with an iron will and Frank's encouragement, he overcame great odds.

Lewis was a star in the classroom, leaps and bounds beyond the others. He especially loved geography and history, with a wanderlust that blossomed from reading about exotic lands while bedridden.

He vowed to travel the world someday, but for now, the focus of their lives was hunting in the wooded hills that rose just beyond their backdoors.

From out of the shadows, came a large, gray hound – deep-chested and ghostly, sucking in air through flared nostrils – followed by a stranger about their age.

Lucky charged the big hound, roaring savagely, then pulled up short. A polite sniffing and tail wagging followed.

"Mind Lucky!" Frank cautioned.

"Easy Race," said the stranger. "Didn't mean to bother ya. Thought he was gonna whup your dog, so I came over."

"Don't kid yourself pal," Frank replied. "You ought to see what he does to the groundhogs he catches in our garden. Where you from?"

"Up over the mountain. The big farm on Hornbeck Road. I'm Tim. I seen you two settin' for squirrel up on the hill last year."

"Is that a coon dog?" Lewis asked.

"He's a champion bluetick hound. Cost me a whole season's fur money to buy him and his sister Pearl. She's at home. I feed 'em only canned food. Mom's against it 'cause it's expensive, but I pay for it. I told her you can't feed table scraps to pedigree hounds. They got papers."

"Lucky used to have papers, too," Frank said. "But he's housebroken now."

Lewis laughed so hard he almost fell off the log.

"I heard your dogs and a horn late one night," Frank said.

RURAL ROUTE

"That's how I call my hounds," explained Tim. "I hunt your side of the hill sometimes."

"How come we never saw you up in the woods?" Lewis asked.

"I didn't want to ruin your watch. Besides, I was after deer."

"Deer?" uttered a disbelieving Frank. "There ain't no deer on this hill."

"There's deer alright," Tim reassured him. "Ever since that big burn on top grew back."

Frank poked the flames with a stick.

"What are you doing huntin' deer in October?"

"I was huntin' with my bow," said Tim. "They started archery season a couple years ago, in '51. I made the arrows myself."

They added more wood and talked for an hour. An occasional loud pop shifted the subject or cued the next hunter to start a new story where another left off, in the way fires have always done. The addition of the third party elevated their previous exploits in the woods from mere experiences to tribal legend, establishing a shared archive of standards by which all other adventures now could be measured and stored. Tales unwritten, but never to be forgotten.

A chill breeze pushed in from the west and enveloped the young men in a gauzy veil of delicious apple smoke, an incense that, on that night, would bind these young hunters for the rest of their lives.

Frank pulled the hubcap from the fire by the chain.

"Help yourself boys."

He speared a potato and ran it down to the house for his father. When he returned to the fire, he sliced off a slab of butter from a dish.

They passed around the gob of butter and salt and pepper. They ate in silence with their penknives, the two friends impressed with the ridgerunner and his hound, and he with their woods savvy. They stared deep into the fire, studying the flickering coals.

"I'll meet you here tomorrow at lunchtime," Tim said. "I'll show you where the deer are."

"You're on," Frank said. "You want these last two potatoes?"

Tim took them and put them in the pockets of his thin jacket.

"I got a long way to go, they'll keep my hands warm until I get home."

IT HAD SNOWED during the night; most of it melted on the ground, but it still clung to branches. It was what is often called an onion snow. After meeting, the new friends headed up through the crabapple woods, up through the maple glade, up past the oak grove to the high side of the regenerated burn, where the snow remained 2 inches deep.

Tim showed them a line of buck rubs, something they had never seen before. Then they slipped into the thicket on a narrow deer trail, pocked with the unmistakable tracks and droppings, and followed it to the fresh beds of five deer that bounded out of the thicket from its far edge.

Their hearts raced after they heard a distant snort and then saw white flags bobbing over the ridgeline.

"There you go," Tim whispered. "There's your deer."

THAT SPRING, Frank and Lewis bought bows just like Tim's. Tim helped them assemble cedar arrows with turkey-feather fletching. Each hunter had a different colored crest: Frank's was red, Lewis's yellow and Tim's blue.

Throughout the summer, they practiced on targets, stalked groundhogs and challenged each other on difficult shots at rotten stumps in the woods. By autumn, they were keen for the hunt.

October waned without a deer being sighted by anyone, and on the season's last day, they decided to put on a slow, silent drive through the burn. They waited for Lewis to post off a deer trail on the opposite side before they still-hunted toward him.

Just as they were about to begin their push, they heard Lewis whooping and hollering like a wild man. Then three does bolted out of the burn, followed by a craggy buck that hesitated, not a dozen yards away.

With reactions honed from many hours of practice, Frank and Tim drew in unison and loosed their shafts. The heavy arrows with razor-sharp broadheads zipped through the buck's lungs inches apart, and the deer went down a short distance away.

Lewis came crashing through the burn a few minutes later, and when he saw them with their buck, he started whooping and hollering again, and they joined in. They yelled and hooted even louder after Lewis settled down and told them that as soon as he had taken his stand, five deer walked into the burn, two of them bucks, and he dropped a fork-horn with a shot in the spine.

Frank and Tim insisted that the other tag the big 8-point, Lewis finally settling it with a coin toss. Tim reluctantly tagged it.

Word spread quickly about their feat, and curious people stopped by, including a reporter from the newspaper. The lead headline on Monday's sports page read: *Young Archers Score on Bucks*. The story included a photo of the trio posing with their bucks and bows.

The backyard fare at that week's fire included venison backstrap, with plenty of scraps for Lucky, even the hounds. Tim now believed there was nothing they could put in a can of dog food that could touch fresh venison. The debate over whose arrow struck the buck first continued and fueled other fires for decades.

That fall, they hunted coons with Tim and his hounds, and the hills rang with their sweet music. At times, Lewis struggled to keep up, but he always managed to get to the treed raccoon and make the shot while Frank held the light and Tim the dogs.

Tim had a masterful touch with dogs, and trained Lucky to be a fine squirrel dog and rabbit rouster. Tim recognized something special in the yellow cur dog, an ancient intelligence that differed from that of his hounds.

That fall, and into the winter, many potato fires burned, the long shadows of the hunters and their dogs stretching out from the fire into the darkness, blurring like spokes on a moving wheel with a molten hub.

And, so it goes that the flaming wheel of youth rolls on quickly.

FRANK BECAME a railroad engineer, and loved bringing the locomotives home down through the river valley. Tim ran a hardware store, then opened the first sporting goods store with an archery shop in the region. He also raised hounds, but for a long time, his companion dog was a yellow dog named Spud.

Frank and Tim raised their families in the same houses in which they grew up, and built a hunting camp up north.

Lewis went on to get a Ph.D in anthropology, wrote books and lectured at universities. He traveled the world as he said he would; Frank and Tim even saw his picture in *National Geographic*.

He sent them bird-shooting gloves from Spain that could turn any briar, an antique silver hunting horn from Scotland engraved with thistles, exotic ocean shells for their kids, Japanese kimonos for their wives. He always closed his letters with: "Keep the home fires burning."

FRANK WRAPPED TWO potatoes in foil, went out back and placed them in the fire. He saw Lewis's bent form scraping along in the autumn leaves before he heard him, having lost much of his hearing after a lifetime of running the big locomotives. The white-haired, bearded professor and the retired train engineer talked until the fire died down. Frank shoveled dirt onto the last blue ember, then they drove in silence up to Tim's farm.

Tim's family filed from the bedroom, where he lay pale and dying. In a raspy and labored voice, Tim said he could smell woodsmoke on them, and Lewis told him about the fire; almost like old times, but not the same without him there.

Tim motioned Frank to move close so he could hear.

"Was your arrow," Frank whispered. "Was your arrow got there first. That was your buck. I get the last word on that."

Frank took the potatoes from his pocket and placed one in each of Tim's cold hands.

"Here you go, we didn't forget about you."

"These will keep me warm," Tim said, "until I get home."

Fresh Tracks

*"There are no unsacred places; there are only
sacred places and desecrated places."*

Wendell Berry

WELL AFTER MIDNIGHT, a doe and her grown fawn emerge from a small patch of woods and browse on the succulent new growth at the edge of the suburban mall. The rows of lights illuminating the parking lot cast an enormous dome of light that obscures the stars. The doe tests the unimpeded breeze that swirls across the macadam, and her fawn imitates her.

Almost every night, they make a circuit by following a tendril of brush from a woods to the north, feeding and resting at the patch of woods near the mall, then returning at first light.

One evening, the deer leave the cover of the woods as usual, but hesitate when the brushy strip they usually follow is gone. They continue on, by habit, across the freshly graded ground toward the distant lights, but turn back when they encounter a bulldozer and other equipment.

The patch of woods near the mall would be cleared in a few days. The only evidence of their presence that remains in that bit of wild ground are some tracks they leave in the black soil.

MAX DROPS OFF his wife at the mall entrance and parks in the upper west corner of the lot, far away from the sea of cars, figuring he'll read the evening paper and work a crossword puzzle while she shops. He rolls the windows down and lets the warm April breeze blow through.

He had forgotten his reading glasses and settles for briefly scanning the headlines. Max looks out the passenger window into the patch of woods where a cardinal sings, and he whistles a fair imitation of its song. The cardinal comes flitting out along the edge, crest up, looking for a rival. Max watches the bird, and then, well beyond it, makes out the silhouette of the decrepit farmhouse in the dense thicket, backlit by the cantaloupe-colored evening sky. It is a profile that comes rushing back through time, as familiar to him as the face of his wife. He had thought the suburban sprawl had claimed the house when the mall was built, but there it stood.

With nothing better to do and time to kill, he walks into the woodlot along a trickling seep, as he had countless times as a boy, to this place, the home of Bill, his cousin and best friend. He stops at the base of a towering sycamore, more than 100 feet high, centuries old. He places both hands on the tree and looks up through its mottled limbs that catch and hold the blush of evening light.

"Old friend," he whispers, patting the tree.

He and his cousin had spent many summer afternoons lazing in the sycamore's branches and, from as high up as they dared climb, they would watch the traffic on the dirt road that bisected this farming community.

Max stands in the shadow of the farmhouse. The roof is sunken in and the floors have collapsed; only the walls remain standing. It is covered in vines, as if the earth was pulling it down, reclaiming the long-surrendered brick and mortar.

Somewhere in the distance, a parking sign, loose in its moorings, wobbles slowly in the breeze, squeaking back and forth. Max is reminded of the pheasant weathervane they had built from sheet metal, and how it squeaked as it turned from the cupola on the barn that stood where his car is now parked. In his mind's eye, he can see the proud swell of the tin cockbird's breast, the long tailfeathers curved slightly in exact attitude.

Plastic shopping bags and paper, blown across the parking lot, are strewn profusely in the bushes and throughout the trees, quaking and rattling in the breeze. But when Max closes his eyes, he hears an older wind rattling the dry, tawny leaves of corn.

MAX AND HIS FATHER walk the dirt lane from their own farmhouse, a half-mile up the road, to join his Uncle Hank and cousin Bill at their home for breakfast and a morning of bird hunting. Max carries his new double-barrel shotgun crooked in his arm, like his father does, while trying to match his father's long strides, step for step.

The dusty dirt lane is a tapestry of pheasant tracks, and he can see birds running across the road ahead.

Max remembers certain days through varied colors, summing up the temperament of the day and emotions and events in a single color. That glorious late October day is remembered as yellow-gold. He recalls walking into the farmhouse kitchen, sunlight

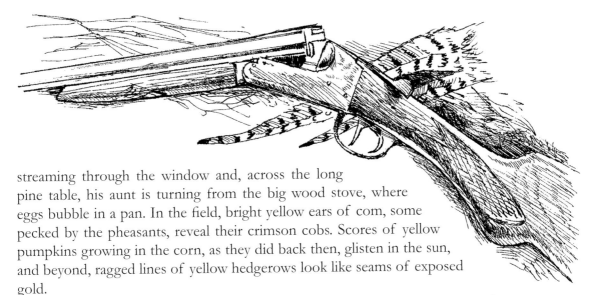

streaming through the window and, across the long pine table, his aunt is turning from the big wood stove, where eggs bubble in a pan. In the field, bright yellow ears of corn, some pecked by the pheasants, reveal their crimson cobs. Scores of yellow pumpkins growing in the corn, as they did back then, glisten in the sun, and beyond, ragged lines of yellow hedgerows look like seams of exposed gold.

The men are in no hurry to get out. The morning chores were done, the frost is burning off and the birds are there. They eat and talk. Max and Bill are eager to try their new shotguns on game. They had saved every penny for months to purchase identical Lefever double-barrel shotguns.

After exhaustive searches through mail order catalogs and sporting magazines, they debated long and hard about which make and model would best fit their budgets. They finally settled on the Lefever, swayed, in part, by the company's longtime advertising slogan, "Who ever saw a broken Lefever?" That line, taken from a testimonial letter sent to the company by a Pennsylvania hunter, was good enough for them. The boys knew they would be hunting together for a long time, and agreed they should use the same gauge, should they need to share shells, but even that decision took days to resolve, and they compromised by settling on the 16-gauge.

They had done much pass shooting on crows during late summer, hiding in the hedgerows as the crows went to roost. The crows slid over their blinds like oil over water, and were fairly easy to bring down, but Max and Bill honed their shooting skills nevertheless, learning proper lead and estimating distance. Pheasants, however, were an entirely different matter.

Max recalls the first rooster that erupted in front of his barrels. It caught him by surprise, flushing from some low grass that wouldn't hold a field mouse, chugging skyward – the Orient Express itself bedecked in feathers – steaming for the clouds. Forgetting everything he learned in the summer crow fields, Max missed wildly.

MAX'S FATHER PUSHES out a hedgerow of blackberry canes, Max on one side, Bill on the other, Uncle Hank bringing up the rear. A brace of cockbirds flushes suddenly, splitting left and right, with Max's and Bill's shots ringing out as one. Both roosters hit the ground at almost the same instant. It would be a golden moment they would talk about for years.

MAX PICKS UP A STICK AND POKES at some brush until it strikes something hard beneath the tangles. He slides the stick under the vines and pries upward, revealing an old millstone with an alternating pattern of lines on the face, filled now with fine moss. He is surprised to see no one has taken it, that it hasn't ended up outside some antique emporium.

Their great-grandfather had brought the stone with him when he had moved from Chester County. It had been in the family for years. The stone was fashioned in the early 1700s and was of no particular use on the farm, serving only as a reminder of their heritage. It made a fine monument, and his aunt had planted day lilies around it. Sometimes on summer evenings, Uncle Hank would sit on the stone, and in his resonant velvet-over-steel voice, tell them tales of redcoats and colonists along the Brandywine River, where the stone had been used in a mill.

Max walks out to the other side of the woods and sees the dozers and a construction trailer parked nearby. Even this sorry patch of woods won't be spared. He turns and walks back through, and as he ducks beneath a limb, he spies a deer track in the soil. He kneels to study it. It is fresh, and the crisp edges of it catch red light from the huge plastic letters of the illuminated mall sign. He is astonished to find deer tracks in the small woods.

Occasionally, they would find deer sign on the farm, and by the time he was a senior in high school, there was evidence that the local herd was increasing and expanding. Max set out alone to hunt deer one morning with a pewtery .32 Winchester Special. It had snowed the day before and into the night, enough to rim his high-topped boots.

He remembers the morning dawned bright and brutally frigid. A huge mass of cold air driven by powerful winds muscled into the valley, its air so cold it could not have come from some distant prairie or northern province, but from another world.

He plodded across the fields towards the big woods, where he had last seen some deer sign. Snow devils jousted playfully across the open expanse, and he walked into one that enveloped him with ice particles fine as diamond dust that reflected prisms of color in the sunlight. He pulled his scarf up over his nose and felt the tug of ice building up on the other side where his breath comes through.

Max walked all day. Late in the afternoon, he eased through a windbreak of staggered pines bordering a lane. He came up and over an embankment above a lane, where the wind has blown the snow, and saw a set of deer tracks. He glanced ahead and caught a flicker of movement in the woods and saw deer moving through the long blue shadows. A small buck hesitated at the cusp of a hollow and the rifle's front bead caught the sun at his back and glowed like a firefly that alighted on the buck's shoulder.

The gun roared, and Max tried to lever another round, but the action was frozen. He unbuttoned his jacket, tucked the receiver under his armpit until it warmed up, then levered a fresh round. He wouldn't need it.

It took him a long time to dress out the buck, his fingered numbing instantly when he stopped. He warmed his hands by holding the big, meaty heart in one hand, then the other, like a hot river stone taken from a campfire. Max slid the deer along the scalloped swells on the lee side of the drifts, where the snow has thinned. He stopped to rest, and when he looked up, he saw his home in the pale violet shadows and considered it the most beautiful thing he had ever seen.

MAX STOPS REMINISCING and looks up from the deer track. He spots his wife in her bright yellow jacket waiting for him at the mall entrance.

A few days later, Max returns to the woods in a pickup, but the woods are not there; neither the huge sycamore, nor even a single brick from the farmhouse. The crew is loading the last dump truck and Max asks the foreman if they still have the millstone.

"You're just in time, it's in that last pile of brush there. You can have it if you want, because it's headed for the landfill. We'll even put it in your pickup for you."

Max walks across the vacant site, now divided with plastic surveyor tape. All that remains is a dark, wet wound where the perpetual seep bled into the black earth.

MAX HAD SOME neighborhood teens roll the millstone onto his wife's flowerbed mound. That night Max dreams this dream: It was of a future time when the days of man had passed. He sits high in a sycamore, admiring the view, taking in the sounds. All around, everything is changing rapidly before his eyes. The mall has sunk from view, and in its stead rises the rim of a dark and endless forest, while shimmering wild fields blanket the parking lots. The faintest stars gain purchase in the dusky sky, and below him a deer walks along the seep.

While Max dreams his dream, the doe and her fawn, persistent creatures of habit, make their way down to where the small woods had been. Without the security of nearby cover, they linger only briefly, then turn and head back. Unless Max's dream holds any element of truth, they are the last of their kind to make tracks upon that once sacred, but now anonymous ground.

Pathfinder

JEFF READS THE same sentence in the hunting magazine three times, but none of it registers, and he lets the magazine flop down onto his chest. He stares at the ceiling, conjuring the image of a deer in a snowstorm in the swirls of cracked plaster, a scenario where he drives the big buck to his grandfather waiting on stand, who shoots the legendary deer and they drag it into camp together. He lies there until the daydream passes and his grandfather's image fades, then sits up, swinging his left leg then the right over the side of the bed.

Jeff's eyes sweep the photos and newspaper clippings tacked to his bulletin board. *Jeff Logan Tourney MVP*, another reads, *Logan Perfect! Fairview Ace Sweetens No Hitter with Homer!* A team picture of the ballplayers holding a banner, "Fairview High School 1949 District II Champs." Scattered among the news clippings are old hunting licenses, hand-drawn maps, and his favorite photo, a snapshot of his grandfather and him dragging in their bucks to deer camp. His grandfather passed away several months after the picture was taken.

He pulls on a baseball glove and pounds his fist hard into the greasy pocket, then, as he does every night, props two pillows against the back of a stuffed chair and stands across the room as if on a pitching mound. He winds up and fires his fastball into the pillow, which receives it with a loud *Whump!* The ball rolls off the pillow and across the carpet, and he scoops it up with his glove. He throws pitch after pitch in the imagined cadence of a game until the pillows are cupped deeply like a catcher's mitt and sweat beads above his lip.

From the top slot of a gun rack Jeff removes his grandfather's deer rifle, a Model 99 .250 Savage. He checks the action, snaps it to his shoulder, and plasters the bead on the chest of a buck leaping from a calendar. He wipes an oily rag over the grayed receiver and barrel and puts the gun back.

From the second rung he takes a baseball bat and rotates the bat from his shoulder several times, staring through the bedroom window, glancing at the backyard fence. He waits for the right pitch and swings ferociously, loses his balance as he pivots on his heel, the momentum of his swing sending him crashing into a wardrobe, ending with a loud clump as he hit the floor.

Seconds later his father bursts in and runs over to him.

"Hey, Jeff, you okay? Here, let me help you up."

Jeff looks away and says, "I can get up myself. I just slipped, that's all."

"Well, be careful. I'll see you at breakfast."

Jeff hears his father whispering to his mother in the hallway, and she peeks in.

"Goodnight, Ma," he says, waving her off.

He missed his grandfather more than ever. He was the one person who wouldn't treat him differently now – not like everyone else has since the accident.

IT HAPPENED 10 months ago, right after his sophomore year. He and Skip, his best friend and the team's shortstop, were hiking by Castle Rock, a towering escarpment in the wooded gap beyond town.

"Race you to the top!" Skip shouted.

They must have climbed the rocks a thousand times when they were younger, the reward a cold drink from the spring at the top that bubbled with the sweetest water in the world. Jeff remembered his route, even though he hadn't climbed it for several years. He had grown taller since then, and his ascent was out of sync. Skip, however, went straight up, quick as a red squirrel up a pine.

Near the top, Jeff undershot a handhold when the tip of his worn sneaker slipped from a crack, and he began to slide, nails raking desperately. A feet-first freefall followed. He would have landed safely on the switchback path that traversed the escarpment 12 feet below, but his right heel caught the tip of a protruding rebar support on a makeshift handrail. The force of his descent drove that rebar right through the heel of his sneaker, straight up through his leg, splintering bones, flaying flesh, exploding his knee.

He opened his eyes days later to undulating fields of snow stretching far before him, but as his eyes focused, he saw that the fields were rumpled bed sheets and that he was in a hospital room, his parents at bedside. Then he remembered, seeing the deep swale in the sheets where his right leg used to be, and he knew his life had changed forever.

He returned to school that fall, but everything was different. Pity was like a contagion that spread among his teachers and friends. He became bitter and withdrawn, spending most of his free time in his room. He skipped hunting season, and didn't go to deer camp with his father. Friends and teammates stopped coming around. Now, in the spring of his junior year, he couldn't wait for school to be over, and even thought of dropping out.

HIS BEDROOM WAS STUFFY and Jeff opens the window. Fickle March breezes, warm then cool – as mercurial as his own emotions. Lightning flashes and thunder rolls up the valley, rumbling along with the 10 o'clock outbound express. A wall of hail hits the side of his family's clapboard house; icy pellets sting his outstretched arms. He scoops a handful from the sill, crunches some in his mouth, rubs the rest on the back of his neck. The air is charged and confused and Jeff becomes restless, his mind pacing the floor, his eyes shifting from wall to wall.

He is tired of the endless days of dreary rain, the too familiar sounds of the slumbering house, of reading about things he could never do again. He unstraps his wooden leg and hangs it on the gunrack and lies in bed, hoping a new dream would find him.

The window he had left open rattles loudly from the 5 a.m. inbound, and Jeff gets up to shut it. Garlands of stars are draped across the dome of the valley – a nice day lies ahead. He opens a drawer and takes out the new riflescope that his grandfather had intended to mount on the Savage. When he looks at the stars through the scope, they stop twinkling, and he sees that some are subtle shades of yellow and pink. Legions of peepers trill in the lowlands, beckoning.

He straps on the leg and gets dressed, then takes the rifle down and slides it into a leg-o'-mutton case. He packs a rucksack with a canteen, a flashlight, a knife and the scope. From the bottom notch of the gun rack he takes his walking stick, then goes downstairs.

His parents come into the kitchen as he packs a lunch. "I'm going to the gunsmith down in Antrim. I want to get the scope mounted on the Savage."

"Let's have some breakfast first and I'll take you," his father says. "Petry's shop won't be open for a couple of hours yet."

"I'm gonna walk. I already have my stuff packed."

"But that's a good 7 miles one way. You sure?"

"I'm sure," he replies, slinging the case over his shoulder. "I'll probably be back late."

"He'll probably be back late," repeats his mother.

They watch him walk across the moonlit yard and slip into the woods.

HE SETS OUT on a boyhood path through an elderberry patch, then takes a tram road that snakes across an oak flat. He finds the old cow path that connects to a dirt lane that runs down the hill. He crosses the highway and several train tracks, then slides down an embankment to the broad, smooth path that follows the river.

The swollen river hisses along in a straight stretch past a huge scrapyard where several antique steam locomotives await the torch, being replaced by the new diesel engines. He passes several farms, then the river curves gently to the west, flowing into the steep forested gorge. The valley lay before him, illuminated by an enormous yellow moon that shows the muscular shoulders of the mountains. His heart leaps at the aching beauty of it and his sudden insignificance, and although he cannot run, his spirit races along with the river's frenzied current.

Jeff walks steadily, watches the sky gray. Gauzy mists hang in the crowns of mottled sycamores and swirl above drowned islands. The river path is flooded ahead, and he crosses

the swampy slough to his right by stepping on grassy hummocks with his good leg and into the water with the other. A great blue heron rises up, and he watches it fly slowly across the river and set down again.

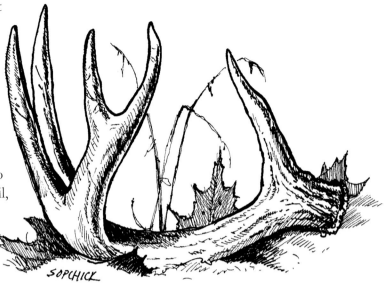

He has to climb a steep, slippery embankment to get to the railbed. He tries a deer trail, but it is too slick. Then he finds another route, pulling himself up on grapevines, but they have too much slack. Finally, Jeff crawls up a rocky gully. He slithers under the roots of a tilted sycamore and comes up onto the railbed on his elbows, pushing along with his good leg. Muddy and tired, he crosses the tracks and sits on an old wooden mine car and eats a sandwich as the valley awakens.

A locomotive chugs by, the engineer blows the whistle. Jeff liked trains, their familiar *click, clack, click, clack* as comforting as breaking waves must be to those who live along a shore. He thought about how all the favorite things of his life were made of combinations of wood, leather and steel; the big engines and ties and rails, his grandfather's rifle, the hiking staff and his bat, ball and glove, and now this artificial leg which just might serve well.

He continues on, the sun warming his back. He stops at a deep ravine that clefts the mountain, and watches a white torrent rush through a culvert. Its roar is the union of all wild voices from high in the uplands, the echoes of autumn's frenzy trapped in ice, buried under winter's snows, released as frothing waters by spring's sun, all of it coming around again as all life strives to.

Just beyond, he finds a big shed antler with five points, but the tallest tine is broken. Farther down the tracks, he finds the other – an exact match, but with all its points. He straps the antlers onto his rucksack and they click and rattle as he walks. He proceeds across the iron bridge into Antrim like some wild, grubby hermit coming down from the mountains after a hard winter.

THE AROMATIC BLEND of oils and solvents and lampblack smoke fills the gunsmith's shop. Petry, the smith, a longtime friend of Jeff's grandfather, drills and taps the receiver and mounts the scope.

Jeff then shoulders the rifle.

"This stock is too short and low for you, Jeff," Petry says. "You're a bigger guy than your Grandpa was. This stock is an older design. I can order an unfinished replacement stock for you for a couple of dollars. When it comes in, I can show you how to finish it."

"It's a deal; I like to work with wood," Jeff replies. "I made a gun rack in woodshop."

Jeff decides to take the other side of the river back. As he walks near a solitary engine idling at the edge of the village, the engineer yells down, "Hey buddy, if you need a lift, climb aboard."

Jeff climbs up the metal rungs with much difficulty.

"You're that fella I saw this morning," the engineer says. "Boy, those sure are nice antlers. I saw a big buck like that cross the tracks the first day of deer season. He came out of a ravine and swam out to a little island on the river. He's a smart one, all right. That rack would be perfect if that point wasn't broke!"

"I was perfect once," says Jeff, who then laughs at the engineer's quizzical expression. "I mean, I pitched a perfect game once, a no-hitter, before I hung up my glove."

"Looks like you still have a couple good innings left in you," the engineer says.

"Maybe," Jeff replies.

Just before the big bend, the engineer slows the locomotive to a crawl and Jeff hops off, but he doesn't fall the way he thought he would. It takes him a long time to cross the railroad bridge's narrow catwalk, one boot in front of the other, the rabid river below frothing and leaping against the trestles.

ALMOST HOME, he stops to rest at the base of Castle Rock. He's hot and thirsty, but his canteen is empty. Jeff looks up, way up, then leans forward against the rock, arms outstretched, palms and cheek pressed against the cool sandstone. He closes his eyes, feels the earth pulsing through the ancient rock, then realizes it is his own heart pushing back against his chest.

He considers climbing the rocks, confident he could, but instead takes the switchback up. On top, he drinks from the cold spring until his jaw hurts, then sits on the edge of an outcropping, legs dangling, looking up through the moonlit valley. In the distance, the angry river is a silver ribbon winding peacefully through the blue hills.

He comes down through the woods, sees the porch light, his parents in the kitchen drinking coffee. He is exhausted, but would rest up for tomorrow – baseball practice started after school Monday and he wanted to be ready.

The Compass Rose

TOM DROVE SLOWLY through the deserted campus and pulled in front of a dormitory, the headlights of his truck raking across a lone figure sitting on a wall. His grandson, Zach, waved, then jumped down.

Tom got out to stretch.

"Hey, Grandpa! 4:15, right on the dot."

"Hey yourself. How'd midterms go?"

"I'm still standin'. What's our agenda for today?"

"Well, the realtor's going to show us several properties that I narrowed down from some listings he sent. If we're lucky, we'll be hunting from our own camp come spring gobbler."

"Is there anything on your agenda about breakfast?"

"Could be, but you'll have to wait. There's some raisin cookies from your grandma in a bag on the back seat to tide you over."

They drove northwest for an hour and a half through the late winter darkness. It had been a tough winter, and the eyes of deer feeding near the roads glowed and blinked like fireflies.

They talked about hunting and guns and the past deer season, and the miles slipped by. Soon, the purple light of day shaped out steep, muscular hills, and on the outskirts of a small village, they pulled into a roadside diner where they were to meet the realtor.

They sat in a booth and ordered coffee. The older man studied the face of his grandson reading the menu and his own muted reflection in the window just behind the young man's shoulder, and was struck by their mutual resemblance. He noted, too, the bright, emergent vigor of youth, and his own paler figure fading into the background. Now that he had retired, he had been thinking about all the time he had to spend with his son and grandson, and wanted more than ever to secure a lifelong dream of owning a camp.

A silver SUV pulled in next to Tom's truck, and the realtor waved to them as he walked by the window.

"Tom and Zach, right?" said the realtor, shaking their hands. "Early birds!"

"He's the early bird," said Zach.

The realtor was a hunter, and had put much thought in trying to match them up with the right place. After breakfast he spread a map on an adjoining table and showed them the properties they would visit.

As the morning wore on, they worked their way through the listings, but nothing really captured their hearts. Perhaps they were expecting too much, Tom thought. The first place was too near other camps; the next, much too small. Another needed major work, and the last was too remote.

"There's one more at the far end of this hollow here, with lots of good hunting right out back," the realtor noted. "It's a bit over your budget, but the owner and his wife have an opportunity on a property in Florida, so there's some strong motivation to sell. It even has an old outbuilding that the owner uses for storage. The outbuilding was the original camp, until the current owner bought it all 20 years ago. He isn't a hunter, just wanted a place to relax on weekends. His wife didn't care for the old camp, so he built this nice cottage instead."

They turned off the dirt road only to have their progress halted by several trees that had blown down across the lane.

"We had a violent windstorm and some flooding here a couple days ago. We'll have to walk up from here, if you don't mind. The power is still out up here, too."

The sight of the devastation stopped them in their tracks. A massive double-trunked white pine had crashed through the cottage, smashing it as if it were made of matchsticks, the contents heavily water damaged.

"Wow!" exclaimed the realtor. "I'll have to call the owner and give him the bad news. It looks like a total loss."

While the realtor talked with the owner on his cellphone, Tom and Zach walked around the clearing and peered inside the old original camp at the edge of the woods. It was full of boxes and plastic storage bins and old furniture covered with drop cloths. Tom walked the perimeter of the building, scrutinizing every detail with his cabinetmaker's eye.

The realtor joined them on the porch.

"Well, I suppose I can't even list it as a fixer-upper," he said, "but if you're interested, it would be a great location to rebuild. Look there," he said, pointing to a flock of turkeys crossing a snowbank on the far side of the hollow.

"You have those birds trained to do that on cue," suggested Tom, and they all laughed.

ZACH'S FATHER CALLED the following week to tell Zach they had just bought the property. "We got a great deal on it. The owner wanted to move on and they reduced the price big time because the cottage was destroyed, and they accepted our first offer."

"So, we're going to build a new camp?" asked Zach.

"Nope. It's the old camp they used for storage that we want to restore. With the three of us working on it, we'll have it shipshape by late spring."

A FICKLE MARCH WIND swept up through the hollow, across the clearing and slammed the screen door behind them. Zach, his father and grandfather stood in the cobwebby gloom. It looked much larger now that it was empty, but appeared to be in bad repair.

"Where do we begin?" Zach wondered aloud.

"It's mostly just superficial," said his grandfather, "and looks worse than what it is. We've got to gut it, skin it and clean it down to bare bones. It'll be fairly simple to get the electric service restored here, and we'll contract the plumbing. Everything else we'll do ourselves."

Tom stayed at the camp, roughing it, and was joined on weekends by his son. They tore off the old aluminum siding to reveal rich brown planking that they stained and sealed. The supports were rock solid oak beams, salvaged from a downstate cigar factory and adapted to the builder's plan. The camp was plumb and level, and the tin roof needed only minor repairs. Tom was impressed by the attention to detail and skill of the builders, and noticed they had even situated the camp precisely on the cusp of the hollow where it caught the first rays of the sun as it rose over the hills.

They pulled the warped paneling from the walls and ripped out the mildewed patchwork carpet and successive layers of linoleum, uncovering a solid, narrow-planked floor black with varnish and grime. Tom worked on the windows, while Zach, who got away for a weekend, helped his father wire the camp.

After the spring term ended, Zach joined his grandfather at camp, and was amazed at the progress. The old cabinetmaker had installed a kitchen all by himself, and the only large task remaining was to sand and refinish the floors.

They took turns running a floor sander in what would be the living room, and the blackened varnish browned and became lighter yet as they worked their way down.

"There's a deer," said Zach.

"Where?" asked his grandfather, glancing out the window.

"Here, on the floor. And there's a turkey over there," he said, pointing to a nebulous shape.

"I see it now," Tom said, moving back and squinting.

He kneeled to examine it closer.

"It's some kind of design," he offered.

He ran a hand-sander lightly in an arc connecting the two animals and saw a curved, segmented border outlined in brass. He stepped off two paces north from the center and worked his way gently down through the varnish, exposing the profile of a bear.

"It's a compass rose," said Zach. "A design they used first on old maps to indicate the directions of the winds. It also was called a wind rose. Today, they're designs that orient direction. There's a huge one set in marble and granite in the library foyer at school."

"This one's about 9 feet across," said Tom. "We shouldn't sand it. Let's do it right and strip the varnish away."

They returned from the hardware store with a solvent and worked late, stopping whenever something new became visible. By midnight, they had revealed a squirrel, a running buck, a drumming grouse, a laurel bloom, a turtle, a fox and an oak-leaf cluster with acorns. They continued on around the large pattern until first light, uncovering a beechnut, a hickory leaf, songbirds, a gun and tracks, each crafted from an alternating palette of hardwoods. In the middle of the compass rose was a space that was slightly lower than the surrounding surface. A plaque, perhaps, that had been removed, or a final piece never completed.

It took several days to refinish the floors and restore and buff the compass rose. Getting it bright and clean late one evening, they applied a final coat of satin urethane, then turned in for the night.

Zach was awakened by his grandfather early the next morning.

"Rise and shine. This isn't a hunting camp until we do some hunting. The gobblers around here have been yodeling all week, especially that old boy on the other side of that knob. So, get your gear on and grab your gun, and let's have a go at him."

They took a deer trail that angled across the hollow, then circled around the knob and set up on the flat at first light. A towhee offered its sweet *Drink your tea* refrain, and was joined by a cardinal that repeated three long and clear notes of cheer.

Soon the woods filled with the waking songs of other birds. Tom added to that chorus with some gentle tree calls, then a few inquisitive yelps. The gobbler double-gobbled several times, and a short time later, they heard him fly down and the muffled plop when he landed.

Zach glanced over at his grandfather and saw the intensity in his steely eyes squinting above the facemask. Eyes that had known a thousand days in the woods. What hadn't he seen? What hadn't he shared with him of that time? Zach knew the camp was much more to him than a place from which to hunt: It was a stronghold against an ever-encroaching world; fertile ground where tradition and legend could root and bloom; a secure haven from which they could look back at an older time and envision days to come; a place where they could reflect and gain perspective of their lives in the world beyond by becoming, as hunters, an integral part of the natural world here.

A breeze nudged the strutting gobbler up and over the lip of the flat like a black balloon come to earth from some faraway place, drifting and dragging through the big timber, its long beard a frayed tether. Then the black orb came closer and pirouetted and danced with the gold shotgun bead, and in the instant when the two overlapped and the gobbler's head rose from its display, Zach shot.

They stopped at the edge of the clearing below camp to admire the gobbler once more, as well as the beauty of the spring woods and how the camp blended in so unobtrusively.

"I think I have a name for our camp," said Zach. "Let's call it 'Wyndwood,' spelled with a 'Y' to give it an old-timey feel. It was the wind that steered us to this place, and the compass rose points out the direction of the winds."

"Wyndwood?" said his grandfather. "I like it. We have one more job today, and then we're finished."

Using a sheet of newspaper and a carpenter's pencil, Tom made a rubbing of the empty space in the center of the compass rose, then placed the rubbing face down onto a piece of leftover birch veneer and burnished it down with a coin, transferring, then scribing the oval. He cut it out with a jigsaw and sanded the edges until it fit the vacant space precisely.

It took another day to finish. In neat script, Zach lettered "Camp Wyndwood" onto the oval, and beneath it, the contour of the surrounding hills with curvilinear lines above, stylized in the way they illustrated winds on ancient maps. He then burned in that design with a wood-burner and varnished it.

"All done" said Zach.

"Beautiful," said Zach's father.

"Welcome to Camp Wyndwood," Tom smiled, and they all shook hands.

THEY WOULD COME TO KNOW the winds in these uplands: The discordant moans they made as they moved through myriad tree cavities across the flat, like aboriginal instruments from another time; a summer breeze in the hemlocks out back, like the hushed voices and whispers of others long gone, who knew and loved these same woods; the steady roar of a frigid northwest winter wind barreling through the night like a dark runaway freight; the playful gusts racing along old tram roads on golden October afternoons.

They would be ushered along by winds of every temperament, and on raw autumn eves after a long day in the woods, they would be lulled to sleep by the soft snare drum chatter of wind-whipped birch branches on the tin roof.

CROSSINGS

Stone Wall Grouse

DEEP OCTOBER, and the uplands are bursting with activity. A ruffed grouse fills its crop with fox grapes, fern tips and a few winterberries, while a trio of gobblers diligently rake the leaf litter across a narrow bench for beechnuts and acorns. Down in the hollow, a buck grates a striped maple at the crossing of two trails, as a porcupine lumbers across a seep and then climbs into a hemlock cavity to rest.

The lives of many wild creatures will cross in the woods this day, including those that travel paths unseen. The aerial flights of blue jays – transporting scores of acorns – crisscross the ridgelines. The route of a gray squirrel as it spirals in stop-and-go motion down an oak trunk. A red-tailed hawk, kiting in the wind, suddenly tucking its wings and dropping through an opening in the canopy, neatly plucking the squirrel from the trunk. Not all paths that meet cross entirely.

Like the thunderous flight of ruffed grouse, most encounters with wildlife are brief, but much may linger. The short essays that follow are impressions and temporal images gleaned from some of those concurrences. They are akin to plein-air paintings, small images painted on location in one sitting. They stand on their own, without need of expansion or further expression.

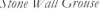

Swan Song

I'M ON MY deer stand at the junction of a deep hollow that intersects a great river valley. Here, tucked away in this fortress of boulders, I'm sheltered from the sleet and wind howling down in the valley.

At midmorning, I hear the high-pitched *woo-ho, woowoo, woo-ho* of tundra swans, and then spot a flock of nine birds that veers into the hollow. Their ranks break and they descend until they are directly above me, suspended like an immense mobile turning in the wind as if for my enjoyment alone.

At first, it seems the swans are only resting a bit in this protected notch, realigning their order, but when dense fog billows into the hollow, I wonder if they had made a wrong turn, having become disoriented upon losing the landmark of the fog-bound river.

They speak to each other continuously in tones soft and harsh, their cries echoing, and I sense impatience and even argument in their wild voices. As they shuffle positions, their great wings fan the ragged mists and I am moved by their pale beauty. They hover like angels convened above holy ground and this hollow is, in my heart, such a province.

The vortex of birds becomes silent for a few

moments, and then an urgent clamber rises, a wild beckoning that speaks of shimmering bays and dark rivers and seamless tundra. So loud and compelling are their cries that could I sprout wings, I would fly from these rocks and join them.

They leave this sanctuary, quickly reassembling into a V formation, and are swallowed up by the scudding clouds.

A few moments later, five deer usher up out of the mists, little more than wild vapors themselves in their gray winter coats. They file toward the ridge, then stand perfectly still, tails clamped down tight, barely distinguishable from the deer-shaped boulders. Only one offers a clear shot, and when my rifle roars, it collapses where it stands.

Both swans and deer have been following the topography of these hills for ages. I wonder if the deer were paused down below, listening as I had, to the swans. Did they also seek meaning in those alien voices, if only for portent of danger? Had they waited for these other-worldly beings to depart before they continued on with the press of the day?

While dressing out the mature doe, I admire its dark face and the sheen of its salt-and-pepper coat. I notice its hooves are worn and scratched like my boots. We are travelers of these same rocky slopes, these deer and I, and I'm privileged to share this journey.

I've hunted this hollow for decades, and recall images of other hunts, still bright and fresh in memory. I know, however, that the progression of all my days in this timeless valley is of little more note than a pale feather falling through fog; my presence, as enduring as a few hairs left on a rutted deer trail.

I drag the deer through laurel and over rocks. Fingers of mist mend our anonymous passage.

Plain Brown Wrapper

A HEN TURKEY walks into the field and begins to feed. She angles across the undulating furrows, appearing from a distance like a brown jug riding the waves of brown waters.

A trio of crows, full of crow mischief, begins to harass her. They each, in turn, dive and swoop, finishing with acrobatic flourishes above her, but she ignores their antics until one flies too near and she flails her wings. This response elicits further torment, for now, the gang has a game. After several minutes of their foolery, she resumes feeding and the crows fly off, a replica flock of shadows beneath them, skimming the ribs of the corduroy field.

The hen continues on, until she is only yards from the edge of the woods where I wait by a scrape line with my bow. The buff tips of her feathers wrap her dark umber form in pale contours, not unlike the edges of the furrows that catch the light and define the topography of the field. Suddenly, she stands erect, alert and unmoving, like a statue fashioned from mud and grit. She sprints away then, darting into the brushy edge, and I wonder why she isn't with other members of an autumn flock.

A veil of high gray clouds eases in, and I still-hunt across a flat thick with grapevines. I flush a grouse, and in some choppings, scare out what sounds like a bear crashing away, but turns out to be just a fat and grizzled groundhog racing to its den beneath a stump. Farther along, I stop at a spring seep that trickles into a tabletop-sized pool and kneel to study the faint rosette tracks left by a bobcat in the exposed silt. Glancing up, my heart skips a beat when I spot a patch of tawny brown moving through the brush. It's a deer, and my pulse takes off again when I see it's a buck, but just out of range. I lose sight of him, then catch only the occasional flick of his tail as he disappears. Late in the afternoon, returning to my stand at the field, I find a single brown feather left by the hen, and when I turn it, a thin wash of iridescent hues reflects the softening light. In the sallow light of day's end, the woods and fields take on the sepia tones of an old, yellowing photograph. Nature's simple and subtle offerings this day have been a welcome respite from the glitz and glimmer of the everyday world.

For only a very few days, late autumn takes on a rich, warm patina that is evident in burnished antlers and the sheen of a grouse fan, and also can be seen in the satiny gloss of oak leaves and brush-whipped gunstocks and in the oily glow of acorns and old boot leather.

These select November days are a gift, a special edition of days that come bound, like the hen turkey herself, in a plain brown wrapper. These are days to be enjoyed at once, every minute relished, for that patina soon fades, giving way to the iron shadows and dried bones of winter, wrapped in white and brittle parchment.

Transgression

IN THE DIM HOLLOW, a ghostly shape appears and reappears as I weave my way down through the oaks and corridors of grapevines. I think it might be the white belly hair of a dead deer, or a dense growth of bracket fungus, and it is not until I am upon it that I see it is a profusion of pale feathers scattered on and around a stump; a veil of feathers finely beaded with dark pearls of blood; the plumage a sizeable bird.

To my surprise, these are the feathers of a bird of prey. I gather a bouquet of breast feathers marked with faint rusty chevrons, long dark-banded tailfeathers, lofty semi-plumes snagged on greenbrier. I can hear the sound of the chase when I wave several barred primaries near my ear. The familiar markings tell me it is a Cooper's hawk.

Searching through the pile, I cannot find a strip of flesh, nor knot of viscera, not a taloned foot nor any bones, save the eyeless head with its steely-blue scimitar beak open yet in defiant scream.

But what has slain this hunter, yanked the feathers from its wings, plucked its breast?

The hawk might have been found dead and scavenged on the spot. Almost one-fourth of Cooper's hawks examined in a recent study had healed fractures, mainly of the wishbone, suffered in violent collisions with tree trunks and limbs in their intense pursuit of prey. Those found dead in the woods may have perished from impalement on a stick, from starvation after breaking a wing or, mercifully, from a broken neck. It is not easy business being a hawk, and sometimes, the hunter becomes the hunted.

To me, it seems a transgression of sorts when one bird of prey kills another for sustenance. It may be that I recognize them as vigilant hunters charged with the difficult work of keeping wildlife populations in check, as if they were all allies united solely for that cause. The cold facts are, though, that Cooper's hawks prey on kestrels, while large owls will sometimes take smaller owls and hawks.

There are no codes or statutes in the laws of survival, no fast rules of allegiance, only dictums spare and broad, beautifully ruthless, without subclauses or addendums: the strong shall survive; hunt to live; seize every opportunity.

Several yards from the stump, a disruption in the leaves indicates a place of struggle. Among the feathers there, a soft feather from the wing of a great horned owl, silent when I wave it. The owl might have taken the hawk from its perch in the night, or possibly as the hawk mantled a songbird it had killed. Owls with young to feed will hunt during the day; a shadow of night passing through the light of day.

Shadows slide up the oaks until only the topmost branches ignite with the last rays of the setting sun, then stand out as sharply etched lines against the evening sky. The hollow fills with cold air. Colors drain from the landscape, blending to a single violet-gray, and the white feathers glow incandescently, even whiter than a deer's tail.

From within the pines, an inquiry: *Hoo-who? Who? Hoo, who?*

"Not me," I reply, dropping the feathers. "It was you. It was you."

The Clearing

THE WEATHERMAN promised a daylong rain. Undeterred by a few raindrops, I set out for a day of bowhunting anyway. A colorful autumn has surged to this point in November. With leaf-fall almost complete, the muscle of the land is revealed: glossy-coated bucks giving chase to does, bears piling on fat, turkeys gleaning the leaf litter, gray squirrels skittering through the canopy along grapevine tightropes. I move slowly, eyes always searching. Every swaying fern, shift of shadow, drifting leaf is noted. But rain was forewarned, and now the drizzle gains strength.

I work my way down the slope and take shelter under a shelf ledge just as the rain intensifies. I wonder if a hunter of old has ever done the same from this very spot. The overhang is the size of a small porch awning and I take a seat on a stack of stones. Water drips from the decorative fringe of ferns hanging over the edge of the rock.

First things first, and that means a brunch of a thick meatloaf sandwich and bread-and-butter pickles. A gob (western Pennsylvanian for whoopie pie) is washed down with hot coffee.

Why save dessert for later?

Since my last visit a year ago, a huge oak has fallen just below, opening up a clearing, offering an unobstructed view.

Among long yellow splinters are half shells of rotted bark scribed on the smooth side by insects, like shards of ancient pottery with a cuneiform-like writing. The iconic profile of a distant

ridge, a flat silhouette in the diffused air, is framed by the slant of tilted boughs, a watercolor painting of sorts, within a watercolor. The air grows chill, and I can sense a slight shifting to November's cold solemnity.

It is a good time and place to take stock of some recent projects, but my review is cut short by a handsome gray fox that threads its way through the branches of the oak windfall. It pads up the long trunk like a dog on a sidewalk, then jumps off and continues uphill. A while later, a small flock of turkeys skirts the clearing, raking clots of leaves back with powerful feet and legs, quickly backing up to claim mast from the exposed ground. I enjoy their barely audible flock talk, their soft clucks and purrs, the piping of the young birds.

The far-off rattle of a train keeps time with the patter of water that runs off a root on the ceiling of the overhang.

The autumn woods radiate beyond their physical perimeter, permeating the bones and mind of the hunter. I clear a like place in my thoughts, an opening void of obstructions; no need to think, to ponder, evaluate, or create.

This is a place to pause and revel in solitude, to simply exist. Like a fox.

Flow

MAKING MY WAY to my deer stand by moonlight, I disturb a flock of roosting turkeys. With every few steps, a bird pitches out, powerful wings slapping branches as they clear the canopy. I wait a few minutes then creep silently along, but others rocket out, slicing across the moon, and sailing down into the hollow.

My stand is in the contorted fork of a windfall, one trunk serving as a stool-height seat, the other as a shooting rest. I hope that the commotion of the turkeys didn't alarm the deer too badly. When I put on my gloves, a grouse flushes from the opposite end of the windfall, curving into a hemlock hideaway.

Right at daybreak, several deer round the steep hillside below. They flow through the thicket beautifully, slipstreaming through the maze of vines and saplings with the same undulating grace of dolphins stitching a seam between breakers. None offers a shot.

There's a great glut of grapes this year, and everywhere robins argue, chase and gorge. Three gobblers gobbling up grapes swing wide around my position. Other birds round the hillside; a downy woodpecker pecks at a goldenrod gall while several chickadees flit and cling acrobatically to milkweed stalks, unloosing a few silky parachutes that lend a festive air to their progress. When a line of geese flies up the hollow, I realize that everything I have seen is moving clockwise around the hill, as if I were standing at a pivotal hub with the forest streaming around.

Later in the morning, a countermovement begins; the Earth coming round the other way. In fits and starts, a red squirrel comes down the shooting rest trunk until it is only inches from my arm. It detours by leaping to a sapling and springing back onto the trunk. Next, a long-legged button buck with cowlicks on its forehead emerges from the witch hazel. It stops and tests the air, time and again, then continues on into the thicket, only yards from my stand.

Two more deer pick their way uphill, weaving a circuitous course through the grape tangles. At my shot, everything momentarily slows, commencing then as I make my way to the large doe stretched out on the leaves. After dressing out the deer, I wash my knife in a seep that trickles from high up the slope. Robins splashing in the laddered pools freeze when a red-tailed hawk passes low overhead. The hawk wheels, and a brace of gray squirrels scrambles to the opposite side of a nearby oak. The press of life here urges me to finish, to hitch to the flow. I tie on my rope and begin the long drag around the hill.

The aroma of Swiss venison steaks rises from the kitchen, drifts through the dining room, rounds the corner and wafts up the stairs to my studio, much in the way the deer worked their way up the hillside. I am reminded that there is no halt in the order of things, no adjournment, no cessation; only a shifting, a transference of momentum.

Once again, I am stirred to move. I lift the lid, ladle the juices over the steaks, and wait.

Upland Aesthetic

I HEAR the nervous *quit-quit* of a grouse coming from a nearby windfall. At my next step, it thunders out low and away, shielded by a wall of beech saplings. I wait a few seconds, then ease ahead. When the second of the pair rockets out, it collides with a swarm of 7½s from my 20-gauge. In hand, I can feel the stout shafts of its folded wings, like the ribs of a collapsed umbrella. It's a fine cock grouse, and I lay it on the log, wings outspread, and sit to admire it.

The grouse's plumage is an artful translation of November's leafy carpet, in somber hues reminiscent of translucent frost on logs and the earthy tones of stumps; even the fiery bits of orange above the eyes are like the few bright leaves that linger in the uplands. Each grouping of feathers is of a different decorative pattern; the subtle chestnut barring on its throat becomes progressively heavier and bolder down through the breast to a stark black and white on the flanks.

Rows of pale, stippled hearts adorn its back and the bars on its black-banded fan are slightly blurred, like soft shadows cast by delicate vines. Complex arrangements of dark and light graphic shapes align to create larger, bolder patterns on its nape and wings. The signature ruff encircling its neck glistens rich blue-black like my gun's barrels. This diverse conglomeration of designs combines as a single entity of exquisite beauty, in the way each visual element of the autumn woods collectively forms a greater and deeper aesthetic.

Form follows function, however, and the grouse's plumage is the pinnacle of camouflage; showing the incredible depth of lights within lights and shadows within shadows, effective at both long, intermediate and close ranges. When a grouse takes off, it is as if a small wedge of the woods itself were suddenly shot from the ground, and is no less startling.

The ruff's first line of defense is the very nature of its habitat, an obstacle course of brush, vines and fallen timber that impede a predator's progress, giving the bird time to escape. If a grouse senses that it is has not been seen, it will often sit tight until a threat passes. Reluctant to fly, it often runs or sneaks off. But when push comes to shove, and flight is inevitable, the explosive percussion of its takeoff interjects sound before sight. Because we try to pinpoint the origin of a loud sound, we fail to track the flight of the bird, and by then, it is gone.

Even experienced grouse hunters occasionally fall to this ruse. Once airborne, a grouse may curve around the trunk of a nearby tree to interrupt the line of its flight. Some say this is an instinctive move, not tactical ploy, but I missed one grouse on three occasions that seemed particularly adept at this evasive maneuver.

With tail fanned and wings blurring like smoke, a grouse in flight is a beautiful thing. It is almost impossible to find an image of a grouse in an awkward or clumsy pose, whether perching, drumming, budding or nesting. Even as it lies fallen on the leaves, it possesses a royal demeanor.

No bird could better serve as the state game bird of Penn's Woods. Those not oriented to its true beauty may initially dismiss it as a brown chicken-like bird, but the ruffed grouse deserves a closer look, and once set to flight, it becomes a living, visible charge that sets to beating the wild heart of the uplands.

Spark

MANY OUTDOORSMEN RECALL certain passages in life by what guns they were using at the time, and although it was very long ago, I remember my pop gun as well as any gun I've owned since.

It was 1959, and I was 8 years old. Bored with being indoors one rainy November day, I went rabbit hunting with my trusty pop gun in a nearby field. Not knowing how to hunt rabbits, I waded through the sodden weeds and took a stand, hoping that an unsuspecting cottontail would hop by. Occasionally, I would work the lever to keep my gun at full charge. The chill rain beaded on the well-oiled gun and seeped through my red hooded sweatshirt.

I stood there a long time. A neighbor who came out on her back porch to shake out a dust mop told me to go home.

"You'll get pneumonia," she hollered.

"I'm hunting rabbits," I yelled back.

This hunt, which began in the spirit of play, took on another guise when older forces began to stir. Hunting is not without protocol, and the Earth offered up its contract — one that I have been bound to all my days since.

I reveled in the solitude, and with senses raw and feral, I seized upon every nuance of the landscape. Borne on the damp air was the fragrance of leaf litter and the sharp spice of crabapples. The weed field was no longer that green and shimmering place of summer adventures, but worn and somber, more to my liking. Branches tossed and clicked in the wind, and I could feel even then the pull of an autumnal tide from the fog-shrouded hills beyond.

The Spanish needles and burdock burrs stuck to my sweatshirt were like medals pinned there for braving the elements. Soaked and shivering, I continued my vigil, but then a sixth sense prodded me to move up through the field – to seek, to hunt.

I took only a few steps when a cottontail bounded away. My heart leapt, as if I had never seen a rabbit before, but perhaps I was seeing for the first time its true wild nature while sensing the same in myself. Out here, both the rabbit and I had assumed different roles.

I followed the white orb of its bobbing tail through the tangles and fired, the pop gun sounding a weak *blaat* that was embarrassing in its benign suggestion of a shot.

I walked back through a long swale of broomstraw.

Everything had changed. Once home, I put the toy gun away.

It is a spark that must ignite the hunter's flame, and for many that spark was the white-hot ember of a rabbit's tail streaking through a weed patch. The fuel that feeds the hunter's fire, though, is a complex blend of things both common and personal, a combustible of such volatility and endurance that once ignited, burns brightly throughout, and sometimes beyond, a hunter's days.

Banquet

AT MY SHOT, the deer bolted downhill in a death sprint, nose-diving in a spray of fresh powder. It was a long way down, and would be a tough drag back up, but I was in no hurry; it was early in the morning and I still had my buck tag to fill, and this was a good spot with plenty of sign.

After tagging and gutting the deer, I trimmed some strips of yellow fat from the ruby-red hams and draped them on the roots of a nearby windfall. I dragged the deer 5 yards uphill, stamped out a stand in the snow and settled in on a log seat.

Within minutes, a band of chickadees was reconnoitering in the limbs above the steaming gut pile. Feeding in typical chickadee fashion, they would drop down in a steady exchange of singles and pairs, picking up morsels then flitting back up to a perch. Another flock of chickadees arrived and discovered the strips of fat, and I was entertained by the yo-yo action of the feeding birds. Other festive diners joined the winter banquet: both red- and white-breasted nuthatches, a downy woodpecker, brown creepers and tufted titmice. A trio of blue jays crashed the party, but stayed only a short time. I was jolted from my reverie when I caught the movement of several deer in the grapevines below, almost forgetting why I was here.

It was of no real matter, though, I enjoy

watching birds as much as hunting deer. Birding is a tonic for the soul, has a high learning curve and sharpens my woods eyes. It's no coincidence that the very best deer hunters I know also are ardent birders, lightning quick at picking up and identifying the slightest movement.

Birding enhances the hunting experience. When things are slow, I watch birds, and in their movements, sense the rhythm of the woods. I bristle when some dismiss this as a waste of time, and I think it somewhat sad to narrow one's interest to only the prize at hand and not the total experience, like watching only the central character in a movie, oblivious to the actions and dialogue of the supporting cast.

A few chickadees flew over to where my deer lay, and after bravely eyeballing me at close range, they alighted on the deer and began pecking at the rim of the cavity. One even perched on the spreader stick that propped the chest open for cooling, peeling threads of meat from the ribs, its pale breast washed in crimson, so unlike the portrayals of birds to which we are so accustomed.

Their voraciousness reminded me of big, white-backed African vultures wriggling up inside the cavity of a wildebeest, shouldering in hard, arguing and gorging before the lion returned to its kill.

When I left five hours later, the birds were still at it. I wrestled the deer across the deep, ribbed drifts of the field, across this snowy veldt, feeling more connected, more integral to the workings of the wild by having providing a banquet for the day.

Scrimshaw

LATE WINTER, 1762. Large, wet flakes fall straight down in the windless woods. A long hunter snugs down the greasy cow's knee protecting the flintlock action of his longrifle. The rifle is carved in a relief of wandering vines sprouting tendrils of inlaid silver wire, and the patch box is engraved with the cycle of a waxing and waning moon. His powder horn is scrimshawed with the storied map of his days, as is his weathered face.

He follows a pair of braided deer tracks leading over a ridge into newly charted country, the fringe of a vast forest of enormous chestnut and poplar, cherry, beech and oak. The diffused light of late afternoon reflects falsely from above, and he thinks perhaps he walks in the light of another time that lingers here from days when no man such as him, or any man, hunted these fabled woods.

The longhunter's gut pinches with hunger, and he dreads the thought of another meager supper of gritty johnnycake and jerky, so tough and contorted, it resembles crude utensils more than food.

He slides among the great trunks, casting no shadow, making no sound. The snow eases to a few errant flakes and he rests on one knee, trying to conjure a deer among the tawny trunks of a windfall. His thumb crooked on the flintlock's hammer seems more a fleshy extension of the hammer itself than thumb, poised there always as it is, ready to set in motion the awesome power of the rifle, and this he does when a bedded deer stands, shaking a blanket of snow from its back.

At the shot, the deer's legs scissor, front then hind, and it collapses into its bed as if it had suddenly decided to rest again. The hunter emerges from the cloud of rifle smoke like some lesser god surveying for life or death, or blood on the snow.

While dressing out the deer, he notes that the curious topography of the entrails is not unlike that of these very hills – undulating hillocks, gentle hollows, domed mountains, deep clefts – a landscape within as well as without. As he works, steam rises from the laddered ribs and mixes with the vapor of his own breath like kindred spirits united, ascending then as one.

The hunter sits within the half shell of a stump, turning a skewer of loin slices on the small, tight fire before him. When the meat chars slightly, he begins to eat, his stomach snatching each offering like a greedy hand. Ever vigilant, he watches the gloomy gaps between the trees and listens for the odd sound beyond the crackling flames.

As one would make an entry in a journal, he scrimshaws a copse of tall trees onto his powder horn and marks the date. Soon he nods, luxuriating with the satisfaction known only to a hunter with a full belly before a fire, the howling world held momentarily at bay.

T HE PAINTING, *Moonlit Trail – Penn's Woods Bison*, illustrates a herd of bison in western Pennsylvania, often referred to as "Westsylvania." There is no archaeological evidence to prove bison existed here, even though towns, rivers, creeks and mountains have the word "buffalo" in their names. Tales abound of herds inhabiting areas throughout the Commonwealth, of sightings and hunts. But not a single shred of concrete evidence has survived, and that is unusual for megafauna that were purported to exist only a few centuries past. When it comes to understanding nature, it is important to not take everything for granted.

In 1681, King Charles II of England bestowed upon Quaker William Penn a large tract of New World land as repayment of a debt to Penn's father. Young William wanted to call it Sylvania, Latin for woodland, but the king had it chartered as Pennsylvania, or "Penn's Woods."

Centuries later, Penn's Woods remains 58 percent forested with 17 million acres of diverse habitats populated by innumerable native species. This accordant landscape of forests, farmlands and waters has a long and storied natural heritage that was assembled by generations of sportsmen, naturalists and woodsmen, and magnified by myriad artists and writers.

So compelling is Pennsylvania's wild and scenic beauty and rich wildlife history, that if one spends a great deal of time exploring its diverse environs, spirits or buried magic of the past just might emerge to be gratified. Perhaps even a herd of bison in late winter grazing on a river plain.

Moonlit Trail – Penn's Woods Bison

Forever from Here

YOU MAY KNOW a place like this. While hunting or hiking, you always go out of your way to stop there: a rock outcropping high in the uplands, where you can see into the valley and beyond, where distant mountains recede like the cobalt-blue hills on hand-painted china, where sky and land blend as one into the atmosphere.

Breathe deep; now exhale, slowly. Again. Now release. The view commands your full attention.

An unobstructed view of a deeply rolling landscape is a satisfying reprieve from the claustrophobic proximities of daily living. We open up, sensing an immediate change in our demeanor as our eyes race to distant horizons. It is easier to understand our station in life when viewing a grand panorama than gazing up at the heavens, into the incomprehensible infinite. And it alters us in profound and sometimes personal ways.

Our forested ridges have few windows that allow unobstructed views, but I know of several such places. They are not the scenic overlooks of touristy waysides, but remote points that demand rigorous climbing to reach, places without signs and railings or the scrawls of vandals.

My favorite place with a view is a remote outcropping of sandstone, scarred and weathered, with a tiered seat of rocks. To get to it, I must follow a long,

circuitous deer trail through thick laurel for some distance, if I approach from on top. The climb from below, up through the boulders, is equally arduous. Either way, the effort is worth it when I emerge from the twisted gray laurel snags dwarfed by the elements and charred, lightning-struck oaks, stepping out onto the mossy clefts and finally, into the open. The world does not unfold, mile upon mile, but is suddenly, startlingly, all there at once.

From here, I have looked down on the shoulders of passing hawks and vultures, listened as five different gobblers opened up almost within the same instant; watched, mesmerized, as a wall of snow seemed to inch its way across the great expanse, then sweep in with a sudden and blinding fury. At other times, I have sat here and thought of others who have stood here through the ages, humbled by the view, thinking thoughts not unlike my own, and of those with eyes yet wilder: bobcat and bear, coyote and raven.

THREE CENTURIES previous, and the vast forest beyond the outcropping is much different than now. The deep hollow below brims with hemlocks and white pines. The distant hills are free of the scars of rights-of-way and roads. No towers with blinking lights or blights of windmills dot the ridgelines. The hand of man, although present, has not yet wrought wholesale destruction. No sounds of plane or train, or the rumble of commerce disturb the lilting birdsong that bubbles up from below.

The dark forest grows darker yet as late summer storm clouds gather in the west, moving into the valley with careful deliberation, like a herd of elk filtering from the black timber into a clearing. The air is heavy and sweet, and three native hunters seek shelter under the overhang where they will wait out the storm. A raven croaks and knocks as it passes by; one of the native hunters mimicking its call exactly.

Leaves settle and all is motionless when a sudden blade of lightning cleaves the sky, arcing horizontally, heating and compressing air that explodes outward in a tremendous crash that rolls far down the valley. The concussive force is deafening beneath the overhang, and the hunters startle, then laugh. The bloated sky sags and collapses in a deluge, while the hunters peer through the silver curtains of rain that define the rock shelter's perimeter.

They sit on their haunches patiently, without speaking, having waited out storms before, and this one seems stalled in the uplands. One hunter picks up a charred stub from an old fire and begins to draw on the flat belly of the overhang as the others watch. He draws a graphic, angular raven, beak agape, wings crooked, holding the zigzag line of a lightning bolt. The others admire and remark at his skill. The one who imitated the raven earlier runs a series of raven *knocks, kraas and quorks* and then says the raven brought the storm, that it carried lightning in its claws and thunder in its belly.

ONE HUNDRED FIFTY years pass, and another hunter moves up the slope below the overhang. Her eyes are yellow-green, expressionless, the pupils contracting and dilating as she walks through pools of sunlight and shadow. The mountain lion winds upward around slides of talus, mouth opened slightly, a glint of teeth showing between black lip and bristling whiskers. The great cat is the tawny color of the rocks, indistinguishable from them when she pauses. She walks up the trunk of an enormous white pine that, after three centuries, had let loose from its sentinel post on the ridge. She pauses by the broad span of the pine's root mass, still clutching rocks larger than the lion.

The cat cups her ears toward a faint shuffling in the leaves and freezes at the approach of a whitetail doe following a trail around the root mass. Sinewy muscles gather as she crouches, the black tip of her tail twitching slightly.

When the doe is but a few steps past, the lion leaps, gathers her feet impossibly on the vertical face of a boulder and launches again onto the back of the deer, jaws clamping down on the back of its neck. In a few moments, it is over. Soon after, she shears and plucks the hair from behind the ribs, where she begins to feed.

After caching the carcass, she climbs atop the overlook and rests, licking, luxuriating in the slanting light of the sun. All seems peaceful, but beyond the farthest pale blue mountain, the woods echo with the steady thud of iron chunking into wood as settlers fell the primeval forest.

I often imagine about life here; the cougar, native elk, wolf and even the bison that might have filtered into this part of Penn's Woods. And I wonder about creatures and plants before that time, because of my discovery of a large section of a scale tree from millions of years ago, down by the creek. It is not hard to imagine the hollow filled with 100-foot-high, fern-like scale trees and the loud clatter of dragonflies with 2½-foot wingspans.

SPEND ANY TIME frequenting an overlook and sooner or later you're bound to see several turkey vultures soaring elegantly within the spiraling thermals, or "kettles" of rising air as the land warms. Look closer though, as it might be its other New World cousin, the black vulture. Black vultures are more compact and hold their wings flat, while turkey vultures show a V-shape, or dihedral confirmation.

Turkey vultures can be identified in flight by their contorted soaring – rocking side to side, an aerial maneuver that varies the amount of lift on each wing. This allows them to fly lower as they search for a meal with their amazing sense of smell, skimming over treetops and undulating terrain where the air is turbulent. Opportunistic black vultures often will be seen higher, flying above the turkey vultures. Often when turkey vultures locate a food source and begin to feed, the more aggressive black vultures muscle in, driving the turkey vultures off.

The turkey vulture is a true master of the wind. I can watch them soar for hours, turning, dishing, silvery undersides of their wings catching the light. And maybe a strange moment of vertigo when they hold steady in the air, motionless, waiting patiently, waiting so beautifully paused in the air for the spinning earth below to bring round its dead.

THIS ROCKY BASTION is home to other creatures, too. The handsome eastern woodrat is a secretive resident that nests here within the flat shelves, an unobtrusive nocturnal denizen of this sandstone keep. It shares the outcropping with timber rattlers, which enjoy the dry southern exposure and the numerous chambers ideal for den sites. On occasion in winter, I've seen coyote tracks leading right up to the edge of the precipice. I like to imagine them howling and yipping, yodeling their music to the world from this point, beneath the star-smeared dome of night.

AUTHOR STEPHEN BODIO, in his book, *Edges of the Wild*, wrote, "New people say the word spiritual a lot. They have never looked long into any void." Lately, there has been much in every branch of the media about spirituality, self-awareness, inner-focus, finding the child within, living in the moment, and lots of other gobbledygook. Centered gurus spout how to gain awareness by proxy, not practice. Be it steaks or spiritualism, they want it neatly packaged and handed to them. Who has time to sit on a rock and think?

While staring deep into a landscape you will at first dwell upon the trees and rocks, clouds and wind, but it is the ability to see so much, all of it together, that is so satisfying. Look hard and long enough, though, and your view within may be as deep and revealing as the one without. You can see forever from here.

Meadow Magic

A LOW-LYING HAZE obscures much of the meadow, and only the tallest weeds poke through it. I come here from time to time, to draw and to hunt. Last deer season, I killed a fat buck from this very seat on the dead split-trunked white pine that had fallen into the field. The temperature that day was zero. Today, deep in the folds of August, it's balmy and humid. One of the trunks on the windfall is slightly higher than the other, making for a comfortable, elevated seat, like sitting on a bleacher.

The meadow is an old, former pasture, steadily being reclaimed by a diverse succession of grasses, weeds, shrubs and trees. The perimeter is indistinct, the edges blending with the encroaching woods. On the northern boundary, is a selectively cut, almost impenetrable woodlot grown thick with raspberries and blackberries. Near the center of the field, a rock outcrop is surrounded by black locust and staghorn sumac. The meadow slopes down to a small, lazy creek which describes its eastern boundary. Beyond the stream is a hillside of some of the oldest and most picturesque white oaks I've ever seen.

Along the creek are peppermint, pokeweed and the showy purple flowers of Joe-Pye weed. Stockades of teasel defend the remnants of an old foundation at the far corner. Turk's cap lillies stand out against dark pines. Chicory, black-eyed Susans and butter-and-eggs add more color, while thistle, mullein and milkweed tower over all. A well-used deer trail winds through a patch of goldenrod.

I call this diverse acreage Windfall Meadow, and intend to spend the day here if I can bear the heat. Better this than the 80-degree difference of my last visit.

QUEEN ANNE'S LACE, also known as wild carrot, is a common Old World plant that grows in the drier reaches of the meadow. In some fields, it grows so profusely that during late summer, entire fields appear to be covered with a continuous white-lace tablecloth. Because Queen Anne's lace dominates an open space so aggressively, it's also known as "Devil's Plague."

Hundreds of tiny snow-white flowers rise on stems of varying lengths from a common center and form a slightly convex plane in an arrangement called an umbel. After blossoming, the umbel infolds, cup-like, and takes on another name, "bird's nest weed." In the very center of the white blooms, on its own stem, blooms a single, indigo flower. An old story is that the dark spot represents a drop of

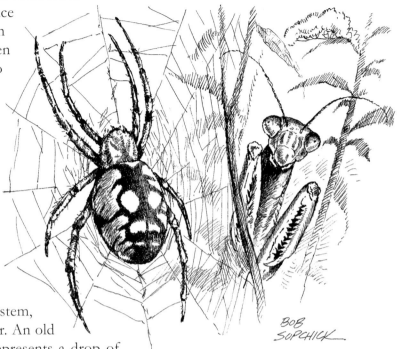

blood that fell from the finger of Queen Anne, an expert lace-maker, when she pricked her finger. The dark bloom, though, is a target bloom, a decoy insect thought to attract pollinators.

A CONFRONTATION between two predators, especially those of different species, makes for an exciting contest of skill and power, especially when the battle takes place inches away. While drawing a yellow-and-black garden spider working on her web, I notice after a few minutes, that I am not the only pair of eyes watching her. From an adjacent goldenrod stalk a praying mantis – also a female – is intensely eyeballing the spider, and I believe that my lovely model soon will become brunch for the formidable mantis.

As predicted, the mantis leaps into the web and in that classic, lightning-like move the mantis is known for, it reaches out to snap up the spider in its powerful sharp-spined forelegs. But the spider is a millisecond quicker, dodges the thrust, dashes next to the mantis' head and wraps it in a swathing band of strong parallel threads from her lower spinnerets. This takes three seconds. A few seconds more and the entire length of the mantis is wrapped and bound fast to the sticky web. I didn't notice when the spider sank its fangs into the mantis to paralyze it, but the mantis twitches feebly and then stops, its fate sealed in a silken shroud.

The outcome surprised me, no doubt. I know mantises well, as my wife has kept them for months in her terrarium. I thought the mantis had every advantage – superior size and strength, expert camouflage and the element of surprise. But actually, the spider had the edge the whole time. It had too many tools. Its web is an extension of the spider's senses. Its spinnerets are tipped with spinning tubes that are like nimble fingers, instantly able to manipulate and configure the threads to deal with any situation.

NO WILD MEADOW is complete without a woodchuck and there are a couple that inhabit the rocky bastion in the center of the meadow. I always find a bit of humor in 'chucks, perhaps it's the way they sometimes appear more annoyed than frightened, or it may have something to do with their stout physique. If you follow a regular route on your country ramblings, some 'chucks become familiar, almost neighborly figures as they head for their burrows when you pass.

About an hour ago, as I am writing this, I took a break to sit on the deck. While sitting near a railing watching some black vultures soar, I happened to look over on the three steps leading off the deck to see a woodchuck sitting on the bottom step, eyeing a big pot of red Gerbera daisies my wife had set out. When I moved, he scampered off the step and dove into a newly excavated burrow beneath the deck. Now what was I writing about being neighborly?

GOLD AND RUBIES, riches beyond belief; goldfinches and ruby-throated hummingbirds, that is, and I am the richer for their presence today in the meadow. Goldfinches are late nesters, raising only one brood a year. Their nesting season coincides with the blooming of thistle plants from which they harvest thistledown to line their nests.

Ruby-throated hummingbirds zip by, up and over the windfall, stopping on a dime to sip nectar or rest for a few seconds before shooting away at 70 wingbeats per second (wps). The bobbing flight of goldfinches seems slow, at 4.9 wps, and crows in steady flight beat their wings slower yet, at 2 wps. But turkey vultures, static soarers, only flap their wings twice, letting the rising thermals over Windfall Meadow provide the lift.

ON MY WAY back, I take a different route through the pine woods to pick up some pine cones as references for a Christmas card I want to make this year. Just beyond the pines is a Big Field of tall goldenrod. As I near the field, I see a round mossy shape in the pine straw that I thought to be a turtle shell, but when I get closer, I see the stitching and discover it's an old softball. This big, level field, just off the hard road, was undoubtedly an informal country ballfield years ago. Part of a rotting backstop juts from the weeds.

The thought of it has a haunting quality. I can almost see the players out on the diamond, hear their catcalls at the batter echoing from the wall of pines. A slow pitch, a mighty swing, the dense thud of bat meeting the ball. The leftfielder backpedals, but the ball is hit too hard and sails into the pines as runners circle the bases. The game is called for a while as several players search for the ball, but it is lost. Until now.

From field's edge, I peg the ball into second base. Two deer bedded in the goldenrod jump from their hiding place and run for home. The ball has finally returned to the field of play, and now, these many summers later, nature reclaims all.

Woodlander

I WAS LOOKING for a used shotgun, a bad-weather double-gun, a "beater" to part the briars in thick and nasty cover; one that had seen honest wear, but was still tight and on face.

After a brief search, I located a seller who had a perfectly fitting 20-gauge boxlock of classic proportions made by Victor Sarasqueta, a well-known Spanish maker. I examined it more closely when I got it home. It was then that I noticed the model name, WOODLANDER, engraved on the bottom of the silvered receiver.

For several days, that word stayed with me. I liked the way it sounded, the images it conjured. It made me wonder who or what a woodlander was or might be.

First, I decided a woodlander was different than a woodsman. An outdoorsman may be adept at some facets of woodsmanship, but a true woodsman is proficient in all manner of woodcraft and can live off the land. A woodsman also is a hunter and trapper, capable of making an underground refrigerator or leather tumpline, knows how to sail tandem canoes and fashion ice-creepers. A romantic figure of frontier days, there are very few real woodsmen today.

Woodlanders are people who always carry part of the woods with them, no matter what they are doing, no matter where they are. The trees, the hills, the wind, are only a blink of an eye or a heartbeat away, but not in the literal sense of proximity. Woodlanders have been shaped by the land, philosophically and spiritually. They have integrated the values learned from their relationship with the natural world to other facets of their lives. Their reverence for wildlife and the land is laminated to a responsibility that they act on selflessly, and in many cases, anonymously.

Woodlanders live in the country, in suburbia, and in cities. They are hunters, birders, trappers, berry-pickers, photographers, insect collectors, journal keepers and stargazers. There are no specific criteria that define a woodlander. There exists no levels of achievement or degrees of recognition for what they accomplish or donate.

They come from every walk of life, but no matter how busy, always find time to make the outdoors some part of their day. They are the elderly or infirm who last spent time in the woods long ago, but walk in their inner woods every day, or share the trail vicariously through you. They are country kids born with birdsong in their ears. They are city kids with birdsong in their hearts, who may not know they are woodlanders until a mentor shows the way.

It is fairly easy to identify woodlanders: they have a certain brightness in their eyes when listening to another's outdoor experiences, a special ring of honest enthusiasm in their words when describing their own. Upon reading this, you may have thought of some woodlanders you have known, and having made it to this point, you may be one yourself.

IT SEEMS PEOPLE have become obsessed with strict categorization, pigeonholing every aspect of their identities into ever-smaller classifications replete with titles, monograms, logos and doctrines that define the parameters of inclusion.

My outdoor pursuits are many and wide-ranging, each building upon the other, but I prefer not being viewed as an outdoorsman or sportsman, as those words seem focused on rod and gun and exclude all other pursuits. I like the ambiguity of being a woodlander. I'll let all the specialized titling to those who must have a nametag that defines exactly who and what they are, and what others are not.

IT IS THE NATURE of woodlanders to share, and one thing they enjoy sharing is a campfire. The dual nature of a campfire is at once both exclusionary and inclusive. It holds the unknown in the outer dark at the perimeter of its light, yet at the same time is inviting, offering warmth and a mesmerizing focal point whereby all those sitting near experience a sense of equilibrium and inner peace.

Much has been written about the psychological associations of humans and campfires, the most prominent being that campfires provoke a fascination among many adults because they never learned to make and master fire as a child. Could not the same be said for other natural elements? What of wind, water, the raw earth, rocks, wood, animals? A lack of understanding and experience of working with and utilizing basic earthly resources has created an enormous gulf between people.

I believe most woodlanders know why wind direction is important when hunting, know how to wade a stream, plant a tree, construct a campfire ring of stones, and build within it a proper fire over which they could grill some backstrap.

No other medium is more conducive to meaningful conversation than a campfire. At a campfire there is no need to fill every moment with chatter. Any words spoken are like firewood added to the flames and are dwelled upon before any response – if needed – is given. The flickering and crackling are cues that provoke all manner of discourse. Straying off topic is encouraged and a lull in the conversation is not deemed as an awkward silence.

Depending how and what they are made of, the characteristics of certain campfires are much like people. Some burn quick, the leaping flames, a hot, bright yellow, and then they are gone. Others have a more substantive armature, producing deep orange and blue flames and an even, moderate heat. Then there are those where the log embers at the base glow a deep cherry-red beneath white ash, offering up serious heat, a fire of endurance that occasionally releases white hot sparks that fire up through it all like flares, high into the night. Woodlanders carry a fire within, too, one fueled steadily by wonder that once started illuminates a lifetime, a fire that may be passed on.

WOODLANDERS ARE CURIOUS by nature, eager to learn, and gather knowledge with the same delight as when they come into a patch of just-ripe blackberries or morels. They strive to know the birds, trees, flowers, stars, fish, clouds, insects and wildlife. They know there is much to learn, and that the joy is in the journey.

Most woodlanders would respond quickly when asked if they have a "totem" or "spirit" animal. Mine is the raven, and the reasons are many; raven lore is steeped in antiquity, literature and art. Wide-ranging and secretive, it is a bird of wilder places and a keen observer. I enjoy its vocalizations and playfulness, its mystery and intelligence. But the raven also represents something greater.

Each wild animal, be it bat or bear, possesses some essence of the wild, some pure element drawn up from the land and expressed in bone and muscle, feathers, fins or fur. One may study the anatomy and natural history of a species, but it is equally important to see and feel that essence to truly know that animal. I recognize it immediately, when, for the briefest of moments, I make eye contact with a wild creature. I have felt the essence of autumn when holding a grouse in my palm, have understood better the progression of night in the muted hoots of an owl filtering through a pine woods.

THE NATURAL WORLD is first realized through individual parts. Next, the connection between those parts begins to form a larger image, and then it all comes together. For some, it is a slowly emerging image that gradually comes into focus. For others, it is all suddenly there, enveloping, vaulting, a living cyclorama in which the observer stands in the very center. It sometimes takes years to see the big picture. But I believe this comes easier to woodlanders.

Woodlanders know how to use all their senses to immerse themselves in the wild. Listen to the faintest rustle beneath a leaf then watch for the vole, brush the stiff wing feather from a wild turkey across your cheek and feel in that stout pinion the power of the whole bird, smell the sweet grass nest left by a cottontail and embrace forever an endless summer. From the evening campfire, taste a tender slice of tenderloin that reveals the wild nature of the animal, and that of the woodland where it lived.

CONSUMERS IN THE modern age often expect immediate returns on any effort or investment. It doesn't work that way with the natural world. It will not always return what is put into it, and is not dependent on reviews. The dilettante is usually disappointed.

Nature, at times, seems to pause to reveal some element of mystery, but it does not halt. It's always in motion, following the cyclical pull of the seasons as the planet spins through time, light and space. Woodlanders are rewarded with the gifts of the wild, because they walk with that flow, not counter to it, and will gladly offer a hand should anyone want to come aboard.

The Nature of Things

THE STUDIOS AND WORKPLACES of artists, writers and researchers begin to take on the fanciful look of a wizard's workshop as the years go by, as do the rooms of many hunters who bring back bits and pieces from their outdoor activities, both natural and manmade.

Professional disciplines require accuracy, and that demands having actual specimens and objects to reference. As both a writer and illustrator, as well as a participant, my studio has been filled to the hilt several times over with curios and botanical, mammalian and avian specimens. This has required a judicious purging every few years. The last entailed a large dumpster in the driveway centered under the studio window, where for a week, all manner of strange things could be seen flying out the window.

I've relegated a large floor chest as sort of a catch-all. A look inside reveals loose game-bird feathers, cicada husks, a white-tailed deer's tail and the legs of a wild turkey gobbler. Squirreled away are acorns, hickory nuts, pine cones and milkweed pods, as well as old hunting licenses, duck stamps and fern fossils, along with owl pellets, pen knives and an assortment of brass shell-casings that conjure memories. Continuing this eclectic assortment are exhibition badges, wildlife pins and patches, a beaver "football," a mantis egg case and a plaster cast of an enormous black bear's track.

All around, on every shelf and cabinet top, or hung on the walls is paraphernalia from the outdoors: Inuit soapstone carvings, antique turkey calls, a Maasai short sword, or *seme*, a mule shoe, hornet nests, antlers, decoys and so much more. These things from our days afield hold some of nature's magic, and collectively release some palpable part of the wild into our everyday lives. What at first appears ordinary becomes extraordinary when the story behind an object is revealed, transporting us to another place and time. Following are a few things that have found a place among my clutter and the stories behind them.

Country Living

The familiar aerial paper nests of bald-faced hornets become visible in late autumn after leaf-drop. Marvels of design, the nests are made of wood fibers that when chewed by the hornets, is mixed with starch in their saliva and becomes a paper-like pulp that can be spread and shaped. Upon drying, it is surprisingly durable and weather resistant. The stucco-like swirls on the hive's exterior show subtle patterns of muted olive, grays and dark ochre hues, depending on the source of the wood fibers. The thick, multi-layered exterior insulates and protects the larvae in the tiered combs inside, and houses the worker females, drones and the queen. The design is a striking contrast of architectural forms with the shell being free-form and organic, while the hexagonal cells of the interior combs are precise geometric units.

Sold as items of country décor in antique shops, the nests often are displayed in kitchens, camps, dens, classrooms and nature centers. Nests, however, shouldn't be removed from a tree until late autumn after a period of cold to ensure the last of the colony has died off.

I have several nests of varying shapes and sizes hanging above a studio window and after discovering a large nest two autumns ago, decided to add it to the display. The nest was built near the top of a small, straight sapling, and resembled an elongated football. Even though it was less than 15 yards off an old farm road, it was difficult to reach, because it was located within a dense thicket of thorny devil's club and recently logged treetops, stitched together with blackberry canes.

After bulling through the nasty tangles, I stopped to size up the nest, which was just above eye level. The weather had been warm with extended periods of rain, so I poked the sapling cautiously with my walking stick and waited. There appeared to be no sign of activity.

With my knife, I cut through the sapling below the nest and just as it was about to topple, a stream of aggressive hornets rocketed out of the hole and hit me full force in the face, stinging, knocking me flat like a punch from a heavyweight. They pummeled me as I crawled, clawing through the logging debris and briars out to the road, where they finally let up. The black-and-white defenders had expertly driven off the clumsy and foolish vandal.

Bald-faced hornets are not true hornets; they are related to black-and-yellow wasps. These hornets have barbless stingers that allow them to sting more than once and a secondary defensive capability of squirting or spraying venom from their stingers into the eyes of invading raccoons, skunks, foxes and bears, causing blurred vision and temporary blindness.

I recovered the nest several weeks later, after a hard freeze, and hung it in the studio. It's a nice addition, but what is brought to mind, aside from my painful encounter, is how similar the nest is to the old, weathered gray barn just down the lane from where I discovered the nest. Now abandoned, the picturesque barn, like the nest, was once an active center of industry and country living in this upland setting.

Cast the Runes

As the antlers of one buck can become entangled and locked up with those of his opponent, much of my career has been locked inextricably to the magic of deer antlers. I've written about them at length, illustrated them, rendered their graceful forms in paintings and spent a lifetime as a deer hunter looking for them atop the head of a buck. After all these years, I still regard antlers with that same fascination shared by hunters since earliest times.

While working on the museum project, part of which would feature an enormous collection of record-book whitetails, the walls of my Midwest design studio were hung with many of America's most renowned whitetail heads. Even though they were certainly impressive, what I found to be just as noteworthy were the incredible stories behind each. In that respect, an old faded mount of a small 6-pointer may be the equal of any museum mount.

A few years ago, I was given a bushel basket brimming with antlers by a woman who had cleaned out her garage. The antlers were from bucks taken by her late husband and some camp members who also had passed on. Each antler was sawed off at the base from the skull plate, probably with some antler projects in mind. I was happy to get them as I use them for reference in my work and my wife enjoys using them in seasonal displays.

I emptied the basket onto a blanket I had spread on my drawing board. Some of the antlers were impressive, a better-than-average representation of mountain bucks one might encounter hunting the northern tier back in the day.

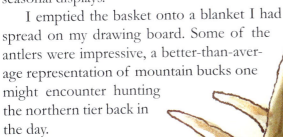

Just as I was about to pair them up, I was reminded of Queequeg, the mysterious harpooner in Melville's *Moby Dick*. The South Pacific native, desiring to learn what fates lie ahead in the pursuit of the white whale, decides to "cast the runes" and produces a small pouch containing pieces of bones carved into shapes and scribed with cryptic symbols. Before casting them onto the deck of the *Pequod*, Queequeg tells the main character, Ishmael, "Bones tell everything."

Gazing into the heap of bones before me, images began to emerge. First, the curved main beams reminded me of the ridgeline contours of the mountains of the northern tier, the spaces between the tines, of the undulating hollows. Some of the antlers had busted tines and all were scribed with scratches and polished burrs that told of battles with other deer, flights through the thickets and the grating of saplings as the buck made rubs.

I looked deep into the shadows within the antler mass, looking for something more. It is of no consequence that I did not know the hunters who took the deer, the name of their camp, or what rifles they used. Soon enough, though, the rich flavor of camp life and the hunt emerged; eggs popped and sputtered in a big frypan while an aromatic fog of woodsmoke, coffee and bacon hung in the cabin eaves. A quick weather check before the hunters dressed. I could see them filing up the mountain to their stands, dark forms against the snow, like ancient hunters from another time. Gunfire in the distance, and suddenly, a legal buck among a throng of does. The hiss of its hide on the snow as it was dragged back, its supple, meaty body slipping over fallen logs. Guessing its weight as it was hoisted to hang on the meat pole. Handshakes all around. A hearty potluck supper and the stories of the day, lore and legend, like one rock stacked atop another, building a wall around this bastion to harbor memories here for all time, or to keep the rest of the world at bay. A last glance at the beloved mountains before heading home.

An antler on a shelf may be only an ordinary decorative element to some. But a hunter may pick it up, and share for a moment, a Potter County mountaintop with a hunter long gone, driven deep in his wool coat as sleet and snow sweeps in hard, just as a sleek buck clears the ridgeline.

Sometimes bones tell everything, and sometimes, not. The memories of the anonymous hunters and the secret lives of the deer would stay locked in these bones forever, and would always belong only to them. One can only imagine about them, but in that imagining, some element of the hunt lives on.

A Matter of Style

Deceiving wild, wary eyes with a decoy and reinforcing it with calling that promises camaraderie, to join others of its kind at a secure place to rest and feed, is an old art that has a special charm. The hunter becomes a member of the flock both visibly and audibly, and then, within the next instant, reveals his predatory self. This is especially meaningful when the decoys are made by hand, as each holds a bit of hope borrowed from the heart of the carver.

Hand-carved waterfowl decoys are great examples of form following function, with some recognized as celebrated works of American folk art. Depending on the carver, condition, style and rarity, some have values well into six figures, while a few have fetched $1 million.

I have three canvasback decoys that were the works of carvers for use on the Susquehanna River. The style of each varies greatly, even though they represent the same species by carvers from the same locale, who hunted the same storied waters. Their styles vary, each an expression dependent on the perception and skills of the carver, each a personal translation guided by eye, mind and hand. In a word, art.

The first decoy features

excellent proportions and captures the bold, robust character of the canvasback. It is high-headed, alert and powerful, a typical gunning-rig pattern and made entirely of wood. The long, ski-jump sweep from the top of the head to the tip of the long bill reads well even from a distance. It has seen much use, yet retains good paint. There is a beauty in the hard-earned patina of longitudinal cracks, fissures, and the raking marks of shot pellets that nicked its black breast.

Next is a decoy from Columbia, Pa., that appears quite primitive in comparison to the classic standard lines and proportions found in the former. This one is blocky, the body carved from a single piece of wood. Its overall shape is that of a big loaf of sourdough bread. It has glass eyes and the thick bill juts out of the head at an odd angle. The breast is flat, instead of rounded, and it lacks a dimensional tail. The styling does not capture a canvasback's majesty, but it has seen some action as evidenced by the 21 shot holes peppering its body. Even though it seems to lack sophistication, it is one of my favorite decoys, given that the naivete of its style elevates it to a highly desirable form of folk art. I wonder if its carver, George Schlotthauer, carved it in his early years before developing into a seasoned decoy-maker, or if its flat, utilitarian design was intentional.

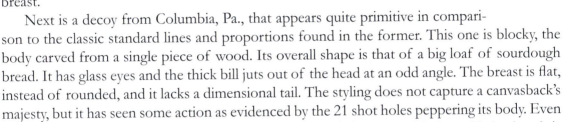

I've painted and drawn the third decoy in still-lifes several times as it is a study in pure grace of form. It has a sleek, low-profile styling and an elegantly shaped three-piece head. The head is nailed on and the eyes are indentations. The body is solid wood with two knotholes plugged with dowels. At first, I thought it was carved as a mantle-piece decoy, because of its slightly smaller size, but it, too, features shot-pellet marks.

Rock On

Almost every camp, lodge, cabin or home of fellow hunters I've visited have one or more rocking chairs. The comfortable motion of a rocker seems to mimic the soothing motion of tree branches or tree trunks swaying slowly in a breeze, or even the rhythmic motion of lake waters lapping a shoreline: back and forth, back and forth.

Rockers first appeared in North America sometime in the early 1700s. Benjamin Franklin is often credited with inventing the rocker, but historical records show they were already in use, mainly in gardens, when he was a child.

Outdoorsman, conservationist and our 26th President, Theodore Roosevelt, would sit in other chairs only as a formality and had rockers in the White House, his homes and ranches. He once wrote, "What true American does not enjoy a rocking chair?"

When I was a boy, my parents would often take me on long scenic drives through the countryside. At the bottom of a mountain, there was a small country store we used to stop at that sold farm produce, homemade jellies and handmade hickory rockers. The first time I sat in one of the woodsy rockers, I was completely enamored.

When my birthday rolled around, my mother asked what I wanted and I immediately told her that I wanted a hickory rocker. She laughed and said, "Those aren't for kids, they're for older people. Wait 'til you retire."

Well, 60 years later, I came across a beautiful handmade hickory rocker, and being semi-retired, brought it home for the studio. It's a great seat on cold winter days for reading, recalling hunts gone by or just looking out the window at winter birds.

You know, things that older people do.

On a table next to the rocking chair is a red sandstone rock, a bit of rubble from author Jack London's ill-fated "Wolf House," a dream home London had built that soon after was destroyed by fire. The stone was given to me by a friend who made a pilgrimage to the site. His instructions were that I should keep it in my studio as it radiates great creative energy. If I should happen to hit a stumbling block, all I'd need to do is place it nearby and a solution would emerge. Conversely, if I had too many ideas, and found it hard to decide, then I was to place it in a drawer. Not that I believe in any of that, but one can never tell when trying to understand the nature of things.

Mountain Time

IT IS PAST MIDNIGHT and I'm writing this by the glow of a big yellow candle that fills the studio with lemon-colored light. My powerful computer, with all its convenient word-processing software, is perched on the writing desk behind me. I like the warm, soft glow of the candle better than the cold light of the monitor, and the click-and-clack of keystrokes so late at night seems too loud.

I pen these words in the fashion of an 18th century scribe, with a crow quill pen fixed with an antique steel writing nib. It is the kind of pen that is dipped into a bottle of India ink and must be held at an exact angle so the pointed prongs of the nib do not catch on the paper, flicking ink, or suddenly regurgitating a black ink blob on the composition of slanted and looping letters.

Writing in this fashion is all about commitment and surety. There is no backspace key, no ability to move entire sentences or delete words. It's like felling a tree with an ax: every measured stroke is automatically calculated through a rhythmic, precise effort. The chips fly and cannot be reinserted, as do the words.

Asleep in the chair, two studio dogs sigh and snore. They won't leave until I'm done. The steel pen scratches like a mouse under leaves and the fox terrier's ears twitch.

I'm writing in this fashion at this late hour because all day long I had been illustrating scenes from nature with this same pen and thought how odd to capture such fleeting images with ink and steel: a cottontail leaping from a weed patch, white-faced hornets buzzing about their nest, a drumming grouse. Each scenario, sparkling with motion, is painstakingly recreated on paper, stroke upon stroke, like weaving one stitch at a time. And now, I hope to do the same through the free-flowing grace of cursive writing.

IT IS OUR nature to hold nature and time in every possible way. On one of the studio walls hang two of my favorite images. The first is a large black-and-white photograph by renowned photographer Ansel Adams, a panoramic portrait of Mount Denali, partially obscured by an armada of clouds. In this photo, the constancy of the great timeless peak is contrasted by the temporal, drifting mass of clouds.

Below the photo hangs a print of a wild turkey gobbler by Ned Smith. The gobbler is running, wings readied, about to launch from the cusp of a ridge. Just the tips of the toes on one foot of the sprinting gobbler touch the earth, and in the next instant it will be airborne. It is more than a skillfully rendered wild turkey print; it's a suggestion of the very next moment in time, when only the ever-watchful mountain remains.

These images remind me that we often live our lives like clouds or turkeys – ephemeral, onward-pressing. But to truly appreciate the headlong flow of the natural world, it is sometimes best to be more like a mountain than a man.

There are certain moments when time – and nature – stalls, as in the deepest part of this cool, still September night. The bulldog casts a baleful look from a bloodshot eye, wondering when I will finish.

A full yellow moon stares plain-faced through the skylight, a lemony twin of my candle. I douse the flame and sit in the moonlight for a few minutes. The black ink blobs scattered throughout the words resemble a flock of crows roosting in a leafless tree. Even though I penned these words in my studio, I did so on "mountain time," when measured time is of no importance – a hitch in time when the perpetual motion of the living world can be dwelled upon, and like dark birds rising from branches, set to flying again.

FOR MANY YEARS I've carried a small gold pocket watch made in 1913 by the Illinois Watch Company. It fits the palm perfectly, has never failed, and keeps exact time. When I lift the back cover of the watch revealing the jeweled movement, or caliber, I am always amazed at the mechanical beauty and genius of the clockworks as it marks time. Time is measured by motion, measured through motion and evidenced by change. When I'm in the woods, I don't like to think of time passing, but evidence of change is all around.

Time is marked and measured in many ways in nature; through the movement of light and shadow, birdsong, insect activity, in seeds, in our own heartbeat. There are certain points when it seems time halts, as in that instant when we shoot at a deer or watch a red-tailed hawk paused in the wind, kiting above a slope. But those are simply moments when our minds and hearts reach a pinnacle point in thought and wonder before continuing on.

Time is invisible, difficult to comprehend, but if there is one earthy medium that describes it best, it would be moving water.

A river is time made visible. So is a creek or brook, a rivulet, or any measure of flowing water within our proximity. Not a vast lake, or swamp or the cauldron of a beaver pond, though.

Even an ocean fails. It's heaving mass of tides mark time, for sure. But as a depository for all waters, it lacks the linear movement of a waterway and is more of a place where earthly time rests before it is ushered out again upon the land.

A prominent part of the ridgeline I hunt protrudes outwards, away from the shoulder-to-shoulder alignment of interconnected hills, like a soldier ordered to step away from a formation. I call it a mountain, but it also can be referred to as a knob or point. Shaped like the robust heart of a black bear, it is replete with a complex network of arteries that carries water from its enormous flat above to the creek far below.

My mountain is like the clockworks of my watch. It powers the creek with seeps, runoffs from violent storms, winter snows, and the slow, steady drip-drip-dripping of countless water drops falling from waxy beech leaves and the ends of twigs and fern tips.

As nature essayist John Burroughs noted, one can usually tell the season just by listening to a creek. The full creek of March when the water is high runs quiet, as the rocks and gravel bars and debris lie beneath the waters. The gurgling of the creek in August is muffled by leaves and grasses and masses of water plants, but the creek in late autumn is loudest as water froths over the exposed gravel, is cleaved by stones, chugs hollowly behind perpendicular logs.

The stuff of fantasy often involves going back in time. This is evidenced in the creek, as water is pushed back upon the main current when striking an object or by an eddy along its periphery, where small whirlpools spin before moving onward. Time pauses, then releases to join the current.

The creek has given me a greater concept of time, and I know more about the creek because first, I understand the magic of the mountain.

A Day So Rare

IT HAD BEEN raining all week without a spot of sun, then, when it seemed the ground couldn't hold another drop, the showers stopped, ending with layers of low-scudding clouds moving quickly from the east below a ceiling of slate-gray clouds sliding south.

I'm up the next morning at 4:30, awakened by robin song and the cheery peal of a cardinal forecasting a sunny day. I have a painting to complete, and scheduled this day to finish it. At midmorning, I open a skylight and birdsong fills the studio. A fragrant, gentle northwest breeze stirs the treetops as the sun dries the sodden ground. A mourning dove alights on the tilted skylight window, as they often do. It moans softly, beckoning me to leave my work and get some sun.

What was originally to be a one-hour birding break progresses to two, then relents to a daylong sketching session as I spot a surprising number of warblers drifting through.

Warbler watching requires patience and

concentration. They are extremely active, and you must anticipate their movements as they weave through the leafy canopy or dense growth of an evergreen. The effort is worth it, though, as their striking graphics and colorful breeding plumage are a delight to the eye.

Several warblers trickle through a towering pine and a brace of hemlocks out back, like a handful of jewels falling through the boughs. A blackpoll warbler works the crevices of bark along a branch, while a yellow-rumped warbler, decked out in harlequin costume, flits below. A chestnut-sided warbler sings its accented song that ends *very very pleased to meetcha*! Ten feet away, a common yellowthroat sings for a long while; its repeated *cheeseburger, cheeseburger, cheeseburger* reminds me it's almost lunchtime.

MY FAVORITE summer bird is the catbird. It seems that nothing escapes its inquisitive nature. If something seems amiss in its territory it is Johnny-on-the-spot, ready for action. One catbird follows me closely as I mow the lawn, chasing the moths that flush in each pass, and whenever I take a break, it perches on the mower handle.

A wasp buzzes across a stretch of lawn with a catbird in hot pursuit. Without slowing, the wasp flies through the gap between two fence slats, but the catbird lifts up and over the fence, and in a wonderfully executed maneuver that would rival a sharp-shinned hawk, it nabs the wasp out of the air and whacks it against a garden slate. The catbird rakes it back and forth across the slate and the hapless insect loses a wing and then is taken into the dark folds of shrubbery.

MY WIFE has more than a dozen birdhouses scattered across our property. Last year, I added one more to that collection that I found at a garage sale. It was made of resin in the shape of a hornet's nest, and the entrance hole was just the right diameter for a chickadee or wren. I hung it from the crab-tree, certain that it would be claimed quickly. It had hardly stopped swinging from its wire when a chickadee began to check it out. I watched for nest-building activity, then noticed that the chickadees opted to nest in a tree cavity just behind the novel birdhouse. So much for my real-estate venture.

THE MOST intense bird species that I see almost every day of spring and throughout the summer is the house wren. Its trickling vocalizations, from early morning until after sunset, are relentless. For more than 30 consecutive years, wrens have nested in a birdhouse somewhere on our deck, allowing close scrutiny.

From a distance, wrens appear to be a drab

monotone of brown. But up close, they are stunning; gradated tones of sepia and umber serve as a base for the fine, vermiculated patterns rendered in a texture that resembles the strokes of a pen.

Wrens are incredible and efficient hunters. After hatching, the wren parents really come into their own, bringing insects to their brood every 20 seconds, as I have timed them. That's a lot of protein. I've watched them dart through the grass, like tiny velociraptors (which means "swift seizer"), snapping up inchworms and other insects.

They are very secretive as the fledglings leave the nest; I've only seen it happen twice. And it isn't long before they gear up for another brood.

HOUSE WREN

WITH EVERY shift of the holidays and seasons, a different wreath finds its way onto our front door. When robins built a nest in the bottom loop of my wife's floral spring wreath, the nest seemed to be part of the wreath itself. From inside the house, we could look out the door's window at the female sitting on her pale blue eggs just inches away.

I closed off the front walkway with a bench and posted a sign for all visitors to come around back. When the young hatched, we got to watch their development. But others were watching, too. The neighborhood band of crows was all eyes as nestlings grow. I've seen them raid the nests of blue jays, grackles, cardinals and newborn cottontails.

On my way upstairs to the studio, I stopped to watch the progress of the robins. I spotted a crow sitting on a bare branch at the top of a silver maple 50 yards away. It let loose its perch, set its wings and just as it swooped up beneath the porch roof to rob the nest, I opened the door. The crow went berserk, as did the robins. But when the dust settled, all returned to normal.

A LOUD *frahnk! frahnk!* is the call of the great blue heron. They are late-day travelers, flying over the house toward the Susquehanna River, catching the last high rays of the sun that has set some time ago. Dusk draws down slowly and the air cools. My eyes are bleary, and I'm satisfied with the day's efforts.

SONG SPARROW

In the afterglow, I'm back in the studio, reviewing my sketches and notes. Right outside the west skylight, the catbirds begin mewing at some intruder in the maple tree and are quickly joined by blue jays and several other birds. It's quite a bit of commotion for such a peaceable time of day.

COMMON NIGHTHAWK

I can't make out what they're fussing about, but when I look into the eye of this feathered tornado, I see a dark shape lying lengthwise on a trunk. It's a common nighthawk, so well camouflaged I have a difficult time picking it out, even with binoculars. Its eyes are half-open, oblivious to the alarmed birds.

After a while, the harassing birds give up, sensing the hawk-sized intruder poses no threat. The nighthawk turns its head and opens wide its big pink maw, almost like a yawn. At dusk, I first hear, then see, several other nighthawks overhead, repeatedly sounding their loud calls, which sound like paint! paint!

The nighthawk launches from the bough, opens its great narrow wings and joins yet others coursing by. *Paint! Paint!* it cries.

Well, I'm too tired and it's too late to start painting now, but I could not pass up an invitation to spend a day with wild birds who proclaim that every day is rare indeed, but especially a day in June spent among their ranks.

Finders Keepers

THE EDGES OF HEAVEN

THERE ARE CERTAIN TRUTHS and realities that fiction can reveal that nonfiction cannot. It helps the reader to better understand others, and ultimately, themselves. A different perspective might open an entire new world. The rich outdoors heritage of Penn's Woods provides many passages for time travel and the stories that follow visit those bygone days.

Coming-of-age stories hold a special place in outdoors fiction, as hunters from any era share much in common during their formative years afield. Mentorship reigns as a significant theme as young hunters rely on a ballast of experience to hold them steady and upright.

In the outdoors, one learns the elements of cooperation, as well as how to function alone. Choices are to be made, responsibilities must be met. Respect and empathy for wildlife, the land and others are part and parcel of the venue.

Gray squirrels have always been a perfect subject when coming-of-age hunting stories are the topic. For years, the gray squirrel has been one of the first game animals that young hunters learn to hunt before moving on to bigger game. Squirrels are plentiful and can be challenging. They can be noisy, curious and quite active. But on some drizzly days, they move quickly and silently, and are gone at the first hint of danger.

In *Finders Keepers*, a brace of grays has been feeding on remnants of harvested corn during the late-winter season, and if the inquisitive squirrel gets a whisker closer to the one possessing the ear of corn, a tussle is sure to ensue.

The Witness Tree

A FARMER IN A YELLOW slicker leans into the slanting rain as he walks, happy to finish the last task of a raw, cold day. He secures a stock gate outside his daughter's bedroom window with wire, knowing that the screeching gate would disturb her sleep.

Back inside, he sits at the kitchen table with a slice of pumpkin pie and hot coffee. His wife braids their young daughter's hair by the fireplace while their son stares out the window. As the chill leaves his bones, the farmer relaxes. All seems right with the world.

"Tell us about the man in the tree," says the boy, refilling his father's cup.

"Please, Daddy, tell us about him," his daughter runs over and also pleads. "Show us his marker."

His children sit cross-legged before him, eager for the story.

The farmer opens a cupboard and takes down a section of warped plank from a row of books. He brushes it off and holds it for them to see the crudely carved epitaph: *HERE I REST AT THE WITNESS TREE; KNOWN ONLY NOW TO GOD AND THESE HILLS*. It was signed *L.B. 1841-1918*.

"When your mother and I moved here in 1939, this farm was wild and woolly," the farmer told his children. "Everything was covered in vines and the fields were full of ditches and weeds. We patched up the barn and fixed up this farmhouse and built a new addition where your rooms are.

"One day, your Uncle John and me were up on the hill repairing the stone wall when we came to this big dead oak. The trunk of that white oak was about 5 feet across, and most of the thicker boughs were broken off and laying in the field. I figured to saw the main trunk off about chest high and leave the tall stump as a stand for deer season.

"It was covered with creeper vines, and after we

cleared them away, we started sawing. Well, we were making good time with the two-man crosscut 'cause the oak is fairly hollow, when I see these words carved into the tree. We thought this person was buried at its base, so we look around and find a low spot. We start digging, but right off we hit a huge boulder. We had a lot to do, so we start sawing again.

"After a while, we stop to rest and I'm mopping my brow when I almost jump outta my skin. Staring down at me from a crack in the tree is a skull. Then I see the whole skeleton in there, and feel bad 'cause we had sawed it right in half.

"That man was inside the tree for almost 21 years. He carved this marker himself, and that oak was his coffin. More than likely he died standing in it. It took some doing, but I discovered that this L.B. was a man named Lyman Baker, and his story began long ago…"

THE YEAR WAS 1850, and 9-year-old Lyman Baker and his younger brother Matthew filled buckets with drinking water then hung them on a yoke across the back of the mule and rode up the hill where their father and several neighbor men were building a stone fence. The boys cleaned clods from the fieldstone for the men, and by the end of the day, the fence had snaked up to a great spreading oak on the crest of the hill.

After supper, the boys ran back up to the solitary oak. Lyman hopped up onto the stone wall, pulled Matthew up after him and they climbed into the inviting arms of the tree. The solemn fields lay in blue shadow, and they climbed higher yet and sat in the rays of the sinking sun.

"If Ma knowed we was this high up in this ol' tree, she'd be awful mad," said Matthew.

Lyman looked at his brother and smiled. Matthew was as skinny as a squirrel and looked right at home in the tree.

"I never saw so much country as this from one place," said Lyman, surveying the panorama of the gentle green river wrapped around the feet of the hills beyond.

A flock of geese on locked wings glided just over them, honking loudly, descending to the river. Their wild, free song was an epiphany for Lyman, swelling in his chest until he thought he would burst. A seed of wanderlust sprouted in him that moment, as surely as the mighty oak had sprouted from an acorn centuries before.

That summer, and in the years that followed, the tree became a sanctuary for the brothers. Their mother had christened the 400-year-old oak the "Witness Tree," because of all the life it had seen passing under and above its boughs.

From their vantage point in the oak, the boys saw a string of small islands on the river, a rocky bluff high on a hill, and tendrils of smoke from distant farms, each landmark noted as a future destination full of possibility. Lofty dreams come easy in lofty places, and the brothers spent hours planning expeditions. Sometimes they just lazed in the branches, imagining the world beyond the rim of their valley.

From those sturdy boughs, they watched their farm grow and prosper, along with other new farms that became part of the patchwork-quilted landscape.

As young men, the brothers were a study in contrast. Lyman was tall and broad-shouldered with the gait of a woodsman, while Matthew was small, rail thin and always scrambled along to keep pace with Lyman. Matthew, however, was blessed with keen vision and a steady hand, and could shoot at great distances with deadly accuracy.

One misty October morning, the brothers were standing side by side in the oak where four huge trunks branched out. They spotted several deer walking along the edge of a field far below. Lyman proposed a plan to stalk them, but Matthew held up his hand to silence him and in one motion, cocked the hammer, set the trigger and braced against a trunk. The still air shattered and a roundball whistled through the mists and through the neck of a sleek buck that never heard the shot.

THE VALLEY SEEMED TO grow smaller every day to Lyman, and he ached to strike out on his own. When he was 19, he left home for the north country, where he found work as a lumberman in Potter County.

It was tough, but satisfying work up there in the Wildcat District, and the boys were a rough bunch. He enjoyed the scenic country, but by the spring of 1861, he was ready to move on. Then news of the approaching war swept through the north woods, followed by a call for volunteers. Lyman jumped at the opportunity to join the 1st Pennsylvania Rifles, better known as the "Bucktails," named for the tail of a buck that each man had killed and wore on his hat.

In a letter home he wrote that he would stop by on his way to enlist.

Lyman and several other Bucktails pulled into the farmyard in a borrowed wagon drawn by mules. Matthew was waiting on the porch with his rifle and pinned to his hat was the tail of a buck he had killed.

One of the Bucktails, remarking on Matthew's

slight build said, "Hard to tell where man ends and rifle begins."

"Can you shoot?" asked another. Matthew looked at Lyman and smiled broadly.

"Some," he said. "See that squirrel settin' on that knot on that big oak yonder?"

"I can see the oak," said the man, squinting.

Using a rail for a rest, Matthew steadied and fired.

After bidding farewell to their parents, they rode on out under the Witness Tree.

"There's the mark of your ball above that knot," said a lumberman.

"And there lies my pa's supper," said Matthew. "Let me fetch this squirrel back and I'll be right along."

While they waited for Matthew, Lyman looked up through the oak at the familiar branches dappled with sunlight. With uncertain adventure looming, and in the spirited company of his brother and friends, it was the happiest day he had ever known.

IT WAS THE worst day he had ever known, that sweltering day of July 3, 1863, at a town called Gettysburg. He and Matthew were part of a small brigade skirmishing with the Confederates along a stone wall. They worked their way toward Devil's Den, and their war became a rifleman's war as each side exchanged fire. The rebels, using muzzle-loaders, were exposed briefly as they reloaded, but the Bucktails were armed with breechloading Sharps rifles and could remain hidden until they fired.

Matthew put on a remarkable display of marksmanship, sending a round through every patch of gray wool visible. The Rebels, seeing that they were being picked off, mounted a terrific charge, and the Bucktails retreated to the stone wall.

Just as they were taking cover, Lyman was sent sprawling by a bullet that hit his boot heel and he crashed headlong into the wall, stunned. Matthew reached back over the wall, and as he yanked Lyman to safety, was hit in the chest.

Lyman held his brother close. Matthew's face was streaked with blue smoke, and his red cheeks paled.

"Someone over there's a fine shot," he said, coughing between words. Then he smiled and said, "It's hard to hit such a skinny person as I was."

And with those light words in that tragic place, the littlest Bucktail died.

BACK HOME, LYMAN NAILED Matthew's bucktail to the Witness Tree. In the years after the war, he made his living as a market hunter on the Susquehanna Flats, then headed north to New York City, where he learned to clerk. It wasn't long before he felt the city closing in, and he turned to the open sea in New Bedford, signing on as a hand on a whaling ship. Years later, when he was traveling in the Midwest, he received word that his father had passed, and his mother had moved to Harrisburg to live with her sister.

In Wisconsin he married, but lost both his wife and child in childbirth. In 1885, he returned to Pennsylvania, clerking in the office of a Pittsburgh ironworks. Four years later, he left the city, volunteering to help the victims of the Johnstown Flood. Then Lyman went north again, finally settling in Clearfield.

When he was 77 years old, Lyman took ill, and set out to see the Witness Tree one last time. He arrived by foot on a frigid November afternoon to find the farm abandoned and growing wild. The oak looked poorly. It was lightning-charred, a bolt having cleaved a wide fissure down its great trunk, bursting its core. Much of the bark had fallen off, and its once great crown held only a few russet leaves.

With a hammer and chisel, Lyman carved his epitaph into the tree, then with much difficulty, he climbed on top of the stone wall and up the tree where the main boughs branched. Lyman chiseled out the lead ball from above the knot where Matthew had shot the squirrel. Very tired and cold, Lyman stepped down into a hollow in the tree to take shelter from the wind.

Lyman dreamed a final dream – a peaceable dream – of the great oak softly rustling in a warm summer breeze, leaves billowing against a blue sky, the wide spreading boughs lifting and falling slowly, becoming then a single motionless image of the tree from afar, a sepia picture fading more and more until there was only gray light.

THE FARMER RAN his hand over the marker.

"We made him a proper tombstone, and a coffin of boards sawed from the oak, and with a prayer, laid the bones of Lyman Baker to rest on the hill.

"Some people stay all their lives in one place – just like a tree – and witness all the things great and small that pass by. Other folks, like Lyman Baker, follow the winds like wild geese. One way is not better than the other, so long as we realize that as much wonder lies in an acorn as in an ocean."

Along the River

CATAMOUNT CREEK, *called "The Cat" by locals, got its name when an 18th century settler killed a mountain lion at the confluence of the two creeks that formed it. Back then, catamount was one of the various common names settlers used for mountain lions; short for cat-a-mountain.*

Beyond its historic origin, though, the river's name would have been equally appropriate if only describing the languid nature of its waters, which were distinctly catlike in their temperament.

Catamount Creek slips effortlessly through the light and shadow of the scenic river valley with the aloofness of a cat, lingering in deep green pools, slinking silently with little turbulence through high-walled narrows, sprawling lazily at several broad flats.

The river's dual nature was displayed, however, in March of 1954 after a rainy nor'easter, on the heels of heavy snowmelt, brought disastrous flooding.

The Cat arched its back, revealing the raw, muscular power of its waters beneath its tawny brown hide as it clawed its way far up the riverbanks, hissing through the reeds and wailing through the narrows.

The rains ended with a ferocious thunderstorm that spawned a great and destructive straight-line wind that roared through the river valley, sweeping the detritus of what remained from the floods into the tortured river.

In the long exhalation that follows devastation, life ventured forth. . .

TWO TEENAGE BOYS in hip waders slog through the shallows of the flooded timber along the river, combing the flats for anything of interest deposited there.

Legion choruses of spring peepers hush in waves as they pass, then start again. On a long, exposed hummock, they spot the shattered stern of a wooden rowboat and are brought to their knees, as if they had discovered a treasure chest, when they find a big green tackle box strapped beneath the stern seat.

"It probably washed down from one of the summer cottages up near Dunlin," says Brian. "There's no name on the lid. We'll split things up if we can't find who it belongs to. If there's a fishing license badge inside, my dad can get the box back to him. It's the right thing to do."

Mark undoes the latches and opens the lid. Opposing multi-tiered trays rise slowly, loaded with the bullion of scores of glittering lures and assorted tackle.

After a thorough search, they find no clue to the owner's identity.

In the bottom compartment was a new Penn Peerless #9 reel. Mark cranks it and whistles. "We'll have to flip or trade for this."

They continue upriver, adding to their growing trove: a tire pump, a long coil of rope and a rucksack with camping tins inside. A large, wicker wash basket hung up on a greenbrier tangle provides a convenient way to carry their hoard. They cut a sapling and run it through the handles, each shouldering an end.

The banks rise steeper as they reach a sycamore grove. Here, they stop to rest, looking out over the river.

"Hear that?" Brian asks.

"Hear what?"

"Listen. There! Hear it?"

Barely discernible above the river's guttural moan is the faint, yet unmistakable, bawl of a hound.

"It's coming from where that big tree fell into the river," Brian says.

They wrestle their way through the brush and mire, then slide down to the root mass of a gigantic sycamore. The tree's crown is hung up on a tall, familiar boulder.

Within the clot of debris piled up against the trunk, they spot a beagle entangled in a great twist of chicken wire wrapped around the treaded ramp of a chicken coop. The dog's hindquarters are in the water, its forelegs atop the ramp.

It bays again, then rests its head on its forelegs in complete exhaustion.

"I'm going out after him," Brian declares. "Hand me that rope."

With the rope, they fashion a makeshift harness and loop it around Brian's shoulders, tie it off on his belt, then secure the other end to the sycamore's roots.

"If I slip, yank me in real quick 'cause that water is real cold and I'll be headed downriver fast," Brian advises.

The smooth, mottled bark of the sycamore is slippery and he straddles the trunk's girth, inching forward as Mark feeds him rope. It is a long way out and he struggles to navigate around limbs that impede his progress.

Almost to the dog, the hound's eyes lock onto his in an expression of complete and unwavering trust, a bond borne in antiquity between man and canine, renews in this unlikely place.

Then, in one motion, Jeff heaves the ramp up onto the trunk, wedging it into the V of a limb.

The hound, lying on its side and unable to rise, lifts and lowers its tail in a single wag.

The sodden, cold hound feels like a hide sack of thawing ground meat.

Jeff feels the pounding of the dog's brave heart beneath his palm as he pets him, then recoils when he sees how the wire has cut deeply in several places across the beagle's ribcage and shoulder.

A white froth rains on him from branches whipping the rabid waters, and the mesmerizing current rushing just beneath the trunk creates a distracting vertigo.

Jeff fights to focus, removing the collar caught on the stubborn wire, and frees the dog from the cruel wire cocoon.

He knows he cannot carry 25 pounds of slippery dog back to shore; one miscue could be disastrous. After cutting several lengths of rope, Jeff lashes the dog to the wooden ramp, then fastens rope to each end of the ramp and ferries the makeshift raft to shore.

They lay the dog in the wash basket and cover his trembling body with their jackets.

"Think he'll live?" asks Mark.

"He'll live," replies Brian. "Let's get him home."

They let everything else there, except the tackle box, and make it back to Jeff's house in an hour.

JEFF'S MOTHER CALLS Doc Evans, then wipes down the dog and covers him with a warm blanket. The vet arrives within the hour, just as Brian's father comes home from work. As Doc examines the dog on the kitchen table, the boys relate their story.

Doc Evans seems concerned. "His breathing seems normal, but we won't know for at least 24 hours," he cautions. "Depends if he aspirated any water.

"We'll warm him slowly, too. Nothing appears broken, but I've got to stitch him up in a couple places.

"He's a 13-inch beagle and looks to be around 3 years old. You say he was tangled up on a chicken-coop ramp?"

"Yeah," Mark replies. "He must've ridden that ramp for miles. Brian towed him in on it. He's like a little captain that wouldn't give up his boat."

"He probably was stranded out on the river for a couple of days," adds Brian's father.

"Keep a close eye on him tonight," advises Doc Evans. "If he starts breathing strangely, bring him in right away. I'll be back around in a couple days. There's no charge. It's not your dog, and if I could, I'd give you both a medal. I'll ask around if anybody lost a beagle. People lost a lot around here."

"HEY MARK, let's call him Captain," suggests Brian. "That's what you called him earlier."

"I like that," Mark replies. "Little ol' Cap, Commander of the USS Chicken Coop."

Brian spends the night dozing in a chair beside the hound, listening to him breathe as manic images of debris strewn in the roiling waters rushed through his dreams.

In the morning, sunlight streaming on his face awakens him.

The beagle, lying on its belly, raises its head and whines, merry brown eyes locking onto Brian's.

"Hey, Cap," he whispers. "Hey, boy."

AS WEEKS, then months pass, Brian and the little beagle, with its buoyant personality, become inseparable.

During dog-training season, it's obvious that the beagle already has a degree in rabbit chasing, and they can't wait for hunting season to begin.

On a frosty Saturday morning along the river in early November, tendrils of gray mist rise from the water, flaring whitely in the slanting sunlight, then evaporating into a translucent fog that hangs above the gentle waters.

Brian, Mark and Brian's father wait patiently in the big brushy flat, what the boys called "The Scouring Pad," as Cap works the thickets expertly.

It isn't long before Cap's yodels ring loud and clear across the flat.

Cap brings the rabbit round and Mark tumbles it from his position atop a hummock.

They call it a morning, after taking five more within a few hours: three ran by Cap and two that were bounced.

After skinning the rabbits and tending to Cap, the hunters sit down to lunch.

"River rabbits are bigger and faster than farm rabbits," says Mark, matter-of-factly, having shot three of the six rabbits that morning. "I lead them a bit more than those farm rabbits that are fatter and slower from eating corn. Any real rabbit hunter knows that. That's why Brian only got one, not using enough lead and missing behind."

Brian takes the kidding in stride. "I thought two of those rabbits you shot were sitting still," he replies.

"Well, the best of us out there today was Cap," Brian's father notes. "He's a real dynamo."

THE BEAGLE LIES in the wicker bed Brian's mother had converted from the wash basket in which they had carried him back.

"You're awfully quiet today, Mom," says Brian.

She looks directly at her son for a few seconds, then speaks.

"We got a call this morning from a man, a retired lawyer from up in Stahlsburg, who wondered if he could stop by later and take a look at Cap. I told him it was all right."

Brian's stomach churns as the blood drains from his face. The dark reality of someone coming forth to claim the dog always lurked in the dim recesses of his heart.

Hoping that this day would never come was always unrealistic, he thought. Someone who owned a dog as special as Cap would eventually find him.

THAT EVENING, Brian sees headlights turn into their lane and a knock on the door follows.

Cap barks and bawls and trots around the kitchen table. Brian's father invites in a slim, silver-haired man.

"Tom Landis," says the old man. "And I knew who that pup was over there before you opened the door. I could tell by his bark. That's my dog!"

The old man kneels on one knee with some difficulty as Cap rushes over, putting his forepaws up against the old gentleman's leg, tail wagging furiously.

"Hey, Gunner; hey, Gunner," he says, his voice quavering. "I thought I'd never see you again." As he strokes the hound's silky ears and neck, his hand trembles noticeably.

They sit down at the table, and over coffee, Mr. Landis tells them how he lost the dog.

"I own a property, an old overgrown farm up by the cottages at Dunlin. I used to train my beagles there. We held a couple of beagle-club trials there, too. Loaded with rabbits."

"Gunner and I took a drive down to the property to see if there was any damage to the old outbuildings on it.

"Gunner chased something back around a chicken coop and that's when that big wind dropped out of the clouds," Mr. Landis says. "In the next instant, the coop and run were picked up, slammed down and blown into the river like matchsticks."

"Trees crashed all around. I got decked with a piece of corrugated tin roofing. When I managed to get up, Gunner was gone.

"I looked hard for days. Then, about a month ago, word came down through the grapevine of two young men who had rescued a beagle from the river, and with a little detective work, it brought me down here."

"Where on earth did you find him?" Mr. Landis asks.

Brian speaks slowly, his words coming hard, weighted with emotion, as he tells every detail of the dog's rescue.

As Brian's mom listens again to the story, tears roll from her eyes. The old man's steely eyes and occasional nod recognize the scope of the boy's heroism.

When Brian is done, Mr. Landis smiles. "Okay, let's talk about flotsam and jetsam.

"According to maritime law that governs the open seas, whenever a vessel loses its cargo, because of a catastrophe, it's known as flotsam," he explains. "But if the crew tosses something overboard intentionally, that's called jetsam.

"Now, if someone recovers flotsam – like Gunner here – that property can be reclaimed by the original owner. If it's jetsam, the one who recovers it can keep or sell it.

"So, from all that legalese, we might determine that Gunner still belongs to me.

The lawyer continues. "But, considering the magnitude of your bravery, and seeing how Gunner has become a member of your family, there's no question he belongs to you."

"Now, let me tell you a bit about your dog," Mr. Landis continues.

"I had been a beagler for many years until I closed down my kennel a couple of years ago. Gunner was my last dog, a companion dog besides a hunter.

"He's the product of a noted bloodline and has won ribbons and trophies. I'll give you his papers and all. His full pedigree name is Tailgunner Mike's Wild Blue Yonder, in recognition of my grandson, Michael, who was a B-17 tailgunner during the war. He flew 27 missions until he was killed in action."

"I can pay you for the dog, Mr. Landis," Brian blurts out. "If you'll accept payments, maybe we can work something out. I work part-time at the store up at the crossroads."

"Tell you what," Mr. Landis replies, "how

about every once in a while, you come up to my property to hunt and help out with a few chores and I'll teach you boys how to run a beagle proper."

"Only if I can change his name back to Gunner," says Brian.

AS IT IS WITH so many hunters lucky enough to have a mentor, the old man was an amazing authority on hunting rabbits with beagles.

During the late rabbit season, Gunner works a bunny through some complex cover for a long time, then loses it.

"That's a Molly," says Mr. Landis. "That rabbit knew every trick in the book."

"What's a Molly?" asks Mark.

"A doe rabbit, a female," he replied. "My Pap used to call them Mollies. A male is called a buck. A Molly is a lot trickier; she knows her neighborhood – all the nooks and crannies, undercut banks, hollow logs, woodchuck holes – better than the buck."

"Is that true, Mr. Landis?" asks Brian. "That the females are smarter?"

"You don't have a girlfriend, do you?" asks Mr. Landis.

"Not yet."

"Well, you'll find out. Come to think of it, that's what's missing here. Another beagle."

THE NEXT SPRING, Brian and Mark meet Mr. Landis at his place along the river to do some habitat work.

"Come over to the truck," the old man says, "I've got something to show you."

On the front seat in a box is a beagle pup.

"There you go Mark, she's yours," he says. "Her name is Molly."

Mark sits the pup down in the grass in front of Gunner who wags his tail and sniffs the pup.

"Now you fellas have a fine brace to chase these big, smart river rabbits," Mr. Landis says.

The pup tosses back her head and let out a clear, single note. Visions of future hunting scenarios run through the minds of the young hunters, images riding the swift current of youthful imagination, in sync with the waters of the river that would always flow within them for the rest of their days.

The Edges of Heaven

THEY FLUTTERED TO THE CITY like drab, nameless moths drawn to the glow in the night sky by the fiery furnaces of a booming post-war steel industry. They came from hardscrabble mountain farms and distant crossroads burgs, from little lumber towns and garden-patch villages strung along threadbare roads, where travelers no longer stopped once the new highways were put in. They moved into the rows of crowded tenements or tried to make the best of the replicated clapboard houses that clung impossibly to hillsides, all painted an even red ochre from the dusty air.

The sounds of country birdsong were replaced by the perpetual screech of steel wheels. The concussion of boxcars coupling echoed through the river valley like the popping of iron vertebrae in the great spine of commerce.

High above the floodplain, on the broad, flat hilltops overlooking the city, the mansions of the lumber kings of an earlier era became the sprawling estates of the industrial barons who refurbished those grand-columned homes with all manner of excess: copper-domed atriums and reflecting pools lined with melodramatic statuary, brick herringbone drives bordered by ornate ironworks and playful topiary. In the cool watersheds far from the city, they built lavish country clubs and sailed on the huge reservoirs that quenched their thirsty mills.

Some quaint country villages held their own, however, far enough from the creep of the expanding populace, yet near enough to reap the benefits of an increasingly mobile society. Echo Valley was one such place, comprised of several stores, a lumberyard, small service businesses, and a gas station and garage, where young Jim Price was working under the hood of a '38 Ford coupe.

The station owner, Schultz, banged on the hood. "Quittin' time, Jimmy. That's it for the week. Gotta get to the bank and pick up the missus yet. Here's your paycheck." The tall, wiry teen wiped his hands on his coveralls and pocketed the check. "Thanks, Mr. Schultz," he said.

"Keep up the good work, Jimmy. Looks like you'll have this beauty back on the street in no time, and in a couple more pays, I won't be takin' the balance out of your checks. You sure got some talent with cars."

Large wet flakes blew into the open bay, beading and running down the sloping black fenders. "Snow for tomorrow. Know what you'll be doin'," said Schultz while swinging an imaginary shotgun. "Let me give you a lift home."

"That's okay. You got things to do. I don't mind the walk."

"Suit yourself, kid. See 'ya bright and early Monday. And, if you could spare a couple rabbits for some pot pie, just remember old Schultzie here."

The round man laughed, rubbing his stomach.

Jim strode up the mountain road, head down against the slanting flakes. The long strides of a field hunter, his face expressionless, like that of a comfortable passenger riding securely in a trusted vehicle.

When he passed the second farm, the black, shiny road gave way to snow-covered gravel. A faint musk of skunk. After another mile, the gravel ended, the road rising steeply as a rutted dirt lane that curved up to his farm on the mountaintop.

Full dark now, the clean, heady scent of leaf litter and indescribable odor of odorless snow. Inside, his beagles bayed.

He flicked on the lights. Electric all the way up here now, put in last year just after his father passed on.

Tip and Maggie ran crazy circles around the overgrown yard, then scrambled up onto the porch and into the kitchen. He stroked and talked to the little beagles. Soft, merry eyes, shiny black noses, each panting and laughing. He fed the dogs first, before he ate.

"Sleep good you two, we'll run 'em hard tomorrow."

THE MORNING DAWNED gray and foggy. He filled the sagging shell loops on his canvas vest and dressed. Tattered brush pants with a pattern of wipe marks from a knife, a greasy red leather cap – more brown than red – pulled down over his shock of yellow hair. He shucked open a well-cared for '97 Winchester that was his grandpa's, then his father's, and now his. Lightning in his hands, though a bit short.

The trio headed out into the misty sea of weed fields and brush-piles. Jim was a skilled hunter and gifted shot, his beagles renowned for their prowess and faultless obedience to their young master.

Jim's mother had died when he was a child, and soon after, his father gave up farming to work in the lumbermill. The farm quickly reverted to weeds and brush-filled hollows, the orchard went wild, the woods blending into the fields, and this suited the budding hunter just fine.

Jim was too young to serve when the war broke out, and by the time he graduated in '48, it was all over. A month after graduation and his father's tragic accident at the mill, Jim was on his own. The farm had been his grandfather's and paid for long ago. He had some insurance money and hired on full-time at the busy garage.

He loved the farm, but lately felt disenfranchised, set apart from a world that he felt was passing him by. He often thought of selling it and moving to the city. Lots of jobs there, especially for someone with his mechanical skills.

The sharp yelps of the beagles knifed through the dense winter air as a rabbit squirted out of a brushpile. It flew like a wild spark, coaxed from the solemn earth by the little dogs that hailed and heralded the fleeing ember that ran before them, driving it back around to their master, who swatted it from the air as it sailed over a crumbled stone wall.

Jim held the warm, supple form in his hand, watched the dark eye glaze, then knelt and let the dogs sniff it, telling them things they loved to hear.

MONDAY MORNING, Jim walked into the garage office carrying a bucket with two rabbits inside, wrapped in newspaper and setting on ice.

Schultz was at the counter, drinking coffee with a man in a neat pinstriped suit. At the pumps was a glistening green Nash Airflyte Ambassador.

"So, you're Jim Price, the rabbit hunter I've been hearing about," said the stranger, extending a hand.

"I hunt some," said Jim

"My name is Tom Gaines, and I represent Mr. Harold Bartram from in the city."

He handed Jim a card.

"Mr. Bartram would like to enlist your services to guide him on a hunt," Gaines explained.

"He's a man with little time, but enjoys the sporting life, and is looking for some local recreation. Mr. Bartram would enjoy the privilege to hunt your farm and, of course, would pay for your time. He has an open slot Wednesday morning, and with your approval, can meet you at your place."

"I work Wednesday, but if he wants to come huntin' with me on Saturday, he's welcome. And I don't need to be paid to go huntin'."

"No, no, no, make it Wednesday," Schultz butted in. "Jim can have the day off."

"I guess it's okay then," said Jim. "Nothin' fancy, though, just rabbits and some grouse, maybe a pheasant."

"Fine. Mr. Bartram will be delighted. We'll be there at daybreak."
The Nash pulled away and Schultz whistled.
"Hoo, boy. You know who Bartram is?"
"Works in the steel business, I guess."
"My dear friend," Schultz said, imitating Gaines, "Mr. Harold Bartram *is* the steel business."

JIM HEARD THE car scraping and spinning on the rutted lane before he saw it, then watched the mud-flecked Nash pull into the farmyard. Gaines opened the rear door, and out stepped the stout, but powerfully built, Mr. Harold Bartram.

He was ruddy-faced, with a fierce red moustache and wire glasses, looking for all the world like Teddy Roosevelt. Camelhair shooting jacket, plus fours tucked into shiny black boots, a necktie.

"A necktie," said Jim to the dogs. "Least he ain't wearin' a pith helmet." Maggie looked up at him.

"If he says 'Bully!' even one time, we're comin' back in."

"Great to be out, and in the middle of the week no less!" Bartram told Jim as he pumped his hand. "Busy times, James! Appreciate your company and generosity."

Bartram strode about, surveying the farm, noisily inhaling great volumes of air.

"Looks like we'll be hunting tight cover today. Let's go with the No. 2, Gaines, the open-bore gun."

Gaines unbuckled the straps of an oak and leather motor case and assembled a magnificent shotgun that glowed with a life of its own. Its twin, No. 1, lay in the velvet-lined case.

"Daylight's burning, let's go!" said Bartram, charging down the lane behind the dogs, Gaines on his heels bearing the shotgun and shell bag.

Jim whistled sharply, and the dogs turned back. Then Jim walked up to the men.

"Here's the way it goes, Mr. Bartram. Gaines here is gonna stay behind. We'll work these fields my way."

After Jim described his plan for the morning hunt, they set out, Jim's one stride to Bartram's two.

As they rounded a corner to the orchard, a grouse flushed back into the woods. Bartram's double flashed and the grouse tumbled into the leaves on the other side of a boggy culvert.

"Nice shot, Harry!" Jim said excitedly. "Mr. Bartram, I mean."

Bartram smiled and broke the gun open.

"Well?" he asked.

"Well what?" Jim replied.

"The bird, son, the bird."

"I don't fetch game, and neither do these dogs. You shoot it, you get it."

Bartram pushed through the greenbrier grunting, then slogged through the culvert and back again, handing the ruff to Jim.

"Cock grouse," said Jim, handing it back to him. "You shoot it, you carry it."

Throughout the morning, the dogs put on a stellar performance. Jim was pleased that Bartram matched each of his successful shots with one of his own, then, to his amusement, realized Bartram was competing with him.

At the farthest reaches of the farm, they took a break on a log pile and the dogs rested. Jim unwrapped a half-dozen rabbit legs, some rat cheese and buttered crackers, and poured coffee from a small Thermos.

"Forget your lunch?" Jim asked.

Bartram nodded, wiped his lips, cleared his throat.

"Well, help yourself to some of this then," offered Jim.

He watched Bartram quickly devour two rabbit legs, sucking the thin bones clean the way he probably did with the bones of his business competitors. Bartram's camelhair jacket looked like chainmail, encrusted with beggar-ticks and burrs, and highlighted with knife wipe marks from gutting his rabbits. The thin silk necktie now served as a game carrier, strung through the hocks of the rabbits, knotted around the neck of the grouse.

Bartram stood, his eyes sparkling, and scratched behind Maggie's ear.

"You know, I've been all over; African safaris for the big five, and at night, champagne dinners and violins on the Veldt," Bartram said earnestly. "A tiger from a machan in India, driven birds in Scotland. The best guides, gunbearers, loaders, skinners, trackers. But I never really hunted, not until today.

"Tell you what, James, I have a proposition for you. I'd like to buy this place – all of it, and make it a private shooting ground. Everything's just right. The best part is, I want you to head it up, with a decent salary to boot. We'll tear down that lobster trap house and build you a fine, warm quarters in the clubhouse. A kennel with pointing dogs, gamebird pens, a stable. Think hard on this James, I am dead serious. I'll send Gaines by for your answer on Saturday."

JIM SAT FOR a long time on the porch steps, long after the red taillights of the Nash dipped over the hill. He looked out at the eternal fields, listened to a cockbird crow, saw a trio of deer ghost through the orchard. He held Tip under his arm, scratching his chest, the air electric with possibility.

Saturday evening, Gaines pulled into the farmyard, followed by Jim's black coupe with Schultz behind the wheel. Jim handed Gaines the much-edited note of his response to Bartram's offer. Schultz gave the keys of the Ford to Jim and told him to drive it in on Monday and slapped him on the shoulder, climbed into the back of the Nash and waved as Gaines pulled away.

Jim got in the coupe, adjusted the mirror and saw a guncase in the back seat. He opened it and inside was Bartram's Parker No.1, and a note with a waxed seal.

Dear James,

I knew what your answer would be before you did. It is my business to know such things, and you have made the right decision. The farm should remain what it is, what it always was, and so should you. I feel you are destined for greater things. I noticed that the fit of your Winchester was a bit short for you, so please accept my Parker No. 1 as a token of my gratitude. I would be honored to always serve as a No. 2 gun to you any day, and hope, from time to time, to be invited back to hunt with you and your wonderful hounds. The car, too, is yours. You did a fine job restoring it, and on our hunt, you should know that you helped restore the hunter in me.

Your friend,
H.B.

Jim walked to the house with the shotgun and the dogs at his heels. From the porch steps he looked at the distant smear of pale light from the city in the eastern sky, knowing that soon enough it would all be here, even way up here at the edges of heaven.

A Blade So Bright

THE BOY AND HIS FATHER sit on a stack of freshly cut black locust logs, sharing water from a quart jar. Around them, lemon-yellow stumps glow, like lanterns placed randomly in the shadowy grove. It's very quiet, save the steady swish of the mule's tail and the clicks and trills of late-summer insects.

From far down the valley comes a low grumble of thunder.

"Let's see if we can cut one more before it rains," the father says.

The boy watches him work. A former logger who helped lay bare entire mountains, his father wields the ax with a practiced precision. The silvery ax flashes with tailing, meteor-like highlights, sending chips as big as saucer shards flying with each stroke. He stops halfway through and hands the ax to his son.

The boy continues with the same sure rhythm and flourishes, and with the last stroke, the tree jumps from the stump, is held momentarily by the canopy, then falls, showering them with the confetti of the small yellow and green leaves. They clean the tree and set it upon the others, all to serve as fenceposts.

The storm, moving in from the west, is outflanked by a phalanx of scudding clouds from the south. Each veils enormous cloud anvils. When the two fronts collide, they exchange cannonades of thunder.

"Let's just sit tight," the father says. "Don't want to take out across the field carrying saws and axes and trailing chains."

Ragged curtains of hail rip through the cornfields, pounding down through the canopy of the grove. They take cover beside their old unflappable mule, which doesn't even blink when a tremendous concussion of thunder shakes the grove.

"We're going to get soaked, Pop. Here it comes."

The rain slants in hard, washing the chaff from their arms and sweat-streaked faces. The deluge slows, then ebbs as the storm shifts away. Just then, a final stroke of lightning strikes a dilapidated stone shed down the slope. The boy slams his eyes shut and yet still sees the ragged after-image of the white-hot bolt on his eyelids.

The small shed is a remnant of another age, isolated from the barn and farmhouse farther down the hill. One wall is blown out and the roof shows a tongue of flame.

"Let's let it burn," the father says. "I was going to knock it down anyway. It'll be easier now."

The following day, the boy explores the ruins. Next to it, a dead black snake is draped belly-up in a crab tree like a discarded rope. There's a curious blend of odors: burned cedar shakes and scorched chestnut, the dank odor of mice and moss and other things that flourish in dark places. Hoops from an exploded cider barrel are curled like apple peels. He finds a rusted handsaw with a flat file welded to its shank.

He takes the fused tools back to show his father. Not one for waste, the farmer knocks the file from the saw.

"We can make you a fine knife from this," he says.

He heats the file in his small forge until it is red hot, annealing the hard steel. After it cools, they lay out the pattern of a hunting blade and begin to grind the shape on the big wheel. Blue and orange sparks fly as the boy turns the hand crank.

Sweat runs down the farmer's face and drips from his nose.

"Files are made of the hardest steel, but I never seen the likes of this," the father notes. "This steel has taken an unusual temper, forged harder yet by that bolt, no doubt."

They grind it a little each day until the shape of the blade emerges, then give it a flat taper. The father fires it again until it becomes red-orange and then quenches it in a vat of water, moving it back and forth, so it does not warp. After hours of polishing, the blade is mirror bright. The boy holds it up and studies their reflection, reasoning that after all their work, some element of themselves is perhaps fixed in the knife forever.

A final tempering, and the blade is ready to sharpen. The boy hones the edge, then strops it thoroughly and oils it, and offers it for inspection.

The father scrutinizes the blade and shaves hair from his arm.

"All it needs now is a proper handle and a sturdy sheath."

While hunting rabbits, the boy angles across the orchard, kicking at brushpiles, when he hears a great commotion ahead. Creeping forward, he comes upon two bucks locked in battle. The rivals strain and pivot, seeking leverage and any advantage, but are evenly matched. Suddenly, there is a loud crack, and one buck, minus an antler, wheels and runs. The boy finds his antler in the tall grass, and sees that it has snapped off, just above the brow tine.

His father admires its heavy beading and mass, then holds it up and looks down the beam with one eye closed.

"Here's your knife handle, this section right here."

On the first day of deer season, father and son stalk along the snowy ridge above the farm. It is late in the day and very cold. The boy carries an old Springfield rifle, and on his belt, the knife rides in a hand-tooled sheath, the antler handle fitted perfectly between brass bolster and butt.

In the valley, smoke curls from the farmhouse chimney, and both think of the hot meal awaiting them. Heading down, they pause in the locust grove to study fresh deer tracks. It seems only yesterday they labored here in the sweltering heat.

The gray form of a buck, head held low, sneaks across a weed field.

"Get ready," the father whispers. "He's coming."

Once again, thunder roars in the grove, and the buck kicks and dashes down the slope, piling up near the foundation of the old stone shed. The boy unsheathes his knife and holds the handle along the buck's broken beam and smiles.

"Well I'll be," his father says rejoicingly. "It's a perfect match."

"Now, let's get him cleaned and hung in the barn."

The knife moves almost of its own accord, and although it is his first deer, the boy makes neat work of it.

After supper, the father shows his son how to skin the deer. He points the knife at the lantern, eyeballing the keen edge, and winks at his son.

JIM ROOTS THROUGH THE bargain crates of odds and ends on a bench outside the auction house. One crate has a stout leather collar and a matching leash that appear almost new, just the right size for Kip, his redbone hound.

He digs deeper and finds a partial box of .25-20 cartridges, which he could also use, and an old knife in a greasy sheath. The blade is bright and wickedly sharp, and he notices his reflection in it. Holding the knife like a razor, he pulls it across the stubble on his face, wipes it, and slides it back in the sheath. The sales assistant asks $2 for the crate, but Jim bargains him down to $1.25, and takes it home.

Jim lives alone, and his life's passion is "a little night music," as his fellow houndsmen call their sport. Kip, now in his prime, is the bass voice of a quartet of hounds that are hunted together regularly.

On a clear and cold November night, the pack trails a big boar raccoon around an oxbow and across the breast of a beaver dam. Kip is in the lead and closing, when the coon bails into the water, followed by the hounds.

The dogs bark treed as the men wade the riffles below the dam. Their carbide headlamps wash a silvery path, not unlike moonlight. The dogs carry on, but Kip is nowhere to be found.

Jim calls, peering into the fathomless corridors between the great ghostly sycamores. He listens hard, thinking Kip might have moved on after a second coon. He glances back at the glassy water and his heart sinks when he sees a single bubble, and then another, break the surface. Jim jumps in from the dam breast. The icy water takes his breath, and he gropes about and grasps the ear of his beloved hound.

Jim tries to lift the dead weight, but a stout aspen pole had slipped beneath Kip's collar when the hound plunged in, and in his struggle, Kip sank farther down the shaft and was held fast. Jim slides the knife under the collar, and in one powerful motion brings the blade through the thick leather as if it were no more than a velvet ribbon.

Once on shore, Jim pushes frantically on Kip's ribs, talking to him. Another hunter blows into the hound's nostrils, but the hound does not respond. Jim steps back while the other men continue.

Oddly enough, at that moment, he thought how much smaller the hound appeared in death. Perhaps the swell of mountain air in the lungs and the rush of a hunter's hot blood and the vigor of the chase shape a hound – or even a man every – bit as much as muscle and bone. Just then, Kip convulses as if a charge of electric had run through him, then hacks and heaves. Jim cradles Kip's head and watches the hound's nose quiver.

The next day, Jim and Kip return to the pond. He spots the glint of the blade in the silt and fishes out that extraordinary knife, which he always keeps within his reach for the next 40 years.

ON THE EVE of the 1971 bear season opener, Toby lays out his gear, double-checking to make sure he has everything he needed for a full day afield, including the prized knife his late Uncle Jim had given him.

Hours later, he is far back in the folds of a Warren County forest. He crosses a pristine creek then climbs a steep hillside thick with pines, where he takes a stand. His home downstate seems very far away, and from his perspective in the primeval setting, he feels he is in an altogether different time.

When he first sees the bear angling up the hill, it is as if it is only a continuance of that forethought, a nebulous image from an older time, until the great black silhouette stops and exhales a plume of vapor.

At that moment, he feels that every aspect of his life outdoors, his deep reverence for wild places, his awe and respect for the bear, the practiced woodsmanship that brought him here, every element, like so many loose strands, is now bound and knotted at this moment.

At his shot, the bear charges downhill, snapping off dead branches and tossing clods of pine straw in its furious descent, finally coming to rest against a huge stump. As Toby dresses out the bear, he occasionally draws the blade through a mossy crease in the stump, wiping from it the fat as he works.

Storing his equipment a few days later, he discovers the knife is missing from its sheath, probably lost when they were dragging the bear across the laurel flat. He can't drive back to search for it, because he's shipping out the next day. He hopes that when he returns from his last tour of duty that he will find it.

Toby doesn't return. And for many years, the knife he had left sticking in the stump stands as an anonymous sylvan memorial to both man and bear.

A FATHER AND SON hike far back in, setting up early on the gobbler they know is roosting in the pines. They sit side by side against a massive stump, but when the bird gobbles from behind, they quickly move around to the other side.

The boy, staring at what first looked like a stub of a branch between them, sees it's an antler, then pulls an old knife from a crack in the stump.

"Look Dad, a knife!"

"I wonder how long that's been here," the father says.

He wipes it back and forth on his pant leg, and sees their vague reflection in the blade.

"Feel that edge, it's pretty sharp."

The gobbler flies down and begins to gobble.

"Now let's hear you work that bird. Start off with your slate, then coax him with your mouth call."

The young hunter groans.

"I left my fanny pack in the truck."

The father searches frantically through his vest pockets and the finds an old slate pot, but no striker. Nearby, he locates a dry branch of the right size, and using the old knife, quickly whittles one end and points up the other. He breaks a small bracket fungus from the stump and pushes it onto one end of the striker, then scrapes the knife blade back and forth, roughening the slate.

He plucks the makeshift striker across the slate and issues forth some crisp clucks, then follows with a few yelps. The gobbler lights right up.

"Get ready," he says to the boy. "He's coming."

In the Gloaming

*"When yet the sun was high,
And smiling in the sky,
Ah! But now it's sinking fast,
In the gloaming."*

A. Hope Thompson

CAM AND HIS BEAGLE hunted across the brushy flat. He had not been up here in many years, but when he recalled an image from long ago, many more followed. Soon they coalesced and ran together like pictures on a reel. Among the maze of saplings and arcing blackberry canes, he was surprised to see that the small gray house still stood, sagging inwards. As he approached, he heard the screech of the porch swing, and when he saw the edge of the swing moving, his pulse quickened, as if expecting to see someone rocking there. But it was only the wind.

The swing hung by one rusted chain, and over the years had scribed the shape of a crescent moon on the floorboards where it dragged. The cracking gray paint on the swing revealed a reddish color underneath. Cam remembered rounding the corner of the house in that distant summer, the bright red swing rocking gently, and he recalled, too, the small, pale boy who sat there, looking out into the hollow through binoculars.

IT WAS A SUMMER UNLIKE any other, and it began with a steelworker strike that started the week after school let out. With all the men at home, the neighborhood never looked better: lawns were mowed regularly, cars waxed, walkways manicured, gardens expanded, fences whitewashed, and when the work was done, there was always time left for playing catch, building treehouses or tuning up bicycles. There was a celebrative air throughout the neighborhood, but as the strike stretched into July, times got lean and part-time work and odd jobs were at a premium.

Cam's father had a friend, Steve Krall, who said he could use some regular help at his repair business, a fix-all place that did everything from blade sharpening to auto repair. To get there, Cam and his father drove to a small village far down the valley, then made a hairpin turn on a gravel road that snaked up the mountain.

Halfway up on a level stretch, they stopped at a wooden tollgate across the road. A sign tacked to the gate read, "All Donations Help Eddie." An old man holding a coffee can came out of a barn.

"Who's Eddie?" asked Cam

"He's Krall's boy," the old man said. "Eddie's about your age, and has been in and out of the hospital ever since he was little. They have lots of doctor bills. His mom passed away about six years ago. She had a bad heart, and so does Eddie."

Cam's father put a quarter in the can.

"I'll be coming up every other day to work for Steve Krall. He said to tell you I don't have to pay."

The old man swung open the gate.

"Go on," he said with a jerk of his thumb.

A kennel of beagles sent up a clamor when Cam and his dad eased into the driveway. The strobe of a welder's torch flashed through the windows of the garage. A minute later, Krall came out, tilting back his face shield.

"Cam, why don't you go find Eddie," said Krall. He's out back waitin' on you. He can show you around while your dad and me get to work. Now listen, he can't run around like other kids. He has to take his time."

Eddie was on the porch swing, studying a distant hillside through a pair of big Navy binoculars. Next to him was a green rucksack bulging with gear, and under the swing, an old beagle with a torn ear.

"Here, look through these," said Eddie. "See those big rocks way out there? We can hike up there if you want."

"All right," Cam replied. "You sure you can do that? Your dad said you had to sort of take it easy."

"Oh, I can do it. There's this path they cut through the woods for me. It's nice and smooth. Here, we'll take my wagon. Old Sarge will come, too."

Eddie put the pack and binoculars in the wooden-backed wagon. Cam grabbed the wagon handle and they went down into the dark hollow.

"You know the names of any trees?" asked Eddie. "I do."

"Yeah. There's apple trees and climbing trees and apple trees that need climbing," said Cam.

"Well, I know most of 'em. Down there by the creek, those are hemlocks, our state tree. It's real cool down there. That tree there is a sassafras and has leaves like a first baseman's mitt, and that one's called ironwood. You could chop at it all day and all you would have is a dull axe when you were done."

They lingered by the creek, watching water swirl under the slat bridge.

"I was born way before I was supposed to, right in the middle of a big snowstorm," Eddie started to explain. "My aunt walked up from down below to help out 'cause no one could drive up or down. We got relatives that live down the mountain, but my dad wanted to live up on top so's they wouldn't be botherin' us all the time.

"Anyway, I wasn't much bigger than a squirrel, and they wrapped me in a hand towel and put me in a shoebox and set me right on top the stove. I'd been sick off and on and had some operations in a hospital in Pittsburgh. Sometimes I get tired. If you can do it, you can try to pull me up the hill in the wagon."

Cam pulled Eddie up the switchback trail, straining in the steep sections, unable to swat the gnats that swarmed his sweaty face. They stopped on a flat and Eddie jumped from the wagon.

"Grab the pack and binoculars and follow me. Sarge will stay here and guard the wagon."

Eddie took off into the laurel like a shot. They followed a rocky deer trail that climbed ever higher, then took a narrow trail that wound around the face of an escarpment until it narrowed to a ledge.

"Be real careful here, It's slippery and there's rattlers here, too," said Eddie.

Nimble as a squirrel, Eddie edged across the rock wall on tiptoes, face in, arms outspread. Cam swung the binoculars around with the rucksack, and with much difficulty, made it across.

Eddie scooted up a gut, where water dripped and tall ferns bowed. Cam struggled to keep up. They hiked another quarter-mile, then Eddie cut down hard to his right and they came out on a big outcrop with a view unlike any that Cam had ever seen before. A quartet of turkey vultures drifted by at eye level.

THE SUMMER DAY STRETCHED FOREVER, a great spreading blanket of green and blue. They talked for hours, looking through the binoculars, eating bologna sandwiches and sipping birch beer sodas.

"My mom, I remember some things about her," said Eddie. "We used to sit on the porch

swing after supper and she would sing. She sang this one song called *In the Gloaming*. Gloaming means twilight. That was her favorite time of day, and her favorite song. I remember some of it."

Eddie sang a few of the remembered verses.

"That's the worst singin' I ever heard," said Cam. "Here come those vultures back, they think somethin's dyin' up here."

"Yeah, it was pretty bad," said Eddie. "My mom, she couldn't sing too good either."

They laughed until they could laugh no more, then shouted out long hellos, Tarzan yells and then their names into the valley. But no echoes returned, as if there was no other world out there, only this great wild valley and this endless summer day.

Cam noticed that the pack was stuffed with cans of fruit and beans, and a small iron skillet, rope and other survival gear.

"How come you bring all this stuff along?"

"Well, I never know when I might just give out, so I like to be prepared."

"You mean give out, like get sick?"

"Or worse, maybe even die. They say I could give out anytime, anywhere. Even right here, and you'd be in real trouble then."

"How come?"

"Because you don't know where you are."

On the return trip, Cam struggled mightily, pulling the wagon over roots and rocks with Old Sarge as an additional passenger. When they reached the house, Cam sagged onto the porch swing.

"You always have someone pull you up and down these hollows?" Cam asked.

"No. You're the first one ever," said Eddie, darting away before Cam could catch him.

THE TWO QUICKLY BECAME BEST FRIENDS. They traded comic books and baseball cards, and Cam brought along an extra mitt so they might play catch. Eddie showed him how to tie off saplings, so, in a couple years, they'd have some nice walking sticks with loop handles.

"Hey, I got something to show you," said Eddie, leading the way to the kennel.

"These are my uncle's beagles, but he keeps them up here where the noise don't bother anyone. Look there."

In a stall was a bright-eyed beagle with a litter of roly-poly pups. They smelled like fresh-cut hay and yipped and whined. Cam had never seen such wonderful dogs.

"These are all champions, like Old Sarge, who is the father. If you want one it'll cost you $10," said Eddie.

"I only have $2," Cam replied.

"Well, I guess two bucks is okay, since we're friends. But don't take that one there, that little one is mine. Her name is Belle. That one there seems to like you. His name is Echo. Can't beat a huntin' dog like that for two bucks."

Cam took the pup to the garage to show his father. The men looked up from under a car hood.

"Did you give Cam first pick, Eddie? That the one you want, Cam?" asked Krall.

"Old Echo, he picked Cam," Eddie replied.

"You know any other kids want a dog? We're given 'em away," Krall announced.

The boys returned the pup to the kennel.

"Given' them away?" Cam blurted out. "I thought these dogs were for sale!"

"Just the pick of the litter is," Eddie countered. "And I only charged you what they call a sales tax. Can't beat a dog like that for free."

THE STRIKE LASTED 113 days. School had started, and Cam visited Eddie on weekends throughout the fall. The following summer, however, Cam's father was laid off, and he went back to work for Krall. The boys had gotten Belle and Echo into fine form, and by autumn they were ready to hunt.

Krall was a reclusive man, burdened by his misfortune, hardened somewhat to the world, and overly protective of Eddie. One November day, he finally relented to an outing with the beagles and young hunters. It was on that hunt that he recognized Eddie's enthusiasm.

Krall's shield for his son fell away when he saw how well Eddie handled the dogs and planned the course of the hunt. The boy was a natural in the field, and a fine shot, too. From then on, the men and dogs and boys hunted every Saturday, and the sweet music of Belle and Echo rang through the valley.

The deer opener found fathers and sons walking a snow-covered powerline. Eddie had insisted on bringing the big binoculars, and stopped often for an obligatory, if not theatrical, glassing of the surrounding woods.

"There's a deer," he said, "and it's a buck!"

They saw the deer sneaking across the powerline, and then it stopped and looked at them. It was very far away. Eddie put his mitten in the fork of a sumac and wedged the forearm of the gun down onto it. At his shot, the deer bucked and ran and piled up at the edge of the woods.

The next year, just before hunting season, Eddie passed away.

Krall gave Belle to Cam and asked if he could hunt deer with them that year. He arrived on the opener to pick them up, as he did every opening day for years to come. During the course of the day, talk would shift to Eddie and to the shot he made on the powerline.

Krall would beam at the telling, the echo of that shot ringing on in legend, perpetuating that shining moment one more time, and they would talk of Eddie, who knew the names of trees and loved his dogs, and marveled at the world through his big binoculars.

CAM WATCHED THE SWING rock in the breeze. Leaves blew across the slanted porch. He and his beagle, Sarge, a descendent of the original, hunted across the flat. He came upon a red maple with an oddly looped trunk; a walking stick tied off and forgotten, grown now.

Time was different up here, he thought. And he thought, too, how in all these good days, that any life, no matter when it is given up to the twilight, to that eternal gloaming, is a life well spent when part of it is shared outdoors with a dog and a friend.

The Cross Fox

EVAN SLEPT IN THE CHAIR with his feet propped on the windowsill, waking occasionally to check the sky. He would leave the city at first light. The heat was off in the second-floor apartment, but he was warm in the depths of his father's wool coat. The coat still smelled like him, of country and city, farmer and ironworker.

He sat up and watched a line of people forming on the sidewalk waiting for the soup kitchen to open. One man had a fire built in a wheelbarrow that he pushed along with him. Their clothes had the same gray patina as the city, their faces the same ashen tone his father had when he died five days before. He recalled his father's withered form, a rind of humanity, lost in this big wool coat, sitting in this same chair. It was the city that killed him quicker than the cancer. It got hold of him and sucked the hope from his bones. The cancer just took what was left.

They never should have left the farm, but his father believed that the ends of the rainbows vaulting over their mountain arced into the city, and that is where they would find their fortune. He rented their farm to Evan's uncle, who worked it for three years. At the funeral, his uncle handed Evan a ring of keys and told him that he was moving his family back east, that the farm was not working out, especially with the Depression on.

Evan made immediate plans to move back.

When the sky grayed, he pried a floorboard up and removed two socks heavy with coins. One held $8 in pennies, the other, around $90 in all, saved from odd jobs and what he got for their few possessions. He tightened the knots and put the money in his coat, shouldered his duffel, and left by the fire escape.

HE WALKED THROUGH the frozen railyard where three old women with buckets were picking up coal spilled from the hopper cars. From a distance, they looked like crows walking about, dressed as they were in their black coats and black babushkas. Evan climbed onto a hopper car and kicked chunks of coal down to them.

He waited by a bridge, and when a line of boxcars slowed, he hopped aboard, helped by a strong hand thrust from an open door. The man's wife and two small boys sat huddled together under a blanket. They were on their way to live with relatives in Pittsburgh.

The train chugged on for an hour and the boys played with a top, trying to spin it as best they could without a string. Evan found some in his duffel, cut a length and cut it in half. He wound the top and set it singing across the floor. He tied the other half in a loop and showed them how to play cat's cradle. When the freight stopped at a crossroads town, Evan stood and bid them well, lobbed the sock of pennies to the young father, and jumped from the car.

He caught a ride north to Punxsutawney, and at a hardware store bargained with the clerk for a Model 92 Winchester in .32-20 from a long rack of guns. The rifle was in good shape, with a clean bore and slick lever action. He bought a hunting license, rubber boots and several boxes of cartridges.

"Let's make it $11 even," said the clerk. "They say you can shoot buck or doe this season."

"I can't wait," said Evan. "I haven't hunted in a couple of years."

Evan got a ride on a lumber truck heading northwest. It was late afternoon when he got out at the intersection of a mountain road and he stood there listening to the wind sigh in the pines. At the top of a rutted lane, his family's white farmhouse was bathed in orange light. From the porch, he surveyed the dark rim of surrounding hills while an owl in the pines welcomed him home.

It snowed hard the next day, and Evan was busy in the toolshed. He found some lumber in the rafters and made a long, narrow hunting sled. The sled slipped easily between trees, and for two days, he hauled firewood in on it. At a nearby village, he bought food and supplies and had a load of coal delivered. A neighboring farmer sold him some chickens and feed.

For Evan, the long, cruel winter of 1930 was an ocean of time for him to get reacquainted with the countryside. He sighted in his rifle, and killed a sleek doe on the first day of deer season. He slid the deer in on his sled and butchered it, then made jerky and smoked the hams.

Late one afternoon, he was down in the coal cellar filling the scuttle, when he caught movement just outside the window. It was a fox unlike any he'd ever seen, black as coal with grayish flanks, its face spotted with white. Evan could see the slit pupils of its eyes, like beetles caught in amber. He saw then that the white spots were not markings or snow, but feathers. The fox picked up a white hen at its feet and trotted off, stiff legged, ears back.

He tracked the black fox relentlessly all the next day, quitting only when the trail wound into a rocky, near-vertical ravine high above a roaring falls.

He dragged himself up the lane in full dark and crossed sparkling fresh fox tracks leading from the coop. A second hen was gone.

He repaired the hole in the chicken coop floor and went to bed too tired to eat.

EVAN WANDERED FAR into the hills that winter, driving every particle of city grime from his pores. He hunted gray foxes and trapped. He took several foxes and would collect the $4 bounty on each. Come spring, he hoped to have enough bounty money for some hogs, or maybe a cow. He always kept an eye out for the black fox, but never saw it.

He came upon a cabin on a distant ridge, drawn to it by a bell-like ringing. A barrel-chested Chow dog came roaring at him from an outbuilding and pulled up short, white teeth bared in front of its blue tongue.

"Khan! Get back!" shouted a tall man peering out of the building. Holding a glowing axe head with tongs, he motioned for Evan to enter.

Evan watched him work the axe head on the anvil, alternately heating and hammering until he was satisfied.

"Huntin' today are ya?" asked the tall man.

"Yeah, for fox. I'm Evan Styles. I got a farm out across from here."

"So, you're the guy's been trackin' up this woods. I'm Tom Prowell. Let's get you some coffee."

A bobcat hung between two gray foxes from a porch rafter.

"That cat pays $15," Prowl said. "The Depression's on, and I never made so much money. More than I ever did at my smithy shop down in Coulter."

Before entering the cabin, Evan unloaded his gun and Prowell asked if he could see it. He worked the action a couple of times and shouldered it, examining it closely.

"Where'd you get this gun?"

"At a hardware near Punxsutawney."

"I'll give you $15 for it – what I'll get for the cat – and I bet that's twice what you paid."

"It's a sweet shootin' gun. Not too big, not too small. Fits me perfect."

"Maybe you want to trade instead," Prowell interjected. "I got a Model 95 Winchester .30-40. Nice deer gun."

Prowell took it down from a rack and gave Evan a closer look. It was in nice shape, but heavier.

"Let me think on it," Evan said.

They talked for a long while, those kindred spirits of the winter woods.

When Evan mentioned the black fox, Prowell's eyes narrowed.

"That's what they call a cross fox. I lost the best hound a man could have to that fox. Belle slipped off a ledge down in the big ravine. I've been huntin' that fox for two years now."

EARLY ONE MORNING after a snowstorm, Evan saw the cross fox mousing in a distant hedgerow. He packed enough things for a day's hunt, and set out on its track. He followed it far up into the hills to a rundown homestead.

While ducking under a windfall, he drove his rifle's muzzle into a snowbank. He unloaded the rifle and leaned it against a log, then hung his coat and pack on a branch. He cut a goldenrod stalk to unplug the barrel, stripping it to the right diameter. As he took a step back, the earth gave way beneath him, and he fell into an old well, landing hard.

He had the wind knocked out of him, and his ribs throbbed, but he was not hurt. He looked up and saw the well was hidden by snow-laden blackberry canes and weeds arced over it.

The inside of the well was glazed with ice from a seep, but only a few inches of water lay in the bottom. The skeleton of a deer unnerved him.

After calming down, he perched on a section of log and assessed his situation. No one would look for him or hear his shouts, and that meant he would have to climb out. Lacking protruding rocks for any handholds, he would have to fashion his own. For that he would need a tool – he'd dropped his knife aboveground before falling – and turned to the deer skeleton.

If he could carve handholds into the sidewalls or even insert bones, Evan figured he could climb up. He was light, strong and nimble, and felt confident his plan would succeed.

It had to; there was no other.

He planned a route, and using a wedge-shaped scapula, he tried to dig into the hardened earth. His progress was slow, but he managed to dig out a suitable handhold. Suddenly, he was very tired, and rested on a short section of the log before falling asleep.

Evan was back at work at first light, and using a round rock, pounded both femurs into the walls, as it was quicker than digging handholds. He made steady progress, and by late afternoon was feeling confident.

The night was long and he was hungry, and he became almost giddy when the benevolent face of the full moon peered in, flooding the hole with blue light. He grew forlorn when it passed over. A fox yapped nearby, and Evan wondered if it was the cross fox.

He worked feverishly all the next day, and when he grabbed a root dangling at the rim of the well, he slid straight down, snapping off the bone handholds. As he lay in the bottom, he thought of a dead deer mouse he found in an empty milk can.

A flock of chickadees showered snow on him, and he found strength in their voices. It was the song of the living. That night, Evan drifted between sleep and delirium and was awakened in the morning by snow that plopped onto his neck. He looked up through the crystals at the face of the Chow dog whose loud barking echoed in the well.

Prowell's silhouette appeared.

"I bet I could offer you a dollar for this rifle right now and you'd take it," Prowell yelled down.

"Maybe,' said Evan. "But I'd like some time to think about it."

"Well, take your time, neighbor. We'll come back tomorrow."

A minute later, a length of rope spiraled down.

AT DUSK, on a warm spring day in June, Evan heard frantic squawking in the henhouse. He grabbed his rifle and from the yard spotted the white form of a hen being carried away by the cross fox. The fox was heading for a crab thicket and Evan swung the bead out in front of the white shape then up a bit and fired. The chicken fell but he didn't know that he had killed the fox until he walked out.

That night, he disassembled the rifle on the kitchen table for a thorough cleaning. When he removed the metal butt plate, he saw some carving in the end grain. It read: "T.P. 1898." This was Tom Prowell's gun, no doubt. He would have been about 16 years old when he carved his initials in it.

The next day, Evan knocked on Prowell's door.

"I got a gun I think you know something about, and a black fox here if you're interested in doing a trade on that '95."

"I don't know," said Prowell, grinning. "That's an awfully old gun and there's no bounty on cross fox. I'd have to think on it."

A Stitch in Time

ALVIN OPENED THE DOORS of the cedar wardrobe and hung his hunting parka and pants inside. "Another season done," he said, figuring this as his 54th. He removed the brimming wardrobe drawer from below and emptied it onto a table, this being a good time to sort out the odds and ends all hunters accumulate over the years.

Each artifact brought back memories and images, vague and crystalline, of places and seasons and people and game. In an old cigar box, he spotted what he thought at first was a coin, but something he hadn't seen in years — an old streetcar token on a small keychain, which rekindled memories of a special deer season from long ago…

ALVIN SPLIT THE LAST of the applewood, then stacked it behind the smokehouse. In the fading light, he raked up the debris and shoveled it into a burn-barrel along with some leaves and watched the pungent plume of white smoke drift over the backyard fence, and across the train tracks. He sat on the bench under the extended roof of the smokehouse, wiping the ax head with an oily cloth, glancing up when Mr. Crowell walked up the sidewalk.

Crowell handed Alvin a bottle of soda and sat next to him.

"Nice work there, young man, I was sorry to lose that old apple tree, but just like me, it's seen better days," Crowell said. "However, we now have plenty of prime wood for the smokehouse."

A westbound freight train rumbled behind them, making conversation impossible.

The old man stood with some difficulty, and Alvin watched him poke at the fire with his cane. Mr. Crowell was his next-door neighbor and had taken Alvin under his wing when Alvin lost his father six years earlier, during the invasion at Normandy. They spent much time together, hunting or working on many domestic projects, such as the smokehouse they had built in Crowell's backyard earlier that year.

They often sat out back for hours, Crowell entertaining Alvin with hunting stories from the old days, and from his 33-year tenure as a streetcar conductor for the Reliable Traction Company. The retired conductor still carried his large Illinois railroad conductor's pocket watch, the same as those issued on regular railroad lines. He kept the watch nested safely in his vest pocket, tethered by a gold chain anchored to an ornate fob.

"It's 5:23; that freight's a little early tonight," he said, snapping the watch lid shut as the caboose rumbled by.

"If you can't go deer hunting anymore, then I don't know if I want to," said Alvin.

"Don't worry about me," said Crowell. "With these bad hips, I'd only hold you back."

"Just walking up the sidewalk is tough enough. Besides, I have hopes of smoking venison – jerky, roasts, sausages – in our new smokehouse. And if you don't get a buck, that's fine, too. You have that day off of school, and there's no better way to spend a vacation day than in the woods."

Alvin frowned.

"It just won't be the same without you," he replied. "Besides, I don't drive, and your Dodge will still be in the shop. How am I supposed to get there?"

Crowell smiled.

"I'll have you up on top of Ginger Mountain before first light. Guaranteed. I just have a few small details to work out."

ON THE SATURDAY following Thanksgiving, Alvin saw Crowell at the smokehouse and went back to see if he needed any help. The bench was heaped with hunting gear, and Alvin was eager to learn of the plan. Crowell came out of the smokehouse patting a small ham.

"For breakfast on Monday, and lunch for you," he said.

The aroma of woodsmoke and curing hams hung heavy in the moist, wintry air. A flat, seamless plane of pale gray clouds stretched above the city, promising snow.

"You'll be able to track 'em come Monday," said Crowell. "Big snow coming, but you'll be ready. Look here, I've been meaning to give you this outfit. This is my old Woolrich jacket with a matching vest and pants from back when I was your size. And here's a rucksack for your gear and lunch, a canvas sleeve for your rifle, and new felts for your galoshes.

"Now let's talk about getting you out to Ginger Mountain and back. I spoke with your mom earlier and she's good with this. You just have to be at the right places at the right times, otherwise you'll be doing a lot of extra walking.

"First, the little gold token on this key chain is my lifetime pass from the Traction Company. Fasten it through a buttonhole on your jacket and show it to the conductor. At 4 a.m., you'll pick up the streetcar down at the corner and it'll take you across town, all the way to the West End. By then it'll be 4:35.

"From there, you'll walk straight out of town one mile to Butterfield Road. My brother Earl – you met him once when we hunted rabbits on his farm – will meet you there in his red Ford pickup at 5. He ought to be done with milking and whatnot by then.

"Now don't dilly-dally, because if you're not there he won't wait long," Crowell continued. "He'll take you up the hard road and then the high dirt road and drop you off way back on top of Ginger Mountain. You'll be there before first light, then you're on your own, with the whole day to hunt your way back down.

"Now make sure you're down off that mountain and back at the crossroads by 5:15. Earl will meet you there and bring you home.

"Most important, though, is that you stay on schedule, and for that you'll need a proper watch. I want you to carry my railroad watch. Just button this fob to the vest and put the watch in the vest pocket. Come over early Monday morning and Mrs. Crowell will have breakfast for you, and a lunch to take along."

ALVIN THANKED farmer Crowell for the ride up the mountain. Several inches of snow had fallen during the night.

"There's a lot more snow comin' our way," warned the farmer. "Now listen, this is an awful big mountain. I know you guys hunted up here before, but when it snows like this, things can all look the same. I don't want to be huntin' you tonight, okay? Now go get a big one."

Alvin checked the pocket watch and set out for a stand of oaks where he had posted last year. At 10 a.m., it began snowing harder and he thought it was time to move. He snuck through a laurel patch and saw three fresh deer beds, but not a tail. When he emerged from the other side, he felt fresh and alive, having shed the husk of the city as a snake would its skin.

The snow slanted in, steering him to the lee side of the mountain, and he watched a line of hunters putting on a drive below, then heard two quick shots. He waited, and 20 minutes later a lone deer, a buck, came up the mountain. Alvin shouldered his father's .38-55, but the buck disappeared in the snow-ladened undergrowth. Alvin soon came upon its tracks and followed them along the ridge.

He unbuttoned his jacket to check the time, and thought it quicker to unhook the watch from its chain and carry it in a coat pocket. The buck's tracks wound through some thick cover, then cut sharply over the ridge to a notched trail that descended gently, angling across the mountain. It was a trail not fashioned by man, but an age-old route carved by the endless progression of animals, large and small, and used by ancient hunters and travelers of older times, and now this deer and him.

Large, compound flakes fell straight down, and there was no sound save the hissing snow; it was like walking in a dream, blurred at the edges. Suddenly, 40 yards out, the hard outline of the buck stood out in stark, splendid relief against the fairyland backdrop. Alvin thumbed back the hammer, covered the deer's dark shoulder with the brass bead and fired. The buck leaped and bolted straight downhill. It was very steep and thick, but Alvin followed the deer's plunging and faltering path easily; he found the sleek 7-pointer piled up against a log 200 yards below.

He had to wait several minutes for his hands to stop shaking before he could dress out his very first deer. Alvin craned his neck and looked uphill, then decided to drag the buck down to the highway somewhere far below. Once there, perhaps some passing hunters would give him a ride to the crossroads. If not, it was only lunchtime, and he felt that he could make his rendezvous with Earl by 5 p.m.

The snow came harder and faster, and even though he was going downhill, his progress was slow. The rugged terrain forced him to angle across a broad plateau, a corrugation of rocky ravines and tortuous laurel jungles. He knew then that he had misjudged the depth and rugged terrain of the mountainside. At dusk, or what he believed was dusk – as the light seemed unchanged throughout the day – he saw the thin, white horizontal line of the highway beyond the trees, still far below. It was half past 5.

The snow was almost knee-deep on the road, and to his dismay, not a single set of tire tracks showed. He figured then that the highway had been closed. Even though it was full dark, he could see well; the slumbering landscape seemed to be softly illuminated from within, as if the snow during its falling had captured and held the dim light of day.

He strapped his jacket and vest to the pack, and with renewed vigor slid his buck right along.

But even young muscles and enthusiasm eventually give out, and his breaks became more frequent. He rested then for a long while, a lonely figure in that desolate valley. Just as he returned to his work, he saw the lights of a vehicle coming down the highway.

"Thought I told you that I didn't want to come looking for you after dark," said farmer Crowell from his seat atop the tractor. "Hey, that's a nice buck. Not bad for a city kid. I'll just drop you at the city limit. You can catch a streetcar there."

THE BRILLIANTLY illuminated interior of the streetcar glowed warmly through the cold blue folds of the storm. The conductor eyed the disheveled young hunter and his deer. "Might have to charge you an extra fare for the deer." he said, followed by a big smile. "Let's tie your buck to the fold-down carrier in front of the car."

As the streetcar lurched into motion, Alvin reached into the coat pocket to see how late he was, and immediately panicked when he didn't feel the pocket watch. He searched frantically through the vest and pack and every pocket several times, but the watch was gone and his heart sank.

Mr. and Mrs. Crowell and his mother were jubilant and relieved upon Alvin's return, but sensed something wrong in his half-hearted smile.

"I lost your watch, Mr. Crowell," Alvin said softly. "I looked again and again and couldn't find it. I took it off the chain and put it in a pocket so I could check the time easier, but I slipped a couple of times and it must have slipped out. I'm really sorry."

"Well, I have another pocket watch, Alvin, and that watch was going to be yours eventually, so let's not worry about it. A watch is only a mechanical device for measuring the time of man, and what you did in the woods today remains outside the pale of time and beyond any measure, as most hunters eventually realize."

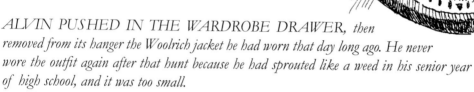

ALVIN PUSHED IN THE WARDROBE DRAWER, then removed from its hanger the Woolrich jacket he had worn that day long ago. He never wore the outfit again after that hunt because he had sprouted like a weed in his senior year of high school, and it was too small.

Now, in his senior years, it seemed once more to fit. He was smoothing it down when he felt a slight bulge and gasped when he pulled Crowell's pocket watch out of a deep handwarmer pocket that he never knew was there. He figured that in all the excitement he had secured the watch in that pocket, mistaking it for the one below.

As he wound the stem, he felt the pulse of the works pick right up where it had stopped, and he thought of how he had lived most of his life between that last tick a half-century ago, and the next tick when it resumed its measure.

He was pleased that he lived those days between fully and fairly, set on course by the good conductor, the best of that time spent with rifle in hand, following deer tracks in the snow.

Brass Mountain

THE FARM is nestled against the foot of the mountain, secure within the great blue shadow that creeps across the fields. Built in 1797, the buildings are a unique blend of Pennsylvania German and Georgian architecture. Constructed of native stone, chestnut and oak, the farmhouse, barn and carriage house are part and parcel of the mountain itself.

The story of the mountain lives on in the buildings: its voice in the creak of floorboards that echo the rub of trees in winter; its cryptic record written within resinous chestnut knots and whorls of wood grain and worm borings; and older tales yet of its earliest history, illustrated by subtle impressions of ferns that decorate the slate roof and the cameos of shells on the stone walls formed in an ancient sea.

Jonathan Crockart walks the long lane from the road to the farmhouse. He looks up at the silhouette of the mountain beyond and is thankful for his prosperity, and to have served as a steward of this fertile ground these 60 odd years. He remembers as a boy when the fields were first cleared, and now, in the twilight of his years, realizes another meaning in the encroaching shadow.

Crockart's father brought his family from England to Philadelphia, and became a successful builder and planner. The senior Crockart was a country gentleman at heart, and developed this valley into a series of profitable farms. Jonathan worked for his father for a few years in the city, but found his true calling in agriculture, and moved with his new wife to the farm manor. They raised two fine sons, both becoming architects, who expanded upon their grandfather's firm in Philadelphia.

IT HAD BEEN A DRY AUTUMN, but several days of cold November rain washes the dust from the lanes. A gray-clad figure moves like a denser vapor within the fog as he wends his way around puddles on the dusky road. He clasps the top of his coat around his neck and leans into the driving slant of rain and sleet.

The traveler halts when he catches a whiff of woodsmoke, then spies the warm glow of the evening fire in the farmhouse. After a fit of coughing, he turns down the lane and circles the house, peeking into each window. At the kitchen window, he spots two loaves of bread and a pie. His tongue slips quickly over his brown and broken teeth, like a nervous mink on jagged rocks.

Crockart's dog growls, and the farmer rises from his writing desk and opens the door before the knocker falls. The man coughs and wheezes, then offers his hand and introduces himself as Titus Peck. Crockart invites the man in, but eyes him suspiciously.

"If I may be so bold as to ask sir, but could I find some shelter in your barn for the night? I was on my way to the village when the winds and fog grew stronger, so's a man could hardly walk, let alone one like myself with a touch of the croup. I saw your light from the road and thought I might…"

Mrs. Crockart breezes into the room, having heard the man's plight. "Of course, you can stay the night!" she offers. "You'll be comfortable in the carriage house. Now get yourself by the fire here, and I'll be right back."

Crockart cringes at his wife's generosity. He, too, was quick to help someone in need, but Peck had an aura of danger about him, and the farmer is unable to determine if it is fever or some pestilence of the soul that burns in Peck's red-rimmed eyes.

Peck sets his greasy pack on the hearth and leans near the fire, an odoriferous steam rising from his wet coat.

Mrs. Crockart invites him to a seat at the kitchen table and serves him a bowl of hot potato soup, ham slices and bread.

"Jonathan, would you build a fire in the carriage house quarters and fetch some water while Mr. Peck dines here and warms himself. I'll brew a fresh pot of tea." Peck wolfs down the food, and as Mrs. Crockart cleans up, he drifts like smoke through several rooms, admiring books and paintings, while his hand, as if it had a will of its own, slips into his pocket a carved ivory letter opener and matching magnifying lens from the writing desk.

Even with Peck settled into the carriage house, Crockart feels they are at risk, especially since they are alone at the farm as the caretaker and his wife had taken leave for a few weeks. There was talk of some thievery in the valley recently, but Crockart had not mentioned this to his wife until now. After she reluctantly retires for the night, Crockart returns to his writing desk and notices that his magnifying lens is missing.

Impossible. He was a man of detail, and would not misplace such a thing. And where was the letter opener? Crockart takes his shotgun from a closet, then loads and primes both barrels. He would stay vigilant all night and, at first light, would roust Peck and send him on his way.

Crockart sits in a chair in the dark, his shotgun lies on the quilt covering his lap, his dog, a restless sentry at the door. Hours pass, and wind-driven rains, like rampaging steeds, race down the valley. Branches claw and rake against the stone walls of the house. Leaves buffet and spiral past the window like cloaked figures. His mind races. He unlocks a trunk and removes a small oak cask that once held blackpowder.

On his way through the sitting room, he stops and takes a small brass statuette from a shelf, a treasured relic from his wife's childhood. It portrays a gentleman hunter standing with a gun under his arm, a brace of pheasants hanging from his belt, a loyal setter gazing up at his master. The brass hunter was a remarkable likeness of her father, a British gunner of some renown. It has no great value, but is the sort of thing a thief might take if given the opportunity.

"Peck will not have this, either," he whispers.

Crockart bundles the brass hunter in canvas and binds it with a cord, then with cask firmly in hand, slips out the mudroom door and into the woods.

The rain stops, and tattered clouds race past the horned moon. Crockart takes a path up through the oaks, and at the first curve, cuts sharply to his left and takes 10 measured strides toward a boulder. He kneels and thumps the ground with a pry bar until he hears a hollow sound. He brushes away the leaves and pries the lid from a cider keg that he had buried years before as a place to secret valuables in a pinch. He sets the cask and figurine into the keg, nails the lid shut, then covers it with leaves and branches.

At daybreak, with shotgun in hand, he raps sharply on the carriage house door. Peck has slipped away, but not before gleaning the room of bric-a-brac.

Crockart is angry, but relieved that they had not been harmed. After breakfast, he becomes very tired, the rigors of the troublesome night settling heavily within his chest. He rests, but when he awakens, he suffers a small stroke. Mrs. Crockart rigs up the buggy, and hastens her faltering husband to the doctor, their dog riding between them.

They pass a pedestrian leaving the village, splashing him with mud. Peck's rheumy eyes fix on them for an instant, and he quickly looks away. She glances back, but the thief has stepped off the road into a thicket.

At the doctor, Crockart rests, whispering nonsense of a brass hunter in the woods, but she quiets him. That afternoon Jonathan Crockart passes away.

Mrs. Crockart sends word to their sons in Philadelphia, but in the days awaiting their arrival, takes ill herself. In a weakened state from her loss, she falls victim to the virulent contagion borne by Peck.

Her sons stand at each side of the bed. She whispers the words "brass" and "mountain" again and again from the depths of her delirium. The next evening, her sons find some solace knowing that their mother now was joined again with their father.

FINDING NO ONE ABOUT, Peck ransacks the Crockart manor house by the light of a lantern. He wrestles an enormous bag stuffed with valuables through a doorway, then slumps into a chair, wracked by fever.

He awakens an hour later, gasping and wheezing from a nightmare vision and stands bolt upright holding an oil lantern aloft, but the floor cants suddenly and he falls to a knee. The walls spin and blur and Peck crashes to the floor.

By morning, all that remains of the stately home are charred and collapsed beams and blackened stone walls. The snow has melted away in a large circle from the heat of the conflagration.

Desiring to be rid of this tragic valley, the forlorn Crockart sons arrange the sale of Crockart Farms. At the wake, they inquire of friends what their mother could have meant by her last cryptic words. No one can fathom a guess, nor would anyone ever know. But from that fateful time in 1858, the mountain behind the Crockart farm became known as Brass Mountain.

A CENTURY PASSES, and the Crockart farm has fallen to disrepair, the fields reverting to wild meadow as the mountain reclaims what had been borrowed. Before sunrise, a rail gang makes repairs at the curve where the tracks straighten for a long run down the valley. They take a break when the sun gains purchase in the October sky. Bill Merrit flings some coffee grounds from his cup, then refills it and watches the sun flood the face of the mountain.

"That's Brass Mountain," says the foreman.

"Good name for it," says Merrit. "Looks like it's made of brass, the way it shines there in the sun. All those oaks and hickories just light up."

"Good huntin' up there," says the foreman. "My boy got a big buck up there last year. You hunt?"

"Yeah, mostly pheasants," Merrit replies. "I got a bird dog, a setter."

"That mountain's public land. I've seen some grouse up there. But this bottom belongs to the farmer just up the tracks. There're ringnecks down here. Just ask, he'll let you hunt."

Merrit stops by to talk to the affable farmer, named Deibler.

"I used to hunt a lot," Deibler says, "but just can't do it anymore. My hips are so bad I just can't. But you're welcome to.

"Now, up there at the foot of the mountain, was what used to be the Crockart Farm," Deibler advises. "There's an old barn up there I use for storage, and an empty carriage house. Look around if you want to. There used to be a big manor house, but it's gone. I stopped planting up there a couple years ago. It's mostly all weeds now, real good cover. Enjoy yourself. I got to cut silage tomorrow, and put some gravel down in my turnaround."

"Well, then I'll see you tomorrow," says Merrit.

"No need to," Deibler replies. "You have permission."

"I'm not gonna hunt," says Merrit. "I'm coming by to give you a hand. I'll hunt next week."

MERRIT CLOSES THE BREECH on his L.C. Smith while Chip, his English setter, splashes through a seep near some apple trees. Almost immediately the dog gets birdy. Merrit eases in, admiring the sculptural form of the white setter against the backdrop of dark weeds. A woodcock rises as if it were suddenly yanked skyward on a string, and at Merrit's shot, the bird puffs and tumbles. Chip retrieves it and they set out across the fields.

Soon after, they put up a rooster that Merrit drops with his second shot. When they reach the carriage house, he goes inside. It's not a big place, but larger than the apartment he and his wife April rent in town. It has an enormous fireplace, broad plank floors, deep windowsills and wavy windowpanes. A steep, walled staircase winds to the second floor, where a window is missing and the walls are plastered with mud dauber and swallow nests.

Merrit looks out the window and inhales deeply, struck by the aching beauty of the rolling fields and robust hedgerows stretching all the way out to the road.

When April comes home from her job at the bakery, Merrit tells her about the carriage house and barn, and that Farmer Deibler said that he would sell it, along with five acres that runs up onto the mountain. They had just started to save to buy a house, but wanted something out of town. Deibler said he would sell it to him for the price of the acreage alone. They drive out that evening to talk it over.

April is a hard-working country girl with boundless energy, and recognizes the potential in the place. She immediately feels a sense of belonging and security tucked up against the mountain. It would take a lot of work to fix the place up, but would be a labor of love.

BY THE FOLLOWING autumn, they have the carriage house fully restored. They converted the carriage bay into a large kitchen where April makes baked goods for several stores and restaurants in town. Merrit and Chip find a whole new world in the pursuit

of ruffed grouse on the slopes of Brass Mountain. Merrit had been raised on a farm, and helps Deibler out in trade for the use of a few additional acres that he clears for a large garden. They have never been happier. Merrit even starts to think of farming full-time.

Farmer Deibler suddenly passes away that winter. His heirs put the farm and its considerable acreage up for sale. Tendrils of civilization from town had shot far up the valley in the last two years, and there was talk of a developer buying the farm. Merrit and April had planned to build a larger home on the footprint of the old Crockart home someday, and wanted to have a family. But that vision, once so dear, blurs like the view through one of the wavy glass panes in the kitchen window. The sellers will not subdivide, and are asking top dollar.

MERRIT AND CHIP ease down Brass Mountain with a brace of grouse. He would bake them in a clay pot with wild apples the way April likes, thinking it would cheer her some.

Merrit sits on a boulder and strokes Chip's neck. He stands and stretches, and as he begins to walk, he drags along a rusted metal hoop caught on the toe of his boot. He thinks nothing of it, because he often finds relics like this in the woods. Then he sees the circular lip of several barrel staves protruding from the ground.

Curious, he pulls out handfuls of leaves and sticks from the barrel and digs out a stiff, moldy cloth with something wrapped inside. He is amazed to find a small brass statue of a hunter and his dog. It is heavily tarnished, but should clean up just fine.

MERRIT SITS AT THE TABLE slicing apples when April returns from a delivery in town. She picks up the brass statue and smiles.

"Where on earth did you find this? I love it. It looks just like you and Chip, don't you think?"

"I found it up in our woods. And something else, too."

Merrit hefts a mossy cask onto a butcher block. Chip's quivering nose inhales the musty scent of the cask, and they, too, can smell it. It was the odor of damp, gravelly earth and leaf mold and autumns past, the rich smell of old things returning to the earth with the promise of new things to come.

Merrit cannot remove the bung, so he pries the studded straps off with a screwdriver.

Chip cocks his head and watches as Merrit places a chisel into a crack and splits the keg open with two hard blows.

April gasps.

Merrit is speechless.

Chip barks and chases down gold coins spilling onto the floor.

MERRIT AND APRIL walk from the Deibler farm that they had just purchased, all the way up to the carriage house. Chip flushes a cockbird that scrambles into the soft blue-green sky, its iridescent feathers gleaming in the remains of the setting sun. They watch it settle into a long level flight. *Kuk! kuk! kuk! kuk! kuk!* it squawks as it alternately flaps and glides across their fields, until it is but a pale mote setting down in the blue shadow of the mountain.

GREAT GUNS

*T*he *Red Glove*, pictured above, is not a photograph, but an oil painting presented through *trompe l'oeil*, a style meant to deceive the eye. It is rendered to present light, form and texture as realistically as possible, using techniques I learned in an Old Masters class. I did this painting when I was very young, and it has its own story. The gun in the painting is a Winchester Model 94 carbine, a .32 Winchester Special and was my first deer rifle.

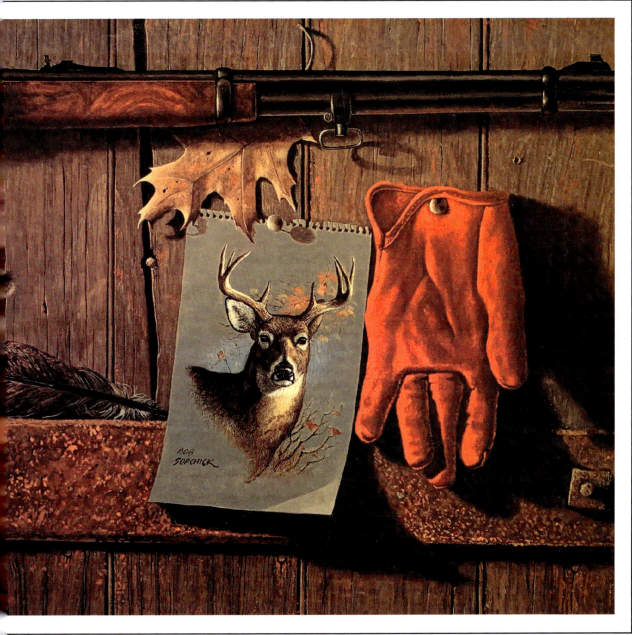

The Red Glove

My parents bought it as a Christmas gift in 1963 at an auto store. New, it cost $85. I hunted hard with that gun and years later, used it as part of this still-life. The painting took on a life of its own, and won two art competitions. It also appeared in several magazines as an illustration for feature articles, among them a three-part article I wrote for *Pennsylvania Game News* called "125 Years of Pennsylvania Deer Rifles."

The red glove in the painting was my father's. His hands were so large, the only gloves that would fit him were cheap, stretchy cotton gloves. In a way, this painting is a story of our time deer hunting together: my rifle, his guiding hand, the deer we loved to hunt.

Every gun has a story, as the guns we own eventually become part of ourselves, with some element of the hunter always remaining in the steel and wood. The following stories celebrate that union.

The Golden Pear

THE GERMAN'S HOUSE SAT farther back than the other houses on our street, tucked up against the woods like a concrete bunker. His immaculate yard was enclosed by a chain link fence, and was patrolled by Max, a vicious German shepherd. Whenever James, Billy and I walked by, we always gave a wide berth to the snarling Max as he followed us along the fence.

The house belonged to a man named Niklas Bauer, but everyone called him The German. Bauer had been a German sniper in World War I. Sometimes at night we saw the light burning in the shop window above his garage, and we created scenarios about him sending secret radio messages to the fatherland while the neighborhood slept.

One summer day, James was demonstrating a new hand-trap by tossing clay birds from my backyard into a hillside out back. Billy, on his turn, disregarded our instructions and sent a clay bird rocketing across several yards, and we watched in horror as its long, slow-motion descent sailed through The German's open shop window. A split second later, the red-faced German appeared in the window, shaking his fist, unleashing a tirade of Old World oaths. From then on, he kept a close eye on us.

Come September, the branches on a trio of pear trees in The German's yard drooped with the burden of luscious golden fruit. The trees were expertly pruned and the trunks whitewashed partway up, as was the practice back then. After hiking up the hill from school, our mouths watered at the sight of the succulent pears. But with Max always on patrol, we dared not reach in to pick a pear, nor did we have the courage to ask the grumpy German if we could have one.

James, like the biblical Adam, became obsessed with tasting the forbidden fruit. Studying the trees through binoculars, he devised a foolproof plan that would not – subject to interpretation – incur the wrath of God or The German.

"I still think it's stealing," Billy protested.

"No, it isn't," insisted James. "Stealing is if he owned a store and you took some of his pears. This is harvesting. When you pick fruit from a tree, it's harvesting, and you, Billy Boy, are gonna be the harvester. Besides, you won't be setting one foot on his lawn."

The plan was ingenious. James and I would play catch on the sidewalk out front, diverting the attention of Max. Meanwhile, Billy would climb the big oak out back and shimmy out onto a branch that overhung The German's shop. When The German walked into the front yard to see what the commotion was all about, Billy would drop down onto the workshop roof, walk the length of it, fill his rucksack with pears from the branches near the roof, and would be gone before The German returned.

All went precisely as planned, until Billy was overcome with bravado. He needed only a few more pears to fill his rucksack and decided to climb from the roof into the pear tree. The German picked up his newspaper from the sidewalk, eyeballing us suspiciously, then with Max heeled, he walked back to the house, underneath Billy, who signaled us from his perch.

Billy waited for them to enter the house, then in a bold move, began climbing down the pear tree. He was going to march right out The German's front gate, and would have made it, too, if his rucksack hadn't hung up on a branch. Billy thrashed about, trying to free himself, and ripe pears began falling. One struck an aluminum awning, and when a screen door slapped back in place, Billy slipped out of his rucksack and bailed out of the tree. He dashed for the gate, but Max came out of nowhere and was on him instantly. Billy turned, and a strange gurgling sound emanated from his throat. Max ran a quick circle around Billy, postured before him, with front legs splayed and rear-end raised, tail wagging wildly, a white, toothy grin on his fiendish black face.

Max wanted to play.

The commotion drew The German, who clamped one of his huge hands around Billy's wrist, and they marched down the walkway. He froze us in our tracks with an icy Teutonic stare, then without saying a word, released his sobbing prisoner.

The next day, we found Billy's rucksack hanging on the gate. Inside were three pears. James and Billy refused to eat the fruit, convinced that it was poisoned. I cut one apart and examined it, then slowly ate a thin slice. Assured that I would live, they ate the pears like starving waifs. Although we agreed that the pears were the sweetest, juiciest pears ever, they were actually quite ordinary. From then on, we steered clear of The German, and he looked upon us with a glint of amusement in his steely gray eyes.

NOT LONG AFTER, we were shooting our .22 rifles at the local range and Billy's gun wouldn't fire. He unloaded it and removed the bolt and started fidgeting with it, when a large shadow loomed over the bench. It was The German.

"Let me see da gun," he requested.

Billy handed him the rifle.

The German examined it and then frowned.

"Firing pin's broke," he said. "When's da last time it was cleaned?"

"A while ago," Billy said. "I cleaned the barrel with a coat hanger."

"Colt hanker?" The German replied incredulously. "Come mitt me."

We followed the German back to his shop. A rack of tagged guns stood along one wall. The neat shop was well equipped with a drill press, a lathe and a band saw. A small forge sat in a corner and next to it, a German army helmet filled with kindling.

Handmade turnscrews and chisels bordered a long bench, and a beautiful rifle stock carved in high relief with oak leaves and acorns rested in a cradle.

"I learnt gun vork when I was a young man in Oberndorf, but den come da war," The German explained. "After da war, I come to America and vork in mill, but always still fix guns little bit here and dere. Now I'm on pension, I vork on dem all da time," he said.

In short order, he had our guns completely disassembled, and showed us how to give them a proper cleaning. He even installed a new firing pin in Billy's rifle. Then he made some adjustments on our rifles, oiled the parts sparingly, and directed each of us on their reassembly.

The German showed us his sniper rifle. He said it was an Imperial GEW98, a 7.92 Mauser. Its claw mounts held a Goerz scope and he now used it as his deer rifle. Bauer always had a buck hanging from his plum tree every deer season.

Hanging above the bench were two framed sepia-toned photographs. In one, a young Bauer beamed proudly, wearing the Iron Cross. Pinned next to the photo was the medal. The other was a formal salon photo. Bauer stood next to a fair-haired girl seated at a table – his wife Frieda. They moved to Pennsylvania in 1924, and Freida had passed on soon after.

"What about this gun?" asked James as he pointed to a pewtery double-barrel shotgun with a broken stock in the rack. "Are you going to fix this gun? It looks pretty bad."

"I can fix," The German replied. "Maybe you boys help, too. Come back und I show you."

UNDER STRICT SUPERVISION by The German, who we now called Mr. Bauer, we cut his lawn and trimmed his shrubs and whitewashed his house. James helped prune his trees, and Billy walked Max every evening. We picked vegetables and pears for him, and helped can them. In addition to earning extra money, he took us through the stages of restoring the shotgun.

It was a 20-gauge L.C. Smith, a lightweight field-grade with good bores, and the action was still on face. Restocking a Smith is difficult, but Bauer soon had a handsome piece of figured walnut installed, or "headed up" to the action, then laid out the stock for shaping. It would have a half pistol grip and splinter forend, with 22-lines-per-inch checkering. There would be no engraving, but after polishing the metal, Bauer case-hardened the action using a series of hardening boxes and charred bone. When he was done, color swirled on the sideplates like prisms of oil on water. He also worked his magic on the barrels, charcoal-bluing them to a deep, lustrous blue-black.

Like a wizard instructing his apprentices in the arts of alchemy, Bauer showed us how to create a breathtaking oil finish on the stock. To halt the penetration of oil into the wood, he used a formula of alcanet root, raw linseed oil, spar varnish, turpentine and Venice turpentine. After the pores were sealed, we oiled the stock using red oil to impart a deep, reddish cast. Every day for a week, one of us stopped by to apply a thin coat of oil with the palm of our hand. Bauer let the stock stand for several days, then applied another coat of raw oil. Several days later, the oil had hardened and gummed over. Then, with a wad of rags, Bauer coated the stock with hard automobile cup grease, sprinkled some powdered pumice onto it and then scoured off the hardened coat of oil. Next, he rubbed it with his bare hands, and it glowed as if captive embers burned somewhere deep in the fathoms of grain.

The next time we saw the gun, it was assembled and lay gleaming in an opened trunk case lined with green velvet. Bauer had inlaid a single gold pear on the bottom of the action. The oval nameplate in the belly of the stock was engraved with our initials.

"This gun belongs to all of you, for your graduation coming up," Bauer explained. "Each vun vill use it for two years, den give it to the next vun. Dis you will do for always, but at da end, you must make sure it goes on to somevun after dat. Da guns, they can liff on, and part of you liffs in dem."

"Who gets it first Mr. Bauer?" asked James.

"Vell now, I got dat figured out," he said, offering a sly smile.

"I giff each of you 10 shells. Only short shells chamber in dis gun. New ones don't fit, so der's no cheating. Take da gun, one at a time, and see who brings back da most crows. Whoever is da best jäger, the best hunter, gets da gun first."

It was late winter, and there was an enormous roost of crows on the other side of the river. James hunted first, setting up near a dump. He put out an owl decoy and a spread of crow silhouettes, returning that evening with four birds.

"I got five, but one fell in the river. I guess that don't count, though."

"Where I come from, four is not fife," said Bauer, followed by his square-toothed grin. My chance came next. I had done some scouting and located a flyway where a steady stream of crows passed through on their way to roost. It was pass shooting, plain and simple. I didn't bother to call or set out decoys, but sat well camouflaged in a hedgerow. I shot only the left barrel, choked a tight-modified, and brought down six birds.

Billy showed up late for his hunt, and was reluctant to go. He was a poor shot, and didn't do well at anything without our guidance. He was wearing a red sweatshirt with the hood tied tight around his face, an old, flat-sounding crow call dangling from one of his hood strings. He pocketed his 10 shells and headed out into the lengthening shadows.

Billy returned at dark – half frozen – and plopped a bundle of crows onto the workbench. There were seven; their legs bound together with the string from Billy's hood. It was nothing less than a miracle. He was a real wingshot, a true jägermeister. Secretly, James and I were proud of him.

Bauer disassembled the gun and we wiped it down and cleaned it. Billy's hands were still numb, and he dropped the stock. It smacked the edge of the stove, putting a crescent-shaped dent right through the checkering. Bauer tried to raise it with steam but it was too deep, and so it stayed.

JAMES WOULD NEVER USE the gun. His family moved to California right after we graduated, and we never heard from him again. Without James around, Billy and I fell out of touch. Once, when I was home from college, I bumped into him in front of his house. He was a soldier on leave, about to begin his second tour of duty in Southeast Asia. He was wearing a beret, and his overcoat sported sergeant stripes.

"Hey, I got something for you," he said.

He brought the cased gun out onto the porch and handed it to me.

"I never used it, and never will. I don't have any interest in hunting."

"I bet you guys always wondered how I got those crows," he said mischievously. "Well, I took the railroad bridge across the river and hid inside an old sycamore trunk until just before quitting time. Hundreds of crows were settling down in that roost. I got four with one barrel, and three with the other. Two shots. I didn't understand until I got back that it was supposed to be a wingshooting thing. I just killed a bunch of birds the best way I knew how. Anyway, it's yours now."

SOMETIMES I HUNT near an abandoned farm. Several pear trees are all that remain. I usually flush a grouse there as they like to feed on the rotting fruit. When I approach the trees, I nervously run a thumbnail along the dent on the stock. At that moment, I think of James and wonder where life had led him, what golden pears he had found. I think of The German, who shared his craft and showed us how to do a thing well. But most of all, I think of Billy. Brave Billy in the pear tree; the runny-nosed kid with his stringer of crows; the soldier who never returned, but lives on in this gun with the others. Just like The German said.

The Tiger and the Dove

"THERE'S A NICE English double I just got in that I want to show you," said Mike, the manager of a Midwest gun shop. "And I know you like 16-bore guns."

He unbuckled the straps of an old oak-and-leather gun case and, after assembling the vintage shotgun, handed it to me. I shouldered it several times, swinging it deftly along the line where wall meets ceiling. The gun was light and lively and fit so well it instantaneously linked mind and eye with bones and muscles.

I examined the best-quality Westley Richards closely while Mike rattled off some features.

"It's an Anson and Deeley hammerless boxlock ejector. Six pounds, three ounces. Doll's head extension; Deeley latch on a splinter forend tipped with a wedge of horn. Deeley ejectors, of course. Best bold scroll engraving with "WESTLEY RICHARDS" scribed in both action banners. Double triggers. Top tang safety with gold inlaid "SAFE." Straight grip buttstock of marbled Circassian walnut with a perfectly blended stock extension that probably replaced a pad. Extra-fine checkering within the side panels with teardrops. Classic checkering pattern; vacant silver oval nameplate. No case coloring remaining; 29-inch flawless black steel barrels choked modified and full with 2 ½-inch chambers, proofed for 1 ⅛-ounce loads. It has a London address of 170 New Bond Street on the concave rib, matching the maker's trade label on the inside lid of the case. It's tight, on face and Birmingham proofed. Has all the patent stampings."

"This could be the perfect dove gun," I said.

Mike grinned.

"Now here's where it gets interesting," he said. "It was originally built to shoot things a lot bigger than doves. Look at the underside of the gun."

I turned the gun over and was surprised to see a tiger engraved on the bow of the trigger guard.

"A tiger?"

"Yes, a tiger," Mike replied. "This shotgun was originally a .450 Express double rifle, used by its first owner to hunt tigers and other game in India. There's a letter in the maker's case

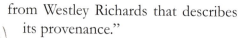

from Westley Richards that describes its provenance."

"What happened to the rifle barrels?"

"No idea. When it came to the States years ago, it arrived as a shotgun. If you're interested in the gun, take your time. I won't have it cataloged and photographed for a week."

IN INDIAN CULTURE, it is thought that one who sees a tiger early in the morning will have courage throughout the day, but I wasn't brave enough to buy the gun. I felt lucky, though, as it's always a treat to see the work of British artisans and designers who balance form with function on the fulcrum of art. I had handled scores of double guns over the years and own a few, but some indefinable aspect of the former tiger gun haunted me for several days, something that padded silently through the tall grass of distant memory.

Back in 1959, when I was a boy, I bought a plastic model kit of a Royal Bengal tiger head that upon completion was mounted trophy-style on a plaque. It was a half-scale model with ears laid back, baring its fangs in a ferocious roar. I hand painted every stripe and marking exactly, carefully gluing each individual whisker at the proper angle. I painted its eyes yellow-gold, with crazed, pinprick pupils. Those eyes burned bright in the dim light of my bedroom, through the forests of the night of boyhood dreams.

That was the era of Hollywood jungle movies, a time when tiger skins were fashionable and celebrities posed in front of their status-symbol rugs. Of all the big cats, tigers were my favorite. I read lavishly illustrated magazine articles of tiger hunts, fantasizing that someday I might hunt one.

That was never to be, of course, as tiger hunting was banned in 1971.

Mustering some courage, and after some judicious trading, I had the gun sent to Pennsylvania several days later.

ACCORDING TO AN OLD Westley Richards ledger, this gun began its amazing journey at the company's Birmingham works, having been built for one honorable Lucit W. Luard. Luard resided at 148 New Bond Street, London, a two-minute stroll from the famous Westley Richards shop at 170 New Bond Street, where he took possession of the .450 Express on April 10, 1884. That date would mean it was originally a Black Powder Express rifle. Smokeless powder was not used in big-bore guns until 1898, when introduced by John Rigby & Co., another venerated London firm.

The .450 Nitro Express case was loaded with Cordite nitro powder and 480-grain jacketed bullets that flew at around 2,100 fps, setting the benchmark standard for all dangerous-game cartridges.

It took the hunting world by storm.

Luard's rifle, although new, already stood in the shadow of obsolescence. It could shoot smokeless loads, though, by using cartridges with carefully reduced loads of smokeless powder to safely replicate the ballistics of the black-powder version.

Luard might have had the still-new tiger gun converted to a shotgun at this point, having moved on to one of the new smokeless calibers, relegating the shotgun for shooting jungle fowl and peacocks.

Aside from its wood extension, the stock had undergone other renovations. I'm fairly certain it originally had a pistol grip and cheekpiece, as I've never seen a vintage double-rifle stock of any other configuration. Both were expertly removed, giving it the classic lines of a fine British shotgun. Barely discernible is a wooden plug inserted where the rifle sling was attached.

Another reason for the conversion may have been political, as the British Home Department in 1905 banned .450 rifles and .450 ammunition from import to India to keep it out of the hands of rebels and insurrectionists who might have pilfered hunters' trunk cases. Perhaps Mr. Luard chose to have it converted those 20 years later for use in driven-pheasant hunts in the English countryside.

Decades passed, and the gun found its way across the Atlantic to a gunner in Florida, then northward, to another shooter in Minnesota, ending up in Missouri. Now, nearly a century and a half since it left the bustle of New Bond Street, it would have its due in the shooting fields of Penn's Woods.

AT TIMES, there can be lengthy lulls in the dove fields before the late afternoon flights begin. Sitting in the shade of an island of trees in the center of the big field during one such lull, I could only imagine how Lucit Luard, holding this same gun in its original form, might have sat for many hours in an elevated tree platform – a machan – watching a bullock tethered next to

the sandy trail that revealed the large pugmarks of his striped quarry.

There was no way to hear the great cat approaching, no way to see it slipping through the lengthening shadows of deep dusk. Perhaps a monkey or bird would set up an alarm, but mostly the tiger would just suddenly be there. And, so it is with doves, too. Sometimes they appear out of nowhere, hard and high from behind, or slow and low unexpected, or in that maddening changeup-pitch flight that befuddles the shooter.

Being surprised by the sudden appearance of game, no matter how prepared we are, is one of the most exciting aspects of hunting.

Another way that Luard could have hunted – and the preferred style of Victorian hunters – was from a platform called a *howdah*, strapped atop an elephant. These hunts were usually extravagant affairs involving a large party of hunters, the Indian hunter-guides known as *shikaries*, elephant drivers or *mahouts*, hundreds of beaters and stoppers and dozens of elephants in carefully orchestrated drives, or "beats."

These lavish hunts for tigers, rhinos and bears were all the rage of British nobility and dignitaries, the royal passion of maharajas and viceroys. But that was not to say it was all fun and games, as occasionally a tiger, as its final act, managed to leap 20 feet onto the back of a squealing elephant, pluck a hunter from the howdah, and drag him down into the tall grass.

Dove hunting, too, is sometimes an elaborate group event, where dozens of hunters take their places around a field, the progressive sound of their shots defining the paths of various flights, like air-traffic-control indicators, the pulse quickens, searching the horizons for birds driven to high speed by the shooting, winging their way to your position.

Dove season is a place where summer coexists with autumn within the same frame.

Radiant heat rising from the fields as mirages concede in late afternoon to a crystalline coolness that ushers in a chill that expands within the vaulting blue shadows. Insect choruses trill, click and serenade both the passage of summer, yet herald the leading edge of autumn.

Doves are released to mark the opening festivities of noted events, and in the hunter's world, it seems quite appropriate that their September flights mark the celebrated openings of hunting seasons to come. Release the doves!

THE CHALLENGES THAT doves present for the wingshooter are many, and it's always satisfying to make a great shot with a favorite gun.

But it is the flight of the bird that is spellbinding. Their flight is always dramatic, always beautiful, no matter if they flutter from a perch to the ground, or streak great distances across a sultry September sky. It gracefully defines the very atmosphere we take for granted.

Sometimes in nature, elements we deem invisible can take on

a perceptible form. Watch a trout muscle through the liquid forces and energies of a stream and the water becomes visible through the trout's flash of fin and turn of tail. The rise and fall of a dove's aerodynamic body, propelled by intricate movements of powerful, whistling wings, defines and sculpts its passage through the vagaries of wind and air, seemingly a less-dense form of water.

THE WESTLEY RICHARDS serves well in the field. With the sun below the trees, a last solitary dove just before quitting time, very high and fast, crossing right to left, is swatted from a tangerine-colored sky. Its momentum carries it into tall grass and thick growth far into a drainage.

I mark the bird but have a tough time finding it.

Startled by a doe bedded there that leaps up in front of me, I stand in the high growth for a few moments. It is as if the gun and I are transported back to tiger country, back into the elephant grass as the beaters close in.

I can almost hear the scream of peacocks and frenzied chatter and howls of macaques, the thunder of fleeing sambar, and then the *swish-swish* of dried grass as a tiger materializes, roaring, yellow eyes angry and determined. I clutch the gun a little tighter and find the dove snagged on a blackberry cane.

I WIPE THE SHOTGUN down and put it into its slot in the gun safe. It has traveled more than 20,000 miles over 134 years to get here, transported by ship, train, horse, elephant, jet and automobile. Its journey is not yet done.

With care, it will service other hunters for another century.

I am glad that, once again, it is out in the fields where it belongs, not a curiosity in a collection that would relegate it to a lesser value.

To me, it will always be a tiger gun, a gift to that boy who loved tigers but would never hunt them, who would realize these many years later that the disparate kinship of the tiger and the dove, separated by time and oceans and continents, could be bound by a hunter's will, his gun and a little imagination.

The Good Shot

TWO HUNTERS, father and son, see a deer trotting just inside the woods on the far side of a weed field. They confirm it is a buck and sneak ahead to look for a shooting lane, easing to a point where the field narrows to 75 yards. The son braces against a tree and, at the report from his .303 Enfield, the buck bolts behind a screen of greenbrier.

The young hunter has difficulty ejecting the round, and his father hurries a few steps ahead and fires his .30-40 Krag just as the buck clears the brush. The buck stumbles and plows into a snowdrift.

"Look here," said Bill, young Vic's father. "We both hit him, right through the boiler room. That was a good shot you made. I really didn't have to shoot. He would have gone down anyway."

Bill watched his son tag and field-dress the buck. It was very cold and beginning to sleet – frozen pellets like rice bouncing noisily off their stiff canvas hunting outfits.

"Mom and the girls will be surprised," Vic said proudly. "They thought we were wasting our time going out on the last day of the season."

"I'll carry the guns and you can get yourself warmed up dragging in your buck," said Bill.

He slung his Krag over a shoulder and cradled the Enfield in his arm. His son's old British rifle had seen better days. He wanted to get him a new rifle for Christmas, but times were a bit lean. The Krag was in good shape and lots of guys used them in the Post-Depression north country. He thought of getting the Krag sporterized for his son, which would be almost like a new gun, but more affordable.

BILL WAS A TRUCK DRIVER for a lumber mill. He enjoyed traveling the routes through the Big Woods, but driving had been difficult this fall, with successive snowstorms that began in late October. On his next run, Bill took the Krag with him and stopped at Ebby's Hardware and Sporting Goods, which he often drove by.

Ebby came out of the backroom, wiping his hand on a greasy leather apron. The gunsmith was an older fellow with a shock of white hair and a bushy moustache. His pale blue eyes peered at Bill over wire glasses.

"Yes, sir?" he said.

"I want to see about getting this Krag sporterized," said Bill. "As a Christmas gift for my boy, if the price is in my reach."

"Let's see," said Ebby, looking at a calendar. "It's December 15, and you want this work done for a Christmas present. Why didn't you wait a little longer, maybe Christmas Eve? All I have to do is wave my magic wand and you could have it right then, with a big red bow wrapped around it."

"I guess I wasn't thinking," said Bill sheepishly. "I could probably give it to him for a graduation gift next spring."

Ebby inspected the Krag and did some figuring on a pad. "It'll have a 22-inch barrel, and I'll replace the military front sight with a gold bead and install a Lyman No. 34 receiver sight. I'll slick up the action and remodel the stock. Then I'll check and refinish the stock and put on a rubber butt pad. We'll take the slack out of the trigger and add a set-screw to make the pull adjustable, then fit eyes for sling hooks on the buttstock and forend band. It'll need to be re-blued, too. A new leather sling will finish it out. It's gonna cost about $35 and that includes two boxes of ammo and sighting it on the range out back."

I paid six bucks for that gun, Bill thought to himself. Thirty-five dollars was a lot of money.

"Alright," Bill said finally. "I'll let it here. I'm not local; I drive truck two counties over. But I'm through here all the time. I'll come by every once in a while, to check in."

Ebby took Bill's name and address and tagged the gun while Bill browsed the aisles. The 'smith watched Bill take some money out of his wallet and count it carefully. Bill examined a wool coat and inspected a pair of boots, then scrutinized a knife display, reviewing his Christmas shopping aloud.

There was his youngest daughter, Penny, but Mary, his wife, had already gotten her gifts. Ellen, their older girl, needed a new winter coat, and Mary said she would need a few more dollars for that.

He and Vic had made Mary a cherry dining table with matching benches for her empty dining room. All it needed was some final polishing, but he had to save $3 for the Yuletide centerpiece with brass candelabra that he had laid back.

Ebby sensed what Bill was deliberating.

"Look here," said Ebby, handing him a store flyer. "You might want to stop by next week when I have my holiday sale. A dollar stretches a little farther then."

GREAT GUNS

VIC MET HIS FATHER at the mill after school to help with the final polishing of the furniture. When they finished, they stood back and admired their work. It was more beautiful than anything they had seen in any store, and made from good Pennsylvania cherry that Bill had hauled himself.

"Vic," Bill said to his son, "pick up that centerpiece tomorrow. Here's the $3 I still owe on it. Bring it home and hide it in the basement."

"I'm one step ahead of you, Dad. I got it yesterday and paid for it with money from shoveling snow."

Bill smiled at his son.

"I have to make a run over to Warren tomorrow morning and won't be back till late afternoon," he told Vic. "Meet me here and we'll load up the table and benches. There's no trying to surprise her with it, but she'll be happy enough."

At five o'clock the next morning, Bill was on the road. He was unloaded by 9 and headed back with a storm at his heels. He had $14, enough for a nice pair of boots for his son and wool socks and maybe a Marble's hunting knife, too.

When he crested the hill, cars were parked all along the road. Must be some kind of sale Ebby's having, he thought, and parked his rig far down the road. He heard gunshots from the rifle range in back of the gun shop.

Ebby was standing behind the counter talking to several men, pointing out the features on a fancy rifle.

"Hey, you're the trucker, right?" asked Ebby. "Bill Adams?"

"Yeah," Bill said. "Just stopped by to pick up a few things for my boy." Ebby went into the back and came out with the newly sporterized Krag.

"It's all done," he said. "Finished it yesterday. Looks like your boy'll have it for Christmas after all. Sighted it in early this morning, and she's dead on."

Ebby handed the gun to Bill. The ungainly military rifle was now a sleek and handsome sporter.

"You must have a magic wand back there somewhere, but I only have 14 bucks along, and it might take me a while to get the rest," Bill said as he shouldered the Krag. "I'll just get him something else for now."

"Tell you what," said Ebby. "You're in the wood business. "Do you ever come across some nice walnut? Straight-grained and fancy, for gunstocks?"

"Sure, we deal in all kinds of wood," said Bill.

"How 'bout this, then," Ebby offered. "You get me some walnut, and we'll forget the balance. I want it sawed into blanks, though. Don't go draggin' some big log in here. Take this gun along for your boy."

"It's a deal, Ebby!" Bill said as he shook the gunsmith's hand. "Say, what's all that shootin' out back?"

"That's the fire company's annual Christmas Eve shoot. Shooters come from all over. Grand prize is that new rifle those fellas are gawking at. Why don't you take that Krag out and give it a try? Ticket is three bucks. Register here and give the rangemaster your stub. The last flight is goin' up real soon. You better hurry."

Bill suddenly remembered the $3 in his coat pocket that he was going to give to Vic for the centerpiece, and visions of his son toting the prize rifle loomed large. Bill was a gifted rifleman — a natural shot. He paid the entry fee, and with the Krag under his arm went outside. A large crowd of shooters and spectators filled the lot, spilling over to the diner next door. When Bill got to the range, the snow was falling steadily. He was the last shooter on the end bench.

The rangemaster quickly explained the rules.

"We have 227, no, 228 shooters this year. Each of you has a target downrange in your lane with your number on it. There are five bulls numbered one through five on each target. You will fire five rounds, one shot at each bull. Bull one is shot from your benchrest. Two is a standing offhand shot. Three is a leaning rest against the post. Four is sitting or prone, your choice. Your target is then tacked to the running deer. The fifth shot is a standing offhand shot at the running deer. There are 10 possible points per bull, and a total perfect score of 50 points. If there's a tie, the closest measured shot to dead center on the fifth bull wins. There's a spotter at each bench to instruct you. Targets are set at 75 yards. Good luck."

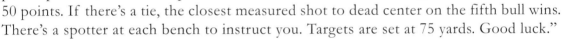

The new Krag was dead on like Ebby had said, and after the fourth bull, Bill had 33 points. When the running deer slid across the range, it was difficult to make out the bull through the swirling flakes. Bill thought of the buck he and his son had shot earlier, and with that image in mind, pulled the crisp trigger.

"We got a high score of 41 here," announced the rangemaster. "That means we have a tie for high score of the day. There was another 41, in the second flight. Okay, here comes the measurement to center on shooter 228's target. Looks like shooter 23 was a half-inch closer. Shooter 23 is the winner."

The storm was intensifying, and Bill quickly headed for his truck.

"Hey buddy," his spotter yelled. "You got second place. Go in the store and pick up your prize."

Ebby was all smiles, and Bill was elated to find that second place was a new Woolrich hunting coat. "Take the size you need off the rack and hit the road," Ebby said. "This storm's a bad one."

THE RIDE HOME was treacherous, and it was after dark when Bill pulled into the mill. Vic was waiting there with the furniture already wrapped in tarps.

Mary had left a note that she and the girls were at the neighbors, and would be home shortly. They placed the furniture in the empty dining room, which had been closed off for the winter. Vic brought the centerpiece from the basement and put it on the table. She would be surprised after all.

Two days later, on Christmas morning, the family gathered in the front room and watched the girls open their gifts. Bill asked Mary to bring in the package he had put in the dining room for Vic. When she opened the door, he heard her gasp. She flung the blinds open and sunlight streamed onto the expanse of polished wood and bounced off the gleaming centerpiece, spraying the walls with a galaxy of golden stars. She sagged onto a bench and placed her hands flat on the polished surface, speechless.

Bill handed his son the package that held the Woolrich coat, then sat next to his wife. The girls each gave their father a small package with a bow.

"Merry Christmas, Daddy," they said in unison.

There was a box of .270 cartridges in each.

Vic left the room and returned with a long box.

"This is for you, too, Dad."

Bill unwrapped the box but could not believe what was inside. It was a Winchester Model 70 Super Grade with a 2 ½ power Lyman Alaskan scope.

"But how?" he asked incredulously.

"I won it, Dad!" Vic replied. "Over at the fireman's shoot by Warren. Nick Thomas and I went over. They said I beat another guy by a half-inch. I was gonna use my old Enfield, but Ebby, who owns the gunshop, let me use a sporter he had in back."

Bill reached under the table and handed his son the Krag with a big red bow tied around the barrel.

"It wasn't by any chance this gun, was it?"

EBBY LOOKED OUT the window and squinted at the mounds of snow left by the storm. He thought of the trucker and his kid and smiled, then sang along with a Christmas carol on the radio.

Quicksilver

FOREVER. I was waiting forever it seemed, for their return, when I'd get to wipe down their shotguns and listen to the account of their day. My father had gone hunting with our neighbor Jack for squirrels and rabbits around the mountain farms. I wasn't old enough, and my father was just learning to hunt, so I'd have to wait. My mother readied a big pot of briny water and spread newspapers out on the long butcher block table along with a pair of shears. She even stropped some knives, as I waited forever some more.

They returned at last light and came into the basement canning room. They stood there momentarily, guns broken open and hinged over their crooked elbows, the smell of the woods and all manner of wildness still about them. I could see weed chaff and leaf detritus caught in the laces of their high-topped boots and beggar ticks and Spanish needles stuck on the corduroy collars of their canvas jackets. They laid out a bunch of bushytails, a rabbit and a grouse on the newspapers. While cleaning the game, they told their stories and saved the tails for me. I put them in a shoebox then wiped down their shotguns.

Five of the eight squirrels and the grouse were taken by Jack. We had dubbed his gun "Quicksilver." It was a pewtery gray H&R single-shot 16-gauge hammerless, and it was quicksilver in his hands. My father said that the real reason Jack always got more squirrels was because he always carried a bag of oyster crackers in his hunting jacket's front pocket, which he snacked on throughout the day. All his munching and crunching proved irresistible to squirrels, which offered easy shots when they came in to investigate.

FOREVER. I was waiting forever for them to finish their second cup of coffee, so we could get into the woods on this, my first squirrel hunt. My new canvas hunting coat was bought several sizes larger so I could grow into it. It was heavy and stiff, like wearing one of those sandwich board advertising signs. I was proud of it, though, and of my hunting license, in its holder pinned on the back, advertising that I was now a member of this timeless fraternity.

I would be carrying Quicksilver, given to me with a cleaning kit in a tin box and an odd assortment of paper shells – a gift for hauling countless wheelbarrows of stones all summer for the long garden walls they built. Jack also gave me a pair of WWI trench boots – the model without the hobnails and heel plate – he had bought at the hardware store years ago. They fit me perfectly, but I wore them only one year before I outgrew them. Like most kids back then, we went into the woods wearing hand-me-downs and carrying military surplus, like some vagabond militia set loose in the uplands.

Once in the woods, we took a stand by a small creek bordered by towering oaks. Shafts of sunlight ignited the russet canopy and it was not long before a squirrel hopped out onto a high limb, surveyed its surroundings, then quickly spiraled around the trunk to the ground. It rustled in the leaves then went right back up the tree and out onto a limb, turning an acorn around in its mouth.

Just as I aimed, it scampered along the limb, the gun's silver bead chasing it, then racing ahead. I fired and the gray fell, then fell some more, thudding onto the leafy carpet. When I picked it up, I saw that it still had the acorn clenched between its teeth. It was a big buck squirrel, grown plump on the mast crop of beechnuts and acorns. When we cleaned it later, we saw it had been killed by a single pellet.

I tacked its tail to the wall of the gun closet under the stairs, then cleaned and wiped down Quicksilver and stood it in the rack. Even though I now owned the gun, I would always consider it Jack's. He had bought it sometime in the mid-1920s, and it had seen lots of use in the 40 years he owned it until it was given to me. A gun can be more than a tool; it's a key that opens the door to the great arena of the hunt, where the oaks and beeches, the musical stream, the chill air, and the gray squirrels all became something different in that context. I saw how it all connected, how, collectively, it was something greater than what I could imagine. The men invited me, ushered me, to that empty seat they had reserved in the glorious woods. And should I wish it, it would always be mine. Forever.

ONE YEAR LATER, I had decided that when hunting squirrels, I preferred the challenge of hunting with a scoped .22 rimfire and bought one with berry-picking money. The gray squirrel had much to do with the legendary skills of colonial marksmen, and since that time, cannot be separated from the guns used to hunt them.

That first rimfire was a Remington M511 Scoremaster with a Weaver B4 scope. In the 50 years since that gun took its place beside Jack's Quicksilver, I've managed to put together some great squirrel-hunting rigs. These included a Ruger M77/22, a Winchester M52 reproduction; another Winchester, this one a M9422 XTR, and finally, a Ruger American, which is a legitimate 100-yard squirrel gun, but in .17 HMR.

There is one other rimfire I enjoy, a vintage squirrel rifle from 1921. The Marlin 20-S slide-action has a 24-inch octagonal Ballard-rifled barrel with fine workmanship throughout. At a touch over 5 pounds, it carries well in the squirrel woods.

Besides sitting and still-hunting for squirrels, another approach that provides a lot of action is walking the open border between a cornfield and the woods. It doesn't matter if the corn has been harvested. I use a double-barrel scattergun for this as squirrels run at top speed for the safety of the woods when they see danger approach. These big corn-fed grays can cover those few yards as quick as a cottontail, so it's nice to have a second shot.

GRAY SQUIRRELS, in their pale salt-and-pepper coats, are dapper animals, but many consider the larger fox squirrel with its grizzled nut-brown coat, trimmed in yellow maize and burnt orange, to be handsomer. On a dark, drizzly November day, when the woods are a deep monotone, the gray squirrel appears especially beautiful, its color the same frost-blue haze of wild grapes.

Once, up north, I was watching a black squirrel, which is a melanistic color phase of the gray squirrel. It was halfway up a tall white pine then vanished in the shadows, only to reappear much closer, climbing a white birch just to my left. It was a dynamic study in black and white, the black squirrel, like a big comma among the other punctuation marks on the white tree.

The gray squirrel is the very spirit of golden autumn, condensed and wrapped in silver. Hunters know that nature moves in cycles, and our days afield often end up where they began. So, it is then that many silver-haired hunters in their golden years end up in the squirrel woods. Ralph Waldo Emerson expressed it best: "A squirrel leaping from bough to bough and making the wood one wide tree for his pleasure, fills the eye not less than a lion, is beautiful, self-sufficing, and stands then and there for nature."

Big Medicine

THICK PATCHES OF FOG, draped like horse blankets over the swaybacked ridges, shift and slide throughout the day, while ragged curtains of rain and sleet sweep across the uplands. Partway up the ridge, a hunting camp sits on the lip of a small flat. Inside, it is warm and steamy. A large pressure cooker chatters on the stove, lending a nervous air to the charged conversation of bear hunters eager for the evening meal and the hunt to come.

Bear season had been closed in 1970, and was only one day in 1971. The closed and short seasons were lamented for some time, but now the hunters are focused on the 1972 two-day season and feel it will be productive; there is lots of sign on the terraced oak flats above camp.

Plans are reviewed over steaming plates of ham, green beans and potatoes. They would put on drives the first day of the season, and on the second, hunt alone. Later that evening, the long plank table is heaped with gear as they make ready.

Young Art Morrow, the newest member of the camp and to bear hunting, thumbs cartridges into the loops of a leather cartridge wallet he had made. Being deskbound at his new job since graduating from college, he is especially eager for the rigors of the hunt.

"Nice cartridge holder," Eddie says. "But those are some awfully small bullets for black bear. I moved up to 250-grainers for my .350 Magnum. What are you using?"

"A .257 Roberts with 117-grain soft-points." Art replies. "I've shot three deer with it. Do you think it's potent enough for bears?"

"Just take a look at the gun rack," Eddie says, pointing with his chin.

Art studies the row of rifles in the anteroom off the kitchen. The first three are Remingtons, a pair of .30-06 pumps and Eddie's .350 Magnum with its laminated stock. The next two, Savage Model 99s, were from different eras; one, a new .358, the other, a straight gripped .38-55. Next is a brush-scarred Marlin carbine in the venerable .35 Remington. His own Remington Model 722 is sandwiched between two Winchesters; a .348 Model 71 and a silvery Model 1895 in .405, with a bore like a stovepipe.

"Don't let Eddie kid you," says John, oldest member of the camp. "Your Roberts is plenty of gun."

John takes the .405 from the rack, flicks the lever, then eases the hammer down and hands it to Art.

"This one's mine. I call it 'Big Medicine;' that's what Teddy Roosevelt called the .405 he used in Africa."

Art nestles the crescent butt plate into his shoulder, finds the bead in the buckhorn sight and centers it on a pine-knot on the wall that had the vague shape of a running bear.

"What size bullet?"

"The 300-grain round-nose is the classic choice," John explains. "It can get the notice of a charging lion or cape buffalo. The year we built the camp, I took a bear with it in Washtub Hollow. It come out of the laurel like a runaway locomotive, and when I shot, he hit the ground and skidded down the embankment nose first into the creek.

"Now listen Art, I know guns and I know hunters, and I sense

that a splinter of doubt is starting to fester in your head. I've seen a Colorado bull elk pile right up with one shot from a Roberts. Eskimos shoot polar bears with .222s – a woodchuck round. When it comes to the moment of truth, doubt is a bad thing. You should have no doubt about your ability to make a killing shot and that your rifle is up to the task. If you'd like, you can borrow Big Medicine here and I'll use your .257."

"I appreciate your offer, but I can't," Art answers. "Besides, I'm not familiar with your rifle and I'd have doubts about my ability to shoot it well."

"You're right," John replies. "But the offer stands in case you change your mind."

THE FOG PERSISTS high on the ridges, so the hunters spend the morning by driving out a series of swamps. On the last drive before lunch, Art is a flanker, pushing out a dense swath of laurel between two huge windfalls. When he comes out on a slight rise, he hears something running in front of him, then sees the brush quiver in its passage. He watches for the white flash of a deer tail. Not half a minute later, he hears the roar of a shot from John's position, and hurries ahead.

"Big bear, Big Medicine!" proclaims John, smiling broadly.

The bruin is piled up against a boulder. Art shakes John's hand, and feels the nervous quake of excitement in the veteran hunter's grip.

Art runs his fingers through the thick, bituminous black coat, studies the wide paws; the creases on the pads are like a maze of trails. It is a handsome bear, the small white blaze on its chest shines like a solitary star in an endless void.

It takes the gang the rest of the afternoon to pull the bear to camp from the bowels of the swamp. They hang it on the game pole and guess it to be around 350 pounds.

That night at dinner, Eddie brings up how he had almost shot a cub.

"It was running full tilt, 30 yards away, and I'd swear it was a full-grown bear," Eddie recalls. "I was leading him like a grouse and was about to shoot, when he slowed and I saw he was just a young one."

"I guess I'll have the right rifle for that job, if they ever make cubs legal," Art surmises.

"There he goes again," interrupts John, slapping the table. "Take Big Medicine tomorrow. I'll be sleeping in."

THE NEXT MORNING, the hunters head their solitary ways in the dark. They plan to meet back at the camp for a late lunch, then clean up and head for home. John had suggested a rugged bit of ground for Art to check out for Monday's deer opener.

Art takes a switchback trail up the mountain, then angles far to his left, to where the mountain curves around. He finds a small flat of towering oaks and grape tangles that overlook a reef of laurel and settles into a windfall.

It's very quiet, save the occasional splat of water drops. A doe slips across the flat, ears back, followed by a fork-horn, and then, a few minutes later, an 8-point. This is definitely his deer stand, Art confirms to himself.

Swirling winds push the raw, moist air, and the dampness creeps beneath his coat and seeps through his skin, settling into muscle and marrow. He shivers and decides to still-hunt along the edge of the laurel, stalking along while warmer blood pumps through his veins.

Suddenly, a bear hustles up over the rim of the ridge, its hide rippling over inches of fat and muscle. It stops behind a screen of scrub oak. Art frantically searches for an opening. The bear swings its head right then left, takes a few steps and pauses again behind a thicket of small birch saplings.

Art stands stock-still. The wind is in his favor, but the bear seems to sense something is wrong. It stares through the saplings the way a caged bear might stare through bars. This, however, is a wild creature, confined only by the boundaries of a great forest. It knows freedoms no man could fathom, its life a journey as raw and epoch as a meteor traveling through a nameless parcel of space.

The bear whirls and runs, angling slightly. Art tries to plant the thin crosshairs of the Weaver K 2.5 behind its shoulder, but the bear is moving fast. He wishes he had borrowed Big Medicine, then he could have placed the bead at the end of the ribcage and let the big slug plow through.

He shoots just as the great black form goes over a log and is swallowed by the dense laurel. Art jacks the bolt back, wishing at that moment he could somehow pull the bullet back through the bore, bringing back that round he fired from a dark chamber of doubt.

Art listens.

Silence. Nothing. He stands there a long while.

A dark comma of earth shows where the leaves were thrown back as the bear dug in, accelerating at Art's shot. He finds a few black hairs that he holds between his fingers, twirling them nervously as he looks about for blood.

The bear is on a well-used game trail. Fifteen yards down that trail, Art finds a spot of crimson; five steps farther, another. Eight steps more he finds a smear of blood on a laurel leaf a foot off the ground. He marks the spot with a piece of tissue and sits down.

He tries to remember exactly where the crosshairs were planted on the bear when he shot, but he cannot halt that single frame in the blur of images. He follows the trail through the thicket for some distance. Then the spots of blood give out.

The trail wraps impossibly around the steep face of the mountain, and through the trees, he can see the silver ribbon of a river far below. A raven sails by at eye level and calls *Quork-quork*, as if beckoning Art to follow, or perhaps it is warning its brother, the bear, that danger is right behind.

Art presses on, to the edge of a great sandstone escarpment. From there, the game trail is little more than an inches-wide line scribed through the rocks. A piece of foamy green moss broken off the edge of a rock might have been loosened by the bear, but for all he knew, it could have been dislodged by a chipmunk.

He hopes he has only grazed the bear. If hit high up, the blood would run over the barrel of the body and down through the thick fur, leaving little or no blood spoor. The wound would plug with fat, and with every other step, the hide would cover it.

The footing is treacherous, and he is far from camp. But Art continues on. In places, he has to hold onto the root handles of yellow birch growing around rocks, like skeletal hands clinging tenuously to life on this precarious ground.

The escarpment is a warren of deep dark fissures, some connected to underground chambers. He shines his flashlight far into crevices, and while pausing near one, he feels the air ushering gently out of the earth, a mustiness of an older time on the expelled breath of the mountain.

He wonders then, if somewhere deep within the rocks, the bear is breathing its last. It starts to rain very hard, silvery sheets pelt the big rocks. He gives up the trail and returns to camp.

NOW, AT 56 YEARS of age, Art is the only remaining member at camp from that old crew. John had left him Big Medicine, and Art had used it on occasion for deer. For the first time in many years, he finally manages to get bear season off. But only three other hunters come to camp.

Art cradles Big Medicine as he walks last in line with the other hunters out the long grassy road on top of the mountain, each dropping off at their respective stands. At the top of Washtub Hollow, Art hangs his pack on the stub of the tree and at first light, sits on a rock slab with the rifle across his lap.

He stares at the pewtery, slab-sided receiver, noticing it is the same hue as the wintry clouds that skim the treetops. A raven passes over, mirrored in the receiver. It erupts with its *kek!kek!kek!* alarm call, as if urging him to look up.

Suddenly, a bear appears loping along on the other side of the hollow, and with the .405 on his shoulder, Art feels as if he is Roosevelt himself, looking ahead for an opening as a Cape buffalo crashes through an acacia thicket.

The bear pivots and offers a poor angle, almost identical to the one of yesteryear. Art feels the cold curve of the trigger against the first joint of his finger and begins to squeeze, then hesitates.

He eases the hammer to safe, tucks the rifle stock under his arm and surveys the sky and the woods.

He senses no rush of power or vault of ego by holding his shot; he is not some lesser god, wielding the power of life and death, only a hunter, an agent in an ages-old venue, a fortunate soul whose path bisected, for one wondrous and shining moment in this boundless woods, with that of an iconic wild creature.

And that, he believes, is truly Big Medicine.

Country Lane Kestrel

Across the Big Field

HUNT AN AREA long enough, and there's usually a landmark there that becomes synonymous with your days afield. It may be an old tram road that wends through the hemlocks as you make your way to a favorite deer stand, a swamp that you must navigate, the ruins of an old farm replete with crumbling stone walls and foundations.

These last 20 years, the main feature and the hub of my hunting grounds is what we simply came to call the Big Field. Nestled within the Allegheny Plateau, it is an isolated mile-long agricultural expanse located at the edge of thousands of acres of prime public land. I often thought as I flew over it from the Midwest how it resembled a tabletop supported on the knees of the hills. In the middle of the field, a swath of trees serves as its centerpiece. Deer, bears and turkeys dine upon the field's bountiful spread, usually planted in corn, soybeans and winter wheat.

To get to where I want to hunt requires a long, pleasant walk on a woods road and a hike across the Big Field, then selecting one of five hollows or the ridges that separate them, depending on what's to be hunted. Sometimes, though, the field is my destination, especially in spring, when turkeys gather to strut and gobble, and in the fall, when bucks work scrapes along its edges.

There's something about the Big Field that's almost magical to me. It's surely tied to how, after a long day of hunting, it opens my mind and soul by offering magnificent views of the surrounding landscapes and the long roll of expressive skies that invite moments of peace and reflection. But also, because my every sojourn across that expanse has become a cherished memory.

WHILE BOWHUNTING one November afternoon, fierce, gale-force winds drive me – along with torrents of leaves – out into the Big Field. Oak leaves swirl with those of cornstalks in a whirling brown and yellow tossed salad. It gathers into a towering mini-twister, and then dances across the field racing right by me before cutting in front.

Suddenly, the wind dies and the leafy dervish sags and falls, and I am showered in confetti. Crows just inside the wood-line cheer like bystanders at a parade, but there is no hero nor dignitary here, save me, a humble bystander to the wonders of nature's mercurial elements.

Bars of yellow light stream from breaches in the seams of dark clouds in the distance, all the way east to the thin blue line of the Allegheny Front. A curtain of sleet and snow sweeps by, painting a swath of the Big Field with a startling, ragged white brushstroke a hundred yards long.

Sometimes nature offers up several incongruous elements within a few minutes, and all you can do is stand in awe at what is described best as performance art of the highest order.

THE UPLANDS OF Penn's Woods are notorious for dense fog, and some fields, especially so. After a day of bouncing a flock of turkeys around Grapevine Hollow, it's time to head back. It had been a drizzly day, and when I get to the flat on top, I am greeted by a wall of dense, white fog. This, however, is no ordinary fog. Such is its opacity that visibility cannot be measured in yards, only at arm's length.

I know which direction to take, as the Big Field lay only 150 yards beyond, but I have to move from tree to tree to maintain a sense of direction. That doesn't work, as I begin walking in arcs and end up at the edge of a steep hollow. Trouble is, there are no hollows between Grapevine Hollow and the Big Field.

It takes me an hour to reach the field. Here, the fog seems even thicker. I don't follow the edge of the field back. Instead, to save time, I follow the border separating a harvested cornfield and emerging winter wheat.

When I stop to regain my bearings in this Great White Nothingness, I am overtaken by a sense of utter detachment. I know where I am, but the only anchor to reality is the grass beneath my boots. I stand as if in a dream. Every step is uncertain; like walking on ice, the mind demanding caution to tread on what cannot be seen.

Continuing on, I am suddenly surrounded by deer feeding like there's no tomorrow.

I've walked right into the midst of them. When I proceed, they bound away, snorting, and, every once in a while, one or two run past me. I jump higher, I'm sure, than a few I almost bump into.

Finally, I reach the main tractor path. The fog thins here, and after a few more steps, I can see the long warp of land all the way out to the far woods. Colors rush forth and earth and sky assume their proper positions. Deep-space perspective returns as proportions realign.

Nature can jog perception in many ways, ranging from rainbows and assorted mirages, flaming waterfalls and sundogs, floating landforms and a dozen more illusions. Today, a simple upland fog creates a field of dreams for the hunter returning to camp. But really, is it not what nature presents at every step?

WE LIKE TO get to our deer stands early, and with a deep snow already on the ground and sunny skies in the forecast, there will be a lot of hunters afield. We're the first ones in the parking area, hours before first light and we take our time as we head up along the western slope of the field.

Near an official Dark Skies region, the Big Field is ideal for stargazing. When we stop to rest at the highest point of the field, we stand in awe at the swarms of stars in colors like oil on water. Meteors momentarily etch the great black expanse with white exclamation points. It's as if we are standing at the edge of creation and that if a single word is spoken, we'd fall off into the heavens from this tiny rock upon which we cling.

The beauty of the day extends into the late afternoon as Dave and I meet not far from the truck, each of us dragging in our deer. The shadows are blue, the slanted light where it strikes the snow, a bright orange. There are no vehicles in the parking area. We load our deer into the truck, but linger, talking of the day, reluctant to leave. It's not easy to give up a day like this. An owl calls. The first star blinks above the Big Field. It's time to go. Time to give the day back over to the nations of night.

I CUT ACROSS the field's corner to set up along its edge for the day's last two hours. I turn for a quick look across the field and there, a hundred yards away, a really nice buck is looking at me. It stands in line with the soft yellow Hunter's Moon that has risen above the treetops. We are like the factors of an equation written on a great sheet of paper. The hunter, the deer, the land, the infinite. Within each element, though, countless variables, shifting expressions and phantom constants abound.

When the buck turns and heads for the woods, so do I, but my boot tip hits a furrow, and for the second time today, I fall. Something beyond clumsiness is at hand, I think, but then, as my father used to say, "Just walk it off." And I did.

Two months later, during the late-winter season, a welcome reprieve after many days of rain, I decide to do a little bowhunting. I hunt the deep, curved western edge. At day's end, I slog along a tractor lane but fall into a puddle and get stuck in the muddy quagmire beneath the surface. I can't get up. No matter how I try – even with the aid of my walking stick – I can't rise to one knee. I have no choice but to crawl the 50 yards back to the woods, where I manage to pull myself up. I do, but realize now that something's very wrong.

AFTER A BATTERY of tests, the neurologists say I most likely have a neurological condition called MMN, a type of motor neuropathy treatable with plasma infusions.

When spring gobbler season rolls around, I'm back up on the Big Field, listening and thinking. I had no real response to the infusion treatments and my condition actually worsened a bit. I lost a lot of strength in my right arm and hand and now walk with a leg brace. I tire easily.

As an ardent researcher, I had resigned myself to the possibility that I had ALS – better known as Lou Gehrig's disease – a devastating, always-fatal affliction. I'd know for certain in a few months at my next appointment.

This hunt, I felt, could in all probability be my last ever. Considering that possibility, I concluded there was one thing I must do: make one final pilgrimage to my deer stand. I struggled a mile to get there, but I did it, sagging onto the log that overlooked the benches below. Warblers flitted through the canopy. A grouse drummed somewhere from the depths of the grapevine tangles. A raven passed, telling me, as always, that it knew I was there.

I sat back and revisited my years here, and they flickered across the hardwoods like fleeting images on an old movie reel. The ghosts of a thousand deer, the forest's unwavering magnificence, the comforts I felt and treasured sitting where I belonged.

Just as I was about to leave, a deer in its red summer coat worked its way downhill and onto the tram road below me. I tried to discern if it was a buck or doe, something I have done many times before. It stopped and looked up, then flipped its tail and sailed down the hill, its white flag waving a final goodbye, as so many have, all the way to the pines.

I make it back to the Big Field by noon and sit near the edge. I always like to be at a field at noon as many gobblers begin searching for company again after the hens of the morning have moved on.

We have seen much wildlife in the Big Field: deer and turkeys, of course, bobcats, eagles, kestrels, bears, coyotes, fishers, geese, scores of songbirds, and even elk. And now, the Big Field offers up one last visitor. A final gift. Three hundred yards down the northern edge, a gobbler steps out into the sun, stretching its great barred wings, then steps out farther, looking all around.

Unable to use a friction call, I use a short, loud tube call that immediately gets his attention, then switch to a raspy diaphragm. He walks slowly in a circuitous route to me, alternately fanning and strutting. He wants the hen to show herself. When he gets closer, he gobbles. Finally, after much coaxing, he's in range. I place the red dot on his neck but can't pull the heavy trigger. My hand is too weak and I can't switch shoulders. A month earlier, I had no problem when sighting in my turkey gun, but things had changed since then. Summoning all my strength, I pulled harder, but yank the sight off target as I fire, missing him cleanly.

It's a long walk back to the truck, and I savor every step. As I walk slowly up the woods road, I wonder if the gobbler was the last wild bird I would ever hear. But nearby, a pileated woodpecker cackles its mad, joyous call of hilarity that seems to ask if I had the time of my life.

Yes, I have.

Every big field that lies before us requires two passages: one across, the other back. I have spent a lifetime traveling across mine, and now it is time to return.

Along the edge of a long puddle is a line of fresh deer tracks. The crisp, perfect hoof print – one of my favorite graphic symbols – is as pure and beautiful as its printmaker. The line of tracks is a cryptic message written in the mire this final day, an invitation, perhaps, to pick them up on the other side.

ACKNOWLEDGEMENTS

THE STORIES, essays and art in this book were selected from a series of columns published in *Pennsylvania Game News* magazine. During the 15 years that these columns ran, I've had the pleasure of working with several editors who opened the doors wide to ideas and expression not often found in state conservation magazines.

I'd like to thank Editor Bob Mitchell who first invited me to create the *Penn's Woods* columns, which ran monthly for more than a decade.

After a 10-year hiatus of designing outdoors stores and museums, I returned full-time to Pennsylvania and was asked by Joe Kosack, *Game News* Associate Editor, if I would be interested in resuming my column for the magazine, which I did.

I'd like to thank PGC Bureau of Information and Education Director Steve Smith, *Game News* Editor Travis Lau, Senior Associate Editor Bob D'Angelo, and Administrative Assistant Patty Monk for their efforts and support in making this book possible. A thank you to designer Fawn Brucker for her assistance on the cover designs.

A special salute to Joe Kosack is due, for his leadership in making this book a reality by taking it to heart, and also for writing the foreword. Thank you, Joe.

I can't express enough thanks to my sister Janet James and her husband, Dave, my hunting partners, who, through their kindness, love and gracious hospitality, made our days together in Penn's Woods a joy beyond words. Also, thanks to my sister Diane Swarney for her support and her husband, Randy, hunting partner and friend.

A thanks to my son-in-law, Drew McDonough, a great student of the hunt, who gave me the joy of outdoor mentorship, enriching my days afield, and who now carries the torch.

To my children, Hillary and Dan, who grew up in my studio, and shared the joys of the natural world.

Many thanks and much love to my wife, Terry, who helped tirelessly, in every way, every day, to help get these words and pictures between two covers. This book is but one project we've worked on together in a lifetime of special projects that identify who we are together.

I'd also like to recognize my father, Richard, who loved nature, and always found the time to take me hunting, and my mother, Sophie, who told us to go.

And to all my kind readers and collectors of art, thank you, woodlanders all.

AUTHOR BIOGRAPHY

BOB SOPCHICK is a multi-talented writer, artist, museum designer, educator and outdoorsman whose creative efforts have garnered dozens of awards. His original art and murals are part of many private and public collections and also have served as limited-edition prints and collectible stamps that have raised financial support for numerous conservation initiatives.

A founding member of the Pennsylvania School of Art and Design, he served there as the chair of the Communication Arts Department for 10 years. A longtime freelance illustrator, his art has graced the pages and covers of dozens of outdoor publications and books until he began to write and illustrate his own columns, among them, the celebrated "Penn's Woods" series for *Pennsylvania Game News* magazine.

Another aspect of his career was serving as a central design consultant for the *Wonders of Wildlife Museum and Aquarium* in Springfield, Mo., as well as the *NRA National Museum of Sporting Arms*.

A lifelong firearms enthusiast and naturalist, he also has written extensively on both sporting arms and natural history. A longtime member of the Pennsylvania Outdoor Writers Association, his favorite outdoor pursuit is hunting for deer, bear and wild turkeys in the uplands of Penn's Woods. Sopchick lives in York, Pa. with his wife Terry.

THE PENNSYLVANIA GAME COMMISSION
A Keystone of Conservation

THE PRIMARY MISSION of the Pennsylvania Game Commission is to manage Pennsylvania's wild birds, wild mammals, and their habitats for current and future generations. That message is profoundly captured in Bob Sopchick's more than 20-year-old design of the agency's logo, which replaced a state-seal logo used by the Game Commission for decades. Overnight, it helped Pennsylvanians better understand what the Game Commission was about, and what its wildlife guardians protected.

Bob's logo uses varying parts of Penn's Woods – some of which also serve as official state symbols – to showcase the length and breadth of the organization's operations. These iconic staples include: the hemlock, our state tree; the white-tailed deer, our state animal; the ruffed grouse, our state game bird; and mountain laurel, our state flower. The bald eagle represents the highly successful restoration of our national symbol within the Commonwealth. The beaver lodge signifies the state's beaver comeback as well as the importance of furbearers. The pair of Canada geese flying over wetlands emphasizes the critical habitat wetlands are to environmental health and the return of Canadas, another restored game species. The mountain range in the distance is probably the most illustrious feature of Penn's Woods.

In all, Bob's logo has represented the agency better than any that had preceded it, using visual attractiveness to help strengthen public understanding about the Game Commission's work. It was a monumental step forward for Pennsylvania wildlife conservation.